Forget &
Forget

Three heroines—they've forgotten
everything...except the power of love!

Forgive & Forget

FORGOTTEN HUSBAND
by
Helen Bianchin

DARK OASIS
by
Helen Brooks

DAUGHTER OF THE SEA
by
Emma Goldrick

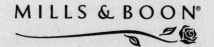

MILLS & BOON®

MILLS & BOON and MILLS & BOON with the Rose Device are registered trademarks of the publisher.
Harlequin Mills & Boon Limited,
Eton House, 18-24 Paradise Road, Richmond, Surrey, TW9 1SR

FORGIVE AND FORGET
© 1998 by Harlequin Books SA

Forgotten Husband, Dark Oasis and *Daughter of the Sea* were first published in separate, single volumes by Mills & Boon Limited.
Forgotten Husband and *Dark Oasis* in 1995
and *Daughter of the Sea* in 1985.

Forgotten Husband © Helen Bianchin 1995
Dark Oasis © Helen Brooks 1995
Daughter of the Sea © Emma Goldrick 1985

ISBN 0 263 81132 8

05-9809

*Printed and bound in Great Britain
by Caledonian Book Manufacturing Ltd, Glasgow*

Helen Bianchin was born in New Zealand and travelled to Australia before marrying her Italian-born husband. After three years they moved, returned to New Zealand with their daughter, had two sons then resettled in Australia. An animal lover, she says her terrier and Persian cat regard her study as much theirs as hers.

Encouraged by friends to recount anecdotes of her years as a tobacco sharefarmer's wife living in an Italian community, Helen began setting words on paper and her first novel was published by Mills & Boon® in 1975. Since then, Helen has written thirty books, and has had nearly ten million copies of her books distributed worldwide.

FORGOTTEN HUSBAND

by

HELEN BIANCHIN

CHAPTER ONE

SHE didn't want to open her eyes. Not yet. For when she did, *he* would be there.

The man they said was her husband, seated in a chair to one side of the bed where she'd been told he had maintained an almost constant vigil for days after her admission.

For the past week he had confined his visits to three each day—early morning, mid-afternoon, and evening.

The nurses had commented on it when they thought she was asleep...and relayed it in informative, faintly envious tones when she was awake. Together with the added news, her initial admission had caused a furore. It appeared that within an hour of being transported unconscious by ambulance from the accident scene to a nearby public hospital all hell had broken loose, and she had been transferred post-haste to this exclusive and very expensive private establishment with its coterie of consultant specialists.

'Elise.'

The voice was a deep, faintly inflected drawl, and its timbre succeeded in tripping her pulse into an accelerated beat.

Damn. Now she would have no recourse but to acknowledge his presence. Her lashes trembled fractionally, then fluttered slowly upwards.

His physical impact was such that it took considerable effort not to close her eyes again in an attempt to shut out the sight of him.

A tall man, whose impressive breadth of shoulder and impressive frame, even in relaxed repose, was intimidating. Broad, sculptured facial features were harshly chiselled, all angles and planes as if etched from stone, and his eyes were so dark that they appeared black—almost as black as his well-groomed hair.

Beneath the cool mantle of his sophisticated façade he bore the look of a hunter, as untamed as a savage jungle beast and just as dangerous.

Alejandro Santanas. Even his name was unusual, and the relayed information she had been given was merely statistical, rather than enlightening.

He was in his late thirties and he headed a financial empire whose very name was regarded with due reverence in the business sector.

A very wealthy man, one of the nurses had revealed, whose entrepreneurial skill ranked him high among the upper echelon of the country's rich and famous.

Elise didn't find it surprising, for there was an inherent degree of power, a ruthlessness lurking beneath the surface, which she found vaguely frightening.

The knowledge that she was his wife had initially shocked and dismayed her, for each individual nerve-end had screamed out in denial that she could be bound to him in any way.

Dammit, she didn't *feel* married, she agonised silently.

Nor did she feel pregnant. Yet there was an ultrasound picture as proof that the seven-week foetus in her womb had suffered no harm.

His child.

Never in a million years could she imagine that she'd fallen in love with him . . . or he with her.

Yet there were wedding-photos taken six months previously to prove their legal alliance, and not once during the many times she'd examined them had she been able to detect anything other than pleasure in her captured smile.

Depicted on celluloid, the top of her head barely reached his shoulder, lending her slender frame a visual fragility. Honey-blonde hair worn in a shoulder-length bob framed a finely boned face, and her eyes were wide-spaced, her mouth a generous curve.

Yet when she looked in the mirror she saw a stranger, with pale symmetrical features and topaz-flecked green eyes.

Losing one's memory, even temporarily, was akin to standing in front of a door to which there was no key, she thought in silent anguish. The answers lay out of reach on the other side.

Amnesia after such an accident was not uncommon, and in her case the condition was temporary. With no indication of *when* her memory would return, she'd been advised that while some patients regained total recall within days, others experienced intermittent flashes over a period of several weeks before everything finally fell into place.

'Good morning, *querida*. You slept well?'

His voice was deep and vaguely husky, and Elise watched with detached fascination as his wide mouth curved into a warm smile.

Why ask, she felt like querying, when you've undoubtedly elicited that information from the attendant sister before entering my suite?

'Yes.' The monosyllabic response held restraint, and she silently examined her need of it. 'Thank you,' she added politely, all too aware of the studied darkness evident in his eyes.

Shouldn't there be some level of recognition deep within her psyche, *anything* that would allow her to *know* him? Even if her mind failed to acknowledge him in any intimate capacity, surely an instinctive sixth sense would force some kind of awareness?

Dammit, she cursed silently. It wasn't *enough* to have to believe that Alejandro Santanas had swept her off her feet in a whirlwind courtship. The fact that they had married a month later in Sydney left too many details unexplained.

A natural curiosity about her background had been partially satisfied by examining a thick album containing family snapshots, although there was a sense of disappointment when not one of them managed to rouse a spark of recognition.

In the past week she had leafed countless times through the many pages filled with glossy prints depicting her from infancy through childhood, highlighting scholastic and sporting achievements, accenting her chosen career as a paediatric nurse. There were photos of her parents, the mother she had lost at an early age, and several of her father, whose affection for his only child was achingly apparent... all the more poignant, given that he had recently died. Holiday snaps taken with friends she was unable to identify. The suburban family home Alejandro informed her she had shared with her father until her marriage. Altogether they encapsulated the past twenty-five years of her life.

'Your hand?' Alejandro queried lightly. 'It is less painful this morning?'

'A little,' she responded stiffly, refusing to relay that her ribs and her shoulder still ached, and that her heavily bandaged right hand, in which surgeons had inserted titanium pins to align several fractured bones, felt stiff in its supportive splint. It could have been worse, the medics had assured her, considering that the other vehicle had run through a 'Stop' sign and ploughed head-on into the passenger side of her car.

'Is there anything you need?'

Elise closed her eyes, then slowly opened them again. 'You send me flowers every day.' Unbidden, her gaze skimmed to the huge bunched masses of exotic blooms—roses, varying in hue from pale cream to the deepest red, their long stems and velvet petals attesting expensive hothouse origin, exquisite arrangements assembled with delicate artistry and dispensed, according to one of the nurses, from one of Sydney's most exclusive floral boutiques. 'And fruit.' A bowl containing a varied selection stood within easy reach. 'I have so many magazines...' She made a visible effort to inject a little warmth into her voice.' What more could I possibly want?'

'To come home, perhaps?' Alejandro queried with teasing indolence, his dark eyes intently watchful as she attempted to veil her startled expression.

Dear God, *no*. It was a silent scream dredged up from some hidden recess deep within her soul. The hospital, this particular suite, represented a sanctuary she was reluctant to leave. Yet she couldn't stay indefinitely.

She swallowed, aware of the slight lump that had risen in her throat, and her fingers began pleating the sheet's hem in abstracted agitation. 'I am to be released?' She looked at him carefully, attempting to read something more from his expression, yet his features were relaxed and his mouth curved to form a warm smile.

'The neurologist and obstetrician have each assured me there is no reason why it should not be this afternoon.'

So *soon*. Why couldn't it be tomorrow, or the day after? At least then she would have time to get used to the idea.

Now, the thought of re-entering the home she purportedly shared with him filled her with inexplicable dread.

It was difficult to pinpoint her reluctance. Was it because there had been no one, other than Alejandro Santanas, to visit her?

She could accept that she had no immediate family, but what of her friends?

Was he such a possessive man that he wanted her entirely to himself, to the exclusion of all others?

She searched his features and saw the assurance evident, the strength of character, and perceived that he was a force to be reckoned with, a man no adversary would choose to have as an enemy.

And as a lover? A shiver of apprehension slithered down the length of her spine. One couldn't live with such a man as he and be unaware of his sexuality... or remain unawakened to her own. Without doubt he would have introduced her to every intimacy, every sensual pleasure, and taught her precisely how to respond in kind.

'Don't look at me like that,' Alejandro growled in husky chastisement.

Elise closed her eyes in silent chagrin, then opened them again, her gaze wide with a mixture of puzzlement and confusion. 'You don't understand.'

The air seemed charged with emotional intensity, and she seemed to be having trouble regulating her breathing.

'You think not?'

She gained nothing from his tone of voice. 'Alejandro——'

'It is no more difficult for you to be faced with a husband you fail to recognise than it is for me to have a woman who is my wife look at me as if I were a stranger.'

In seeming slow motion she watched as he clasped her uninjured hand and lifted it to his lips, and a gasp emerged from her throat as he gently turned it palm upwards and buried his mouth in the soft hollow.

Acute sensation arrowed with unerring accuracy to the core of her femininity, flooding it with a heavy languorous warmth, and she was held mesmerised by the depth of emotion evident in his eyes.

'Do you have any conception what it does to me to see your eyes dilate with apprehension every time I touch you? To be aware you would prefer my lips brush your cheek, rather than possess your mouth?'

The room, its contents, faded to the periphery of her vision, and she could only look at him, unable to utter so much as a word, the moment seemingly freeze-framed in time.

The knock at the door proved an anticlimax, and she hurriedly tugged her hand free as the kitchen orderly carried in a breakfast-tray.

'Morning,' the woman greeted cheerfully as she placed the tray on the bed-trolley, then slid it into position before turning towards the man seated close to the bed. 'Can I bring you some coffee, Mr. Santanas?'

Alejandro's smile curved the edges of his mouth, deepening the vertical creases that slashed each cheek. 'Thank you, no.'

Elise watched as he unfolded his lengthy frame from the chair. Leaning forward, he covered her mouth lightly with his own, and her lips trembled beneath the brief contact.

'Your discharge is scheduled for two o'clock. *Hasta luego, querida.*'

For one crazy second she felt strangely bereft, almost wanting more than that fleeting touch, and something flickered in the depths of his eyes before it was successfully hidden, then he straightened and moved towards the door.

Elise watched his departing figure with perplexity. The warmth of his lips against her own, the restrained degree of passion that lay just beneath the surface had stirred her senses, almost as if some inner being were intent on forcing recognition.

'There you are, Mrs Santanas,' the kind-faced kitchen orderly declared as she undid a mini packet of cereal and added it to the bowl of fresh fruit. 'Which spread would you prefer on your toast?'

Hospital routine ensured that there was little time in which to brood, Elise accorded wryly, for within ten minutes of the breakfast tray being removed a nurse arrived to assist her in the shower, followed by the doctor's round, physiotherapy, morning tea, the daily visit from the hairdresser—arranged, she had been informed, by her husband.

It was a thoughtful gesture, although she couldn't help attempting to analyse his motivation. And that proved detrimental, for it only brought her relationship with Alejandro Santanas to the fore, and incurred a renewed bout of soul-searching.

It seemed ludicrous to doubt Alejandro's depth of caring when there was every evidence of his devotion in this room: the cards carefully placed together in the drawer of her bedside pedestal, each bearing 'Love', written in black ink, and signed 'Alejandro' in a powerful slashing hand.

More importantly—did *she* love him? Certainly she'd married him, but was *love* her motivation?

Dear heaven, she wasn't the sort of woman who had deliberately contrived to trap a wealthy man by using feminine wiles...was she?

Elise closed her eyes in silent anguish, then slowly opened them again.

'Time, *patience*,' the neurologist had stressed solemnly. Yet such an answer was as frustrating as it was ambiguous.

Lunch was a delectable bowl of beef consommé, followed by thin slices of roast beef with accompanying vegetables, and segments of fresh fruit for dessert.

Apprehension began to knot in the region of her stomach, only to intensify a short while later as a nurse entered the suite.

'Your husband will be here to collect you in half an hour,' she informed Elise with a bright smile. 'I'll help you dress, then pack your things.'

I don't want to go, an inner voice screamed in silent rejection. Several jumbled thoughts raced through her head. Perhaps she could dream up a mild complication—the onset of a headache, her hand—*anything* that would delay her departure.

Yet even as she contemplated such an action she dismissed it as futile and, pushing the bedcovers aside, she slid to her feet, watching with detached fascination as the nurse moved to extract clothes from a nearby closet.

Sage-green trousers in uncrushable silk, a cream silk blouse, wispy briefs and bra in matching cream silk and lace, low-heeled shoes. Each item looked incredibly expensive, and undoubtedly was, given the evident reverence with which they were handled.

Elise stood still as her nightgown was removed, an exquisite garment in peach satin-finished silk and lace, which made up a set with its matching négligé.

Obediently she stepped into the briefs and helped draw them up, then the trousers.

'I'll use the outermost clip,' the nurse declared as she carefully slipped the bra into place before adding the blouse. 'If it's not comfortable, we'll take it off. Would you like some help with your make-up?'

There was a case holding everything imaginable, but all she'd chosen to use over the past week was moisturiser and a pale lipstick. Perfume? Her fingers hovered near the curved glass bottle of Dior, then retreated. She hadn't bothered to use it in hospital, so why begin now?

Elise watched with idle fascination as the nurse extracted a valise and began filling it with all her belongings.

'Please,' Elise intervened as the girl caught up a variety of glossy magazines. 'Keep them.'

'Are you sure?'

'Yes. And the flowers,' she added. 'Divide them among the day and night staff. And the fruit, the chocolates.'

The nurse's features mirrored her gratitude. 'Thanks. They'll be appreciated.'

Elise's mouth curved into a soft smile. 'You've all looked after me with great care.'

They had, despite it being their job to do so. Yet there had been a marked degree of dedication to this particular patient.

Because of the man whose very presence demanded nothing less? Or was it the faint air of mystery, the haunting vulnerability of the attractive girl who had occupied this suite?

'Sister will be here in a moment to formally sign you out of the hospital system.'

Elise murmured something suitable in response, and gazed sightlessly after the nurse's departing form.

Why did she feel so uncertain and so damnably insecure? A natural reaction, an inner voice assured her, in tones remarkably like those of the consultant neurologist.

The door swung open and she turned towards the ward sister, accepted the relevant appointment cards, and listened to the professional advice which concluded with, 'Don't attempt anything too strenuous too soon.'

'I will personally see that she doesn't,' a faintly accented masculine voice assured her from the doorway, and Elise turned slowly to face her husband.

The business suit he had worn that morning was absent, replaced by dark trousers and a polo shirt unbuttoned at the neck. The casual knit fabric emphasised his breadth of shoulder, the long sinewed sweep to his taut waist, and revealed powerfully muscled forearms liberally sprinkled with dark hair.

His smile was warm, and Elise idly watched the nurse's reaction with detached fascination, aware of the faint appreciative gleam evident beneath the professional façade.

Did all women respond to Alejandro Santanas in this way? Elise wondered silently. Such thoughts were hardly conducive to her peace of mind, and she stood very still as he moved towards her and brushed his lips against her temple.

'I have the car waiting outside.'

Her indecision must have been apparent, for his gaze narrowed slightly as it took in her pale features and the degree of uncertainty evident in her deep green eyes.

'You have no need to feel apprehensive,' he assured quietly.

Are you kidding? she wanted to scream. I'm being taken to a home I can't remember with a man I feel I hardly know.

With a sense of desperation she sought to elicit some sort of recollection—*anything* that would provide her with a measure of reassurance.

Yet there was nothing, and she cursed herself afresh for attempting to force a situation over which she had no control.

'If you'd care to follow me,' the ward sister suggested, 'I'll accompany you to the main entrance.'

His frame seemed to overpower hers as they traversed the carpeted corridor, and her stomach executed a series of painful somersaults as she caught sight of a large, expensive-looking vehicle parked immediately adjacent to the main doors.

Indisputably his, it looked as powerful as the man who owned it, and she slid carefully into the passenger seat, unconsciously holding her breath as he leaned forward to attend to her seatbelt.

His hand brushed against her breast, and her pulse leapt, then set up an agitated beat as he carefully fastened the clip in place, leaving her feeling helplessly trapped.

Oh, God. She had to control her over-active imagination, she counselled silently as he closed the door and crossed round to slide in behind the wheel.

The car eased forward and she experienced the insane desire to tell him to stop and let her out, which was crazy, for where could she go?

Minutes later the large vehicle emerged into the steady stream of traffic, and with a sense of resignation she focused her attention on the scene beyond the windscreen.

Houses constructed of bricks and mortar; neat garden borders bearing a variety of brightly coloured flowers; carefully tended lawns; trees lining the streets, their wide spreading branches providing shade from the sun's shimmering rays; numerous electronically controlled intersections; shops.

It all appeared so normal, so everyday. Yet none of it looked familiar.

Some of her tension must have made itself felt, for Alejandro turned slightly and cast her a discerning glance.

'You are uncomfortable?'

Her eyes widened slightly as she met his dark gaze, and she uttered a polite negation before he returned his attention to the road.

The car's air-conditioning reduced the force of the midsummer heat, and Elise breathed a silent sigh of relief as he activated the stereo system, glad of the music's soothing qualities, for it precluded the necessity to converse.

With seeming fascination she observed the quality and style of the houses lining the wide arterial road begin to change, from small, dark, weathered brick structures sited on small blocks of land to those of larger and more stately design.

Old mingled with new, their elegant façades revealing a visual attestation of wealth.

The celluloid print Alejandro had shown her of their home in suburban Point Piper revealed a large double-storeyed mansion overlooking the harbour. How long before they reached it?

'A few more minutes,' Alejandro told her quietly, almost as if he knew the passage of her thoughts.

CHAPTER TWO

THE large vehicle slowed to a halt before a set of ornate steel gates which opened at the touch of an electronic modem, then closed just as quietly behind them as Alejandro eased the car along a wide sweeping driveway.

The double-storeyed house was an architectural masterpiece in cream cement-rendered brick and floor-to-ceiling tinted glass, its tiled roof a dazzling silver-white, and set well back from the road in beautiful sculptured grounds, whose neat garden borders and profusion of flowers and shrubs were visual proof of a gardener's loving care.

The car drew to a halt at the main entrance where an impressive set of heavy panelled doors was offset by a pair of large ornamental urns, and once inside Elise was unable to prevent a faint gasp in awe of the spacious foyer.

The central focus was a tiered marble fountain, complete with gently cascading water, above which an ornate crystal chandelier hung suspended from the high glass-domed ceiling which lent spaciousness and light. A wide double staircase curved up to an oval balcony from which opposing hallways led to two separate wings.

Exotically designed panels of stained glass in the huge atrium shot brilliant prisms of multi-coloured light on to the pale walls, magnifying their pattern in an ever-changing sweep controlled by the direction of the sun's rays.

'It's beautiful.' The words slid unbidden from her lips, and she moved forward to pause at the marble fountain. 'Were you responsible for the design?'

His eyes were dark, almost still, then he smiled. 'To some degree—yes. I consulted with numerous experts in order to achieve this result.'

She put out a hand and trailed her fingers through the water, soothed by its soft flow against her skin, then she turned slightly towards him.

'You must entertain a great deal.'

His slow smile held warmth. 'There are occasions when it is more relaxing to invite business associates to one's home,' he responded indolently.

'With their wives?' Where did that come from? A natural assumption, she assured herself silently. Successful men had wives or mistresses. Some presumably had both.

Did Alejandro possess a mistress?

He took the few steps necessary to her side and placed a hand beneath her elbow. 'Let us go into the lounge. Ana will have made tea, and prepared a few delicacies to tempt your appetite.'

At the silent question mirrored in her expression, he added quietly, 'Ana takes care of the house and does the cooking. Her husband José looks after the grounds, the cars, and acts as general handyman.'

His nearness bothered her more than she was willing to admit, and she walked at his side as he ushered her into a beautifully furnished room which commanded a splendid panoramic view of the inner harbour.

Expensive works of art were spaced at intervals on the silk-covered walls, and provided an elegant backdrop for the magnificent Chinese rugs that covered the marble floor. Predominantly pale blue, employing a delicate mix of cream and the palest pink in their patterned design, the large rugs were a perfect foil for the cream-upholstered sofas and chairs, the rosewood cabinets and profusion of glass-topped occasional tables.

No sooner had Elise selected a single chair and settled comfortably into its cushioned depths than a pleasantly plump woman of middle years entered the room, wheeling a trolley on which reposed two steaming pots, milk, sugar, cream, and various plates containing a selection of small cakes, pastries, and delicate sandwiches.

'It is so good to have you home again,' Ana greeted as she poured tea, added milk and sugar, then placed the cup and saucer within easy reach on a glass-topped table beside Elise's chair.

'Thank you.' It seemed strange to be faced with a woman she must have dealt with on a daily basis in the six months of her marriage.

'I will make dinner for seven o'clock. Is there anything special you would like?' The smile broadened with pleasure. 'You have often complimented Ana on her chicken soup.'

Elise injected warmth into her voice. 'Chicken soup will be fine.'

'And afterwards? An omelette, with mush-rooms, some cheese, a little tomato, ham?'

'That sounds delicious,' she qualified, watching idly as Ana poured coffee into a demitasse and handed it to Alejandro before leaving the room.

The tea tasted like liquid ambrosia, and Elise took a small sandwich, savouring the delicate smoked salmon and cream-cheese filling, accepted another, then declined anything further.

'More tea?'

'Please,' she acceded gratefully, watching his lengthy frame unfold from the chair. His move-ments were measured and concise, his hands sure and steady as he refilled her cup and replaced it within easy reach.

'Have you lived here for very long?' The need to converse seemed paramount, and her fingers shook slightly as she lifted a hand and smoothed back an imaginary lock of hair behind one ear.

His eyes flared slightly at the nervous gesture, and she made a conscious effort to dampen the edge of panic threatening to assume unmanageable proportions.

'A few years. I had the original house removed, then began from scratch.'

She felt as if she were on a conversational roller-coaster that she couldn't stop. 'During the past week I've looked at photograph albums which mean very little, and you've provided essential information. Tell me more about how we met, and why.'

His smile assumed musing indulgence. 'The need to fill in some of the gaps?'

'There are so *many*.'

'And you are becoming impatient.'

'Frustrated,' Elise corrected. 'I seem to have a hundred questions.'

'All of which you want me to answer at once?'

Her eyes took on a haunted quality. 'I *need* to know.'

'You walked into my office demanding a minimum five minutes of my time.'

'*Why?*'

'Your father had borrowed extensively from my merchant bank, and you refused to accept my decision not to extend the loan or the term.'

She digested the information slowly. 'You own a merchant bank?'

'I have many investments,' he revealed solemnly.

'Was I successful in overturning your decision?'

He seemed to take his time in answering. 'You could say we eventually reached an understanding.'

'You asked me out.' This much she knew, because he had told her.

'You opposed me as no other woman had, questioning my business acumen and condemning me for my lack of compassion.' Warmth gleamed in the depths of his dark eyes. 'Your fierce loyalty impressed me, and I was sufficiently intrigued to insist we share dinner. Within twenty-four hours I had persuaded you to marry me.'

'And arranged for the wedding to take place a month later.' Dear God. Such omnipotence was devastating. She found it vaguely shocking that she had given her consent. 'Am I supposed to believe you're an honourable man, or go with reality?'

One eyebrow slanted in mocking cynicism. 'Which reality would you prefer, *querida*?'

'You have the advantage,' she managed, with a degree of sadness. 'While I possess none.'

'Finish your tea,' he commanded quietly. 'Then I will take you upstairs to rest.'

She wanted to say that she wasn't in the least tired, but the thought of being free from his disturbing presence for an hour or two was attractive, and she replaced her cup on its saucer.

'I have a house overlooking the ocean at Palm Beach. It's an ideal location for you to relax and recuperate.'

'You mean for both of us to stay there?' Not *alone*, surely? she agonised, aware that he had caught the fleeting emotions apparent on her expressive features.

He lifted a hand and brushed warm fingers across her cheek. 'Of course. Your welfare is very important to me.'

For some inexplicable reason she felt the faint stirring of apprehension feather insidiously down her spine.

Why? she queried silently as they moved towards the magnificent staircase. Yet with every step she took, her sense of anxiety increased.

The entire floor was covered in thick-piled powder-blue carpet, providing a cool tranquillity that was pleasing.

Elise caught glimpses of rooms employing muted shades of pale green and peach, delicate pinks and greens, the softest shades of blue and cream, all so beautifully co-ordinated that she began to suspect he had enlisted the services of an interior decorator.

The master suite held a king-sized bed and two finely crafted rosewood chests of drawers, with matching cabinets and bedside pedestals. The drapes and bedcover were of a bold design in cream, pale lilac and blue.

She watched as he crossed to the bed to turn back the cover, then with deft movements he retrieved several pillows from a cabinet and assembled them into a comfortable nest against the bedhead.

'There's an intercom device on the pedestal,' Alejandro informed her as she slid off her shoes, then sank back against the pillows.

The breath caught in her throat as he lowered his head and brushed his lips against her own in a provocative caress before straightening and moving back a pace.

'I'll be in the study for an hour or two. If you need anything, just activate the intercom. Rest well, *querida*,' he bade gently, then he turned and left the room.

There was a collection of magazines conveniently placed within easy reach, and Elise idly browsed through two before discarding them, her eyes heavy with a weariness she could no longer fight.

Her sleep was dreamless, and when she woke it was to see Alejandro standing a short distance from the bed, his eyes dark and faintly brooding as they examined her pale features.

'I'll have Ana bring you a tray.' He reached out a hand and tucked a stray tendril of hair back behind her ear. 'Come,' he commanded, sweeping the sheet aside. 'I'll help you undress.'

No, a silent voice screamed from deep within. 'I should be able to manage,' she voiced in strangled tones.

'I doubt it,' Alejandro returned, his eyes darkening measurably at her evident reluctance. 'Think of me as a nurse,' he drawled, taking in her clear-eyed resolve with a narrowed gaze as she got to her feet.

No nurse of the male species could possibly look as he did, nor create such havoc with her senses.

Calm deliberation was evident in his actions as his fingers undid first one button, then another.

'The thought of a man you can't remember removing your clothes,' Alejandro pursued in a silky voice, 'a man who as your husband has lain with you every night in this bed, tasted every inch of you, and placed the seed of his child in your womb... *frightens* you?'

'Unnerves me,' Elise corrected shakily, almost hesitant to voice the words that had tortured her since she had been made aware of her pregnancy. 'Had we *planned* to have this child?'

His eyes took on a gleaming warmth as he leant down and brushed his lips to the edge of her mouth. 'The choice and timing of conception was your decision.' His fingers freed the third button, then moved to the fourth. 'Rest assured, I could not be more delighted.'

The last button slid undone, and she stood helplessly still as he slipped the silk blouse free from her left arm, removed the sling supporting her injured right hand, then carefully drew the blouse free.

When he reached for the clip fastening on her bra she was unable to prevent an intake of breath or govern the erratic beat of her heart, and she would have given anything not to be dependent on his help.

'Close your eyes, if you must,' he advised with amused indulgence. 'Unfortunately I cannot do the same, for fear I might cause you unnecessary pain.'

He was amused, damn him! Resentment flared, lending her eyes a brilliant sparkle as she sprang into barely restrained speech.

'You think I enjoy being dependent on you?' Stupid tears welled up and threatened to spill.

'Your reticence is somewhat misplaced,' he chastised as he freed the clip, then eased the straps off each shoulder, and his eyes narrowed as she lifted an arm to cover her breasts.

A protesting gasp escaped from her lips as he caught hold of her left wrist and carefully pulled it away.

She closed her eyes, aware of her bruised shoulder. The colour had changed from dark red to purple. Now it was a deep bluish-green.

'*Por Dios*.' The soft curse slipped into the stillness of the room, and his eyes darkened in silent anger as he saw that the bruising extended the length of her ribs on the right side.

The silence stretched between them, and began to play havoc with her nerves.

'It could have been worse,' she offered, and saw his expression harden into a frightening mask.

'Yes,' Alejandro agreed with brutal cynicism. 'That young fool behind the wheel could have been responsible for your death.'

His eyes travelled to the soft swell of her breasts, and she remained helplessly still as he trailed gentle fingers over their rounded contours, shaping first one, then the other, before brushing a thumb-pad across one tender peak.

Elise gasped out loud as pure sensation shot through her body, arrowing down to focus at the junction between her thighs, unleashing a multitude of feelings she wasn't sure how to handle.

A distressed whimper escaped her lips. 'Please,' she begged, her eyes clouding with anguish as he traced a path to the soft hollows at the base of her throat, then lingered over the rapidly beating pulse for a few heart-stopping seconds before trailing up to rest at the edge of her mouth.

'You look so incredibly fragile, it robs me of breath,' he ventured slowly, his dark eyes so deeply piercing it seemed as if he possessed licence to see into the depths of her soul.

Elise swallowed convulsively, and let her lashes flutter down to form a protective veil, only to have them fly open as the tip of his finger slowly outlined the generous lower curve of her mouth, teasing the soft fullness until it parted involuntarily, allowing him to continue the sensual probe.

A slight tremor shook her slim frame, and she was powerless to move as he slowly lowered his head to close his mouth over hers in a provocative, sensual tasting that was so incredibly gentle it almost made her weep.

Some deep intrinsic need prevented her from moving away, and she bore the light sweep of his tongue as it explored the sweet recesses of her mouth, creating an acute sense of loss as he slowly withdrew. For several long, timeless seconds her eyes were held mesmerised by his, then his lips curved into a slow, warm smile as he reached for her nightgown and eased the straps over her injured hand, then her head, before pooling the silk at her waist while he removed her trousers and briefs.

'Do you need help in the bathroom?'

'No,' she refused, infinitely relieved that this was an area there was no need for him to invade.

'I'll be back with a tray in ten minutes.'

Oh, dear God, she breathed silently as the door closed behind him. What was happening to her? How could she react so damnably with someone her conscious mind failed to recognise?

She had made no effort to move away from the touch of his mouth, merely stood mesmerised as he had initiated a sensual foray that had played havoc with her vulnerable emotions.

'There are two dinner-plates,' Elise declared with a slight frown as Alejandro re-entered the room and set the covered bed-tray into position across her lap.

One eyebrow lifted in quizzical query as he subjected her to a long, considering look from beneath dark-fringed lashes. 'You imagined I would leave you to eat alone?'

She had hoped he might. He emitted a sensual vibrancy that was intense—*dangerous*. To envisage him as a lover was sufficient to set alarm bells jangling inside her brain, awakening feelings deep within that raised questions she had no desire to answer.

'Eat, Elise,' Alejandro commanded. 'Before the food becomes cold.'

Obediently she picked up the spoon and started with the soup, then when it was finished she used a fork to dissect the omelette.

It was impossible not to be aware of him as he sat a few feet distant in a comfortable chair. His movements were economical, and her eyes were drawn to the strength of his jaw, his mouth.

Remembering how that mouth had felt against her own brought a flood of soft colour to her cheeks, and she couldn't help but wonder what it would like to be kissed by him... really kissed, not the controlled brushing of his lips against hers that had been little more than an affectionate salutation.

He looked the sort of man who would *consume* a woman—with a deep, drugging passion that gave no quarter, demanding an abandonment so complete that there could be no room for reticence.

She did not know the measure of her own personality, or the strength of her emotions. Yet even in her wildest imagination she couldn't imagine acting like a wanton in his arms.

He had said he had tasted every inch of her. He couldn't mean...

'You have finished?'

His query startled her, and she met his unfathomable gaze with widened eyes. 'Yes. Thank you. I'll be fine now,' she added quickly in dismissal, and saw his eyes narrow slightly as he removed the tray.

He regarded her steadily, his expression revealing, and there was latent steel beneath the velvet tone of his voice. 'The bed is sufficiently large to accommodate both of us.'

The thought of sharing the bed with him made her stomach knot with unenviable nerves. 'I'd prefer a room of my own.'

'No.'

It was a categorical refusal. One that made her uncommonly resentful. 'I think——'

'Don't *think*,' Alejandro advised with dangerous softness, and her eyes acquired an angry sparkle.

'How can I *not*?' she declared, with a degree of asperity. 'I have no knowledge of you in any sexual sense. I know I'm not ready to resume intimacy. Dammit,' she flung heatedly, 'I can't even remember if we're——'

'Sexually compatible?' he drawled in silky query. 'I assure you we are, *mi mujer*. Passionately, primitively so.'

The retort she wanted to fling at him died in her throat as he began unbuttoning his shirt. No matter how hard she tried she couldn't prevent her gaze from focusing on him, watching beneath lowered lashes as deft fingers competently dealt with remaining shirt-buttons before moving to free the belt at his waist. Seconds later the shirt was tossed over a nearby chair, closely followed by his trousers.

It was impossible not to be aware of his impressively muscled frame: broad shoulders, chest tapering down to a trim waist, slim hips and long, powerful thighs.

Something deep inside her stirred, then slowly unfurled at the sight of his chest, liberally covered with whorls of dark hair which arrowed down over a taut waist to disappear beneath black silk briefs.

'Are you going to join me in the shower?'

He had to be joking!

Elise's eyes widened measurably, then grew dark as her gaze shifted to a point somewhere beyond his right shoulder, and she was powerless to stop the faint flood of colour covering her cheeks as her imagination ran riot.

'I can cope on my own,' she managed in strangled tones, hating him as he calmly scooped her to her feet.

She wanted to hit him, or at the very least hurl abuse at his merciless head. Sparks of topaz accentuated the green of her eyes, and her chin tilted in open defiance. 'I hate having you play nursemaid,' she said with a degree of anguish as he carefully undressed her.

'I refuse to stand by and have you inflict further damage on your shoulder out of a foolish need for modesty.'

The tone of his voice should have warned her, but she was too angry to take any notice. 'And I dislike the thought of a husband who practises voyeurism.'

He stiffened, his large frame an awesome sight as he held himself severely in check. Anger emanated from every pore, and his eyes were so dark that they resembled polished onyx. 'Perhaps you should give thanks to the good *Dios*,' he intoned in a hard voice. 'If it were not for your injuries, I would teach you a lesson you would not easily forget.'

As he had in the past? Dear God, was he an abusive man? she agonised in shocked silence. Her features paled at the thought, and she heard him utter a string of viciously soft incomprehensible words.

'Go and have your shower, Elise,' he commanded with dangerous silkiness.

She needed no second bidding, and her mouth set in mutinous lines as he followed her into the bathroom and switched on the water, tested its temperature, then stood aside as she stepped into the large stall.

Despite the rising cloud of steam she was aware of his presence a few feet distant on the other side of the glass screen, and she gritted her teeth against rising anger, feeling no remorse for taking longer than necessary before closing the taps.

He was waiting as she slid open the glass door, and her eyes waged a silent battle with his as he stepped forward and removed the waterproof covering from her bandaged hand, then collected a towel and began blotting the dampness from her body.

'I'm quite capable of completing the task,' Elise said tightly, and almost swayed beneath his long, intent gaze.

Did he have any idea of how vulnerable she felt? How damnable it was to have to stand naked before him and suffer his ministrations?

'Of course,' he drawled with hateful amusement as he discarded his briefs and stepped into the shower.

There was an enviable selection of toiletries to choose from atop the long marble vanity unit, and after making use of a few Elise collected a large towel and was about to secure it sarong-wise around her body when the water stopped.

Seconds later the door slid open and Alejandro emerged from the stall.

Elise hastily averted her eyes from the electrifying image of his superbly muscled frame, with its generous mat of curling chest-hair arrowing down in a fine line past his navel to join the hair couching his manhood.

There was something incredibly erotic about glistening water droplets caught in male body-hair, the fluid grace of strongly honed muscle-fibre moving beneath satiny, lightly bronzed skin.

The degree of restrained power in repose was an intensely disturbing entity, and her fingers shook as she caught up a brush and stroked it vigorously through the length of her hair, increasingly aware of his every action as he towelled himself dry.

As he reached for a black silk robe she stepped quickly into the bedroom, almost succeeding in donning her nightgown before firm fingers eased the straps over her injured hand, and she stood helplessly still as the silk hem whispered down past her hips.

Impotent resentment darkened her eyes, and Alejandro cast her a long, thoughtful look which she found increasingly difficult to hold as the seconds ticked slowly by.

He lifted a hand and slid firm fingers beneath the hair at her nape, then in seeming slow motion his mouth claimed hers with an element of possession she instinctively knew would harden should she attempt to pull free of him, and she swallowed convulsively as pleasure overtook warmth, touching each nerve-end as it coursed through her body.

She felt strangely afraid—not of him, but of herself, and the wild sweetness that swirled within, encouraging a response she was hesitant to give.

His tongue sought out every secret recess, every ridge, before lightly stroking her own tongue in an erotic dance that reached deep into her feminine core, unleashing emotions almost beyond her control.

She was slowly melting, awash in a sea of delicious sensation, totally unaware of voicing a faint murmur of regret as he slowly lifted his mouth from her own.

'Into bed, *querida*,' Alejandro bade firmly.

Within minutes of her head touching the pillow her eyes became heavy, and it was easier to give in to somnolence than fight it.

Alejandro stood for a long time in contemplative silence, his gaze dark and brooding as he surveyed her finely boned features, the sweep of blonde hair, the delicate texture of her skin, the long, thick eyelashes and the sweet curve of her generous mouth, softly swollen from his kiss.

A muscle tightened at the edge of his jaw, then he reached forward and switched off the lamp on the nearby pedestal before crossing to the other side of the bed to ease his long body carefully between the sheets.

Seconds later he snapped off his own lamp, and focused his attention on the shadowed ceiling.

CHAPTER THREE

THE heat of the summer sun was reduced to a comfortable level by the car's air-conditioning, and Elise leaned back against the leather-cushioned seat as Alejandro slotted a disc into the stereo system.

'This is a beautiful car,' she commented with genuine appreciation as it swept noiselessly along the arterial road heading north.

'A Bentley,' he enlightened her, shooting her an amused glance.

'It looks expensive.' The words slipped out unbidden, and his eyes narrowed slightly.

'A luxury that affords me pleasure,' he responded in a soft drawl that sent a shivery sensation feathering down the length of her spine.

As I do? Is that all I am to you . . . a possession?

Permitting her thoughts to travel such a path was both fruitless and detrimental; it served no purpose.

'You have been remarkably docile all morning,' he relayed musingly. 'I could almost believe you are treading eggshells.'

'I woke early, and couldn't get back to sleep,' she proffered, for it was no less than the truth.

He slanted her a frowning glance. 'You should have woken me.'

'Why?' She attempted a smile, and almost made it. 'So we could both have lain awake?' How could

she tell him that she had experienced a gamut of
emotions as she had watched him sleep? His
strongly etched features had been barely visible in
the darkness and then, as the dawn sky began to
lighten the room, she had been held spellbound by
the stark beauty of his countenance in repose. The
harshness was gone, his jaw and mouth relaxed,
and his lashes curled slightly, their length and shape
dark and lustrous. Fascinated, she had wanted to
reach out and place a finger against the edge of his
mouth, to trace a slow pattern over the firm curve
and watch him stir into wakefulness, to open his
eyes and witness their warmth as he caught sight
of her. Instead, she had feigned sleep the instant
he looked like rousing, and only stilled the pretence
when she had felt him rise from the bed.

Afterwards she had managed to dress herself, and
on descending the stairs a startled Ana had immediately led her out on to the terrace to join
Alejandro for breakfast.

'The car I was driving . . . was it badly damaged?'

Alejandro slowed the Bentley to a halt at a set
of traffic-lights, then turned to slant her a probing
glance.

'You are more important to me than any vehicle.'

Was she? 'You didn't answer the question.'

'It will be several weeks before you gain medical
clearance to get behind the wheel of a car. And,
when you do, it won't be a fashionable sports
model. Meantime, José can drive you wherever you
need to go.'

She looked at him in stunned silence for several seconds before venturing in protest, 'You can't be serious.'

'Unequivocally.'

Elise added another quality to his character. Inflexibility. 'Are you usually this ... overbearing?'

'Protective,' he corrected. 'You could have lost the child. Worse, I could have lost *you*.'

The lights changed, and his attention returned to the road ahead. As the Bentley gathered speed Elise evinced an interest in the passing scenery.

There were many coves and inlets, picturesque beaches, crisp sand, softly waving tree-branches stirring beneath a gentle breeze, and an expanse of glorious blue sea that stretched out to the horizon to merge with the sky.

'How long before we reach Palm Beach?'

'About forty minutes, depending on traffic.'

It was just after midday when Alejandro swung the car into a driveway leading to an imposing double-storeyed house overlooking the ocean.

It was the antithesis of what she had imagined a beach-house to be, and once inside there was a sense of unreality as he led her through several rooms on the lower floor. Beautifully furnished, it was almost as magnificent as the Point Piper mansion. There was even a swimming-pool adjacent to the terrace— almost a decadent addition, given the accessibility of the ocean a few short steps distant.

The upper floor held four bedrooms with *en suite* facilities, and as she followed Alejandro into the largest suite Elise couldn't help but wonder how frequently he made use of the house.

'Do you come here often?' she queried, watching as he deposited their bags.

'Whenever I can manage a few days away.'

Crossing to the large picture window, she moved the curtain fractionally to admire the view. Sun-dappled water, a few cruisers anchored offshore, young children, supervised by their mothers, playing happily in the sand. 'It looks so peaceful.'

She sensed rather than heard him move to stand behind her, and sensation stirred deep within, lending an awareness that made her feel acutely vulnerable. His body warmth seemed to enfold her, and all the fine hairs on her skin rose up in instinctive self-defence.

'The precise reason why I bought the place,' he told her.

'An escape from the wheeling and dealing of high-powered executive city living?'

Was that why she felt such an empathy with the house? Because it represented a refuge? From what...*whom*? The man who owned it?

She gave a sudden start as his hands rested lightly at her waist, and there was no way she could disguise the frisson that shook her slim frame as his lips settled against the curve of her neck.

'Alejandro...' Her voice faltered, then regained a measure of strength. 'I'd like to go downstairs,' she said, on a note of desperation. He was too *close*, much too close. It bothered her, and she couldn't reason why. 'Lunch,' she elaborated, and felt immeasurably relieved when he disengaged his clasp and moved fractionally away.

'Then we shall eat. The fridge and pantry are well-stocked.'

Elise turned slowly to face him. 'You're going to play cook?'

He lifted a hand and trailed gentle fingers across her cheek, letting them slide down the edge of her jaw to tilt her chin.

She gazed at him in mesmerised silence, taking in the hard planes and angles of his broad facial structure, the vertical crease that slashed each cheek, the powerful sweep of his jaw, the wide mouth.

'You find the prospect of being alone with me so daunting?'

He was teasing her, and suddenly it seemed so unfair that he had the advantage while she had none.

Indecision and a fleeting sense of mild panic coursed through her veins, visible in the dilation of her eyes as she gazed at him.

His eyes darkened and became almost black. 'Little fool,' he growled gently. 'You look at me as if you are struggling with fear. What manner of man do you imagine I am?'

'I don't know,' she was forced to own, aware that it was nothing less than the truth. Of all the details she had been made aware of, few had given a hint of his character.

'Come,' Alejandro directed, releasing her chin. 'We'll go down to the kitchen and find something to eat.' He bent down and brushed his lips against her own with the lightness of a butterfly's wing. 'In a few days you will become accustomed to having me around.'

Somehow she doubted it. Yet she accepted that she had no choice but to try.

In the kitchen he retrieved cooked chicken from the refrigerator, divided it into portions, and placed several on a platter to heat in the microwave. Then he prepared a wholesome salad with a deftness Elise found surprising. Within a matter of minutes there was food on the table.

'Please,' she protested as Alejandro began filling her plate. 'That's too much.'

'Eat what you can,' he bade easily, employing his cutlery to divide her food into bite-sized segments which she could manage with a fork.

There was a studied intimacy in his actions, a familiarity she tried desperately to recognise, yet she could recall nothing that gave a hint of the many meals they must have shared together.

'Why the slight frown?'

'Did we socialise much?' she ventured, quickly qualifying the question. 'Both your homes are large.'

'It is all too easy to gather a coterie of acquaintances who are active on the social circuit,' he answered. 'Unless you become selective, it is possible to spend three nights out of every seven at one dinner party or another.' His eyes assumed a teasing warmth. 'Since our marriage, I have chosen to entertain only when necessary, and much prefer dining *à deux* with my beautiful wife.'

Yet a man of his calibre would be in demand, his friends many and varied. Her position as his social hostess seemed a foregone conclusion.

'Why not eat?' he suggested quietly. 'The chicken will become cold.'

It looked appetising and, aware of her own hunger, she picked up her fork and speared some chicken, then salad, repeating the action until she felt replete.

'Some fruit?'

She selected an apple, its white flesh crisp and tangy, and when she'd consumed it she sat back in her chair.

'Iced water?' Alejandro queried, and she shook her head in silent negation. 'Why not go upstairs and rest?' he prompted gently. 'I'll take care of the dishes, then join you.'

'Your solicitude is overwhelming,' Elise said quickly, alarmed at his intention. 'But hardly necessary, when you must have calls to make, people you should contact.'

His gaze was remarkably steady, and a faint smile lifted the edge of his mouth. 'And you prefer to be alone,' he drawled.

'Yes,' Elise answered honestly, and glimpsed a degree of humour lurking in the depths of his eyes. *Because you scare the hell out of me*, she added silently. *Every defence mechanism I possess screams out a warning of one kind or another, yet I'm unable to fathom why.*

It was a relief to reach the sanctuary of the bedroom, and she selected a magazine, then sank back against the pillows.

She dozed, and when she woke there was a note, scripted in black ink, signed by her inimitable husband, informing her that he was in the study.

It took only minutes to freshen up and go downstairs, and Alejandro glanced up from a sheaf of papers he was examining as she entered the study, a slow, teasing smile curving the edges of his mouth.

'You look rested,' he commented musingly, and her heart tripped its beat, accelerated for a few seconds, then settled into a steady pattern.

His smile was lazy, extending to the depths of his eyes, and he rose to his feet with a lithe indolence, crossing round the desk in a few easy strides.

His head lowered to capture her lips with openmouthed gentleness, and she felt like crying *Don't* out loud as she stood helpless against the trembling sensation slowly consuming her body. The desire to sway towards him shocked her, and she experienced a mixture of emotions as his lips left hers.

Relief, dismay—*regret*? She didn't want to analyse her emotions, and she gave a shaky smile as he caught hold of her hand.

Alejandro exchanged long trousers and shoes for shorts and Reeboks, insistent that Elise discard sandals for Reeboks too—an action which set the butterflies inside her stomach fluttering into a nervous dance as he hunkered down to effect the change.

It was a glorious afternoon, the sun's summer warmth caressing her skin as they wandered slowly along the hard-packed sand, which was still slightly damp from an outgoing tide. A gentle breeze teased the length of her hair, causing a few tendrils to drift across her cheek.

There was a sense of freedom apparent, a lightness resulting from confinement in hospital for the past ten days, and she allowed herself several shallow breaths in order to drink in the salty smell of the ocean, the cleanliness of unpolluted air.

A few children were at play in the distance, their chatter and laughter barely audible as they darted back and forth, heads bent in their quest for seashells.

It was good to be alive, Elise decided with a slight smile, only to have the smile slowly fade with the realisation that, had Fate been unkind, her loss would have included the right to life of her unborn child.

An arm curved lightly round her waist, and she turned towards him, her eyes wide as she searched his strong, firmly etched features.

Some degree of her inner anguish must have been apparent, for his hold tightened fractionally, and his lips brushed the top of her head.

She was supremely conscious of his close proximity, aware of his warmth, and the security his powerful frame afforded.

They continued walking until Alejandro drew to a halt. 'This is far enough, I think.'

Elise viewed the short distance they had travelled and wrinkled her nose at him. 'I feel fine,' she protested, not wanting to return to the house just yet. 'Look,' she exclaimed, as a large golden retriever loped along the water's edge. 'Isn't he beautiful?' The dog's movements were poetry in motion, measured lolloping strides that sent his long golden hair flowing back from his young body.

'Beautiful,' Alejandro agreed, and when she turned towards him she saw his focus was centred on her, not the dog.

The breath caught in her throat, and for several long seconds her eyes felt impossibly large, then she smiled, a tinge of humour lifting the edges of her generous mouth. 'I don't suppose I could persuade you to walk a bit further?'

'No,' he refused lazily, and his eyes held amusement as he looked down into her upturned features.

'So, this is it for today?'

'Don't sound so disappointed.' He lifted a hand and tucked a flyaway lock of hair behind her ear. 'There's always tomorrow.'

Without a word she turned slowly and walked back to the house at his side. Once indoors, he led the way through the kitchen. It was warm, and she felt in need of a long, refreshing drink. She watched as he extracted two glasses, filled each with fruit juice, and held one out to her.

'You have enjoyed your taste of fresh air and sunshine?'

'I don't think anyone fully appreciates the choice of freedom to move anywhere at will until that choice is removed.' She lifted the glass and took a long swallow of the icy liquid, watching as he followed her actions.

There were several chairs and two sun-loungers positioned on the wide, partly covered terrace, and Elise moved outdoors and sank gratefully into one of the loungers. The sun was beginning to lose some of its warmth, although the house provided sufficient protection from the breeze to make sitting outdoors a pleasure.

'Your face has regained a little colour,' Alejandro observed as he chose the other lounger close by, and she bore his scrutiny with equanimity.

'Another two weeks of this, and I'll resemble a sybarite,' she said, with a tinge of humour.

'Your welfare is very important to me.'

The quietly spoken words stirred her sensitised nerve-ends, and she examined his features carefully. 'I hesitate to think at what cost,' she ventured slowly.

Something flickered in the depths of his eyes, a fleeting emotion she was unable to define before it was successfully hidden. 'I retain eminently qualified personnel.'

Whose positions within the Santanas corporation Alejandro would instantly terminate should any one of them fail him in any way. The knowledge was an instinctive judgement that needed no qualification, and she was silent for several long minutes.

'It's difficult to comprehend that there was a time when I knew everything about you,' Elise confessed.

'While now there are only gaps?'

'A deep, yawning abyss,' she corrected with a faint grimace.

'Which you would like me to fill?'

'You did that to some extent while I was in hospital.' Details, facts. Not the personal things she desperately wanted to know.

'So, *querida*,' he mocked gently, searching her intent expression, 'where would you like me to begin?'

'I think…with you. Where you were born, when. Your family. Things you enjoy doing.'

'An extended biography?'

'The condensed version.'

His eyes held warm humour, and his soft laughter transformed the hard-chiselled bone-structure, so that for a brief moment he appeared almost human, she decided, as he lifted the glass to his lips and drained the contents in one easy swallow.

'My father was born in Andalucía, the son of a wealthy landowner. My mother was a descendant of the French aristocracy. After their marriage they emigrated to Australia, where I was born. A year later my mother died in childbirth. Papa never fully recovered emotionally, and my paternal grandmother flew out for an extended visit, only to stay on and raise her only grandson. It was because of that good woman's determined strength that I stayed at school and received the education my father insisted I endure.'

He paused to shoot her a faintly whimsical smile. 'I was known to display rebellion on occasion.'

Elise had a vivid mental picture of a tall youth whose broad bone-structure had yet to acquire its measure of adult musculature.

'At university I acquired several degrees associated with business management and became part of my father's financial empire. At the lowest level,' Alejandro qualified drily. 'A Santanas son was accorded few advantages, and I spent several years proving my worth. A fatal accident ended my father's life, and I was catapulted through the ranks to a position on the board of directors.' He spared her a faintly cynical glance. 'The next few years were—difficult, shall we say? Men with years of experience do not view kindly a young man taking control of a string of multinational companies, or making decisions that oppose their way of thinking.'

Elise looked at him thoughtfully, seeing the strength of purpose, the chilling degree of hardness apparent, and barely controlled the faint shiver that threatened to slither down her spine. 'You succeeded.' As if there could be any doubt.

His expression did not alter for several long seconds. 'Yes,' he acknowledged with wry cynicism.

Had she been his social equal? Somehow she didn't think so.

'I have little idea of what my childhood was like,' she proffered with pensive introspection. 'The photo albums you brought to the hospital reveal events of which I have no recollection. I can only piece together the visual impression of a happy childhood. A mother I can't remember, whose passing must surely have caused my father great grief. I don't even know the extent to which I missed her. Or whether boarding-school was a happy experience or a lonely one.' She paused, her eyes dark with reflected intensity. 'I chose paediatric nursing as a career, but I don't know if I had a boyfriend, or several. Or what sort of life I led before I met you.'

'I doubt the existence of many boyfriends in other than a platonic sense,' Alejandro put in with indolent humour. 'You were relatively inexperienced.'

Her eyes sparked with resentful resignation. 'A fact you no doubt soon remedied.'

His husky laughter was almost her undoing. 'With immense pleasure, *mi mujer*. You proved to be an apt and willing pupil.' He leaned forward and brushed his mouth against her own, his eyes gleaming with humour as she reared back from his touch. 'Time to prepare dinner, I think.'

An hour later they sat down to soup, and followed it with grilled steak and salad, electing to watch television until Alejandro deemed it time to retire to bed.

Elise had little option but to accept his assistance, and she stood, head bent, lower lip caught between her teeth, as he began freeing her clothes.

There was something incredibly sensual in having him tend to the buttons on her blouse, the fleeting touch of his warm fingers as they brushed her sen-

sitised flesh. To have him unclip her bra and feel
his light touch against each breast.

Last night should have prepared her for the pro-
tracted intimacy of standing part-naked in front of
him. Yet, try as she might, she was unable to control
the shallowness of her breathing, or prevent the
faint colour heightening her cheekbones.

It was a relief to escape into the *en suite* bathroom
and shower alone, and she took as long as she dared
before emerging to find Alejandro waiting to towel
her dry.

She wanted to say she could manage, and for a
moment she almost did, but one look at his dark,
brooding features was sufficient for her to realise
that such an action would be the height of
foolishness.

The instant her nightgown was safely in place she
made to turn away, only to have her movement
stalled as her chin was caught between a firm thumb
and forefinger.

'*Don't,*' Alejandro began in cautionary remonstrance, 'erect obstacles where none exist.'

The soft drawl matched the faint mockery evident
in those dark eyes, and a lump rose in her throat
that made it difficult for her to swallow.

Her mouth trembled, and she felt the ache of
unshed tears as she searched the strong masculine
features, noting the grooves that slashed his cheeks,
and the tiny lines fanning out from the corners of
his eyes.

'How can you say that?' she queried in strangled tones, feeling at a loss to cope with the force of his compelling masculinity.

He lifted a hand and traced a finger down the slope of her nose, then traversed the tip to settle on the curve of her lip.

'Easily,' Alejandro assured her as he lightly stroked the soft fullness of the lower contour before exploring the generous line above.

His touch was provocative, light, and sent warning flares to each separate nerve-ending as a deliciously warm sensation slowly radiated through her whole body.

I could close my eyes and become lost, thought Elise, swayed by emotion and held in its invasive thrall. There was a part of her that hungered for the touch of his hands, his mouth, and she had the most insane desire to plead with him to turn the erotic images into reality.

A soft moan whispered from her throat as his mouth closed over hers, teasing, tasting, in a gentle exploration that brought her body close to his in an involuntary movement as he carefully deepened the kiss.

It was heaven, she decided hazily, filled with such agonising sweetness that she felt as if she were melting, boneless. *His*.

She wanted more than the mere fusing of their mouths. Much more. It was almost as if some secret part of her was privy to a knowledge that eluded her conscious mind, and she gave a tiny despairing

moan as his tongue slowed its masterful stroking
dance with her own as a prelude to retreat.

As he lifted his head her eyes clung to his, wide
and almost trance-like, for several long seconds
before his features swam into focus.

Elise glimpsed the passion held severely in check,
the deep slumbering emotion that darkened his
gaze, and something else she couldn't quite define.

Her lips were swollen and the inside of her mouth
so acutely sensitised that she wondered if she was
capable of uttering so much as a word.

Never had she felt so hauntingly vulnerable, or
so fragile. A pulse thudded visibly at the edge of
her throat as the blood drummed through her veins,
and she lifted her left hand, only to let it fall helplessly to her side.

'Bed, I think,' Alejandro decreed, his eyes narrowing as he glimpsed the effort it cost her to retain
some measure of control.

His hand cupped her left shoulder, then slid to
her breast, slipping beneath the silk to shape the
tumescent mound with exquisite care.

She felt it swell beneath his touch, the peak taut-
ening in sensitive arousal, then his mouth assumed
a wry humorous twist as he lifted both hands to
frame her face.

'Television, or would you prefer to read?'

It took considerable effort to summon a faint
smile as she allowed him to lead her towards the
bed. 'Television,' she declared unevenly. 'Providing I get to choose the programme.'

'Brave words, *querida*,' he teased lightly. 'You will probably be asleep by the time I have shaved and showered.'

She was unable to still the faint fluttering of butterfly wings inside her stomach, and her gaze became pensive as he stripped down to his briefs, then crossed to the *en suite* bathroom.

He was an enigma, Elise decided thoughtfully as she endeavoured to concentrate on the images flickering across the screen.

Darkly intense, almost frightening. Yet he could be gentle and considerate. A difficult mixture to comprehend, she accepted silently, wondering if there had ever been a time when she had understood him.

Thinking about it made her tired, and her lashes drifted down as she lapsed into dreamless oblivion.

CHAPTER FOUR

THE days ran one into the other, each following a similar pattern to the one preceding it. They rose early, dressed, and went for a walk along the deserted beach, then returned to eat a simple breakfast out on the covered terrace, after which Alejandro would disappear into the study for an hour.

It was his only concession to maintaining a check on business interests, and although there was a phone in the car, and a mobile cellular unit tucked into the pocket of his shorts whenever they moved away from the house, only once did either ring. His instructions on each occasion had been chillingly brief.

Occasionally he would pack a picnic lunch and drive to one of the neighbouring beaches, or a designated park. Sometimes they stayed at home and watched videos. Late each afternoon they embarked on a leisurely walk along the beach.

With every passing day the pain in Elise's hand lessened, the bruising faded, and she was soon able to don and shed her clothes without help, something she considered to be a milestone.

Alejandro appeared to be attuned to her every mood, watchful that she didn't become tired, and able to coax her into laughter with very little effort at all, until gradually she began to relax and regard him with hesitant affection.

She became accustomed to the light brush of his fingers across her skin, the touch of his hand on her arm, cupping her shoulder, resting at the small of her back or curved round her waist. The light touch of his mouth against her own was something else, and more than once she was barely able to suppress a tide of sensation as he instigated a teasing kiss. At night she no longer felt uneasy when he joined her in bed, nor did she attempt to pull her hand away when he threaded his fingers through her own.

Yet all the time she was aware of his restraint, the latent passion just beneath the surface of his control. Occasionally she glimpsed evidence of it in the darkening of his eyes, felt it in the sudden quickening of his pulse.

The knowledge made her nervous, tugging at something hidden deep inside her. It generated a waiting expectancy that sent tiny flares of fire surging through her veins, set her fine body-hair on edge, and curled insidiously at the core of her femininity.

The weekend came and went, with a series of scattered showers which kept them indoors. Monday dawned fresh and clear, with not a cloud in sight.

'I thought we'd pack some food in the car and head north,' Alejandro declared as she cleared the last of their breakfast dishes and watched as he rinsed and slotted them into the dishwasher.

'What time do you want to leave?' Elise queried with an alacrity that curved his mouth into a slow teasing smile.

'Allow me an hour in the study. Around ten.'

It was a glorious day, the sun high in an azure sky, with a soft breeze tempering the midsummer heat.

Alejandro brought the car to a halt and switched off the engine. The view out over the park was one of tranquillity, with several large trees lining the grassed verge. Bleached white sand bordered the eastern boundary, and the surface of the lazy outgoing ocean tide shimmered in the early afternoon heat.

'Hungry?'

Elise turned towards him and offered an easy smile. 'Ravenous.'

The park was almost empty, and Alejandro slid from behind the wheel and walked to the rear of the vehicle to retrieve a rug, cushions and a picnic hamper from the capacious boot, choosing a smooth patch of grass beneath a nearby tree.

Minutes later Elise sank to her knees and watched as he began apportioning food on to two plates.

Cold chicken and salad, with crusty bread rolls and fresh fruit, presented a veritable feast, and she picked up a chicken leg and bit into it with relish.

'Your appetite is improving,' Alejandro commented in approval, and she wrinkled her nose at him.

He sat stretched out beside her, his powerfully muscled legs tanned by the sun. His feet, like hers, were shod in Reeboks.

Looking the antithesis of a wheeling, dealing multinational corporate leader, he had ignored designer leisurewear in favour of cut-off jeans and a loose cotton shirt. The effect was devastating, she conceded as she allowed herself a circumspect appraisal, all too aware of the effect he had on her equilibrium as she admired his chiselled jaw, the firm sensual mouth, then slowly raised her eyes to meet the dark intentness of his gaze.

There was a latent indolence apparent, a studied watchfulness that was wholly sexual. She could sense his potent chemistry, like a magnetic force field, and something stirred deep within, pulsing through the tracery of veins, triggering nerve-ends until her whole body became caught up in the thrall of physical awareness.

'A sip of wine?'

'It will make me sleepy,' she protested as he extended the patterned flute to her lips. There was something incredibly intimate about placing her mouth to the rim where his had been only seconds before, and she savoured a small quantity of the excellent Chardonnay, letting it slip slowly down her throat, then followed it with several long swallows of iced water.

'Would that be such a bad thing?'

She sensed the faint humour in his voice and her eyes widened slightly. It would be so easy to reach out and touch him, to place fingers against that

hard jaw and explore the vertical crease slashing
each cheek. She wanted to, badly.

Almost as much as she wanted to feel his mouth
against her own, his hand shaping her breast. A
long, slow prelude to a passionate overture. Except
that she wasn't sure if she was ready for the finale.

Such wayward thoughts were infinitely dangerous
to her peace of mind. In an effort to shut them out
she turned her attention to the horizon, aware of
his deft movements as he extracted a fresh peach
and began peeling it.

What was he like as a lover? Passionate,
primitive, *shameless*. Dear Lord in heaven, could
there be any doubt?

'Elise?'

She turned at the sound of his voice, and her
fingers shook slightly as she took a segment of fruit
from his outstretched hand. 'Thanks.'

It was deliciously cool and juicy, and she followed it with a glass of chilled mineral water.

If she lay back and closed her eyes, maybe it
would stem this inner restlessness. She hadn't taken
into account the soft sea breeze, the sun's warmth,
or their midday meal. Together they had a sop-
orific effect, and it took only minutes for her to
slip into a light doze.

Elise woke slowly, passing through the threshold
of sleep to a state of nebulous consciousness, aware
that the slight feeling of lethargy had dissipated. It
was difficult to tell whether it could be attributed
to the recuperation process or her pregnancy.

Perhaps it was a combination of both, she decided lazily as she let her eyelashes sweep slowly upwards.

Alejandro lay sprawled in a half sitting position within touching distance, his head propped in one hand as he faced her, and she blinked as he lifted a hand and trailed gentle fingers down the edge of her jaw.

'Pleasant dreams?'

She couldn't recollect even one. 'How long have I been asleep?'

'Almost an hour,' he responded, and her eyes widened in disbelief.

'You should have woken me.'

'Why?' he asked, watching the play of emotions across her expressive features. 'There's no need to hurry home.'

Elise stared at him, aware of the sheer physicality of his powerful body and his ability to make her feel infinitely fragile. There was a warmth evident in those dark eyes, a latent sensuality that was deeply disturbing.

It was as if she was being drawn to him by some invisible magnet, and she became increasingly confused as her emotions swung like a pendulum between cautious acceptance and denial.

Logic reasoned that a man of his considerable means could easily have hired a nurse-companion for her and continued to devote most of his energies to an extensive business empire. Yet he had not chosen to delegate. Surely such an action was sufficient evidence of his caring? Why this instinctive niggling doubt that persisted despite every effort to rationalise and dispel it?

'Ready for some exercise?'

Her eyes cleared, and a smile curved her mouth. 'Yes.'

With easy lithe movements he rose to his feet, extending a hand to help her, then he stowed the hamper in the boot and followed it with the rug and cushions.

They walked in companionable silence, and Elise lifted her face to the sunshine, loving the soft afternoon breeze as it came off the sea, the slight tangy smell of salt refreshingly evident.

There were young children playing close by, three beneath the age of five, and a lovely plump baby sitting on a rug beneath the shade of a wide beach-umbrella.

Elise looked at the baby's bright eyes, the wide smile and happily flailing arms as the young mother deftly exchanged one nappy for another.

Something tugged deep inside her, a wistful longing that came from nowhere, and she made no protest as Alejandro curved an arm around her waist and pulled her close to his side.

Unbidden, her own fingers traced a light path across her waist, then paused in an unconsciously protective gesture.

Would their child be a dark-haired imp inheriting his father's genes, or a flaxen-haired angel who would steal her father's heart? Without doubt their child would be fortunate enough to lead a privileged existence.

It was late afternoon when they arrived back at Palm Beach, and Elise wandered through the house while Alejandro checked the fax machine and made a few calls.

She found her way into the informal lounge and picked up the remote control unit, flicking from one television channel to another in a bid to discover something worthy of her attention. At this time of the afternoon most of the programmes were designed to educate or amuse children, and she discarded the unit in favour of a magazine.

'Would you like to eat out? There's a variety of restaurants within a short driving distance.'

Alejandro's entry into the room had been soundless, and she glanced up in surprise as he crossed to stand within touching distance.

In public? The idea held definite appeal. '*Yes.*'

His soft laughter held a degree of quizzical warmth, and she swallowed convulsively as he caught hold of her hand and lifted it to his lips, kissing each finger in turn before slipping inward to caress the softness of her palm. The sensation sent tiny shock-waves radiating from her feminine core, and she shivered at the lambent warmth evident in those dark eyes so close to her own.

Releasing her, he slid both hands beneath her blouse to free the fastening of her bra. His fingers were warm, his touch deft, unleashing a number of sensations she found difficult to ignore.

It would have been all too easy to lift a hand and pull his head down to hers to initiate a long, sweet kiss. Except that if she did, it wouldn't stop there.

'If you continue to look at me like that for much longer,' Alejandro drawled, pressing a finger to the soft lower fullness of her lip, 'I'll take it as an invitation to join you in the shower. Afterwards,' he promised huskily, 'where and when we eat won't be a consideration.'

Colour stained her cheekbones and she turned away from him, forcing herself to walk to their suite with unhurried steps. Once there, she gathered up fresh underwear and entered the bathroom.

The water's warm spray soothed her fractured nerves, and she stayed longer than necessary, emerging to towel herself dry, then don lace-edged briefs.

Alejandro was in the process of tucking a shirt into his trousers when she entered the bedroom, and she consciously averted her gaze as she crossed to the capacious wardrobe to select something suitable to wear.

Black silk culottes, slim-heeled black sandals, and a long white sleeveless button-through silk top, she decided as she extracted the clothes from their hangers. It was a go-anywhere ensemble that was both comfortable and elegant.

Elise stepped into the culottes and pulled them into position at her waist, then reached for the top as Alejandro crossed to her side.

'No bra to fasten?'

'The top is fully lined,' she explained, intent on closing the buttons. She lifted her head and her eyes clashed with his dark, disturbing gaze. A spiral of sensation began in the region of her stomach, radiating a wealth of sensual warmth which she found difficult to ignore. Dampening it down, she forced her voice to remain steady. 'I won't be long. I just need to brush my hair and apply basic make-up.'

'You look about sixteen.'

She managed a shaky smile. 'Much too young to be married and pregnant to a man like you.'

'*Por Dios*,' Alejandro drawled. 'Why a man like me?'

Levity, surely, was an appropriate weapon, and she used it without hesitation. 'If you're going to swear, at least do so in English,' she chastised with mock severity.

He laughed softly and brushed his lips against hers. 'You *are* beginning to recover,' he mocked drily. 'Soon you'll be challenging me at every turn.'

Dear heaven. She'd been that brave to cross verbal swords with him ... that *foolish*?

'If you're ready,' he suggested easily, 'let's go and eat.'

She moved into the bathroom, brushed her hair until it resembled a curtain of pale silk, stroked translucent gold shadow on to each eyelid, then applied lipliner and gloss.

When she emerged Alejandro was waiting for her, an impeccably tailored reefer jacket lending an air of sophistication she felt at a loss to match.

The restaurant he chose was Italian, small, delightfully intimate and filled with a variety of beguiling aromas that teased her taste-buds. There was also a tiny square of parquet floor and a man of middle years playing a soft romantic ballad on a small electronic keyboard.

Elise ordered tortellini with mushrooms served with garlic bread, while Alejandro opted for pasta with a marinara sauce, and afterwards she sat back feeling replete.

'Dessert?'

She shook her head. 'I couldn't fit in another mouthful.'

He seemed totally at ease, and she couldn't help being aware that his presence caused a flutter of interest among several of the female patrons.

How could she blame them? He was a superb male animal, who possessed more than his share of sexual magnetism. Inherent good looks and an overwhelming aura of power made him a spellbinding challenge few women could ignore.

The lilting music and warm convivial atmosphere of the restaurant were persuasive, and she cast him a faintly wistful smile.

'Would you like to try the dance-floor?'

She looked helplessly at the small square of parquetry that held one couple, then inclined her head in silent acquiescence.

Minutes later she wasn't so sure it was a good idea. Her right hand lay supported between her breasts, while the fingers of her left hand rested against his shoulder. His hands were loosely linked behind her hips, forming a protective cage, and this close she could sense his body-warmth beneath the sophisticated mantle of his clothes.

His movements were sure, fluid, his strength a potent entity as he guided her with effortless ease. The keyboard player sang a hauntingly slow ballad, and to her surprise her steps didn't falter once, although her breathing quickened in tempo with her fast-beating pulse.

Warm heat spread through her veins, suffusing her body until she was aware of every sensory pleasure-spot, and a deep aching need that cried out for his touch.

She felt his hands shift to curve over the slight swell of her bottom as the ballad finished and another began, even more poignant than the last. Seconds later, she felt the brush of his lips against her hair as they trailed down to settle at her temple, and her stomach executed a tiny somersault, then went into a series of crazy flips as his warm breath stirred a few stray tendrils close to her ear.

Slowly she lifted her head, her eyes skimming the broad column of his throat to take in the firm contours of his mouth, the straight patrician nose, the sculpted cheekbones, and lastly his intensely dark eyes.

What she glimpsed there deepened the colour already staining her cheeks, and her mouth trembled slightly as she sought to put some distance between them.

He immediately loosened his hold, allowing one arm to curve lightly round her back as he led her from the floor.

'Another drink?' Alejandro queried when they were seated.

Something cool, *icy*, she qualified silently. 'Please,' she accepted. 'Lemonade with a dash of lime.'

He ordered coffee for himself, and she sipped the contents of her glass, contrarily wanting the evening to be over, yet strangely hesitant to leave the restaurant.

Why so apprehensive? she reiterated to herself as the Bentley cruised smoothly towards Palm Beach. There was no medical reason why they shouldn't resume intimacy, and to be so racked with nerves was ridiculous.

'Do you want to share?'

The sound of his voice startled her, and she turned towards him in silent query.

'Your thoughts,' Alejandro elaborated as he eased the large vehicle into the driveway, then activated the remote control to raise the garage doors.

Dear heaven, had he guessed? What would he say if she said she was scared stiff... of *him* in the role of lover? More than likely he would be mildly amused, she decided wretchedly.

As soon as the car came to a halt she released the seatbelt and slid to her feet, waiting as he sprang the locking system before crossing to her side as they entered the house.

Once indoors she made straight for the stairs, only to come to an abrupt halt as his hand closed over her elbow and he turned her round to face him.

His eyes were faintly hooded, his tone a deceptively soft drawl. 'You're reacting like a skittish kitten, unsure whether to leap and run, or stay.'

'Perhaps because that's how I feel.'

'You find my touch abhorrent?'

Oh, my, nothing like aiming straight for the jugular. 'No,' she disclaimed quietly. 'But I'm not ready to sleep with you.'

'We already sleep together.' His voice was so dangerously quiet that it sent an icy shiver scudding down her back.

Dull pink streaked her cheeks. He was fully aware of the havoc he was creating, and she hated him for the deliberate assault on her ambivalent emotions.

'You know that isn't what I meant.'

He caught hold of her chin between thumb and forefinger, tilting it so that she had to look at him.

She couldn't articulate a single word, and it was difficult to swallow the lump that had suddenly risen in her throat. Her eyes felt large and impossibly wide as she watched his head descend, and she was incapable of movement as he angled his mouth to settle over hers in a kiss that claimed his possession, savouring it in a manner that alternated between gentleness and restrained savagery.

Elise told herself she should be shocked. Instead, she became caught up in a tide of deep primitive need.

One hand cradled her face, the other cupped her bottom as he pulled her hard against him. Evidence of his arousal was a hard, throbbing entity, and she gave a faint moan of protest as his mouth took on a light teasing quality, then slowly withdrew.

She could only look at him, totally ignorant of the deep slumberous quality evident in her eyes. Her lips felt swollen, and she could have sworn they trembled beneath the intentness of his dark gaze.

It was as if time stood still, for she wasn't conscious of anything except the man: his eyes, the sensual curve of his mouth, the hard planes of his jaw, the strength of his chin, the texture of his skin.

He didn't say a word for what seemed an age, then he leaned forward, swept an arm beneath her knees and lifted her against his chest.

Sensation curled deep inside her stomach and began radiating through her body as he mounted the stairs to the upper floor.

On entering their suite he closed the door, slid off her shoes, then carefully set her down on her feet. Lifting a hand, he slowly traced the contours of her mouth, probing the softness with a gentleness that made her catch her breath.

'I want to make love with you.'

Her eyes dilated and her pulse began to kick in a quickened beat. She wanted to voice her nervousness, but the words never left her lips.

His eyes held hers as he shrugged off his jacket and tossed it over a chair, then he loosened his tie and discarded it before unfastening the buttons on his shirt. Next came his shoes and socks.

Elise couldn't look away as his fingers unbuckled his belt, slid free the slim metal clasp, then freed the zip on his trousers.

Black silk briefs rode low on his hips, barely containing the turgid rigidity of his manhood, and awareness arrowed from her feminine core, focused and so intense that she was unable to suppress a slight shiver that spiralled down her spine.

Slowly he closed the distance between them, took her left hand in his, and led her to the bed. His touch was warm and strong, and she uttered no protest as he sat on the mattress's edge and drew her close.

Her eyes were almost on a level with his, and she felt mesmerised by the dark gleaming passion evident as he lifted a hand and lightly traced the contours of her face.

The touch of his fingers against her skin was electric, and she swallowed convulsively as they trailed down the column of her throat and traversed a path to the edge of her top.

He freed one button, then the next, until the edges hung loose, and she uttered a faint gasp as he brushed the full curve of her breast.

'The thought of doing this has driven me to edge of sanity,' Alejandro said huskily. 'All evening, every movement you made emphasised their unfettered state.' With extreme care he eased the blouse free and tossed it to join his discarded clothes.

'Beautiful,' he whispered, gently shaping the creamy fullness, testing its weight as he lightly circled each sensitised peak.

Acute sensation curled deeply inside her stomach, and her throat began to constrict as he leaned forward and took one peak into his mouth, rolling it with the roughened edge of his tongue until she felt it swell and harden beneath his touch.

A low groan locked in her throat as he bestowed a similar attention on its twin. Then she gasped out loud as he began to suckle deeply, drawing from each tender peak an erotic satisfaction she had no conscious urge to deny.

When at last he lifted his head, she met his gaze through half closed lids, and she stood quite still as he reached for the waistband of her culottes and began easing the silk down over her hips to pool at her feet. Satin and lace briefs followed, and she felt heat sear her body as he conducted a leisurely appraisal.

He lifted a hand and trailed gentle fingers up over her ribcage, then slowly traversed her hip, slipping to caress the slight roundness of her bottom before brushing a path to her thigh.

His eyes never left hers, and Elise felt her own dilate as he sought the soft, curling hair, then followed its upper line, caressing, moving back and forth, until her whole body began to sing like a finely tuned instrument.

Slowly his hand lowered until he reached the junction between her thighs, and she uttered an audible gasp as he initiated an intimate exploration she was hesitant to accept.

'Am I frightening you, *querida*?'

Fear wasn't quite the word she would have used to describe her feelings. Excitement, exultation, to name only two. 'No.' The single negation emerged as a whispered gasp.

His touch proved an erotic torture, and she shuddered as an initial spasm caught hold of her and spiralled out of control.

'Alejandro.' His name on her lips was a deep, husky groan.

Dear God, such sweet magic. It was like being taken straight to heaven and shown a hundred different delights.

'Gently, *querida*,' he cautioned as she reached blindly for him.

The soft sounds emerging from her throat were incomprehensible, and she was hardly aware of him easing her down on to the bed.

He carefully moved her injured hand into a comfortable position, then stretched out at her side.

His mouth sought hers in a long, slow, drugging kiss that alternately teased and tantalised, and she began to tremble as his lips began a path of erotic discovery so that it was all she could do not to cry out as he nuzzled the entry to her innermost core.

Brazen, she admitted silently as she climbed to dizzying heights. Shameless. Hopelessly, helplessly passionate and disruptively sensual. She never wanted it to end, yet the spiral of sensation was so incredibly acute she wasn't sure how much longer she could maintain any restraint.

It was the most intimate kiss of all, a deep, drugging oral simulation of the sexual act. A sensual gift so exquisite, so incredibly generous that she wanted to weep from the joy of it.

Slowly his head moved, and he began raining a trail of open-mouthed kisses over the plane of her stomach, upwards to caress the soft underswell of each breast before fastening on one sensitised peak.

Then he raised his head to look down at her, taking in the slumberous darkness of her eyes, the soft pink that coloured her pale features, and her parted lips.

Elise lifted a tentative hand to the dark springy mat of hair on his chest, and she traced his shoulder, played delicately with the strong cage of his ribs before moving involuntarily down to the taut flat planes of his stomach.

She felt the muscles clench, and unconsciously her tongue edged out and ran a tentative path along her lower lip.

'*Dios*,' Alejandro cursed in husky remonstrance. 'If you don't stop *now*, I will pass the limit of my control.'

She looked at him carefully and glimpsed the latent passion, the heated desire barely masked.

A feeling of power raced through her veins, building until she felt like a goddess in charge of something so infinitely precious, so rare that only *she* could grant him the release he sought.

With deliberate slowness she trailed her fingers to trace the length of his distended shaft. Fascinated, she afforded it a gentle tactile exploration, feeling it engorge further beneath her featherlight touch.

'I don't want your control.' Her voice was a husky enticement, and she heard his deep despairing groan followed by the sound of silk being torn from hair-roughened skin.

'Dear God,' he responded piously, 'I doubt you would condone my lack of it.'

With extreme care he prepared her to accept him, and she arched instinctively, welcoming the intrusion as he gained entry. The feeling was intense as moist tissues stretched to accommodate his length, and she exulted in the total enclosure.

It was almost as if this were their first time together, and she experienced a sense of wonder in his possession.

As crazy as it seemed, she could *feel* the blood vessels engorge as she encased him, the spasmodic action of inner muscles as they sought to encourage and match his rhythm.

It was almost as if her body recognised what her conscious mind was reluctant to accept, urging a blatant display of passion that was vaguely shocking.

With the grace of an uninhibited Circe she traced the length of his spine, then gently kneaded his tightly muscled flank. Almost of their own volition her fingers trailed to his hip, then began a slow exploratory inner path to the highly sensitised base of his sex.

Gently, very gently she squeezed the sensitive glans, and exulted in his indrawn breath. Not content, she initiated a seeking path with her lips until they discovered a sensitive male nipple, and she suckled shamelessly, nipping occasionally with her teeth until she felt his powerful body shudder in the initial throes of sensual ecstasy.

She wanted . . . Dear heaven, what *did* she want? More, *more* than this carefully controlled pacing. All of him, plunging deep inside her in a torrent of wild strokes that would take them both to the heights.

Elise was hardly conscious of the soft sounds emerging from her throat as her body reacted with instinctive ease, lifting, angling with a will of its own as she intuitively matched each and every one of his movements.

His hands on either side of her shoulders braced his weight, and she met his mouth hungrily as it closed over hers, his kiss so deep, so consummate, it mirrored the sexual act itself in an erotic joining that culminated in a wild journey to the centre of her sensual universe.

Her mind might deny any conscious acknowledgement of her primeval soul, but every sensitive chord in her awakened body was attuned to this one man, honed by his expertise, tutored with a mesmeric passion that surpassed every restrictive boundary.

There could be no vestige of doubt that she was *his*. The traitorous proof was apparent in every sensitive nerve-ending, the acute vibrancy that thrummed through her veins, heating her blood to a fervent flame of desire that could only lead to a conflagration of all the senses. *Passion*—pagan, primitive, and wildly erotic.

When it was finally over, she was so emotionally enervated that she doubted her ability to move so much as a muscle.

She felt tinglingly alive, as if every nerve-ending had become acutely sensitised by his touch, yet drowsy and deliciously spent. Languid, she corrected, smiling as she felt his lips caress the curve of her neck, then slip down to bestow an open-mouthed kiss on each breast in turn.

He was...magnificent, she acknowledged dreamily. A tender lover, caring, considerate of her needs. Had *he* enjoyed himself with her as much as she had with him? Was he satisfied, complete? Somehow she couldn't bring herself to ask.

She felt him move, and she shifted her head to look at him as he retrieved the support for her arm and carefully fixed it in place.

His eyes were dark, slumberous, and her own skittered to a point somewhere beyond his left shoulder.

'Don't,' Alejandro chided huskily as he cradled her head and forced her to look at him, 'attempt to hide what was an intensely beautiful experience for both of us.' His thumb probed the swollen softness of her mouth. *'Exquisito.'*

He slid down to lie beside her, gathering her close so that her head nestled beneath his shoulder. With minimum effort he caught hold of the sheet and drew it over them. 'Go to sleep, *querida*,' he bade her gently.

Yet she couldn't, not for a long time. Instead she lay still, listening to the steady beat of his heart.

Had it always been like this, right from the beginning? Or had it taken time and practice to reach such a pinnacle of sexual satisfaction?

Sadly, she didn't know. There was just the aching acceptance that her body remembered what her mind could not.

CHAPTER FIVE

THE beach was peaceful, with the merest breeze slipping in from the ocean to caress Elise's skin and tease the length of her hair.

The water was a deep blue, its surface smooth in the distance, cresting as it neared the shore to swirl foam-laced over the hard-packed sand.

A strange feeling of ambivalence held her in its spell...and a degree of sadness. She felt safe here. Secure.

The past ten days had been idyllic: lazily spent sunshine-filled days and easy companionship, long moonlit nights and gentle loving.

Tomorrow they were to return to Point Piper. Next week she was to begin physiotherapy, and there were appointments with the obstetrician and neurologist. Within a very short time Alejandro would drive into the city each morning to spend most of each day in his office atop one of Sydney's inner-city modern architectural masterpieces, and she would be alone...

An office. Atop a modern city architect-designed building...

She saw it clearly.

A large, sumptuously furnished room, clean lines, expensive prints on the walls, and a wide expanse of tinted plate glass with splendid views over the city and harbour.

An encapsulated vision of a room with a tall, broad-framed figure leaning against the edge of a large executive desk. Alejandro, his expression harsh and forbidding, his silent anger a vivid entity.

She was there, recapturing her anger...his. Hearing the words with frightening clarity.

'My respect for your father,' Alejandro declared in a dangerously soft, slightly accented voice that was chilling in its intensity, 'allowed you to get past my secretary and buy five minutes of my valuable time.' Dark eyes became icily dispassionate. 'I suggest you make good use of it.'

'My father doesn't know I've initiated a personal appeal,' Elise assured him in immediate defence.

'It makes no difference. My decision is irrevocable.'

The words were clipped, hard, and horribly final. 'How can you say that?' she demanded, launching into passionate speech. 'He deserves——'

'Another chance?'

'Why don't you let me finish a sentence?' she parried with mounting antipathy, and encountered his visible cynicism.

'Four minutes and thirty seconds doesn't allow for verbose explanation.'

She wanted to hit him. She almost did. Yet there was something electrifyingly primitive beneath his sophisticated façade that warned her that he would retaliate in kind without the slightest qualm.

'Without your help, my father faces bankruptcy,' she enlightened him starkly, and glimpsed no visible change in his expression.

'I head a multinational corporation which has a complex variety of investments throughout the world. Although I retain a controlling percentage, as director I am responsible to a number of shareholders. Your father's latest appeal for a further extension resulted in extensive feasibility studies. The findings negate any possibility of directorial board approval for either an increase in borrowings or an extension of time.'

Elise felt her misgivings increase at his inflexibility. 'He's ill,' she stressed with a sense of desperation. 'Conclusive tests reveal the necessity for heart surgery.'

'I cannot gamble with my shareholders' money.'

The hard unyielding words brought a rush of anger she barely managed to contain. Don't blow it, an inner voice cautioned. 'My father is a very proud man for whom honesty and integrity are sacrosanct. Hansen Holdings has been a family company for three generations,' she informed him with commendable steadiness, given the short rein she held on her temper. 'It will kill him if he loses everything in a bankruptcy action.'

His expression did not change. He was a superb tactician, watchful, waiting for her to plot the next move. There was no doubt he would win the game, but for the moment she was still a player, even if he held all the cards.

'Commendable sentiment isn't sufficient reason for me to grant the extension your father requires.'

He was an obdurate, unfeeling monster, she decided with bitter acrimony. Truly *el diablo*. Pride lifted her chin and lent her eyes a fiery sparkle. 'What would you consider to be sufficient reason?'

His eyes darkened fractionally, and she was unable to look away. His intent gaze had a mesmeric effect, and a slow heat suffused her body, reaching deep to unleash an entire gamut of sensations she was loath to recognise.

A deep insistent burr was almost an anticlimax as it broke the fraught silence, and Elise watched as he reached for the in-house phone, privy to the brusqueness of his voice as he checked the time and intimated he was on his way.

Replacing the receiver, he moved away from the desk. 'I am needed in the board room.'

She endeavoured to keep the desperation from her voice. 'Please . . .'

His eyes seared hers, lancing right through to her soul. After what seemed an interminable silence, he drawled, 'Have dinner with me tonight.' He named a well-known restaurant. 'Meet me there. Seven-thirty.'

Her lips formed a single negation, only to have it remain locked in her throat.

'A test of filial loyalty, wouldn't you agree?' He moved with lithe ease towards the door. 'My secretary will see you out.'

*   *   *

A shiver shook Elise's slim frame as the image disappeared and, no matter how hard she concentrated, it was impossible to recall.

Alejandro paused beside her, his expression intent as his eyes raked her pale cheeks. 'What is it?'

She lifted a hand and smoothed a stray tendril of hair back behind her ear. Slowly she turned towards him, her eyes shadowed and pensive.

'I was in your office.' She drew in a deep breath, then relayed a description. She looked at him, puzzlement creasing her forehead. 'I was appealing to you to extend my father's company loan,' she explained shakily. 'You were angry,' she revealed slowly. 'We both were.'

She'd felt it, *breathed* it in those few brief minutes, a palpable entity so vivid it made her feel terribly afraid.

His expression was impossible to fathom. 'How much were you able to remember?'

Was that why she'd married Alejandro? To save her father?

Her head began to reel, and she drew a deep breath in a conscious effort to stave off a spell of dizziness.

'You were called in to a board meeting,' she revealed slowly, trying desperately to recall the elusive image without success. 'I can remember walking to the lift, stepping into it,' she said helplessly. 'But that's all.'

His hands lifted to cradle her face, then his mouth closed over hers in a light tasting that elicited little response. It was as if her mind were still caught up with the desire to recapture the past, and she didn't offer a word as they made their way back to the house.

Elise found it difficult to shake off an inclination towards introspection for the rest of the day, and even during dinner she was unusually quiet.

'Anxiety won't help hasten the return of your memory,' Alejandro advised as she pushed her plate aside.

She glimpsed the inherent strength apparent, and her eyes took on a shadowy quality. 'I can't help the feeling of defencelessness that has always lurked in the background,' she revealed slowly, holding his gaze.

'You have no reason to be uncertain. About anything,' he added with deliberate emphasis.

She wasn't quite so sure, but at the moment she had little option but to accept his word.

He rose to his feet and began collecting cutlery and stacking plates. 'Sort through the video cassettes while I take care of the dishes.'

Elise wandered into the informal lounge, and after some deliberation she selected an action movie that threatened to swamp the viewer with lots of thrills and spills.

Alejandro walked into the room just as the previews concluded, and as she made for one of the single chairs he tugged her down on to the two-seater beside him.

With maximum ease he adjusted their positions so that she rested between his thighs and leaned back against his chest. His hands moved to link together over her lower abdomen.

The desire to stay there overcame any willingness to protest, and she forced herself to concentrate on the superbly fit male actor on screen as he launched into a daring choreographic karate routine with his opponent.

Elise must have fallen into a doze at some stage, for when she woke she was in bed and it was morning.

After a leisurely breakfast Alejandro tossed their bags into the boot, locked up the house, and drove back to the city.

'You look so much better,' Ana beamed with approval as she greeted them on arrival, and her pleasant features creased into a genuine smile. 'It is good to see the colour in your face again.'

Elise's mouth curved with a certain wry humour. 'Alejandro has been feeding me up and taking me for walks along the beach.'

'I will serve lunch early. Your appointment is at two, *sí*?'

It was all going to start: the daily physiotherapy sessions, the visits to specialists, and soon there would be no reason for her not to rejoin Alejandro on the social scene.

Elise was unable to still a feeling of instinctive apprehension, and although she did justice to a bowl of Ana's chicken soup, she toyed with the salad, picked at the bread, and opted to conclude the meal with fresh fruit.

Perhaps José would drive her to the physio-therapist's rooms, leaving Alejandro to retire into the study for the rest of the afternoon.

However, it was her inimitable husband who slid in behind the wheel.

'There's no need for you to come in with me,' she essayed when the Bentley eased into a parking bay adjacent to the main entrance.

'I'll confine myself to the waiting-room,' Alejandro conceded with amused tolerance, and she wrinkled her nose at him in silent admonition as he followed her in to reception.

The physiotherapist explained precisely what exercises he wanted her to do, and why—muscles lost their elasticity if they were not used, resulting in stiffness, gradual loss of mobility, and pain.

Elise completed the simple exercises with super-vised care, and at the end of the session Alejandro drove her home.

Traffic was congested, some drivers more impatient than others as the lines of cars slowed to a snail's pace. Tempers rose, horns blared and engines roared in protest. Then slowly they began to move again.

The Bentley had just begun to pick up speed when Alejandro hit the brakes. Elise was conscious of several things at once: Alejandro's arm anchoring her against the seat an instant before the car lurched on impact, and the sickening sound of crunching metal. She registered dimly a string of viciously articulated Spanish words, then Alejandro was leaning over her, his features harsh as his hands cupped her face.

'Are you all right?'

She was in another car, a white sports model, behind the wheel, passing through a computer-controlled intersection. There was an instantaneous reaction as she slammed on the brakes and wrenched the wheel in a desperate bid to avoid hitting the oncoming vehicle. But it was too late. There was a sickening crunch of metal. Her head hit something, and then there was darkness.

'*Por Dios.*'

Elise felt as if her eyes were far too large for her face as she attempted to re-focus them and shut out that horrific vision.

'Are you hurt?'

She registered Alejandro's voice, deep, dark and throbbing, then she saw his face, anxiety etching every line, his eyes almost black as they attempted to see beyond the mask her features had become.

'Elise.' His fingers were gentle as they stroked each cheek, and she blinked once, twice, then she was back in the present.

'I'm—fine,' she attempted, through lips that trembled badly. She met his intent gaze, and swallowed the sudden lump that seemed lodged in her throat. 'Really,' she assured him shakily as she defended herself against eyes that seemed to pierce her soul.

'You remembered the accident.' It was a statement, not a query. 'All of it?'

Her lips seemed strangely dry, and she edged out the tip of her tongue to moisten them. 'Just—a blur of blue hurtling towards me, the moment of impact.'

His eyes never left her face, and her mouth trembled slightly as he reached for the car-phone, punched in a series of numbers, requested the police, and gave a brief description of the accident and location.

Elise could only stare straight ahead as Alejandro pushed open the door and slid to his feet, and his hard inflexible tones combining with those of the man who had tempted providence by making an erroneous move barely penetrated her conscious mind.

Was this how her memory would return? A series of brief isolated incidents every few days?

Seconds later Alejandro slid in behind the wheel, and Elise bore his intent scrutiny with equanimity.

'I'm OK,' she assured him. 'Is there much damage to the car?'

'*You* concern me. Not the car,' he said bleakly.

At some stage she heard the distant wail of a police siren, then it came close, red and blue lights flashing. Doors slammed, voices.

It wasn't until they arrived home that she saw the broken light and its surround, the deep gouges and scratches. The sight of them brought on a wave of nausea, and she only just made it upstairs in time.

No protest she made prevented Alejandro from calling in the doctor.

'Dammit, this is *normal*,' she uttered fiercely, and saw his expression measurably harden. She lifted her hands in mock surrender. 'All right, I give in.'

An hour later she barely refrained from reiterating the doctor's reassurance, and the only concession she made to resting was to recline on the sun-lounger beneath a shade umbrella at the pool's edge.

The next few days assumed a regular routine as Elise attended the physiotherapy clinic and kept an appointment with the neurologist.

Alejandro rose early, spent an hour working out in the downstairs gym, followed it with several lengths in the pool, then after breakfast he closeted himself in the study until Ana served lunch.

An urgent telephone call on Friday morning necessitated his presence in the city, and Elise rejoiced at the thought of spending the day alone.

The physiotherapy session was scheduled for mid-morning, and after lunch she settled down to leaf through a supply of the latest glossy magazines.

Tall, perfectly proportioned young women modelling beautiful clothes, she perceived as she flipped idly through the fashion pages.

One model in particular caught her eye, and she wondered at her instinctive fascination with a long-haired brunette with classical features and cool dark eyes.

Without any warning those same features seemed to come alive, and it was like watching a re-run of part of a film depicting an isolated incident in her life, Elise decided, momentarily freezing as images crowded her brain. So clear, so hauntingly vivid.

Alejandro, Elise and Savannah seated together at a table, aiding one of several charities Alejandro was known to support.

Savannah. The hauntingly beautiful model who had been Alejandro's close companion for several years before Elise had been thrust into the limelight as his latest conquest.

Now Savannah seemed intent on proving she still held Alejandro's interest by indulging in a little game of subtle flirting, a fact which was not lost on Elise.

It was extremely difficult to maintain the semblance of a smile as she spooned morsels of delectable fruit from the elaborately presented dessert.

Jealousy was a terrible emotion, she conceded, as she picked up her fork and speared a segment of orange with more force than necessary. With little provocation, she could have killed Savannah for her blatant attempt to capture Alejandro's attention. As for Alejandro... She would have liked to do temporary harm to a vulnerable part of his anatomy.

Perhaps he sensed her antipathy, for he turned his head and his eyes gleamed with mild amusement as he met her calculated smile.

Without a word he reached for her hand and carried it to his lips, kissing each finger in turn as she seethed with silent anger.

How dared he? She wanted to walk out and take a taxi home. As it was, she barely managed to preserve a calm front for the remainder of the evening, and the instant Alejandro brought the Bentley to a halt inside the garage she burst into angry speech.

'In future you can choose whether you partner Savannah or your wife,' Elise railed in fury.

'You expect me to display ill manners by ignoring a friend I have known for several years?'

'Heaven forbid,' Elise said sarcastically.

'You have no reason to be jealous.'

She slid from the car as he moved out from behind the wheel, and it gave her the utmost satisfaction to slam the door.

'I am not jealous. I simply refuse to be part of a *ménage-à-trois*.'

Alejandro began to chuckle, and the husky sounds of his amusement acted like flame placed too close to combustible octane.

Elise threw her evening bag at him, and followed it with one evening sandal, then the other, each of which he neatly fielded and slid into the pockets of his jacket.

'So you want to play?'

He reached her far too easily, before she had gone more than a few steps, and she gasped in outrage as he lifted her effortlessly over one shoulder and carried her indoors.

'Put me down!'

He walked through the foyer to the stairs, gaining the upper floor with galling ease, seemingly uncaring as she beat her hands against the broad expanse of his back.

In the bedroom he tumbled her down on to the bed, discarded his jacket, then captured her wildly scrambling form by the simple expedient of covering it with his own.

'Damn you,' Elise vented as she struggled impotently against his superior strength. 'I hate you.'

'I love the way you hate, *mi mujer.*'

'Sex. Lust,' she qualified. 'Bought and paid for.'

He went curiously still. 'I suggest you retract that vilifying statement.'

'Why? Does the truth penetrate your conscience, Alejandro?' she taunted, only to cry out in shocked surprise as his mouth closed over hers with punishing force.

What followed was a form of retribution he actively encouraged her to share, their mingling anger resulting in wild, untamed sex that gave no quarter . . . for either of them.

'Elise?'

The sound of Ana's voice seemed to come from far away, and Elise dragged her mind back to the present. Her heart pounded inside her chest, and her skin was damp with the fine sheen of sweat.

'I have just made tea. Would you like some?'

Somehow she managed a suitable response.

Dear God. This was the most explicit span she'd experienced. The memory of it was so vivid, the act so primitively savage that it was all she could do to prevent herself from being physically ill.

I don't want to remember any more. Not if total recall means a revival of anger and dissension.

The friendship, the special closeness which she and Alejandro had shared at Palm Beach seemed part of a distant fantasy.

Instinct warned her that she was teetering on the edge of reality, and a chill feathered over her skin, raising all her fine body-hairs in protective defence.

CHAPTER SIX

IT RAINED most of the weekend, squally wind-driven showers that beat against the windows, bringing much-needed water to the city's depleted dams and providing relief against the seasonal threat of bushfires.

Alejandro taught Elise the basic skills of chess, checkmating her so many times that she declined to allow him further victory as she opted to trounce him at cards. That too was a disaster, for, although she won twice, she suspected that it was only because he deliberately set out to lose.

Monday dawned bright and clear. The Bentley went in for repair, and Alejandro took the Porsche into the city.

Elise attended physiotherapy after lunch, then José drove her across town for her appointment with the obstetrician. They arrived early, and she opted to check in rather than wait in the car.

The senior nurse greeted her warmly. 'Doctor has a patient with him, Mrs Santanas. He won't be long.' Elise took a seat, selected a magazine, and began leafing through the pages. An article caught her eye, and she read it with interest.

Minutes later she glanced absently at another, and froze. Two frames featuring Savannah adorned facing pages, and with a tiny gasp of shock everything suddenly fell into place, almost as if someone had depressed a camera shutter, then released it to reveal a moving photograph to view.

With horrified fascination she watched it all unfold.

Dear heaven, no. *No*. The negation seemed to thunder inside her brain over and over as she desperately sought to stop the images appearing one after the other like a rolling reel of Technicolor film.

It wasn't true. None of it. There was some terrible mistake. A shocking joke played by a devilish hand.

If she sat still, perfectly still, the images would disappear, and she could walk out of here without becoming an emotional wreck.

Her stomach churned as the impact of recurring memory took effect, and she only just made it to the powder-room in time.

Afterwards, she leaned her head against the cool tiles for several minutes as she stared sightlessly at the beautifully appointed bathroom.

She didn't feel like facing anyone, much less a skilfully perceptive medical professional who would doubtless take one look at her pale features, note her elevated pulse-rate, and begin a line of questioning she had no wish to answer.

Elise wondered what sort of reaction she would generate if she simply walked out, slid into the waiting car, and bade José take her home.

Home. Hell's teeth, how could she go *there*? How could she not? she decided dully. If she requested José to take her anywhere else, it would only be a matter of minutes before José alerted Alejandro, and then what? A confrontation?

She had so much anger to expel. Such a degree of inner rage.

With deplorable ease her mind slid back to the ill-fated dinner she had shared with Alejandro Santanas only hours after launching a personal appeal for him to stave off her father's imminent fall into bankruptcy...

Elise arrived five minutes late and was escorted to Alejandro's table where, within minutes of ordering iced water, she immediately launched a further attempt on Joseph Hansen's behalf.

'What inducement do you intend to offer me?' He lifted one well-shaped eyebrow, his expression assuming world-weary cynicism. 'Yourself, perhaps?'

It took mere seconds for his words to sink in, a few more for her to throw the contents of her glass at his face. She rose to her feet in white-faced fury, then stormed from the restaurant... only to have to return when she discovered that she had left her evening bag on the table.

When she reached for it, his hand closed over hers.

'Sit down.'

'I have nothing to say to you!'

'Walk out on me a second time, and any chance you might have will be gone.'

Every instinct screamed for her to turn away from him, and it was only the image of her father that persuaded her to resume her seat.

'You care for your father very much.'

'If I didn't,' she responded flatly, 'I wouldn't be here.'

'Enough to give your personal guarantee to investment from my private funds?' His pause was deliberate. 'Become part of the deal?'

She felt cold, and barely in control. 'In what capacity?' If he said as his mistress, she would tip the soup in his lap, then walk away. This time she would make sure she had her bag. And hell would freeze over before she would willingly exchange so much as a word with him should their paths meet again.

'My wife.'

It was the last thing she had expected him to say. 'You're insane.'

He subjected her to a long, steady look before venturing in a hateful drawl, 'Two million dollars as an unconditional gift in exchange for two years of your life.'

'No.'

'You sign a pre-nuptial agreement relinquishing any claim on my assets in lieu of the two million dollars I advance to your father on the day of our marriage,' he continued as if she hadn't spoken.

It was totally crazy. 'No.'

'Handsome recompense for an act of mercy.'

'My father would never condone it.'

'He need not know, if you act a part.' His eyes never left hers. 'You have twenty-four hours to reach a decision.'

She gave it, within mere minutes of his deadline.

The marriage of Elise Hansen and Alejandro Santanas took place a week later.

'If it were not for my father,' Elise vented with restrained vehemence as she attached her signature to the marriage register, 'I would never have agreed to this diabolical arrangement.'

'I have no doubt.'

'What if I refuse you?' she flung at him later that night when they retired to their hotel suite.

'A no I should interpret as a maybe?' Alejandro queried. 'If my foreplay succeeds in arousing you to a state of sensual desire?'

'You damned egotist,' she spluttered.

Afterwards she hated herself, *him*, for proving that sex and love were two entirely different emotions.

It had taken only weeks to discover the existence of Savannah and learn that the glamorous model had been and, rumour had it, still was Alejandro's mistress—a revelation deliberately designed to shatter her confidence. At the time, the vindictive gossip did not hurt at all. The pain came later.

Four months after her marriage her father suffered a heart attack, partly recovered, only to incur a second massive attack in a matter of weeks.

The night he lay so ill in hospital after the initial attack she forgot to take the Pill. By the time she realised the implications of her lapse it was too late, and her worst fears were confirmed when a home pregnancy test showed positive. A doctor's appointment merely verified it.

For two weeks she suffered the tortures of the damned. Then, early one morning, soon after Alejandro left for the office, she simply threw a few clothes into a bag, slid in behind the wheel of the Porsche Carrera and headed north.

Ironically, she had only cleared the outer suburbs when another car ran through a 'Stop' sign.

She could vividly recall her reaction as she slammed on the brakes and made a desperate effort to avoid him; the sickening sound of colliding metal; a shuddering jolt that threw her against the door. Then nothing.

Elise's head was throbbing so badly that at first she didn't hear the repeated knock at the door.

'Mrs Santanas? Are you all right?'

Oh, God. How long had she been in here? Five minutes . . . ten?

'Yes. An attack of nausea,' she reassured the nurse shakily. She'd have to pull herself together. She looked and felt like death. 'I'll be out in a minute.'

'Doctor is ready to see you. Can I get you a cool drink? A cup of tea?'

There were disposable toothbrushes and toothpaste thoughtfully provided, and she made use of both before applying lipstick and running a comb through her hair. 'Tea would be lovely. Thanks.'

Ten minutes later she sat in a deep cushioned chair facing a small middle-aged man, who viewed her over half-moon spectacles resting halfway down the bridge of his nose.

'You're pale, and your pulse-rate is elevated,' he declared quietly. 'Care to tell me what's bothering you?'

'The baby——'

'Is fine. The mother, however, is giving me cause for concern.' He subjected her to a lengthy appraisal, then ventured gently, 'Your memory. Have you experienced any recurring flashes?'

She wanted to deny them, for, if she pretended they hadn't occurred, she might somehow fool herself they were part of some horrid nightmare that had no place in reality.

'A few,' she admitted cautiously, unwilling to relay that her memory had returned in full.

'You've found them distressing?'

Partial truth was infinitely preferable to truth in its entirety. 'I guess it's a natural reaction. My husband has been able to fill in some details, but not all.'

'I think I should call him.'

'*No*. No,' she hastened quickly, aware of his sharp interest. 'Please.'

He looked thoughtful. 'He has been very concerned about you.' He didn't add that Alejandro Santanas had insisted on a full report after every one of his wife's consultations. 'I think it would be best if I see you again in a fortnight. Finish your tea.'

José was waiting in the car when she emerged, and as soon as he caught sight of her he moved quickly round to open the rear door, then, when she was safely seated, he slid in behind the wheel.

'Is there anywhere you would like to go? A little shopping, perhaps?'

She had money, and sufficient credit-card buying power to walk into any store and purchase literally anything. For a moment she was tempted to indulge in a splurge that would raise her husband's eyebrows when he received the bill. But she had an entire closet full of fashionable clothes, enough shoes to wear a different pair every day for a number of weeks. Perfume, toiletries, make-up. Even jewellery. Alejandro had been exceedingly generous, given the circumstances of their marriage. She related such generosity to the need to project the image of a successful man's wife.

'Double Bay, José,' she instructed on a sudden whim. 'Alejandro is entertaining a business associate tonight, and I have an inclination to buy a new outfit.'

'*Sí*,' José concurred with a friendly grin. 'I shall take you there.'

The car slid forward, moving out into the flow of traffic, and Elise leaned back against the cushioned seat and closed her eyes against the onset of images crowding her brain.

'Would you like me to accompany you?'

Elise blinked at the sound of José's voice, and hastily caught hold of her scattered thoughts as she established that the Bentley was parked outside one of several exclusive boutiques known for their designer labels and expensive price-tags.

'No, thank you, José.' She cast him a warm smile. 'Why don't you have coffee somewhere? I'll be at least half an hour.'

She was twice that time and more, requiring special authorisation when it became apparent that she was unable to sign the appropriate credit slips.

They arrived home only minutes ahead of Alejandro, and she moved quickly upstairs to their suite in the hope of avoiding him... at least momentarily. If she hurried, she might be able to seclude herself in the shower.

She managed it, but only just, and when she emerged into the bedroom he was in the process of discarding his clothes.

Her eyes encountered his, then skittered away as he pulled off his shirt and took the few necessary steps to reach her.

For a few more hours at least, she had to act a part. After their dinner guests departed, she could unleash her inner rage.

The need to say something—anything—seemed paramount, and she rushed into speech. 'José took me to Double Bay. Shopping,' she elaborated, indicating the assortment of brightly coloured carrier bags at the foot of the bed. 'I felt like wearing something new tonight.' He was within touching distance, and she injected warmth into her smile as he lifted both hands to cup her face.

His mouth closed over hers, warm, hungry, possessive. She could feel her own unbidden response, the unfurling deep within as he drew her close in against him.

When he lifted his head it was all she could do to meet the dark intentness of his gaze, and she felt her lips tremble as he gently rubbed his thumb back and forth across the kiss-swollen curves.

One hand traced a path down her neck to trail the edge of her silk robe, parting it to slip inside and caress the full curve of her breast. 'What did the obstetrician have to say?'

How did she answer that? With extreme care, a tiny voice warned. 'He reassured me that the baby is fine.'

Her breasts felt heavy, their peaks taut and aching. It wasn't the only part of her that ached. *Dammit*, how could her body react in such a traitorous fashion?

His eyes seared hers, dark and analytical, almost as if he knew precisely what had happened and was waiting for her to tell him.

Could the obstetrician have called him? The possibility wouldn't surprise her. 'I—suffered a bout of morning sickness.' She paused, then made a light attempt at humour. 'In the middle of the afternoon.' She was not such a good actress that Alejandro would be fooled for long. 'I had another memory flash.' It was an extension of the truth. 'It shook me up a little.'

'Poor *niña*,' Alejandro soothed, brushing his lips against her temple. 'If you don't feel up to dinner tonight, I will contact André and have him meet me at a restaurant.'

'No,' Elise said quickly, adding, 'Ana has gone to a lot of trouble.' She didn't want to wake in the depths of night when he slid into bed and reached for her.

She wanted a confrontation. Dammit, she wanted to launch a full-scale war against him. But not when they had a guest due to arrive for dinner in—how long? Less than an hour?

'Shouldn't we get ready?'

Alejandro drew back and gave her a rueful smile. 'I need to shower and shave.'

The dress she had bought was a slim-fitting sheath in a brilliant red uncrushable viscose and linen mix, its hemline resting just above the knee. A clever panel of red beaded embroidery elevated the simple design to the glamorous, and matching beaded shoes completed an ensemble that shrieked a top Australian label.

Alejandro entered the bedroom as she put the finishing touches to her make-up, and with practised ease he attended to the hook on her bra, then assisted her into the dress. The long zip-fastener slid home, and she slowly turned to face him.

'Stunning,' he pronounced, his eyes gleaming with indolent appreciation as they roved over her slim curves. 'Do you need help with your hair?'

'I thought I'd wear it loose.'

She crossed to the dressing-table and caught up her brush, stroking the length of her hair until it shone. Ear-rings were too difficult to attach with one hand, so she discarded the idea.

André Valery was a tall, handsome man in his late thirties, charming, with Gallic appreciation for the opposite sex.

'I have been looking forward to meeting the woman who managed to slip beneath Alejandro's armour.' He lifted his glass in salute. 'I congratulate you.'

Dinner was a success, for not only had Ana excelled herself with superb culinary offerings, but the delicate baiting each man indulged in bore the stamp of a long friendship.

'You realise our fathers were business associates? *Oui*. It is true. For some years we spent holidays together. Gstaad. St Moritz. One year Alejandro was packed off to join my family in Paris.' His eyes twinkled with wicked humour. 'We were young, gregarious, and, I think, a little too adventurous for our own good.'

'Don't indulge in tales, André,' Alejandro drawled, 'or I may feel compelled to relay a few of my own to Anne-Marie when next I see her.'

'Anne-Marie,' André returned, with a Gallic shrug, 'is in no doubt as to what manner of man I am.'

'Are you about to destroy my illusions?' Elise queried lightly, and incurred his slight smile. His eyes, however, assumed inscrutability.

'What illusions do you refer to, *chérie*?'

'That you might be an exception to most successful men and have chosen not to have both wife and mistress?'

André's gaze didn't waver, and she met it fearlessly, aware of the sudden stillness in the room. 'If a man values his family, and his wife meets his needs,' he offered quite gently, 'why would there be the necessity for him to take a mistress?'

She was stepping into dangerous territory, but she didn't care. 'The challenge it represents, perhaps? Excitement?' She managed a careless shrug. 'Would you consider it fair for a wife to expect her needs also to be met?'

Alejandro's voice was pure silk. 'You are lodging a subtle complaint, *querida*?'

It took all her acting ability, but she managed a light incredulous laugh. 'How could I begin to fault you?' She reached out a placating hand, and sat quite still as he took hold of it and raised her fingers to his lips.

It was a deliberate gesture, and she glimpsed the dark gleam in his eyes, a watchfulness that sent warning flares licking the taut edge of her nerves.

He knew. Perhaps not precisely *when* her memory had returned, but there was no doubt he was aware that she had experienced a total recall.

'Shall we adjourn to the lounge for coffee?' Alejandro suggested smoothly.

Somehow Elise managed to get through the rest of the evening. If André sensed that her conversation was a little too bright, he gave no indication.

'You must excuse me,' André said at last. 'It is late, and I must return to my hotel.' He crossed to her side. 'Thank you for a most enjoyable evening.' He took her hand and lifted it to his lips, then held it a fraction longer than was necessary. 'Alejandro must bring you to Paris,' he said gently. 'It would give Anne-Marie much pleasure.'

'Indeed,' Alejandro concurred as they moved through to the front of the house.

Elise turned away from the door the instant the car's tail-lights cleared the gates, acutely conscious of Alejandro's actions as he re-set the alarm system.

Apprehension prickled at the back of her neck as she made for the stairs. The anger that had lain dormant since this afternoon rose to the fore, darkening her eyes and reining her mouth into a firm line.

Entering the bedroom, she slipped off her shoes, then reached for the zip-fastening at the back of her dress.

Alejandro came into the room as she began a third fruitless attempt to slide the fastener down, and she didn't utter a word as he crossed to complete the task.

With extreme care she stepped out of the dress and placed it over a nearby chair, watching out of the corner of her eye as he discarded his jacket and removed his tie.

'When did it happen?'

His voice was quiet, deadly, and she turned slowly to face him, unwilling to prevaricate.

Eyes as dark as onyx were filled with a chilling intensity, and her chin tilted fractionally as she prepared to oppose him.

'This afternoon. In the obstetrician's waiting-room.' Her eyes sparked with green fire. 'A photograph of Savannah in a magazine acted as the trigger, giving me total recollection in slow motion.'

His expression darkened fractionally, and he reached out a hand, catching hold of her chin between thumb and forefinger, tightening his grasp when she attempted to wrench it away.

Elise's eyes flared a brilliant topaz-flecked emerald in unspoken challenge. *'Why?'* she demanded. 'Why did you deceive me?'

He held her effortlessly, his expression an inscrutable mask. His silence angered her immeasurably.

'Dammit, *answer* me!'

His eyes became bleak, and his voice sounded as dark as the depths of his black soul. *'When* would you have had me reveal facts?'

She suffered his raking scrutiny with angry defiance as she waited for him to continue.

'While you lay in a hospital bed injured and afraid?' he pursued relentlessly. 'When you first came home?' His eyes dared her to refute him. 'Should I have destroyed your trust? Refused you reassurance and affection?'

'You took advantage with a calculated play on my emotions,' she cried, raw with pain.

'We made love,' Alejandro corrected harshly.

'We had *sex*.'

'A carnal coupling?' His voice was lethal. 'Based on greed and the gratification of a primitive urge?'

Dear God, it hadn't been like that. Ever. No matter how hard she fought, she had been entrapped from the moment of confrontation in his office. One look, and she'd been shaken to the very roots of her being by the mesmeric quality of his masculinity. Aware, with the depth of self-knowledge, that Alejandro Santanas possessed the ability to render her helpless as no other man could. She had hated him for it, hated herself for her own vulnerability. But, most of all, she had hated the circumstances that bound her to him.

She wanted to cry out a rejection, but the words choked in her throat. 'The night of the accident,' she revealed bleakly, 'I'd decided to leave you.'

His eyes speared her. 'How long did you imagine it would take before I tracked you down?'

'I intended to see a lawyer and file for separation.'

His features hardened measurably. 'You hate me so much that you would attempt to deny me knowledge of your pregnancy, my child's existence?' His voice lowered to a dangerous silkiness that sent tiny shivers along her spine. 'Or did you plan an abortion?'

'*No*,' she jerked out in shocked denial, re-asserting in a hushed tone, 'No.' The thought had never entered her head.

He was silent for several interminable minutes, and when he spoke his voice was hard and held unaccountable bleakness. 'The child you carry is as much mine as yours. Uniquely *ours*. Our son or daughter deserves to be more than someone we fight custody for in a law court.'

'I married you because I couldn't stand by and see my father emotionally and financially beaten. It would have killed him.' She had to take some consolation from the knowledge that the last few months of his life had been happy. 'You engineered a diabolical game,' she accused him fiercely. 'I should have damned you to the depths of hell and walked away.'

He regarded her steadily for what seemed an age. 'Yet you didn't,' he reminded her, his gaze alert beneath partly lowered lids. 'You accepted the arrangement as a challenge, and attempted to score against me.'

That had been her intention. At first, she had fooled herself that she was succeeding. Except that somewhere along the way she had fallen in love with him.

'Displaying beautiful manners in public,' he went on in musing reflection, 'while behaving like a virago when we were alone.'

Her eyes were dark and accusing. 'A fact you deliberately withheld from me.'

'If you remember,' Alejandro pursued, 'I made no pretence that we shared an idyllic relationship.'

'You said we argued occasionally!' Elise flung, hating his skilful employment of words.

'Frequently,' he corrected. 'The resolving of such arguments was always——' he paused deliberately '—satisfactory, wouldn't you say?'

That was an understatement. In bed, they had always been in perfect accord. In the beginning it had been a source of anguish, for she found it difficult to condone the degree of her emotional involvement with a man she professed to hate.

'Our marriage breaks all the rules,' she offered wretchedly, her eyes stormy with anger, and her hand shook as she lifted it to push hair back from her face.

'The reason for its existence remains the same,' he said in a hard voice.

She looked at him carefully, aware of his immense strength of will, the arresting elemental quality that made her feel suddenly afraid. 'You can't mean for the marriage to continue?'

'Indeed,' Alejandro declared inflexibly. He subjected her to a long, level appraisal. 'What is more, I insist that you honour the two-year term listed in our pre-nuptial agreement.'

Anger emanated from every pore in her body. 'That's barbaric!'

'Perhaps.' His smile was a mere facsimile, his eyes dark and forbidding.

'You expect me to act a part?' She felt like screaming with indignant resentment. '*Pretend*?'

His expression was resolute, and his voice held infinite mockery. 'You have managed admirably for the past seven months.'

'*Six*,' she flung back angrily, incensed by his imperturbability. 'I cannot be held responsible for the past one and a half.'

He lifted a hand and brushed light fingers along the edge of her jaw. 'Relieved of the barriers of your animosity for a few short weeks,' he said, 'there was no reason to generate hatred for your Spanish *esposo*.'

She closed her eyes, then slowly opened them again. 'There wasn't meant to be a child!' It was a cry from the heart.

His voice gentled as he caught hold of her chin and tilted it towards him. 'Nevertheless, there is. Its unexpected existence is something I refuse to consider as anything other than a very special gift.' His thumb lightly caressed the lower edge of her lip. 'For several weeks we were able to dispense with any hostility.' His eyes darkened measurably. 'Friends, as well as lovers.'

Her eyes glittered with anger, sheer emerald flecked with gold. 'We can never be friends!'

A smile tinged with wry mockery tugged the edges of his mouth. 'Perhaps at this moment you do not believe so.' Dark eyes gleamed with cynical humour. 'Why don't you get into bed?'

Her pulse tripped its beat and measurably quickened—as a result of anger, she assured herself, not passion. 'I don't want to go to bed, and I especially don't want to share a bed with you.'

'We share, Elise,' he insisted in a dangerously soft voice, 'as we have done from the beginning.'

His threat wasn't an idle one, and she looked at him in silent mutiny for several long seconds. 'If you touch me, so help me, I'll *hit* you,' she vouched with low-pitched vehemence, and, turning away from him, she caught up her nightgown and crossed into the bathroom to remove her make-up.

Her fingers shook so badly that the cream got into her eyes, and she dabbed frantically at it before sluicing her face.

Alejandro was in bed when she emerged, stretched out, his arms crossed behind his head.

Elise eyed him warily as she slipped in beneath the covers and closed her eyes. Seconds later she heard the snap of the bedside lamp as the room was plunged into darkness.

Slowly her lashes swept upwards, and for a long time she stared sightlessly ahead, discerning shadows and a thin strip of moonlight threading between the curtains as her eyes adjusted to the grey light of night.

She was acutely aware of every sound, her own breathing, his, and she knew the moment when Alejandro's steadied and assumed a deep rhythmic beat.

Tomorrow, she promised as her eyelids became heavy and began to flutter down. Tomorrow she would launch an attack about the depth of his involvement with the glamorous Savannah.

CHAPTER SEVEN

ELISE woke late to discover that Alejandro had already left for the city. His absence provided an anticlimax, for there was a fine edge to her inner rage that longed for the satisfaction of a full-scale confrontation.

'Alejandro asked me to tell you that you are both to attend a formal dinner to aid charity this evening,' Ana conveyed as Elise sat down to a solitary breakfast.

The Santanas Corporation was a well-known benefactor, and Alejandro lent his personal patronage to selected organisations. Elise had attended several such dinners in the past, and her heart sank at the thought of mingling with Alejandro's sophisticated coterie of acquaintances.

Without doubt Savannah would be present, and Elise hated being an object of conjecture as certain guests speculated on the latest developments between the Santanas scion, his wife, and the glamorous model who had been his constant companion for years before his sudden marriage to a virtual unknown with no social background.

Elise entertained no doubt that Alejandro's absence from the social scene for the past six weeks had been duly noted and commented upon, details regarding her accident embellished and explicated.

It seemed coincidental that she was to have the bandages removed from her hand today. After this afternoon, physiotherapy would be reduced to weekly instead of daily sessions. Soon the only evidence would be a thin scar on her hand.

The thought of regaining her independence was a heady one. After today, she would be able to drive again. There were a few friends she needed to contact. *Siobhan*. Realisation suddenly hit her that her dearest friend might be anxious not to have heard from her at all in the past six weeks.

As it was, she had no idea whether Siobhan was still working days at the Royal Children's Hospital, or if she had crossed over to night duty. If it was nights, the answering machine would be on and she could leave a message.

Elise checked the time, then finished her breakfast and moved quickly upstairs to use the bedroom telephone.

Siobhan picked up on the third ring, her voice jubilant on discovering who was on the other end of the line, and they talked for the best part of an hour before Elise reluctantly had to conclude the call in order to keep her appointment with the orthopaedic surgeon.

'Let's meet for lunch—*soon*,' she insisted.

'I'm a working girl, remember?' Siobhan teased. 'However, I'm off the next two nights. Is tomorrow soon enough?'

Elise gave an exultant laugh. 'Tomorrow it is. Just name the place, the time, and I'll be there.'

An hour later José deposited her outside the consultant orthopaedist's rooms, and thirty minutes later she walked out *sans* protective half-cast and bandages. The specialist sanctioned a return to driving, advised care with her hand, and suggested a further appointment in a month.

Now all she had to do was determine which car she could use as her own. There had been no mention of the white Porsche or its fate. Surely it couldn't have been smashed beyond repair? With the Bentley out of action, Alejandro was taking the Porsche Targa into the city, which left the Pajero wagon for José. She would have to broach it with Alejandro tonight.

After lunch she went through the contents of her wardrobe in an effort to reach a decision over what to wear to dinner, and after much deliberation she narrowed the choice down to two, eventually selecting a stunning fitted gown in deep emerald. The colour matched her eyes, highlighted the creamy texture of her skin, and proved a vivid contrast to her blonde hair.

It was almost four when José delivered her home from physiotherapy, and at five she took a shower, washed her hair and had Ana curl fat rollers into its length before attending to her nails.

Alejandro entered the bedroom as she began applying make-up, and she met his studied appraisal with equanimity.

'How is your hand?' He moved towards her, and Elise felt an immediate awareness of his close proximity.

Without a word she displayed the pink scar. 'I'm sure you've already received the specialist's report.' She hadn't intended to sound quite so cynical.

His eyes narrowed fractionally. 'Yes.'

'You also know that I am able to drive again,' she offered, watching as his head lowered down to hers.

She averted her head so that his kiss landed on her cheek, and almost at once he caught hold of her chin, anchoring it as he covered her mouth with his own in an invasion that brought forth a muffled entreaty he chose to ignore.

When he finally lifted his head she silently damned him to the depths of perdition.

The desire to rage against him was paramount, and, drawing in a deep breath, she launched into attack. 'I'd like to become independent again, rather than have to drag José away every time I want to go out.'

Alejandro slipped the knot free on his tie and began unfastening the buttons on his shirt. 'That is part of his job.'

Her eyes assumed a brilliant hue as anger began to unfurl, and it took considerable effort to control her temper. 'Have you assigned him as my gaoler?'

'You're being fanciful.'

'Am I?'

He looked every inch the power broker... indomitable, lethal, inflexible. 'Are you intent on having an argument?'

She wanted to throw something at him and have it cause mild bodily harm. 'I find it difficult to condone almost everything you do where I am concerned.'

He pulled his shirt free and tossed it down on to the bed. '*Almost* everything, *querida*?' One eyebrow slanted in silent mockery. 'Should I take that to indicate there is some hope for me?'

'Don't be so damned facetious,' she condemned fiercely, seething with helpless indignation as she glimpsed his amusement.

'We need to leave in half an hour. Can this discussion wait?'

'Until when, Alejandro?' she taunted, holding his gaze without any difficulty at all. 'Next week, next *month*?'

'Tomorrow.'

It was a better concession than she had hoped for, and she viewed him steadily for several long seconds as her anger began to dissipate.

'Where is the dinner being held tonight?'

One eyebrow arched, and his mouth assumed a degree of cynicism. 'The Sheraton.'

Some devilish imp prompted her to ask, 'Will Savannah be there?'

'I imagine so. She likes to attend most of the events.'

'In order to see *you*.' It was nothing less than the truth.

'Savannah has many friends, most of whom are active on the social circuit,' he drawled, and his faintly mocking tones brought a resurgence of anger.

'I can't think why you didn't marry her.' Elise endeavoured not to sound bitter. 'She would have leapt at the chance!'

'Perhaps,' Alejandro conceded, watching the play of emotions across her expressive features. 'I chose not to ask her.'

'One can only wonder why.' Her eyes deepened in colour and became faintly reflective. 'She's beautiful, poised, and she comes from the right social background.' It was amazing that her voice sounded so calm.

His eyes gleamed with sardonic humour. 'Many women of my acquaintance fit that description.'

'Several of whom are wealthy in their own right,' she pursued, uncaring that she was treading dangerous ground. 'Poor Alejandro,' she added lightly. 'Were you afraid their prime motivation was an advantageous financial merger? Or, if their independent wealth was sufficient for that not to be a consideration, could there have been distaste that they were merely lusting after your body? Not to mention your——' she hesitated deliberately, then finished with considered delicacy '—impressive skill in the bedroom.'

'Only in the bedroom, *mi mujer*?' he mocked cynically. 'I retain a vivid recollection of several enjoyable...encounters, shall we say?' he suggested, slanting one eyebrow. 'When we shared the shower, the spa.' His eyes gleamed as soft pink coloured her cheeks. 'Shall I continue?'

'You've had plenty of practice, damn you!'

'You are jealous, *querida*, that any one of my former lovers might possibly have meant more to me than you do?'

Elise felt her eyes widen with shock. Was she so transparent? Could he be aware of how much she hated the thought of his splendidly muscular body engaged in the act of lovemaking with another woman...? *Women*, she corrected. Past and present.

'How could I be jealous,' she countered, with as much pride as she could muster, 'when you clearly defined the reason for our marriage, allocated a price-tag and specified a time-limit?'

'That bothers you?'

It bothered her like hell, but she was damned if she would admit to it. 'About as much as the fact that you've chosen to retain Savannah as your mistress.'

'The term *mistress* conveys a woman kept by a husband while still co-habiting with his wife.' His eyes were dark, and held latent anger. 'You imagine I would insult you in such a manner?'

I don't know. 'I'd appreciate it if you would at least keep the...*liaison* discreet.'

There was a perceptible pause, one in which it seemed that even a pin falling to the floor would result in cacophonous sound. 'Am I to understand that you give your sanction to such a relationship?'

No. The silent negation screamed inside her head. It took tremendous effort to effect a slight shrug. 'Would anything I say make a difference?'

He appeared to be marshalling his anger, confining it beneath a mantle of superb control. 'We have a dinner engagement,' he reminded her icily. 'I suggest you get changed.'

The thought of sitting through a formal dinner in the company of some of the city's social glitterati was more than she could bear. 'Forgive me, Alejandro,' she said with bitter cynicism, 'but I can't bring myself to play pretend tonight.' Her eyes sparkled with emerald brilliance. 'I'm sure you can come up with some valid excuse that will explain my absence.' A devilish imp prompted her to add, 'Savannah will be delighted.'

He looked at her for what seemed an age, his expression a compelling mask from which she inwardly shrank. 'You tempt me to the brink of violence,' he said in a voice that was so dangerously quiet it raised all her fine body-hairs in silent fear.

Without a further word he discarded his clothes and strode into the bathroom. He didn't slam the door, and she found that infinitely more disquieting than if he had resorted to an outward display of anger.

Ten minutes later he emerged, a towel hitched low over his hips, and she moved hastily to her feet as he began to dress.

'Ask Ana to prepare you something to eat.'

'It's her night off,' Elise managed in a stilted voice. 'I wouldn't dream of disturbing her.' She crossed to the door. 'I'm quite capable of fixing something myself.'

She didn't wait for Alejandro to respond, and on reaching ground level she made her way to the kitchen.

The refrigerator was well stocked, so too was the pantry. It was just a matter of making a decision. An omelette would suffice, with cheese, tomato, ham, mushrooms... Not that she felt in the least hungry. If anything, the thought of food made her ill.

She removed a skillet, assembled the ingredients on the bench-top, then chopped, sliced and diced with methodical stoicism.

Alejandro entered the kitchen as she turned the omelette on to a plate, and she willed her hands not to betray her as she turned down the gas.

His raking appraisal unsettled her more than any words he could have chosen to utter, and she turned away from him as she carried her plate to the wide servery bench, then returned to collect cutlery.

She sensed rather than heard him move, and seconds later she felt his hands close over her shoulders as he turned her towards him.

For one achingly long moment their eyes clashed, then his head lowered in seemingly slow motion, and a strangled cry of dissent lay imprisoned in her throat as his mouth closed over hers in a hard merciless kiss that tore at her defences and reached right down to the depths of her soul.

It became a ruthless invasion that bordered on violation, and when at last he lifted his head, she could only stand in shocked immobility. If he had wanted to punish her, he'd succeeded, she decided numbly.

She felt raw, her whole body consumed by an emotional pain so intense that it was almost a tangible entity. Her eyes began to ache, then glistened with tears she refused to allow to fall.

His features were harsh, and with a muttered imprecation he turned and strode from the kitchen.

Minutes later she heard the muted sound of a car engine start up, then its refined purr diminished as it reached the end of the driveway.

She hugged her arms together, and tried valiantly to maintain a measure of control.

How long she stood there she had no idea, for she had no sense of the passage of time as she attempted to rationalise the foolishness of pitching her strength against a man whose physical and emotional strength were infinitely superior to her own.

It was only the prosaic need for food that refocused her attention, and with determined resolve she collected cutlery and systematically divided the cold omelette into bite-sized portions, forking them automatically into her mouth.

When she had finished, she cleaned the skillet, rinsed the plate and cutlery, and placed them in the dishwasher.

The house seemed incredibly silent, the lounge much too large for her to sit in alone. Feeling thoroughly unsettled, she wandered into the informal *sala*, collected a magazine, and sank into one of the deep cushioned seats. The pages were not able to capture her interest, and she discarded the magazine, choosing instead to use the remote module to switch on the television. Surely there would be something she could become involved in, she thought with despair, as she clicked one channel after another.

Two half-hour comedy shows provided some light relief, but her appreciation of the humour portrayed was only superficial, and when they were over she roved between the channels in search of a movie that might prove interesting.

There was not much selection, and she crossed to the cabinet and browsed through the collection of videos, discarding all but one. It was a dark Gothic piece that had earned critical acclaim, but she found it too intense, and was quite pleased when the credits finally rolled.

Elise crossed back into the kitchen and filled a glass with ice from the freezer, then added orange juice and slowly sipped the contents.

What time would Alejandro come home? If he came home, a tiny voice taunted. Dammit, of course he would. He had never stayed out before, so why would he begin now?

Maybe because you virtually gave him *carte blanche* to spend time with Savannah, the same tiny voice reminded her with devilish glee.

A glance at her watch revealed it to be after ten, and with sudden decisiveness she finished the juice, then made for the stairs. She would have a shower, then go to bed.

Twenty minutes later she slid beneath the cool linen sheets, snapped off the light, and closed her eyes.

Sleep did not provide the release she craved, and half an hour later she gave a muttered groan and slid out of bed, choosing to curl up in a chair close to the curtain-draped window.

How did one reconcile the heaven of loving Alejandro Santanas, and the resultant hell of knowing he could never love her? Elise reflected as she gazed sightlessly round the darkened room.

Like a moth at a flame, she had been struck by the lightning of instant attraction, aware of the swift invasive pull of sheer physical desire, and engulfed by its powerful magnetism.

By day she had fought him, hating him for being able to hold her captive to her own desire, hating herself for being so easily entrapped by the dictates of her own flesh... By night she lost the fight and revelled in the magic of his touch.

Would it ever be any different between them? It had been, she reflected sadly. For six short weeks she had believed him to be a caring, loving husband. A man who had devoted all of his time to her, and shown her incredible *tendresse*.

Had it been real? Or merely an act? She would probably never know.

Oh, hell, she cursed, as her eyes filled and tears began to trickle down both cheeks. She hardly ever cried. Except when her father had died. Dammit, her hormones must be raging some sort of inner war with her emotional heart. To be this stricken with tears was crazy.

Futile, she amended, timeless minutes later when she appeared all cried out. The spent emotion made her sleepy, and she snuggled deeper into the chair and rested her head in the curve of one arm.

It was there Alejandro found her, and he stood for a long time looking down at the graceful arch of her slender neck illuminated by the bedside lamp, the softness of her hair as it clung to her neck, the slender curves beneath the simple white cotton nightgown. And the faint evidence of tears.

Slowly he discarded his clothes, then he crossed back to the chair and carefully lifted her into his arms.

Elise stirred, aware in the depths of her subconscious that something was different. Whereas the cushioned chair was softly padded, now there was the warmth of hard muscular flesh beneath her head. She was aware of a deep rhythmic heartbeat, and an arm curving her close against a long male body. Fingers traced a light transient pattern over her hair, and she felt the brush of lips against her temple.

A soft sigh emerged from her lips, and almost in reflex action her arm crept out to encircle his waist.

His mouth was beautifully chiselled, and she knew exactly how it felt against her own. Even thinking about it brought alive the flicker of desire, igniting from her central core and licking treacherously along every nerve in her body.

Of its own accord her head angled slightly, the soft curves of her mouth parting to accept a kiss that began with incredible gentleness. Teasing, provocative, and profoundly seductive.

There was no thought of denying him, or herself, and she exulted in each caress, the overwhelming bewitching rapture as he guided her towards fulfilment—seismic, earth-shattering, a surrender to the sensual delights of passion.

It was the one level on which they communicated. No discord, no sense of disappointment. Just beautiful intimacy. Sex, she corrected, all too aware of the difference.

'Drop me anywhere along Oxford Street, José,' Elise declared. 'It's a beautiful day, and I feel like walking.'

The Pajero eased through the traffic-lights and pulled into a parking bay. 'What time, and where shall I collect you?'

'I'll get a taxi back,' she said lightly, unwilling to put a curfew on the day. Who knew how long lunch with Siobhan would extend? And besides, she might want to explore the shops for a while.

'Perhaps you will ring when you are ready?' José suggested on an anxious note. 'Alejandro would insist.'

Alejandro could insist all he liked! 'I'll let you know,' she conceded, feeling only slightly guilty that she had no intention of calling José. She proffered a warm smile, then opened the door and stepped down on to the pavement, waiting only a few seconds after he pulled out into the traffic before making her way towards the next street.

Siobhan was waiting for her, and they hugged each other as if it was years instead of several weeks since they had last seen each other.

'You look fantastic,' Siobhan declared as they entered the restaurant. The maître d' took them to a table with views of the harbour, handed them each a menu, then left them to make a selection. 'How is your hand?'

They ordered mineral water, deliberated over what they would eat, ordered, then attempted to continue where they had left off the previous afternoon.

Three hours later they shared the bill and wandered out into the fresh afternoon sunshine.

'The shops?' Siobhan hazarded with an irrepressible grin, laughing as Elise concurred with alacrity.

It was after five when they parted, promising to phone to arrange another lunch together the following week.

Taxis were in high demand, and the queue at the nearest rank was a lengthy one. Securing a taxi within half an hour looked to be impossible.

Damn, Elise cursed, aware that she should have taken the peak hour into consideration. Maybe a rank in one of the neighbouring streets would offer her a better opportunity.

It didn't. If anything, it was even longer. There wasn't much choice except to ring José.

She reached into her bag, then made a wry grimace on discovering that she had left the compact mobile phone at home. Locating a telephone booth took several minutes, and she had to wait for two people in front of her to take their turn in making calls.

Finally she got through, and the signal only sounded twice before the receiver was lifted from the hook. However, it wasn't José, or even Ana, who answered, and her heart took on an agitated beat.

'Where are you?'

Alejandro sounded so coldly furious that it was all she could do not to snap back at him.

'Downtown city. All the taxi ranks have horrendous queues.'

He appeared to be summoning control, and his anger emanated down the line. '*Where*, precisely, Elise?'

'Tell José I'll wait in Elizabeth Street, the Park Street end.'

However, it was the black Porsche which pulled into the kerb some thirty minutes later, not the Pajero.

One glance at Alejandro's harsh features was enough to determine that a battle was about to commence.

Alejandro leaned across and opened the passenger door. 'Get in.' His voice sounded clipped, and Elise slid in beside him and fastened her seatbelt.

It took the next change of lights before he could ease the Porsche ahead of the traffic, and their progress was hampered by the sheer number of vehicles vacating the city.

'I planned on being home before now.' It was a statement, not an apology.

'Obviously.'

Anger rose to the surface as she turned towards him. 'Dammit, Alejandro, I won't allow you to put me in a gilded cage!'

Something flickered in the depth of his eyes. 'My position in the business arena is well-reported in the Press.' A muscle tensed at the edge of his jaw. 'In today's society there are a few fanatics who take pleasure in targeting those who lead a high-profile existence. Consequently, I take extreme care to ensure any possible risks are kept to a minimum.' He spared her a dark glance, then returned his attention to negotiating the traffic. 'Hence the necessity for security measures. The reason I insist you always carry a mobile phone, and each vehicle has a car phone. A need for someone—myself, Ana, José—to be aware of your whereabouts. For protection. Not restriction.'

She lifted a hand in angry agitation. 'If I'd had my own car, this wouldn't have happened.'

He didn't say anything. He had no need, Elise decided darkly as the car cleared the city confines and traversed Bayswater Road. The traffic thinned slightly as they reached Double Bay, and ten minutes later the Porsche swung through the wide double gates at the entrance to the Point Piper mansion.

The garage doors lifted at a touch from Alejandro's remote module, then the car slid into place between the Pajero and a stunning red top-of-the-range Mercedes sedan.

'Yours,' Alejandro told her as she cast it an admiring glance.

Her stomach executed a slow flip, and she turned slowly towards him. 'You bought it for me?'

His expression was unfathomable. 'José will take you for a test-drive tomorrow.' He unclipped his belt and slid out from behind the wheel.

Elise did likewise, pausing long enough to run tentative fingers over the red satin-smooth paintwork. 'It's beautiful,' she said quietly and, taking a step towards him, she reached up and placed a fleeting kiss on the edge of his chin. 'Thank you.'

His mouth curved to form a wry smile, and his eyes assumed a darkness she found impossible to fathom.

'Your hand,' Alejandro asked quietly. 'How does it feel now the bandages and plaster have been removed?'

'A little strange. Stiff,' she elaborated with a slight shrug. 'Physiotherapy helps.'

'Shall we go indoors? Ana will be waiting to serve dinner.'

She needed to freshen up, and use the bathroom. 'Give me ten minutes.'

Elise took time to change into silk trousers and a matching top, then ran a brush through her hair. A quick slash of pink restored colour to her lips.

Her expression was vaguely pensive as she joined Alejandro in the dining-room, and she spooned her soup with little real appetite and merely picked at the tender beef with its accompanying vegetables.

'Not hungry?'

Elise looked at him carefully, examining the strong bone-structure, the assemblage of muscle and skin that moulded his features into compelling attractiveness.

Before the accident she would not have had the least compunction about beginning an argument with him. Not only that, she would have delighted in doing battle, exulting when she succeeded in rousing his temper. It was madness, because she could never win against him.

Now she seemed hell-bent on following a similar path. His brand of caring during their time together at Palm Beach, his tender affection, had wreaked havoc with her emotional heart. Worse, it had destroyed the very core of her resentment.

'No,' she answered at last, pushing her plate to one side.

'Have some fruit.'

Elise looked at the selection Ana had placed in the bowl, then shook her head. She reached for her glass, miscalculated, and water pooled across the table.

'Oh, hell,' she said shakily as she collected a napkin and began mopping up the excess. What was wrong with her, for heaven's sake?

'Leave it.'

She rose to her feet. 'I'll get another napkin.'

'Leave it, Elise,' Alejandro commanded silkily. Stupid tears pricked her eyes, and she blinked furiously in an effort to prevent them from spilling over. Any second now she'd make a fool of herself, and that would never do.

She moved from the table and had taken three steps when a hand closed over her arm.

'Let me go. Please,' she begged in bleak despair, hating the degree of vulnerability evident as he tilted her chin.

'When you tell me what is disturbing you.'

She closed her eyes against the sight of him, then slowly opened them again. 'I didn't deliberately stay in the city in order to cause you concern.'

'I wasn't aware I implied that you had.' He cupped her face between both hands and brushed a thumb-pad across one cheek.

Dear heaven, why did she feel so acutely sensitive where he was concerned? A few days ago she wouldn't have thought it possible that she would find it imperative to offer him any explanation or proffer an apology. Now she was doing both.

However, soul-searching wouldn't achieve anything, for there was no easy resolution.

'Thanks for the car,' she managed unevenly, and glimpsed his faint smile as he watched the fleeting emotions chase across her expressive features.

'What good manners you have, *mi mujer*,' he drawled. 'I shall look forward to a more—passionate shall we say?—expression of your gratitude.'

It took considerable effort to keep the pain from her voice. 'Payment in sexual favours?' she queried, and saw his eyes darken.

'You little fool,' Alejandro responded with deadly softness as his mouth fastened over hers in a kiss that was meant to punish.

A silent cry of impassioned entreaty remained locked in her throat, and it seemed an age before he lifted his head.

His eyes speared hers, and she became trapped beneath the degree of latent sensuality evident, a primeval recognition that had everything to do with the senses.

Her mouth quivered, its soft curves faintly swollen from the ruthless force of his own, and she cried out a single negation as he swept her effortlessly into his arms.

In the bedroom he let her slide down to her feet, and she wanted to vent her rage against his deliberate seduction as he gently cupped her face.

Eyes that were impossibly slumberous held her own captive, and helpless frustration welled up inside her as she became caught up in mesmerised fascination.

Did he know how difficult it was for her to accept the traitorous desire she experienced in his arms? The breath seemed to catch in her throat, and her eyes clung to his, bright with anger, yet intensely vulnerable.

A hand slid beneath her hair, urging her close as his lips trailed across her forehead, then moved slowly down one cheek to settle at the corner of her mouth, teasing, gentle, and incredibly erotic as he conducted a sensual tasting that made her ache for more.

Beneath his sensual mastery a deep flame flared into vibrant life, and she gave herself up totally to the delights of unbridled ardency.

Elise made no protest when he set about freeing her clothes and his own, and her body arched of its own accord as his mouth began a supplicating path over every inch of her body.

She was barely conscious of the tiny sounds emerging from her throat as she began to plead with him, wanting, needing his total possession.

When at last he gave it, she cried out, welcoming his mouth on hers with hungry passion as acute sensation spiralled towards a mutual climax that explored the heights of primitive satiation.

Sexual ecstasy at its zenith, she accepted drowsily a long time later as she drifted towards sleep.

CHAPTER EIGHT

ELISE revelled in her independence, and chose to take the Mercedes out each day.

On one occasion she visited the ward where she had worked at the Royal Children's Hospital, after which she drove by the old brick house she had shared for years with her father.

It looked different, she reflected with a tinge of sadness. The small front garden no longer existed, the curtains had been changed, and the door was now painted a brilliant green.

Was it only nine months since her world had been turned upside-down? In some ways it seemed much longer than that.

It was impossible not to ponder what her future might hold, and that of her unborn child. She wanted... What *did* she want? Alejandro's love? Was it such an impossible dream?

The blast of a car horn interrupted her thoughts, and she set the Mercedes moving away from a street that no longer held a place in her life.

Lunch, she decided, feeling suddenly hungry, after which she would head towards Double Bay to browse among the many boutiques. She might even visit a beauty salon and indulge in a facial. Then she could look for a suitable gown to wear to an

136

important end-of-year function to be held the following evening in an inner-city hotel.

After an extensive search she discovered exactly what she wanted, added matching evening shoes and bag, and tried not to blench as she signed the credit slip.

Alejandro's appreciation of her choice was plainly evident as she bore his appraisal mere minutes before they were due to leave the house the next evening.

'I won't be able to let you out of my sight,' he drawled, and she proffered a teasing smile.

'Likewise.'

'Indeed?'

His eyes held latent passion, and something she dared not define. A tiny flame flared deep within and flowed through her body. 'Shall we leave?'

'So many beautiful women,' Elise murmured as they entered the hotel ballroom some thirty minutes later. 'Wearing a fortune in clothes and jewellery in a personal quest to outshine one another.'

Alejandro cast her an amused glance as one of several hostesses hurried forward to check their tickets and indicate their table position.

'Careful, *querida*,' he drawled. 'Your claws are showing.'

She offered him a winsome smile. 'It's one thing to show them, and quite another to use them.' Unlike Savannah, who didn't hesitate to do both, she added silently as she paused at Alejandro's side while he exchanged pleasantries with an acquaintance.

The ballroom had the capacity to seat eight hundred patrons, with ten guests assigned to each circular table. An impressive annual event, it was a draw for the city's social élite who came primarily to be seen. The promoted charity, the reason for such a gathering, was incidental.

Perhaps that was being a little unkind, Elise decided as she took her seat a short while later. Committee members affiliated to any charity organisation worked tirelessly to put something like this evening's soirée together, and deserved an accolade for their efforts.

Two seats at their table remained empty, and Elise's fingers tightened on the stem of her glass as she overheard who was due to join them.

'Savannah is always late, darling. She likes to make a grand entrance.'

Savannah's presence tonight was a foregone conclusion, but only someone with a twisted sense of humour would have placed the glamorous model at the same table as Alejandro and Elise Santanas. It was too contrived to be coincidental, and Elise could only conclude that Savannah herself had engineered the seating arrangements.

The lights dimmed, a spotlight hit the podium, and the charity's president extolled the amount raised and its purpose. Tonight's guest speaker was a well-known dignitary who would begin his speech at the dinner's conclusion, after which music would be provided for guests to dance.

The spotlight faded, the lights returned, and there was Savannah, looking absolutely stunning in jade silk that clung lovingly to every curve. The man at her side wasn't someone Elise had previously met, and she pinned a smile firmly in place as Savannah performed an introduction.

Was it her imagination that their table was the cynosure of all eyes? Perhaps not, she conceded, although there could be no doubt Savannah's presence would be viewed with interest.

'Elise. How are you? Quite recovered from your accident, I hope?' The slightly bored tone was offset by a seemingly sincere smile which did not reach her eyes as Elise made a polite rejoinder. 'Alejandro missed you dreadfully at last week's dinner.' The smile deepened and became deliberately secretive as she switched attention. 'Didn't you, darling? Quite the devoted husband. If he hadn't been a featured guest speaker, I doubt if he would have come.'

Elise was saved from having to respond by the arrival of a waiter bearing a basket of bread rolls, and when the first course was served she dutifully spooned the delectable potato and leek soup until it was finished.

Faced with a choice of fish or chicken, she opted for the former, and forked each mouthful with studied care. Every so often she paused to sip iced water from her glass, acutely conscious of Savannah's presence directly opposite.

Incredibly beautiful: there was no visible flaw in any one of her perfect features. Nature had bestowed with a bountiful hand, while good fortune had ensured that she'd been born into wealth. A modelling opportunity had landed in her lap at a tender age, and the rest, as they said, was history.

Elise had viewed her with extreme caution the moment they had first met, and nothing had occurred in the interim to change her mind. The model was an ensnarer of men, making it very plain that Alejandro Santanas was her prime target. His marriage was dismissed as of little account, merely a mild irritation soon to be dispensed with.

'Some wine, my dear?'

Elise turned towards the man seated on her left, and shook her head. 'It's kind of you to offer, but no.'

'You're getting by with water, darling?' Savannah queried, effecting a faint *moue*. 'Are you driving?'

Alejandro shifted slightly in his chair and caught hold of Elise's hand, lifting it to his lips. His eyes gleamed with warmth as he gently kissed each fingertip in turn before enfolding her hand in his.

She wanted to wrench her hand free, but even as the thought occurred, his own hand tightened measurably in silent warning, and she had no recourse but to smile. Damn him, he was little more than an elegant savage behind that sophisticated façade. Ruthless, she added, suppressing a slight shiver as she caught sight of Savannah's fixed stare.

'You're not *pregnant*, are you, darling?'

Only Savannah would ask such a question, and Elise held her breath as Alejandro met the model's seemingly innocent gaze.

'Yes, much to my delight.' There was no doubt about the element of steel beneath the silk-smoothness of his voice.

The arrival of dessert was an anticlimax, and Elise picked segments of fruit from their meringue nest, then pushed the plate to one side, choosing tea as the guest speaker took the podium.

Afterwards a DJ provided background music and encouraged guests to step on to the dance-floor. Savannah and her partner were among the first, moving through the steps with effortless ease.

She looked so—sophisticated, and so very sure of herself. Her features were faintly sultry, and Elise had no doubt that the model knew precisely the effect she was having on her partner.

The question was whether it was having the desired effect on Alejandro.

Elise cast him a surreptitious glance, and was disconcerted to meet his hooded gaze. She offered a tentative smile, afraid he might have deduced the pattern of her thoughts, and she blinked as he reached out and threaded his fingers through her own.

'Would you like to dance?'

Part of her wanted to quite desperately, for she badly needed the sanctuary of his embrace. The other part recognised the danger of having her body pressed against the hard powerful impact of his own.

With a word of assent she rose to her feet, moved out on to the floor and into his arms.

The music was slow, and her steps matched his in perfect unison. Magic, she mused. Was it possible for one human being to be addicted to another? Held in thrall as if the essence of him were some powerful narcotic?

He diminished every other man in the room, possessing an inherent ruthlessness, honed by experience and enhanced by the degree of his success.

It held a fascination that men recognised and women viewed with the speculative interest of their sex. To some it was an invisible magnet, activated by the excitement of discovering if the man, freed from corporate restraint, was as skilled at lovemaking as he was at adding millions to his investment portfolio.

An immensely sophisticated man, yet there was the hint of an untamed quality, a primitive savagery held rigidly in control.

A faint shiver feathered down her spine with the knowledge that he would be devastatingly heartless as an enemy.

'Cold?'

His voice was a soft caress against her hair, and she murmured a faint negative.

'Someone just walked over my grave,' she offered, with a droll attempt at humour.

'Savannah?'

She missed a step, and gave an inaudible gasp as he enfolded her close against him. It was a far from conventional hold, and she tilted her head to meet the dark inscrutability apparent in his gaze.

'You're too astute for your own good,' she offered in a strangled voice.

'Is that a disadvantage?'

She chose not to answer, and when the music changed she moved back a pace and suggested they return to their table.

'I need to use the powder-room,' she murmured, aware of the effect of several glasses of water. She caught up her evening bag with the intention of doing a few running repairs to her make-up while there.

'Do you want me to escort you?'

She directed at him a slow smile of amusement. 'I'm not a child, Alejandro. What can happen to me?'

What, indeed? she could only query silently several minutes later, when she emerged from a stall to find Savannah examining her make-up in front of the long mirrored wall.

'Playing to win, darling?' Savannah queried softly.

'Every time, Savannah,' she managed evenly as she took out lipstick and ran colour smoothly over her lips.

'You're very... small,' Savannah opined with a total lack of graciousness. 'A petite size eight?'

There had to be a purpose to this conversation, and determining her dress size was totally irrelevant, Elise reflected as she recapped the lipstick and turned to face her aggressor.

'Alejandro is so...' Savannah trailed off delicately.

'Well-endowed?' Elise suggested, deliberately manufacturing a stunningly amused smile. 'A distinct advantage, wouldn't you agree?'

Dark brown eyes glittered with dangerous venom as the model released a tinkle of soft laughter. 'He's a lusty animal, darling.' Her gaze focused on Elise's trim waist. 'Pregnancy is hardly flattering, especially in the latter stage. I can't imagine he'll practise celibacy, no matter how temporary.'

'And you'll be there for him to turn to?'

'Of course, darling.' She paused, then sharpened the verbal barb for maximum impact. 'As I have been, and always will be.'

Elise felt sickened, and it took considerable effort to summon a light smile. 'I really must go back to the table.' She turned away, only to give an anguished gasp as Savannah caught hold of her injured hand.

'Don't underestimate me.'

'I never have,' Elise assured steadfastly. 'Will you please let go of my hand? It's still quite painful.'

Savannah's grip momentarily tightened, and her eyes gleamed with a malevolence that changed her features into a hard mask.

For a few shocking seconds Elise thought she wouldn't be able to cope with the pain, then Savannah flung her hand aside with a pitiless laugh.

'I'd hate to hurt you unnecessarily.' Collecting her evening bag, she swept out of the powder-room.

For several minutes Elise was locked into immobility as she tried to control her shaken emotions. Her hand throbbed, aching with an intensity that clouded her eyes and took the colour from her face.

'Are you all right?'

The light feminine voice held concern, and Elise dredged up a faint smile.

'You're very pale. Perhaps you should sit down for a few minutes? Shall I fetch your husband?'

'No. No,' she reiterated quickly. 'I'll be all right in a few minutes.'

'My table is next to yours. We'll walk back together, shall we?'

Elise was supremely conscious of Alejandro's intent gaze as she resumed her seat. To her relief there was no sign of Savannah or her partner.

'Would you like more tea?'

She doubted if she would be able to drink it. 'I've had enough, thanks.' In more ways than one, she added silently.

'Do you want to go home?' His voice was quiet, and there was no escaping his penetrating appraisal.

'Not yet,' she managed with commendable calm. To leave now would amount to an admission of defeat, and she was damned if she would give Savannah the satisfaction.

Most of the guests were drifting from one table to another, and Elise gave an inward sigh of relief when another couple joined them. The man, a business associate of Alejandro's, launched into an in-depth discussion with him, while the woman engaged Elise in innocuous conversation.

It was twenty minutes before they left, and Elise cast Alejandro a startled glance as he leaned an arm across the back of her chair.

'It's almost eleven. We've done our duty. Shall we leave?'

'If you want to.'

Without a further word he made their excuses, then began leading the way from the ballroom. Several acquaintances sought his attention and, although he paused momentarily to offer a few words in polite response, he didn't linger.

It was a relief to reach the car, and once inside Elise simply leaned back against the leather-cushioned seat as Alejandro eased the Bentley up to street level and into the steady stream of traffic vacating the city.

Her hand still throbbed, although with less intensity, and the pain had subsided to a deep nagging ache. Bearable, she conceded, but only just.

Music emitted from the stereo speakers, and she closed her eyes as the car sped smoothly towards Point Piper.

Once indoors she made straight for the stairs, discarding her clothes as she entered the bedroom. When Alejandro appeared, only a bra and briefs shielded her from total nudity.

'Want to tell me what upset you?'

Her eyes held a hint of defiance. 'Not really.'

'Savannah followed you into the powder-room, and emerged minutes ahead of you.'

'How observant of you to notice.'

He crossed to stand within touching distance. 'I notice everything about you,' he drawled, sliding a hand beneath her hair to cup her nape. 'The way you respond when we make love. What makes you smile. How your eyes cloud with pain,' he said quietly.

'Savannah and I exchanged a few words.' She attempted a shrug, and met his gaze unflinchingly. 'Is there any reason why we shouldn't?'

His eyes darkened fractionally. 'None at all.' His hand slid forward, and his thumb caressed the soft outline of her mouth.

His touch was an erotic force, and she fought an inner battle not to succumb to his subtle brand of foreplay as he reached to unclasp her bra, freeing her breasts from the scrap of silk and lace.

The burgeoning peaks ached for his touch, and a faint moan escaped her throat as he stroked the creamy fullness before paying attention to each dusky peak.

His hands slid down her ribcage, over her waist to slip beneath her briefs, carrying them down over her hips with effortless ease before transferring his attention as he removed his own clothes.

Then he reached for her, both hands framing her face as he lowered his head.

His mouth was an erotic instrument, and she welcomed his kiss without reserve, exulting in the liquid warmth coursing through her veins. Her whole body seemed alive with acute sensation, and she moved close against him, needing the physical contact. Most of all she wanted to be swept away by primitive desire, to become so lost in the rapture of his lovemaking that Savannah and her hateful words would be pushed beyond the periphery of rational thought.

It was almost as if he knew, and a low groan of delighted anticipation emerged from her throat as he drew her down on to the bed and began conducting a leisurely tasting of every sensual pleasure-spot.

She exulted in the degree of eroticism he skilfully bestowed, the depth of emotion she experienced beneath his touch, so that when he finally took her it was all she could do not to cry out with joy.

Afterwards she lay curled into the curve of his body, delightfully sated and on the verge of sleep.

Elise woke later to find that Alejandro had already left for the city, and she indulged in a leisurely stretch before sliding from the bed. So far she had been very fortunate, for, although she occasionally experienced a slight queasiness on waking, it had not developed into morning sickness.

After a refreshing shower she dressed in shorts and a top, then ran lightly downstairs to the kitchen.

'Morning, Ana. Isn't it a beautiful day?'

'*Sí,*' the older woman answered with a warm smile. 'I will get your breakfast.'

'I'll do it.' Cereal, fruit and toast, with orange juice and tea, were simple enough to assemble. Besides, she'd looked after herself for years, and valued a degree of independence.

Elise enjoyed a leisurely breakfast, browsing through the morning papers, then when she had finished she moved outside for a walk round the gardens.

The flowers were beautiful, grown in colour coordinated borders that were a visual delight: delicate pinks and whites, brilliant reds and yellows, then carefully clipped shrubs. There were a number of urns gracing the steps leading down from the terrace, and a splendid concrete tiered bird-bath was the central feature of a square expanse of manicured lawn.

Beyond that lay the swimming-pool with an adjacent cabana which housed a bar and changing-rooms.

It was a magnificent property, the architecture and landscaping in perfect harmony. Its location and beautiful views out over the harbour indicated a value she was hesitant to calculate.

Was it any wonder that Savannah coveted the man who owned it? His position in the city's social scene was unquestionable, and there were few women who were not fascinated by rich and powerful men. Some even sold themselves in a quest for fame and fortune.

As she had. Although not for fame or fortune. Her father... Dammit, such introspection was dangerous. It led nowhere, and achieved nothing except to highlight her own insecurities.

Love was a mixture of heaven and hell. Especially when you were not loved in return. The physicalities of lovemaking were there, but not the emotional commitment.

Would it ever be any different? *Could* it be? Sadly, she didn't think so.

Elise wandered down to the swimming-pool and sat in one of the chairs positioned beneath a wide sun-umbrella. The sun felt warm against her bare skin, and she leaned her head back and closed her eyes.

'Elise? It is ten-fifteen.'

She came sharply awake at the sound of Ana's voice, amazed that she could have lapsed into a light doze.

Her hand had swollen slightly and was beginning to show signs of bruising. There was also a degree of pain when the physiotherapist supervised her exercises, a fact which he noted, adding an admonition to be more careful. There didn't seem much point in assuring him that it was not self-inflicted.

At home she ate the chicken salad Ana had prepared for lunch, then she changed into a bikini, selected a book, and wandered out to sit beneath a shade-umbrella by the pool.

It was almost six when Alejandro arrived home, and Elise cast him a warm smile as he entered the lounge.

'How was your day?' she asked lightly, and was unprepared for his brief hard kiss.

'A series of meetings, appointments.' His tone was dry, his eyes dark and inscrutable. 'I'll change. Then we'll have a drink before dinner.'

'I'll go and check with Ana.'

The table was already set, and there was a delicious aroma emanating from the kitchen.

'Vegetable soup,' Ana informed her as she stirred the contents of a saucepan. 'Paella, with fresh fruit to finish.'

'Sounds wonderful. Can I help with anything?'

'It is all under control,' the older woman beamed companionably. 'I will serve in fifteen minutes.'

Elise wandered towards the lounge, and was busy watching the televised news when Alejandro entered the room.

He looked vaguely satanic in casual dark trousers and a polo shirt which highlighted the olive tint of his skin and emphasised his length and breadth. 'A cool drink?'

She glanced towards him and her breath caught in her throat as she glimpsed the hard demeanour just beneath the surface of his control. 'Please,' she managed evenly, returning her attention to the television.

She turned as he reached her side, and instead of handing her a glass he placed both down on a nearby pedestal.

'Let me see your hand.'

He knew. *How*? The physiotherapist? There was no one else who could have told him, she reasoned silently.

'It's a bit stiff,' she admitted with a helpless shrug, unwilling to extend it for his inspection.

'Some bruising, pain and reduced mobility,' Alejandro stated with dangerous softness, 'consistent with the hand being compressed.' He reached forward and carefully caught hold of her arm. His intent examination filled her with a peculiar sense of dread, and she almost died at the savagery apparent as he seared her features. 'Savannah?'

She swallowed nervously. 'What if I accidentally knocked my hand?'

His expression became inscrutable, and his voice contained dangerous indolence. 'Did you?'

Evasion of the truth was hardly wise, for there was already visible evidence of bruising. 'No.'

He said something vicious beneath his breath in Spanish, then lifted a hand to cup her jaw. His finger traced a gentle pattern over her lower lip, probing slightly before moving to caress her cheek. His eyes became dark, their depths unfathomable as he searched her features.

'My relationship with Savannah was...' He paused fractionally, then said deliberately, 'Mutually convenient.'

Mutual need, Elise qualified, sickened at the picture that conjured up.

'Marriage was not something I had considered until you stormed into my office in a state of fury and began hurling accusations and making allegations.' His smile held wry cynicism. 'Over dinner that same evening I decided I wanted your loyalty, your fierce pride, your honesty.'

He had deliberately tested her, and it rankled unbearably.

He brushed her mouth lightly with his own. 'Eventually—your love,' he added quietly.

He had placed the chess-pieces on a board, and played the game with infinite patience and skill. She hurt too much to let him know that he had won.

'Along with good health, love is something that money can't buy,' Elise declared carefully, and glimpsed a flicker of pain in the depths of his eyes, so fleeting that she wondered if she had imagined it.

'The time between being informed of your accident and discovering the extent of your injuries were the worst minutes I have ever spent,' he assured her ruminatively as he took possession of her mouth in a kiss so incredibly gentle that she simply closed her eyes and gave herself up to the sensual eroticism of his touch.

It seemed an age before he broke contact and slowly lifted his head.

It took enormous will-power to step away from him, and her voice was not quite steady as she offered, 'Ana will be ready to serve dinner.'

'Then let us go in and eat.'

CHAPTER NINE

IT WAS a week later that Elise entered the elegant Double Bay salon and checked with Reception.

'Raphael will be five minutes, Elise,' the stunning blonde told her with a bright smile. 'He's running a little late. Perhaps you'd care to take a seat? Would you like some tea or coffee? Orange juice, mineral water?'

Elise shook her head in silent negation, adding a polite, 'Thanks,' before selecting a chair.

A year ago—make that nine months ago, she corrected mentally—she wouldn't have been able to afford to walk into this exclusive hairdressing salon. To have had Raphael himself apply his artistic cutting expertise to her hair would have been unthinkable.

The name Santanas opened doors, commanded respect, and produced a desire to pander to any whim with such obsequious effusiveness that it was almost obscene.

Elise reached for one of several thick glossy magazines and began flipping through the pages, noting the elegant models, the beautiful clothes, designer make-up, articles written in stylish prose, a feature profile on one of Australia's social doyennes, another profile on a top designer, and the usual society pages with a run-down on recent events with accompanying photographs.

She skimmed over them without interest, only to be riveted by a frame depicting Alejandro with Savannah at his side.

Her stomach gave a painful lurch, and she took a deep breath as she willed herself to check the magazine's date of issue. The event highlighted was a dinner organised specifically to raise money for a well-known charity.

Oh, hell. Why did she have to pick *that* particular magazine? She could have remained in ignorance. Besides, she silently attempted to reassure herself, the photograph was probably the result of coincidence, taken when Savannah just happened to be standing at his side.

And pigs might fly, she added mentally. There was nothing innocent in any one of Savannah's actions. The way Savannah was gazing at him in open adoration was positively sickening.

'Elise. How are you, darling? Sorry to keep you waiting.'

She closed the magazine and rose to her feet with a ready smile. 'Raphael.'

An extrovert, he delighted in the portrayal of exaggerated mannerisms, creating an erroneous image that was in direct contrast to his true personality. White harem-style trousers and a fine white muslin artist's shirt with numerous tiny pleats fanning out from a deep yoke gave the illusion of adding to his lean frame. A diamond stud adorned one ear, he wore a diamond signet ring on his left hand, and a religious medallion suspended from a thick chain hung low against his chest. Long black hair was sleekly plastered against his scalp and caught together at his nape to form a ponytail.

'Your hand? It is still giving you pain?' He drew her towards the far end of the salon and seated her at a basin.

'It aches a little.'

Raphael's personal attention was rare, and Elise, by virtue of being Alejandro's wife, appeared to be one of the favoured few.

She wrinkled her nose as he sluiced water over her hair and applied shampoo, rinsed and repeated the process with conditioner, then towelled it dry before leading her to a mirrored cubicle.

'You are able to drive again?'

'The specialist says I can. Alejandro would prefer José to continue in the role of chauffeur. Although he has compromised and bought me another car.'

'He is being protective, hmm?'

'You could say that,' she agreed with suitable dryness.

Raphael picked up his scissors and comb, and went to work. 'Don't knock it, darling,' he cautioned wryly. 'Men are not usually protective unless they care.'

Alejandro's brand of caring was linked to their unborn child. *She* was merely a secondary consideration.

Or was she? From the beginning his lovemaking had generated a desire for her pleasure as much as his own, and there had never been an occasion when she had felt—*used*.

When had she fallen in love with him? Sadly, Elise couldn't pinpoint a single moment when the revelation had hit. She was aware only of its stealthy possession, and the agonising knowledge that her life would never be the same without him.

'Tonight is the exhibition of fine art held in one of the Woollahra Galleries,' Raphael informed her. 'You are attending, of course.'

Alejandro was a known patron of the arts, and he had a reputation for adding one or two paintings each year to his collection of works by Australian artists.

The evening's event included cocktails and hors-d'oeuvres, and attendance was strictly by invitation.

'Yes.'

'A notable occasion,' Raphael proffered as his scissors moved with crafted expertise.

Without doubt, she agreed mentally. The social glitterati would be present, together with members of the Press, and several photographers, each attempting to outdo the other.

She had even bought a new black gown. Sleeveless, its simple slim-fitting style was enhanced with intricate silver embroidery on the bodice. A high scooped neckline precluded jewellery, and there were matching shoes and evening bag.

Raphael reached for several fat rollers and positioned them in place, collected a magazine for her to read, then moved towards Reception to greet the next client.

It was almost four when Elise emerged, another half-hour before she brought the Mercedes to a halt beside the main entrance of Alejandro's Point Piper home.

She could hear the shower running as she entered their suite, and she stripped down to briefs and bra, collected a silk robe and slipped it on, then she crossed to the dressing-table to attend to her make-up.

Alejandro entered the bedroom, with a towel hitched low on his hips, as she applied the finishing touches, and she watched in mesmerised fascination as he moved to her side and bestowed a lingering kiss on the soft curve of her neck.

His touch sent warmth tingling through her veins, and her expression held a faint wistfulness as he stood behind her and viewed their mirrored reflections.

'What time do you want to leave?' she queried, unable to tear her gaze away.

'Fifteen minutes. The traffic will be heavy.' His hands rested on her shoulders, then slowly slid down the front edges of her robe to slip beneath the silk and gently tease the softness of her breasts. With tantalising care he began to brush the pad of his thumb over each sensitive peak.

Elise felt them swell and harden, and she gave a soundless gasp as his fingers slid to unfasten her bra.

'Alejandro——'

'Humour me,' he said huskily. His eyes held hers captive, their depths alive with leashed passion. 'I have thought of little else all day. The intoxicating texture of your skin, its delicate perfume, the way your beautiful eyes soften when I touch you.'

Sensation spiralled from her feminine core as intense sexual awareness swept through her body. All he had to do was pull her into his arms and she would be lost.

'Shouldn't we get ready?' she asked in a strangled voice, and glimpsed the edge of his mouth twist in a gesture of wry self-mockery.

'Indeed.' His hands lingered, then slowly withdrew to settle briefly on her shoulders. 'If I kiss you, we'll never leave this room.'

'In that case, perhaps you'd better get changed and let me finish my make-up,' she suggested shakily, and he laughed, a deep, soft, husky sound that sent goose-bumps over the surface of her skin.

'Eventually we will return home, *mi mujer*, and then we shall resume where we have left off.'

'If I'm not too tired.' It was a tame attempt at denial, and didn't fool him in the least.

'I promise to do all the work, *querida*.' His lips brushed her temple, then slid down to nibble an earlobe.

Not all, she promised silently as he moved away and selected underwear, a dress-shirt and black trousers that formed parts of a sophisticated shield for the primitive strength of his body. Socks, shoes came next, and when he reached for the immaculate bow tie she hurriedly transferred her attention and picked up a shiny gold tube with which to stroke pastel colour on to her lips.

Her choice of perfume was her favourite, Evelyn, a subtle rose fragrance that imbued the skin with immense delicacy.

Five minutes later she slipped into the gown, and she stood perfectly still as Alejandro slid the zip-fastener into place.

'You look beautiful,' he complimented as she stepped into the elegant evening shoes.

Collecting her evening bag, she turned towards him and proffered a faint smile. 'The women will vie with each other for your attention,' she anticipated lightly.

'I have no control over inherited genes,' he responded in an amused drawl. 'And the only woman I am interested in is you.'

For now, Elise added silently, wishing she could believe him. It would be incredible to feel truly secure in a man's love, to know without any element of doubt that you were adored, and that even if he displayed visual appreciation for another no other woman had a chance of capturing his heart.

Such a hope belonged in the realms of fantasy, she decided ruefully, as the Bentley became part of the flow of traffic entering the inner-city perimeter.

Reality was a combination of harsh facts and formidable statistics which existed as irrefutable proof that love did not always last forever. The first heady bloom often flared brilliantly, only to diminish all too frequently to a state of prosaic affection.

The car slid to a halt, and Elise's eyes widened with the realisation that they were stationary. The car park was brightly lit, and there were sounds and movement as guests vacated their cars.

Alejandro caught her elbow in a light clasp and led her towards the main entrance. Inside, several guests mingled in small groups, and there were several smartly uniformed waiters and waitresses proffering drinks and bite-sized food.

Almost at once Alejandro was greeted by the gallery owner and engaged in conversation, and Elise found herself drawn into a civilised debate on the advantages of free artistic expression over the confines of conformity.

'Do you enjoy Alejandro's artistic taste?'

Oh, hell, she wasn't even sure which artists he favoured. The paintings hanging on the walls at Point Piper and Palm Beach were visually pleasing, although a few were a little too modern for her own enjoyment.

'Mostly,' she agreed. 'Although he has a Pro Hart of which I'm not particularly fond.'

'My wife is a traditionalist,' Alejandro relayed smoothly. 'Her taste runs to Max Boyd.'

'Oh, my dear. Hart is quite brilliant.'

'So are a number of other noted Australian artists,' she offered firmly. 'It's very much a personal choice, don't you think?'

'There's an excellent piece you really must see. Expensive, but worthy of investment.' He riffled through the catalogue pages and brought the item to Alejandro's notice, then made his excuses as someone else demanded his attention.

'I happen to like Max Boyd,' Elise protested as Alejandro's amused gaze rested on her expressive features.

'So do I,' he assured her, and, placing an arm round her waist, he directed her towards a display. 'Shall we begin viewing?'

Some paintings verged on the bizarre, others resembled caricatures of design over brilliant slashes of colour. One in particular looked as if a child at kindergarten level had indulged in a totally wild battle with numerous pots of multi-coloured paint.

'What do you think?'

Elise turned towards Alejandro and endeavoured to present a considered viewpoint. After several seconds she voiced with restraint, 'I'd prefer not to answer on the grounds that anything I say could be overheard, taken into account, and held against me.'

'A remarkable nonconformist piece,' Alejandro drawled knowledgeably, and her eyes danced as she nodded in silent agreement. 'Shall we move on?'

'Please.'

There were a number of guests present whom she had met before, and for the next hour she exchanged pleasantries, accepted an invitation for an upcoming fashion parade, deferred to Alejandro on no less than three dinner invitations, and she was just beginning to find the evening a relaxing venture when she glimpsed a familiar head several feet distant.

Savannah. As if by design the guests shifted position so that the model's body profile was in clear view: a stunning figure, attired in a flamboyant gown that on anyone one else would have looked totally outrageous.

Elise forced herself to meet Savannah's intent gaze, and for one brief second she witnessed unadulterated venom before it was masked. A slight smile appeared in acknowledgement before Savannah turned towards her partner, and Elise was unable to prevent a slight shiver.

Did Alejandro know Savannah was here? It was a distinct probability.

'More mineral water?'

'Thank you.'

'We should be able to get away in less than an hour. We'll go on to dinner afterwards,' Alejandro said quietly.

'Have you already booked?'

He named a well-known restaurant famed for its fine cuisine. 'You would prefer somewhere else?'

'Quiet, out of the way, with little chance of meeting anyone we know?' she suggested hopefully.

'I can recollect a few.'

Suitable for clandestine meetings? Damn, she had to stop resorting to destructive introspection! 'Of course, we could buy a take-away meal on the way home.'

'Anything in particular?'

'Chinese?'

His eyes gleamed with humour. 'I'll cancel the restaurant from the car.'

'Thank you.'

He lifted a hand and brushed his fingers lightly across her cheek. 'Just where precisely do you intend we eat?'

She looked at him with undue solemnity. 'Dressed like this?' she enquired innocently. 'At the dining-room table. Where else?'

'We could always change first.'

'And eat out on the terrace?' She offered a singularly sweet smile. 'What a wonderful idea.'

The depths of his eyes took on a dark brilliance. 'Minx. Remind me to extract due penance.'

'You wouldn't dare.'

A slow, wicked smile tugged the edges of his mouth, and his voice held infinite indolence. 'Just watch me.'

Every bone in her body began to feel liquefied at the thought of precisely how he would exact atonement. 'I think,' she said unsteadily, 'we should attempt to continue our viewing, don't you?'

'An excellent suggestion.'

It was after eight when they left, and almost nine before Alejandro garaged the car. The plastic carrier bag with its various containers emitted a mouth-watering aroma, and Elise slid off her shoes the moment they entered the house.

'You intend to change before we eat?'

She cast him a studied glance. 'This gown cost a small fortune.'

'So did my suit,' drawled Alejandro.

'Perhaps you should exchange it for something less formal.'

'And save on the dry-cleaning bill?'

'Naturally.'

'I gather eating in bed would be considered the height of decadence?'

She failed miserably in suppressing an impish smile. 'It would be such a shame to waste the food.'

'The terrace?'

Her eyes twinkled with devilish humour. 'Think of the moonlight.'

He shrugged out of his jacket and placed it over a nearby chair. 'Plates, cutlery, glasses?'

She pretended due consideration. 'I guess we could opt for informality,' she decided as she picked up her shoes and made for the staircase. 'Two forks, two glasses.' She began mounting the stairs, then paused to look down at him. 'Do you think you can manage that?'

He removed the bow tie and loosened the top buttons on his shirt. 'Don't be too long, *querida*,' he warned gently, and her mouth curved into a guileless smile.

'Patience, Alejandro.' She turned and slowly traversed the remaining stairs. In the bedroom she slipped out of the gown, then dressed in silk culottes and a loose top.

Minutes later she walked out on to the terrace to find Alejandro seated at one of the outdoor tables, a portable lamp providing essential light, the food displayed in its various containers, and a slim flute of wine within easy reach. His shirt was undone almost to the waist, the cuffs rolled halfway up his forearms.

Elise sank into a chair opposite, dipped a fork into chop suey, and savoured a mouthful with suitable enthusiasm, then repeated the process. 'Isn't this better than eating in a restaurant?'

He forked a prawn into his mouth, then shot her a musing look. 'This is quite good.'

'Don't sound so surprised.' She met his gaze and wrinkled her nose at him in admonition. 'The trouble is you've been thoroughly spoilt, with a personal cook and professional chefs to pander to your gourmand taste.'

'Planning to re-educate me, Elise?'

'In some areas it mightn't be a bad idea.'

'And what areas are those, my darling wife?' He sounded distinctly amused, and dangerously indolent.

'You could do with a lesson in humility,' she said with mock severity.

'Where you are concerned, I am remarkably humble,' Alejandro claimed solemnly. His eyes held hers, and she couldn't look away as he lifted his glass in a silent salute before placing the rim to his mouth.

He sounded sincere. Almost as if he cared very much. The breath caught in her throat, and she found it difficult to swallow.

Her fork was suspended in mid-air, and she slowly replaced it on the table, her appetite gone.

He leaned back in the chair, his large frame displaying an indolent grace that was deceptive, for there was a watchfulness apparent, a leashed air she found infinitely disturbing. 'Lost for words, Elise?'

She looked at him for what seemed an age, wanting more than anything to move into his arms, to lift her mouth for his kiss. But she seemed locked into immobility, and there was a strange ache in the region of her heart.

There was so much she wanted to say, yet she felt hesitant, afraid that if she revealed too much it would render her vulnerable.

'Shall I make coffee?' Even her voice sounded breathy and uncertain, and she cursed her own insecurity.

'No coffee,' Alejandro said gently. 'I'll dispose of these containers, then we'll go to bed.'

Bed. That was her downfall. It was where she sold her soul and lost control.

'I'm not tired,' she offered quietly, and glimpsed his faint smile.

'Neither am I. Sleeping wasn't exactly what I had in mind.'

She rose to her feet and gathered up the cutlery and glasses, then carried them through to the kitchen.

Alejandro followed, and she heard him locking the outer doors and setting the security alarm.

It was a simple task to load the dishwasher, and she had just finished when he entered the room.

He looked vaguely piratical: dark trousers, deep olive skin, dark hair, in stark contrast to the white shirt. And tall. He almost seemed overpowering, and, while she craved his touch, there was a part of her that cried out against any sexual subjugation.

She watched as he despatched food down the waste-disposal unit, then dropped empty containers into the pedal-bin before washing and drying his hands.

In silence he turned and caught hold of her hand, leading her through to the lounge, where he selected a compact disc and slid it into the disc player.

Soft music emanated from the speakers and Elise looked at him speechlessly as he drew her into his arms.

Crazy, she thought, as he pulled her close against him and began to drift slowly round the room. She felt his lips brush her hair, followed by the warmth of his breath against her temple. His heartbeat was strong beneath her cheek, and her hands crept to link together at the back of his waist.

The music was so slow and dreamy that after several minutes they hardly bothered to move at all, and simply stood still in the dim light reflected from the foyer.

His kiss was so incredibly gentle that it almost made her cry, and she offered him her mouth, exulting in an erotic tasting that excited without demand.

When the music finished he raised his head and subjected her to a long, searching gaze, then he placed an arm beneath her knees and carried her up the stairs.

Elise wanted to cry, and when he lowered her to her feet in the bedroom, tears shimmered like crystal droplets in each corner of her eyes.

Without a word he led her to the bed and sat down on its edge, then he drew her to stand between his thighs.

Her mouth began to tremble, and there was nothing she could do to prevent the slow downward path of a single tear as it overflowed.

Alejandro lifted a hand and halted its passage with the pad of his thumb before moving to trace the outline of her mouth.

'I was almost hesitant to question the cause,' he drawled gently. 'Do you want to blame it on ambivalent emotions?'

'I guess that's as good a reason as any,' she owned shakily, and almost died at the wealth of passion evident in those dark eyes so close to her own.

'I need you,' he said gently. 'Every day in my life. All night long in my bed.'

Need. Need had to be better than *want*, didn't it? And 'every day in my life' sounded permanent. As in forever?

She wanted to say, '*I love you*.' But the words wouldn't emerge.

He pulled her on to his lap and kissed her, then carefully eased her on to the bed.

Her arms lifted to curve round his neck as she gave herself up to the magic only he was able to create. Soon she was filled with an agonising sweetness as her body began to respond to the exquisite *tendresse* of his touch, and she throbbed with intense awareness when he entered her, glorying in the mutual joy of complete possession as they journeyed towards a mutual fulfilment of the senses.

It was a wild sweet pleasure tempered by raw desire. Erotic, primitive, yet so incredibly sensual she was held captive in its thrall . . . *his* without any equivocation.

On the edge of sleep she was conscious of his arms enfolding her close, and she gave a tiny sigh of contentment before drifting in a dreamless state that lasted until morning.

CHAPTER TEN

'ELISE. There is a telephone call for you.'

Very few calls for her came through the house phone. Alejandro rang direct on the mobile net, likewise the few of her friends to whom she had given the number. Perhaps it was the obstetrician's receptionist rescheduling her appointment.

'Who is it, Ana?'

'Siobhan Barry.'

If Siobhan was calling at this time, it meant she had the day off. Perhaps they could meet for lunch, Elise mused as she crossed to the nearest handset.

'Siobhan. How are you?'

There was a brief silence. '*Savannah*, darling. Did Ana get it wrong?'

A chill feeling settled in the pit of her stomach. Even allowing for misunderstanding, Savannah's surname was vastly dissimilar to that of Siobhan. Which meant Savannah had deliberately set out to deceive. There could be little doubt as to why.

'Is it essential we have this conversation?' Elise managed steadily, and heard a faint intake of breath down the line.

'I suppose you think you're clever,' Savannah opined viciously.

It was a game that had to be played out to its conclusion, Elise decided, saddened that it should have even begun. 'Perhaps you'd care to elaborate.'

'You poisonous little bitch. You had to tell him, didn't you?'

Elise closed her eyes, then slowly opened them again. 'If you're referring to my hand . . . blame the physiotherapist,' she managed carefully, 'and Alejandro, for insisting on a first-hand report every time I visit any member of the medical profession.'

There was a long pause. 'Watch your back, darling.'

'I always do.' Without hesitation she replaced the receiver, only to lift it again and dial a memorised number.

A sleepy voice repeated the digits, and Elise felt a surge of relief. 'Siobhan? How about lunch?'

'I didn't get to bed until three, you impossible person. Must it be today?'

'We could make it a late lunch,' Elise persisted, and heard Siobhan's laughing approval.

'Name the time and place, and I'll meet you there.'

'One-thirty. Doyle's at Watson's Bay,' she returned without hesitation.

They met within minutes of the appointed time, and managed by good fortune to be shown to a table overlooking the beach. After the serious business of ordering was completed, they settled down to exchanging news, something which lasted through the starter, and well into the main course.

'You're positively blooming,' Siobhan complimented quietly. 'Your hair, your skin. Everything about you. I couldn't be more pleased everything is working out.'

Elise managed a bright smile that didn't fool her friend in the slightest.

'Not quite, huh? What's the problem?'

'I didn't ask you to meet me to discuss any problems.'

'Hell, no. You love my wit, my charm.' She leaned forward, her expression pensive. 'I refuse to believe it has anything to do with Alejandro. Savannah?' she hazarded.

'Why not Alejandro?'

Siobhan shot her an old-fashioned look. 'My God, you really can't see it, can you?' she queried, shaking her head in silent disbelief. 'Did you never wonder why I didn't visit you in hospital?' Her expression sobered. 'Alejandro requested—*requested*,' she insisted, 'I stay away until you regained your memory.' Her eyes took on an earnest fervour. 'He rang me every day to let me know how you were.'

Elise could only look at her in shocked silence. Why would he do something like that if he didn't want to make the most of an opportunity to repair her perception of him? It was crazy. Yet only last night...

'Go figure, Elise,' Siobhan advised gently. 'And, if you're still in any doubt, ask yourself why he insisted on marriage, when it would have been infinitely more simple to install you as his mistress.'

It was almost four when they left the restaurant, and a short while later Elise garaged the car, then moved lightly indoors.

Ana was busy peeling vegetables as she entered the kitchen, and she uttered an appreciative sound as the delicious aroma of roast chicken assailed her nostrils.

'Anything I can do to help?'

Ana's smile, like the woman herself, was warm and friendly. 'Alejandro rang. He will be home early. If you must do something, you could set the table.'

Afterwards she took a long, leisurely shower, then dressed in a white silk blouse and tailored straight skirt. She was putting the finishing touches to her make-up when Alejandro entered the bedroom.

Elise offered him a tentative smile, then concentrated on colouring the lower curve of her mouth. Her eyes widened as she saw his reflected image in the mirror, and she stood perfectly still as he turned her round to face him.

'I had a call from the physiotherapist. It appears you forgot your appointment this afternoon.'

Surprise flitted across her features. Damn, it had completely slipped her mind. 'I'll ring tomorrow and offer my apologies. I met Siobhan for lunch.'

His eyes pierced hers. 'Ana said Siobhan phoned. Strange,' he continued thoughtfully, 'when the only number she has is linked to your personal mobile.'

Elise lifted her hands, then let them fall to her sides in a helpless gesture. 'Savannah rang, and tricked Ana that she was Siobhan, then attempted to have me believe Ana had made a mistake over the name.'

'Do you want to tell me about it?'

'Not particularly.'

'Elise——'

'Don't, Alejandro. Please.' She felt so incredibly vulnerable that if he touched her she would shatter and fall in an ignominious heap at his feet.

Even now, the pain was still there, yet she managed to hold his gaze with dignity. Dared she risk all and reveal how she felt? Expunge the anguish, and pray that Siobhan was right?

Drawing a deep breath, she took courage in both hands and began.

'I need to tell you that I viewed my father's death as a ticket to escape a marriage I considered to have been arranged in hell. The night he lay so ill in hospital, I forgot to take the Pill. Ironic, wouldn't you say, that he should die within hours of my discovering I might be pregnant?' She bit the edge of her lip to prevent it from trembling, and the breath caught in her throat as he lifted both hands to frame her face.

'So you ran.' His thumb traced the edge of her lower lip. She swallowed involuntarily, and his eyes narrowed faintly as he witnessed her nervous reaction.

'I considered I had no choice.'

'*Gracias*, Elise.' There was a bitterness apparent that tore her apart.

There was no doubt he desired her, but desire alone had little to do with need, *love*. 'After the accident,' she began shakily, 'you were always there, the image of a devoted husband.' Her eyes searched his, seeing the darkness apparent, the faint tenseness as he waited for her to continue. 'When my memory returned, I felt betrayed. I had trusted you,' she cried in an anguished whisper.

He was quiet for a long time. 'There was no reason for you to distrust me.'

'You perceived it as a game,' Elise went on with incredible sadness. 'With me as the pawn.'

'From the beginning,' he corrected quietly, 'you were the prize.'

'Prey,' she countered. 'Ruthlessly hunted, and relentlessly lured into a trap.'

His gaze was unwavering, intense, and impossible to read.

'You acted a part,' she accused, and saw his eyes darken.

'Never,' he assured her after a long silence, and her features paled.

'I don't believe you.'

'No? You perceived our lovemaking as a calculated coupling without any depth of emotional involvement?'

It had never been that, not even in the beginning. '*Love* isn't a prerequisite for satisfactory sex.' She felt as if she were breaking up inside, her body slowly shattering with each successive word he uttered.

He was silent for what seemed an age, and his voice when he spoke sounded like silk being sliced by the finest tempered steel. 'You can describe what we share as merely clinical satisfaction?'

She looked at him carefully, seeing the strength apparent, the hint of passion in the depths of those dark eyes. 'No,' she owned at last.

His thumb trailed to her cheekbone, explored the faint hollow beneath, then slid to rest at the corner of her mouth. '*Por Dios,*' he declared huskily. 'An admission.'

Time stood still, and she was willing to swear that her heart stopped beating for several seconds before kicking in at a quickened pace as the pad of his thumb slid halfway along her lower lip to rest there momentarily before gently compressing its fullness.

'And *this,*' he drawled with emphasis, as his hand shaped one sensitised breast, deliberately tracing a provocative pattern back and forth across its aching peak, 'is your body's reaction to the caress of any man?'

Dear God, no. *You,* she vowed silently. Only you.

His eyes were dark, almost black, gleaming like polished onyx as he reached into her mind and so easily read what was there.

'Impossible, of course, for you to comprehend you are the love of my life?'

The silence was so total that she forgot to breathe, then her chest lurched as she drew in the first of several deep ragged gasps of air.

'They're only words, Alejandro,' she managed shakily, wanting desperately to believe them.

'They are all I have left.' His eyes were dark, unguarded, and filled with a depth of passion that made her senses reel.

'Your amnesia provided me with a heaven-sent opportunity to begin afresh. Without the barrier of your animosity, it became possible for you to believe you were the very much loved wife of a man who clearly adored you.' He paused, and his touch was so gentle that it made her want to cry. 'I prayed your memory loss would last long enough for those weeks we had together to make a difference.'

'The baby——'

His finger pressed closed her lips, and his eyes were incredibly dark. 'Make no mistake, *querida*. The child you carry is a wonderful bonus. But it is you I care for. *You*.'

She shivered at the soft invasive pull on her emotions as his fingers slid to her nape and angled her head towards his.

'Please—*don't*,' she whispered in anguish.

His head lowered to hers, and his breath was warm against her lips. 'Why not, *querida*?'

Her stomach lurched, then curled into a painful knot as his mouth brushed hers. She couldn't have moved, even if her limbs had been willing. 'Because I can't think when you do that.'

She sensed rather than glimpsed his smile. 'Is it so important that you *think*?'

The tip of his tongue touched the corner of her mouth, savoured the indentation, then lightly traced the full curve to the centre. Liquid fire coursed through her veins, igniting each separate nerve-end until her body seemed one vibrant entity.

'If I don't,' she managed in strangled tones, 'you'll simply sweep me into oblivion.'

She sensed his smile, and heard the faint husky growl emerge from his throat. 'Would that be so bad?'

His mouth was creating the sweetest magic with her own, a slow, tantalising prelude to what must surely follow, and her body began to heat, every nerve-end flaring into vibrant life as her soul reached out to his.

'Alejandro...' His name escaped her lips in a shaken gasp as he drew her close in against the swollen evidence of his desire.

It was almost as if he needed to absorb her—flesh, bones, the very essence that made her unique—and she could feel herself slowly melting, slipping inevitably down into a glorious pool of swirling warmth where there was only an acute perception of the senses, the sweet promise of two souls perfectly in accord merging and becoming one.

With a sense of desperation she dragged her mouth away from his, aware in a moment of complete lucidity that it was because he allowed it.

Her lips felt soft and swollen, tender, and they trembled slightly beneath the moistness of her tongue as she unconsciously ran its tip along the lower edge.

His eyes flared, watching the movement with mesmerised fascination.

Almost as if he could not restrain himself, he leaned forward and brushed his lips against her temple, then pressed each eyelid closed before trailing down to the edge of her lips. His touch was as light as a butterfly's wing, caressing, loving, and she wanted to cry out against his flagrant seduction.

'I expressed my adoration with the touch of my hands, my mouth...my body,' Alejandro declared. He lapsed into Spanish, then repeated the words softly in a language she understood. Erotic, explicit, undeniably earthy. Yet heartfelt, and without any pretence.

Soft colour flooded her cheeks, and her lips trembled as a low husky chuckle emerged from his throat.

'Have I shocked you?' he mocked gently.

A wicked smile curved her generous mouth. 'Did you intend to?' she queried, offering deliberate temptation as she lifted her arms and linked them carefully at his nape, only to gasp as his mouth closed over hers with deep, drugging possession.

He gave no quarter, and she expected none as she met and matched his ardour, exulting in the feel and taste of him, the heavy thudding beat of his heart as it pounded against her own in unison, the sheer sensation of knowing he was hers. It was a heady power, one she knew she would never choose to abuse.

Minutes later she cried out as his mouth left hers to trail down her throat, and she arched her neck to allow him access to the sensitive hollows, gasping as he teasingly nipped delicate skin, then slid to begin an open-mouthed suckling at one silk-covered breast that caught her slender frame in a paroxysm of sensation.

'You are wearing too many clothes, *mi mujer*,' he chastised huskily minutes later as his fingers began to deal with the buttons on her blouse.

'Hmm,' she agreed with a delicious smile. 'So are you.' Her eyes danced with wicked amusement. 'There's a problem,' she announced with seeming regret, and felt his fingers still as he looked at her in silent enquiry.

'Ana is serving dinner at seven.'

His eyes darkened with ill-concealed humour. 'Next,' he murmured huskily, 'you'll tell me you're hungry.'

She wrinkled her nose at him. 'We could eat first, then retire early.'

'Flattering, to be relegated second to food.'

'I promise I'll make it up to you,' Elise declared, and he smiled, the creases deepening as they slashed each cheek.

'Interesting.'

'It will be,' she teased. 'It's the reason I need to keep up my strength.'

His fingers moved to refasten slowly the buttons on her blouse, then he kissed her with such incredible gentleness that it was all she could do not to wind her arms up around his neck and tell him to make love to her *now*.

'Then let us go downstairs and sample what Ana has chosen to serve us.'

They ate a leisurely meal, deliberately pacing themselves, each increasingly aware of the moment they would rise from the table and go upstairs to their suite.

There was a sense of anticipation that became more acute with every passing minute, a sensual teasing as they indulged in a playful game.

More than once Alejandro paused in the process of eating to lift his glass and utter a salute in a drawled collection of Spanish words that required no interpreter to define them.

'After your son is born, you'll have to censor your words,' she chided with an attempt at severity, and failed miserably beneath the liquid warmth of his gaze.

'I have no intention of withholding from him how much I adore his beloved *mamá*.'

She had a mental image of a small dark-haired boy with mischievous dark eyes, running, laughing, infinitely loved by his parents. And later, God willing, there would be a little girl for him to protect and adore.

Elise speared the last segment of fruit from her plate and lifted it to her mouth, biting the firm flesh of deliciously fresh melon with a delicacy that brought a brilliant flaring to the eyes of the man seated opposite.

'I suppose you are going to insist I take coffee?'

Her eyes openly teased his, sparkling with unguarded humour. 'Caffeine,' she explained knowledgeably, 'is supposed to stimulate the brain.'

His dark gaze became languid, a displayed deception that didn't fool her in the slightest as he queried in a silky drawl, 'And it is my *brain* you particularly want to stimulate?'

She swallowed the last of the melon, then ran the edge of her tongue lightly over the curve of her lips. 'I would be disappointed,' she declared with slight emphasis, 'if you proved less than . . . capable,' she finished delicately.

His eyes became faintly hooded, and the edge of his mouth assumed an upward curve. 'Witch,' he responded with deliberate lightness as he sat back in his chair and savoured his wine.

Aware of his propensity to conduct a leisurely lovemaking, extending her pleasure to a point where she became wholly, solely *his*, before tipping them both over the edge into a state of passionate oblivion, she wondered at the wisdom of baiting him.

At that moment Ana entered the room and began clearing the table, her movements sure, deft, and unobtrusive.

'That was a lovely meal,' Elise complimented gently, and was rewarded with a pleased smile.

'*Gracias*. Will you have coffee here, or in the lounge?'

Elise glanced towards Alejandro, who merely raised one eyebrow in silent mockery as he transferred the responsibility for a decision.

'Would you mind bringing it out on to the terrace? It's such a beautiful evening.'

'My wife is a romantic,' Alejandro drawled, sparing Elise a long, thoughtful glance that curled her toes.

'The evening sunset,' Ana agreed with a slight nod. 'Such lovely colours.'

'Indeed,' he acknowledged, and his beautifully chiselled mouth widened slightly as he got to his feet and crossed round to assist Elise from her chair.

Seconds later, as they moved out on to the terrace, his arm curved lightly round her waist, its warm strength a tangible entity that crept through her skin and seemed to liquefy her bones.

The swimming-pool looked intensely blue in the soft fading light, its surface reflecting a mirrored sheen that was duplicated on the waters in the inner harbour.

Elise's gaze wandered out towards the horizon where ocean met sky, breathing in deeply the clean sea-air as she savoured the slight breeze that teased her hair and faintly stirred the leaves on various trees.

Alejandro shifted slightly to stand behind her, his hands linking protectively over her thickening waist as he drew her back against him.

She felt his lips brush her hair, then slip down to settle in the hollow at the edge of her neck as he teased the delicate flesh. Soft tremors shook her slim frame, and she leaned into him, loving the hard muscularity of his solid frame as he enclosed her within the cage of his arms.

To rest against him like this was heaven, and she was aware of the promise of passion, the strength of his control as he simply held her, content to allow her to savour the magic of nature as the sun slowly disappeared beyond the horizon in a brilliant flaring of orange and gold tinged with purple, before the silvery sky slowly darkened to an inky velvet.

The chink of crockery in the background was an intrusive sound they both acknowledged, and together they turned and slowly wandered towards a wide, cushioned two-seater as Ana poured Alejandro's coffee, then filled a glass with water from an iced pitcher for Elise.

'Goodnight, *señor, señora.*'

Alejandro sent Ana a warm smile. '*Gracias. Buenas noches.*'

When the housekeeper had returned indoors he leaned forward and spooned sugar into the dark aromatic brew, stirred, then cradled the cup in his hands.

Elise was strangely pensive. They had cleared up so many misconceptions but——

'There is something on your mind?'

It was a light, teasing query, and, suddenly brave, she took courage in both hands. 'Savannah.'

'What is it you want to know?'

His voice was a wry drawl, and in the semi-darkness it was difficult to gauge his mood. 'You were her lover?'

'Yes.'

It hurt more than she cared to admit, even now.

'A long time ago,' he qualified.

'She implied——'

'Innuendo coupled with distorted fact is a dangerous combination,' Alejandro interposed drily.

She had to ask. 'Did you love her?'

He didn't hesitate. 'No. Nor did she love me.' His eyes pierced hers, dark and faintly brooding.

Elise stared out into the darkness, hardly aware of the tracery of dimmed lamps that sprang to life around the grounds, highlighting the gardens.

'She still wants you,' she opined slowly.

'Savannah dislikes conceding defeat.'

She recalled the cruelly spoken words, spiteful in their intention, deliberately chosen to destroy by a woman who was unlikely to find personal happiness with any one man.

Elise rose slowly to her feet. 'If you've finished your coffee, I'll return the tray to the kitchen.'

'I'll take it.' He moved with lithe ease, and once indoors he activated security before following her through to the rear of the house.

The kitchen gleamed from Ana's meticulous care, and it only took a few minutes for Elise to load their cups into the dishwasher and rinse out the coffee-pot.

She was conscious of Alejandro's studied gaze, and she tilted her chin to meet it, her eyes clear pools of liquid emerald ringed with gold.

There were words she wanted to say, achingly poignant and straight from the heart, yet they seemed locked in her throat. For a moment she hesitated, then she slowly extended her hand and caught hold of his, threading her fingers through his own. 'I want to make love with you.'

His fingers tightened, then he raised her hand to his lips, and Elise saw the blaze of emotion evident in the darkness of his gaze. Deep, heartfelt, and electrifyingly primitive.

Then he curved an arm beneath her knees and lifted her high against his chest.

A slow, burning excitement unfurled deep within and radiated through her body until she felt achingly alive. 'I can walk,' she protested with a soft laugh.

His smile was a thing of beauty, warm and passionate, his eyes almost black. 'Indulge me.'

Her lips were so close to his throat that it was an irresistible temptation to rest them against the warm pulsing cord and savour the deep thudding beat. Gently she circled it with her tongue, then drew it carefully into her mouth.

'Do you want to be ravished *here*?' Alejandro threatened huskily as he gained the stairs.

Elise gave a soft exultant laugh and bestowed a rain of soft kisses along the edge of his jaw. 'The bed might be more comfortable,' she teased, loving his strength, the sheer force of his raw masculinity.

On reaching the main suite he let her slip gently to her feet and drew her close within the circle of his arms.

His mouth closed over hers with infinite gentleness, then hardened as she melted against him, taking possession of her mouth in a manner that left her in no doubt of his feelings.

At last he lifted his head, and she could only look at him in mesmerised wonder as his fingers worked the buttons on her blouse, then dealt with the clasp fastening the contoured strip of silk and lace supporting her breasts.

They felt heavy, each dusky peak swollen as it ached, hungering for his touch.

'You're beautiful.' He traced the curve, shaping it with a reverence that brought the prick of tears, and she blinked rapidly to dispel the threatened spill.

Slowly she lifted a hand and trailed her fingers along the strong thrust of his jaw, tracing the firm chin, the faint indentation, then the chiselled shape of his mouth.

Nothing—no one—mattered. Not Savannah, nor any of the other women who had inevitably shared part of his life.

Who was it who had said you had to make each day count?

The quote and its source eluded her. The message, however, did not.

Her eyes searched his, seeing the watchful stillness in those dark eyes, the hint of pain. 'I tried very hard not to love you,' she declared in a voice that was unbearably husky. She swallowed the sudden lump that rose in her throat. 'I don't remember when it changed, only that it did,' she continued, without any pretence at hiding her emotions. 'Now I know I can't live without you.'

Alejandro reached for her, his hands shaking slightly as they slid to frame her face. 'I want to love you, be with you, for as long as it takes to reach forever. *Dios mediante*,' he vowed huskily.

'Yes,' she agreed simply, her heart in her eyes as she brought his head down to meet hers, and there was the hint of an impish smile softening the curve of her mouth as it parted to receive his. 'Are we through talking?'

'Definitely,' he murmured as his mouth closed over hers, his actions proving more than mere words could ever convey...

Helen Brooks lives in Northamptonshire and is married with three children. As she is a committed Christian, busy housewife and mother, her spare time is at a premium but her hobbies include reading, swimming, gardening and walking her two energetic, inquisitive and very endearing young dogs.

Her long-cherished aspiration to write became a reality when she put pen to paper on reaching the age of forty, and sent the result off to Mills & Boon®. Her first book was published in 1992 and, since then, her twenty-eight novels have been published in over twelve different languages.

DARK OASIS
by
HELEN BROOKS

CHAPTER ONE

'KIT! Where on earth are you? Everyone's absolutely frantic here and David's been tearing his hair out. As well he might! Are you all right, for goodness' sake?'

'I'm fine.' Kit took a long, deep breath. She didn't even want to hear David's name. 'It's over between us. Did he tell you?'

'Yes.' Her friend's voice was scathing. 'He's such a fool, Kit, he always has been, even if he *is* my brother. To mess about with Virginia of all people—*Virginia*! Never has a name been more un-apt, or at least the first six letters.'

'Emma...' Kit closed her eyes briefly and prayed for her voice to sound cool and calm despite her racing heart. 'I don't want to discuss it. I found them in bed and our engagement is over. That's it. End of story. Now, I've arranged for my half of the rent for our flat to be paid——'

'But where are you?' Emma interrupted urgently. 'You wouldn't do anything silly, would you?'

'Of course not!' Her voice had risen and she breathed deeply before speaking again, her tone a few decibels lower. 'I'm having a short holiday in the sun to think where I'm going to go from here, that's all. I'll contact you in a week or so, OK? Bye for now and take care.'

She put down the receiver and leant back against the small booth in the hotel lobby, shaking violently. The brief phone call had brought David vividly to mind and it was as though his face were there in front of her, his mouth a snarl as she had faced him in the doorway of the flat they were buying together for their intended marriage four months away, Virginia's naked body hidden from her sight now behind the closed bedroom door that he had slammed shut as he had raced after her. 'Damn well listen to me!' He had pulled the towelling dressing-gown more tightly round him as her large grey eyes flicked disgustedly over his rumpled appearance.

'There is no point, David.' She was working on automatic, she knew it, but she blessed the shock that was keeping her from disintegrating in front of him. 'And I think this belongs to you.' As she deliberately removed the diamond engagement ring from her finger and held it out to him, his pale good-looking face flushed red, a hint of unease and panic replacing the aggressive bravado with which he had met her stunned face.

'Don't be so stupid,' he spat angrily. 'You're not throwing me over because of that?' He flung back a contemptuous hand towards the closed bedroom door through which she had walked so innocently minutes before. 'I was just easing myself; she was available—Kit!' He caught hold of her arm and she was made to turn without a word. 'Kit, you can't mean it? We're getting

married, we've got this flat, furniture, everything——'

'Keep it.' Let me get out of here with a little
dignity, she prayed desperately. 'Keep it all.' She
was tall at five feet ten, her slender figure carrying
an unmistakable air of cool composure, and she
had never been more glad of it as she met him
eye to eye, her mouth curling with contempt. 'I
wouldn't marry you now if you were the last man
on earth.'

The torrent of abuse that followed her as she
made her escape polluted the very air, mixing with
the picture on the screen of her mind of Virginia's
sprawled naked limbs beneath David's heaving
thrusting body, and now, as Kit relived the sickening episode, she felt the need to breathe in some
fresh clean air. As she left the pleasant coolness
of the air-conditioned building and stepped into
the Moroccan heat, it was like stepping into an
oven, the iridescent blue sky shimmering with
heat. *Casablanca*. Kit squared her slim shoulders
as she walked towards the little red convertible
she had hired for her stay, pushing the bitter hurt
and painful humiliation back into the closed box
in her mind. She'd face that, and the tangles that
would undoubtedly ensue over the little design
business Emma, David and herself had started
eighteen months ago, later. Enough of licking her
wounds; today she was going to explore, and if
tonight in the quiet of her room she cried hot,
angry tears again, well . . . only she would know.

She travelled southward along the Atlantic
coast from Casablanca making for Essaouira,

meaning small fortress in Arabic. The hotel
manager had fired her interest, explaining that
the large harbour in the town had been used for
thousands of years, ancient Romans frequently
visiting to obtain a brilliant colouring material
produced from shellfish and used for dyeing their
robes purple. Ancient cannons still lined the main
street and, after wandering its length, she turned
into a quieter area. But, then, just as she felt the
hairs on the back of her neck prickle a warning
about the footsteps behind her, a heavy blow on
the side of her head turned the light into splintered glass, and as her shoulder-bag was wrenched
from her arm she fell. Fell into a hot blackness
that seemed to race up from the dusty ground to
consume her.

She came out of the buzzing whirl of unconsciousness slowly, very slowly, aware of a sick
pounding in her head that dominated all her
senses and made her limbs like lead. 'Can you
hear me? Try and open your eyes.' A deep male
voice and a cool hand on her burning forehead
registered on her bruised mind, but as her eyelids
fluttered in obedience the piercing light drove
them instantly shut. 'No matter. I am going to
lift you now but you are perfectly safe. Do you
understand me?' She couldn't reply, and in the
next instant she was being carried. She knew she
ought to try and open her eyes again, to speak,
but somehow it was so much easier to slip back
into that soft enveloping darkness...
    'Try and hang in there this time.'

'What?' As she forced her heavy lids open, the cool shadowed room made it easier to fix her wavering gaze on the hard male face in front of her.

'You have been slipping in and out of consciousness for the last few minutes.'

He was dark and magnificently male, his voice the one she had heard before. The accent teased her mind. French? Italian perhaps?

'Just lie still and try to concentrate on my face only until the dizziness stops,' he continued softly. 'OK?'

It was more than OK. If Michelangelo's *David* was beautiful, this man's face was stunning. His gleaming hair was a thick tawny brown worn unusually long, almost down to his shoulders. High, hard cheekbones, straight nose and sensual, almost cruel lips below eyes that were the same tawny gold-brown as his hair completed a picture of such aggressive, vibrant masculinity that Kit felt her toes begin to curl.

But who was he? And where was she? And why did she feel so desperately ill? 'Please . . .' As she tried to struggle into a sitting position on the wide leather couch on which she was lying, he moved quickly, his body carrying the same powerful grace as a beautiful wild animal.

'I said lie still.' His voice was firm and cool. 'You've received a nasty blow on the head so just take it easy.'

'I have . . . ?' As her voice trailed away on a little gulp, she felt hot tears of weakness and pain prick against her eyelids seconds before he spoke again.

'And do not dissolve on me, not yet.' He fixed her with that hard tawny gaze that reminded her of the piercing stare of one of the big cats watching its intended prey. 'I need to know your name, hotel, something. You are a tourist, I think?' His voice was cool and steady and quite unemotional.

'A tourist?' Her tongue felt too big for her mouth. 'I don't know.'

A tourist? The panic that had been at the back of her mind ever since she had opened her eyes began to claw at her throat with strangling fingers. She could be a tourist. She could be anything. She didn't remember.

'Just relax.' He saw the naked horror in her eyes and recognised it for what it was. 'You're clearly concussed, which is not surprising in the circumstances. Unfortunately the animal that did this to you also took your bag, so we have no identification to help us. I was hoping when you awoke you could provide a few answers but as it is——' he shrugged massive shoulders slowly '—the police will have to sort it.'

As he leant towards her she cowered instinctively into the bulk of the couch, flushing as he eyed her sardonically with cool raised eyebrows before wiping her face and mouth gently with a damp perfumed cloth. 'As I said, relax.'

He stood up from his crouching position at her side and it registered on her just how tall he was, well over six feet, inches over, and with a powerful hard frame that would win first prize in any Mr Universe competition. 'My name is Gerard Dumont, by the way,' he added lazily as he folded muscled arms to stand staring down at her impassively. French. Yes, she should have known. 'And you are...?'

'I...' Her voice trailed away as her eyes widened. 'My name... I don't know it.' She raised agonised eyes to the gold of his. 'I don't know who I am.'

'This is not a difficulty; do not panic.' The pronunciation of his words and correct English in that broken accent was incredibly attractive, she thought faintly as she struggled for composure. 'The bump will heal and then you will remember.' He smiled suddenly and she drew in a hard short breath of air. He was something. He *really* was something. Did he know the effect he had on women? She looked into the darkly tanned handsome face silently, mesmerised by her own unaccustomed helplessness and vulnerability and the frightening loss of memory. She had to try to remember. She must remember something. 'The police are on their way, incidentally.' He eyed her lazily. 'It would seem you were perverse enough to be, how you say, mugged at the same time as a rather large jewellery robbery was under way in the middle of the town. Needless to say, you were not considered the immediate priority.'

'Oh.' Her head felt as though it was going to explode any minute. 'Where am I?' It was the ultimate stage response to fit the situation, but for the life of her she couldn't think of a less unsubtle rejoinder.

'In my office.' The gold eyes narrowed a little. 'Can you not remember anything at all? Look down at your clothes; they may produce a spark. It would be preferable to the mountain of questions the police may ask. Subtlety is not their strong point here.'

She glanced down at her legs stretched out in front of her encased in light white cotton trousers, the cut impeccable, and tried to focus her whirling thoughts into some sort of order. Her feet were shod in slender coffee-coloured sandals that matched her waist-length blouse exactly, and again she noticed that both items seemed expensive. Well, fine. She obviously wasn't destitute, but who on earth *was* she?

'No.' She sank back against the couch and shut her eyes again. 'I'm sorry.'

When the police arrived a few minutes later she discovered one thing; she couldn't speak the language. Fortunately the two police officers seemed quite fluent in English but she couldn't tell them much, repeating the same thing over and over again until her head spun.

'I think the lady needs to see a doctor,' Gerard cut into the interrogation after a time, his hard face autocratic.

'Do I have to go with them?' She looked up at him, her large grey eyes suddenly terrified at the thought of leaving the only person she had any knowledge of, albeit a slight one, in this strange country.

'You will be quite safe.' His tone was slightly abrupt, preoccupied, and she noticed as he spoke that he glanced at the heavy gold watch on his wrist before meeting her eyes, a small frown wrinkling his brow.

'I suppose I will.' She wasn't aware her voice was sharp, but he couldn't have made it more clear that she was an awkward inconvenience and everything in her rose up in immediate opposition. 'You must be a very busy man, Mr Dumont; please don't let me keep you. Thank you for your kindness.' The words were grateful, the slight edge to her voice anything but. And then he looked at her, really looked at her, for the first time and grey eyes met gold, the former defiant, proud and very dismissive and the latter narrowed with surprise. 'Have you finished for now?' She spoke directly to the older policeman, a plump hard-faced individual in his middle fifties with eyes of stone. 'Then if you wouldn't mind taking me to the nearest hospital, we'll sort things out from there.'

Was she used to directing people like this? she asked herself faintly as she stood gingerly on her feet, her head thudding. It didn't feel unnatural so she supposed she must be. She felt terrified, sick and desperately helpless but this man Gerard had made it perfectly plain he didn't want to get involved, and she was blowed if she'd beg—she'd sort it out herself. She suddenly had the feeling she'd been doing that for a long, long time. Tears prickled under her eyelashes again and she blinked them away quickly. She'd cry later.

'Look.' Gerard steadied her with his arm round her waist as she stood swaying in the cool, air-conditioned room. 'Please do not misunderstand me. I have an important appointment, that is all. I——'

'Thank you, Mr Dumont.' She moved out of his hold on trembling legs and offered him a slim hand, her chin high. 'I hope you won't be late...' As the blackness took over again she just heard him growl something in muttered French that sounded incredibly rude as she fell, and then there was nothing, nothing but this soft enveloping darkness that cushioned her buzzing racing senses in the thick blanket of unconsciousness.

She awoke to the sterile neutrality of a small white room that smelt of antiseptic and carbolic, and the realisation that she had tried to surface several times before from the crazy world she had in-habited for the last little while, a world of whirling images and alien voices all of which were dominated by grinding, unrelenting pain in her head. But there was no pain now. She moved her head slightly on the hard pillow and winced as a flash of something hot spiked into her brain. Well, not if she kept still.

There was a buzzer connected to a long wire lying on the white counterpane next to her right hand, and she pressed it carefully before her eyes moved to the small narrow window at the end of the room. The grey light filtering through the louvre blinds suggested it was either dusk or dawn and she realised with a little dart of anxiety that she had no idea which it was. Or *where* she was. Or—and here the thought became a hard thudding in her chest—who she was. She shut her eyes tightly and prayed for calm. She remembered falling in that hot dusty street and hitting her head on the rough jagged kerb. She remembered being helped into a cool shaded room and she remembered... Her thoughts stopped abruptly. Yes, she remembered Gerard Dumont. And then, as if her mind had conjured him up, the creaking of the door brought her eyes open and there he was, closely followed by a small nurse.

'Ah, you are awake.' The smile was as devastating as she recalled and her limbs turned to water. 'The doctor thought a few hours' sleep would put you to rights.'

'Did he?' She glanced round carefully as she hitched herself up slightly in the bed, finding that if she moved slowly her head still belonged to her. 'I'm in hospital?'

'Just an overnight stay,' he said coolly. 'And do not start imagining the worst. You have concussion and——' He stopped abruptly.

'And?' But then the nurse took over, popping a thermometer in her mouth which stopped further conversation as she took her blood pressure with bright impersonal efficiency.

He leant back against the wall as the nurse went about her ministrations, arms crossed and big body relaxed as he watched her with tawny narrowed eyes. She found his presence incredibly unsettling, and as her cheeks began to burn so did her temper. Surely he didn't have the right to be in her room like this? This was a hospital, for goodness' sake. And she didn't even know the man. She'd be having a bed-bath next to complete the indignities! And he *had* wanted to be rid of her.

As soon as the thermometer was out of her mouth she spoke carefully, her eyes veiled. 'I appreciate your help, Mr Dumont, but perhaps it would be better if you left now? I don't want to inconvenience you further. I'm fine and this is a hospital, when all's said and done——'

'A private nursing home actually,' he corrected coolly, levering himself off the wall, with a nod and a smile to the nurse as she left, and walking lazily over to the side of the bed to survey her with an expressionless face. 'And as I am paying the bill, I do not foresee a problem.' He knew exactly how she felt about him, she realised with a little shiver.

'You're...?' She stared aghast at the tall figure watching her so closely. 'But why? There are hospitals here, aren't there? I mean——'

'I know what you mean.' He smiled, but there was no warmth in the twist of his mouth. 'And before that active little imagination runs riot, let me assure you that I have no designs on your body.' There was something almost contemptuous in the gold eyes as they ran over her slender form under the white bedclothes. 'I prefer my women with a little more meat on their bones and definitely more submissive.'

I bet you do, she thought angrily as her eyes sparked. I just bet you do. And I'm glad you know I don't like you!

'Nevertheless you asked for my protection before you passed out at my feet, and that is exactly what I have given you, so please do not agitate yourself.' The hard gaze was piercing as it roved consideringly over her hot cheeks. 'Also the hospital here is perhaps not quite what you were used to in—England? Do you come from England?'

'I think so.' She stared at him as the anger drained and the enormity of her problem took hold again. 'I must do. I look English, don't I?'

'To the tips of your feet,' he assured her gravely. 'And your demeanour is all English.' Somehow she felt it wasn't a compliment and again her temper was ignited.

'What exactly does that mean?' she asked hotly.

'Cucumber-cool and twice as self-contained,' he said smoothly, the dark tanned face slightly amused at her indignation. 'You do not like this description?'

'I can live with it,' she returned shortly, and then felt immediately ashamed of her ingratitude. But then . . . she didn't trust him, not one little bit. Why would a complete stranger pay for her to be cared for in a private hospital anyway? There was a catch here, she just knew it. Or was she generally just distrustful of people and men in particular? she asked herself silently. She didn't know, she just didn't know. The panic rose hot and fierce.

'Is there a mirror anywhere?' she asked weakly, as she glanced up from her musing to find the strange gold eyes intent on her face.

'You look delightful——'

'I don't care what I *look* like,' she said sharply before wincing as the pain shot through her head again. 'I just want to see...to see who I am,' she finished miserably.

'Of course.' Suddenly the hard face softened. 'I will call the nurse to take you to the bathroom in case you should feel a little unwell again, yes?' He paused as he walked over to the door and turned again, his eyes searching her white face slowly. 'You *will* remember soon, little one, have no fear about that. The police are making enquiries and soon someone will notice you are missing.'

'But perhaps I'm here by myself?' she said weakly. 'Perhaps I've rented a place even? I could have.' She stared at him, her eyes wide and the pupils unnaturally dilated. 'I could have a child waiting for me, pets, anything. I don't *know*, do I?'

'This is true,' he said gravely, 'but if you try to remember too hard I think it will be even more difficult.'

'That's all very well for you to say,' she said tightly. 'You aren't me, are you? Not that this would have happened to a man, I suppose,' she added bitterly.

'You think the male sex is impervious to being attacked?' he asked quietly, his eyes narrowing at the look of resentment darkening her face.

'Not necessarily, no.' Her eyes met his again. 'But you sure as hell have things your own way most of the time. Women are just appendages of a man's ego, that's all...' Her voice trailed away as she realised what she had said. What had made her feel like that? She felt something large and dark looming in the background and shut her eyes tightly. She had to remember.

'I will fetch the nurse.' She didn't look up as he spoke, and as the door shut behind him she opened her eyes slowly as she sank back against the pillows. This was a living nightmare and one from which there was no awakening. She put her arms round her middle and hugged herself tightly as the panic clawed at her stomach, sending it churning sickeningly. She was exposed, vulnerable, helpless... Her heart began to thud crazily, and when the little nurse knocked and entered in the next instant she could have kissed her, so pleased was she to have another human being in the room to counter the monsters in her mind.

She was quite steady on her feet as she made her way along to the bathroom on the arm of the nurse, and after insisting that the small Moroccan girl wait outside and promising twice not to lock the door, she walked gingerly over to the cloudy square mirror above the small white washbasin and peered at herself with bated breath.

A pair of large, grey, darkly lashed eyes stared back at her nervously and then continued their inspection of the reflection. Small, straight nose, a somewhat wide generous mouth, she noted wanly, and all set in a clear skin that was real peaches and cream. Thick, sleek, chestnut-brown hair with more than a touch of red in its silky depths gave an explanation of the freckles scattered across her nose, and the short bob was expertly cut, complementing the fine features and upward tilt of her chin. Altogether reasonably attractive, although she would never win any beauty contests, she thought slowly, and it didn't mean a thing to her. It could have been the face of anyone, the face of a stranger. *What was she going to do?* She sat down on the loo and put her head between her hands as she tried to think. She was all alone in a foreign country... or at least she thought it was a foreign country. For all she knew, she lived here. She groaned softly. Surely the police would find out something soon? They had to, this was horrific. And that man, Gerard Dumont. Why did she have this feeling that she had to be rid of him at the earliest opportunity? That he spelt danger with a capital D? Could she trust her instincts? They were the only thing she had right now.

He was waiting in her room when she returned with the nurse, his big frame stretching lazily as he stood up at their approach, his whole demeanour casual and relaxed but his eyes hawk-like on her face as she passed, although he said not a word as the nurse settled her back into bed.

'I fetch the breakfast, yes?' The small girl smiled cheerfully. 'And then you feel a million dollars with plenty of zow?'

I wouldn't bank on it, Kit thought silently as she smiled a dutiful response as the nurse left the room.

'The police phoned.' Gerard Dumont settled himself back on the stool by her bed that he had vacated a minute before, and she raised her eyes reluctantly to his. 'No luck yet, unfortunately; it would appear you are the mystery girl. The doctor will be along shortly to examine you, but if all is as he thinks there is no reason why you cannot leave this morning.'

'To go where?' she asked blankly as her mind raced. Was there a British embassy near here? But then she wasn't even sure she *was* English.

'Well, I do have an idea there as it happens,' he drawled slowly, lifting dark brows as he watched her carefully, his face cynical and cool. 'But maybe it would be better for you to eat your breakfast first and——'

'I would prefer to hear anything you have to say right now,' she said firmly, her chin setting at a determined angle that brought an amused gleam into the glittering gold-brown eyes trained on her face.

'As you wish.' He stood up abruptly, walking over to the small narrow window and lifting the blind aside so that a shaft of sunlight spilled into the austere room, catching a million tiny particles in its radiant light. 'I was going to suggest that it would seem logical for you to remain resting somewhere until either you regain your memory or the police find out who you are, yes?'

'I suppose so.' She glanced at the broad back warily. 'And?'

'And that would pose a problem, or at least an embarrassment, as you have no money that I know of?' He turned to face her, his eyes slits of gold light.

'You know I haven't.' She stared back, hard. 'But I can assure you that once all this is sorted out I will reimburse you for every penny you've spent——'

'Do not be ridiculous.' This time his voice was harsh, and she blinked twice before opening her mouth to respond, but he continued swiftly. 'The money is incidental, as I am sure you are aware. I was merely stating facts.'

'Well, now you've stated them I still don't understand——'

'It would seem practical for you to be my guest until you are recovered sufficiently to take charge of your own affairs,' he said expressionlessly. 'There are several guest-rooms at my home in Marrakesh, and as I am a prominent and well-known figure in business circles I am sure the police would be happy to——'

'*You must be joking*!' Tact and diplomacy fled out of the window as she reared up in the narrow bed like a small lioness. 'You must think I was born yesterday, Mr Dumont! So that's what this has all been about, the private room and so on! Well, if you expect me to pay for my expenses in the fashion that is as old as time, you can forget it, mister! I know your sort—believe me, you're far from being unique! I'd rather spend the next few days, weeks or months in a prison cell if necessary compared to what you're suggesting. Just what do you think I am——?'

'I think you are a very absurd young lady.' The icy voice cut short her passionate outburst as though with a knife. 'Impolite, churlish, ridiculous... Need I go on?' He was angry; she couldn't believe *how* angry. 'Do you seriously think that I am so short of female companions that I have to spirit one away to my home—is that it?' He wasn't shouting, in fact his voice was very controlled and infinitely cutting. 'If you want me to be brutal, I do not find you sexually attractive at all. The offer was one of friendship, from one member of the human race to another in distress. That is all. *That is all.*' He glared at her and took a long deep pull of air before continuing. 'Now you have made your feeling perfectly clear, and so I will—— '

What he would or would not do they never found out because at that moment Kit's control finally snapped. The flood of tears and sensation of utter and absolute desolation blinded and deafened her to everything but her own misery, and as she raised her hands to cover her face, her body shaking helplessly, she could hear the sound of her own wailing but could do nothing to control it.

'*Mon dieu...*' His voice was a low growl but the next moment she had been lifted wholesale out of the bed and on to his lap as he sat down on the ruffled covers, holding her tight as he swayed back and forth as one did soothing a devastated child, his voice low and soft now and speaking a crooning stream of endearments in French of which she understood not a word but found infinitely comforting to her terrified mind. And she *was* terrified, she acknowledged faintly as the hard male bulk of him banished the frantic fear for a time. Nothing, *nothing* could be worse than this monstrous, gut-wrenching dread that she would never remember who she was again, that she would be left in this strange, alien half-world where even her own face was that of a stranger, with no memories, no recollection of a past life and with only an empty, uncertain future to look forward to.

CHAPTER TWO

QUITE when she began to find Gerard Dumont's closeness disturbing rather than comforting she wasn't sure. It might have been something to do with the warm male fragrance emanating from the massive frame, a mixture of spicy aftershave and a faint lemony smell, or it could have been the controlled power in the huge body enfolding hers, or even the sound of his voice, deep and seductively attractive as he murmured in his native tongue. Whatever, as the storm of weeping passed she began to feel acutely uncomfortable and vaguely threatened. But there was another emotion there too, one that made her skin tingle and her stomach tighten with a dull ache she didn't recognise.

'I'm sorry.' As she made to move off his lap he let her go instantly, his eyes searching as they washed over her face.

'Have you any idea where all that hostility comes from?' he asked levelly as he stood up and drew back the covers for her to climb back into bed. 'What has happened to make you feel so threatened by the male species?'

'Threatened?' She stared at him wide-eyed, horrified he could read her so easily. 'I don't feel threatened——'

'Yes, you do.' He eyed her impassively and she was conscious of his great height again as he gestured towards the bed. 'Get in. The nurse will be bringing your breakfast in a moment.'

'I don't feel threatened.' She ignored his instructions with obstinate determination. 'This has all just been unsettling, surely you can understand that?'

'I told you that the doctor confirmed concussion?' His voice was low and moderate but with an underlying thread of steel. 'And undoubtedly you have a secondary complication resulting in amnesia. However...' He paused and gestured towards the bed again, his mouth thinning as she still refused to acknowledge the command. 'However, the blow to your head was not severe enough for this continued loss of memory.'

'Are you saying I'm making it up?' she asked hotly as her skin burnt with anger. 'I can assure you——'

'Of course I am not saying that,' he interrupted sharply, 'and for my sake if not yours please get yourself into this damn bed. I do not relish the prospect of picking you up off the floor again and you look distinctly feeble.'

'Thank you *very* much,' she intoned furiously, as sheer temper enabled her to march across the room and climb into the bed more quickly than she would have thought possible in view of her trembling legs and throbbing head.

'What I *am* saying, or rather what the doctor is saying, is that there is something that is causing

you to block out your past,' Gerard said slowly.
'Something that you do not wish to remember,
something that would cause you great pain——'

'Now it's you who's being ridiculous,' she said
quickly as a spark of something blindingly menacing flashed across her mind before sinking back
into her subconscious. 'You are,' she continued
faintly as the dark shadow crept back into that
inner mind. 'I had an accident, I was attacked——'

'Of course you were,' he said softly, 'no one
is disputing that, but the accident has merely allowed your mind to hide behind this incident,
take refuge if you like.'

'No, I *don't* like.' She glared at him, far more
shaken than she would admit. 'Are you saying
I'm unbalanced, is that it?'

'*Mon dieu* . . .' The exclamation was made in
the form of a curse. 'I have never met such an
awkward, difficult——'

'And where is this wonderful doctor who has
made such a profound diagnosis without even
telling me?' she asked angrily. 'Do I actually get
to see him or what?'

'After breakfast.' The nurse had just entered
carrying a loaded tray, her bright black eyes
flashing from one angry face to the other before
concentrating on the food with lowered gaze and
a tactfully bland face. 'I'm joining you, is that
all right?'

'Fine; you're paying after all.' She regretted the
coarseness of the retort as soon as it left her lips
and raised her eyes instantly to his face, her

mouth trembling. 'I'm sorry, that was awful. *I'm* being awful, it's just that——'

'Eat your breakfast.' His tone was firm but not unkind, the hard handsome face expressionless.

'I don't think I could eat anything——'

'You will, if I have to force-feed you every mouthful,' he replied softly, still in the same firm, emotionless voice.

She glared at him angrily and then met the full force of the startlingly cat-like gaze that suddenly told her she would lose this particular battle if she persevered. She gulped, gave him a blazing scowl that could have melted stone at thirty paces and gave in, discovering as she bit into a warm crusty croissant that she was hungry after all.

He didn't speak again until she was finishing her second cup of coffee, and when he did she jumped so violently that most of the semi-hot liquid left in the cup splashed on to the white covers. 'Have you made a decision?'

'A decision?' She raised her eyes to meet his, knowing exactly what he meant but playing for time as her mind raced back and forth seeking a solution to the impossible situation.

He shook his tawny head slowly as he stretched lazily on the stool, his face dark and sardonic and his mouth twisted with cynical amusement. 'Yes, a decision,' he intoned drily. 'And do not insult my intelligence by asking what about. I really could not take that.' As he stood up his bulk seemed to fill the small room, dominating the white surroundings with a menacing energy

that suddenly made her breathless. 'I have to go.
I have an appointment at nine.'

'Oh, right...' She raised a hand to her face to
brush back a lock of hair and was annoyed to
see it was shaking, and then felt doubly humili-
ated when she saw Gerard had noticed it too.

'Do I terrify you so much?' His voice was soft,
and as her eyes flashed to his she saw he was not
smiling, that all amusement and mockery had left
the hard masculine face. 'I do not wish to do so.
You remind me of a little bird I found some
months ago fluttering along in the road with a
broken wing. It pecked me several times when I
picked it up, due to its great fear, and then——'
He stopped abruptly and she stared at him, fascinated by the thought of this giant of a man
bothering about something so small and insig-
nificant as an injured bird.

'And then?' she asked quietly.

'Its heart simply stopped beating.' There was
something in his eyes she couldn't read, something veiled behind the startling hypnotic gaze
trained on her face. 'If it had just relaxed a little,
trusted me a little, I would have been able to help
it.'

She licked her lips nervously and then stopped
abruptly as his eyes followed the gesture, lingering on the tremulous curve of her mouth.

'That is all I wish to do with this little bird.'
He smiled very slowly but for the life of her she
couldn't respond. 'Just help out. But——' he
walked to the door and opened it quietly, turning
with his hand on the brass knob to glance back

at her again '—if you do not want to come to my home then you do not have to. It just seemed obvious, that is all. The doctor will be along shortly and I will return at lunchtime, when you can tell me what you have decided. If you choose to avail yourself of my hospitality you must be ready to leave then. Otherwise——' he shrugged Latin-style '—you may stay on here while you make other arrangements.' And then he had gone, the door shutting with a firm click only to open again a second later. 'One more thing—my sister lives with me in Marrakesh so you will not be entirely without a chaperon.' The heavy eyebrows quirked mockingly. 'Not that you will need one, of course.'

Alone again she stared at the closed door with a small frown wrinkling her brow. 'Not that you will need one.' She sank back against the pillows feeling both disgruntled and relieved. He obviously didn't find her in the least attractive, that much he had made crystal-clear. And that was good. Of course it was. She brushed an inoffensive crumb savagely off the sheet. She could just imagine his taste in women; voluptuous, sexy, possessing good bodies and the knowledge of how to use them. Big breasts, generous hips, pouting mouths... The mental description suddenly sparked the ghost of something in her mind, an image she couldn't drag out of the misty darkness to examine more closely before it had gone. She stared blindly across the small room, her face white with strain. Perhaps she had been more right than she knew when she asked if Gerard thought she was unbalanced; this certainly couldn't be normal. She groaned softly as she turned over on her side to await the appearance of the all-knowing doctor. Well, one thing was certain; there was no way, no way at all, she was leaving this place with Gerard Dumont, sister or no sister.

They left the clinic at precisely half-past three in the afternoon, and after the relative coolness of the air-conditioned building the white heat outside was overpowering.

'All right?' Gerard's eyes were tight on her face as they walked to his car, a low-slung sports model in jet black that looked as if it would bite if provoked.

'Fine.' She wasn't, of course. The heat was amazing but it was the dazzling brilliance of the blazing light that was causing problems, sending sharp little pinpricks of pain through her head as though it were being methodically stabbed with a keenly pointed blade. But even that wasn't the main reason for the trembling that seemed to have taken over her limbs and the palpitations that were causing a violent, irregular beating of her heart and a sick churning in her stomach. It was him. This virile, overwhelmingly masculine man at her side who dwarfed her not inconsiderable height by a good six inches and exuded an air of pure unadulterated sensual magnetism that was both dangerous and darkly attractive.

Why had she ever agreed to leave with him? she asked herself silently as she slid into the

beautiful car just as her legs felt as though they
wouldn't support her for another second. She
hadn't meant to. But somehow...somehow he
had swept all her objections aside with cool logic
and a distant kind of friendliness that reassured
even as she wondered if it were genuine. The call
from his sister had helped too. She glanced at
him now as he slid into the car at her side. 'Why
did you ask Colette to phone me?' she asked tentatively. 'I mean——'

'I know what you mean,' he said mockingly as
the sleek car growled into life. 'And you are right,
partly...' He turned to eye her briefly, his face
cynical and closed. 'You thought I had used her
to promote what I wanted, is that it?' She stared
at him without answering, wondering if it were
too late to jump out of the car and run back to
the relative protection of the impersonal clinic.
'Well, maybe I did, but it is for your own good,
let me make that perfectly clear. This is a foreign
country, or we'll assume it is a foreign country
until we find out differently,' he added as she
opened her mouth to make that very point, 'and
one does not always play by the Marquis of
Queensbery's rules here.' The tawny gaze was
glittering now, reflecting the sun's brilliance as
he held her wide grey eyes mesmerised. 'You are
very definitely the bird with the broken wing at
the moment, however much you dislike the
analogy, and as such prey to all kinds of dangers.
Do you know that in some quarters you would
fetch a king's ransom?'

'What?' She couldn't believe she'd heard right for a moment.

'Make no mistake about it.' His mouth was harsh now as his gaze wandered over the red-brown hair and pale creamy skin. 'With your English looks and that air of untouched virginity, you would be snapped up within days.' He leant back in the seat as her mouth twisted in disbelief. 'You do not believe me? That alone tells me I was right. A babe among wolves...'

Was he going to sell her to some sheikh or white-slave trader? Was that it? She stared at him dumbly, unaware of the terror in her eyes. She had authorisation from the police to stay with him. They knew where to contact her. Lots of people did. Surely he wouldn't have organised all that if he intended——

'Colette exists.' His voice was very dry now as he read her thoughts. 'My home exists. I am a perfectly normal man who would not have slept particularly well at night if I had let you be cast adrift into an uncertain world. The telephone conversation with Colette was satisfactory?'

'Colette?' She pulled her thoughts together and moistened paper-dry lips carefully. 'Yes, of course.'

'You can spend some time talking with a female companion of your own age and perhaps something will be remembered, a spark that will unlock the door, yes?' He put a very large hand over hers resting on her knees, and she forced herself not to jerk away although his touch fired the alarm button. 'Now we have to drive to the small airfield where my plane is waiting. It will not take long.'

'Your plane?' She began to feel slightly hysterical. This wasn't happening to her, it couldn't be. She still wasn't quite sure how she came to be sitting in this prowling beast of a car with its master, anyway. As his hands moved to the leather-clad steering-wheel and he manoeuvred the powerful car out of the tiny hospital car park, she forced herself to think rationally, to get her emotions under control. She had made enquiries, independent enquiries, that morning with the police and the surprisingly sympathetic doctor, who had spent some considerable time with her trying to probe for something, anything, from her past, all to no avail.

She had discovered Gerard Dumont was an eminently respected businessman in Morocco, owning several businesses in Casablanca, Essaouira and Marrakesh involving the processing of fish and fruit, as well as his own fleet of freighters for goods to be sent overseas, and homes in each of the towns. He was enormously wealthy, a dignified and decorous citizen of the land his parents had moved to before he was born and altogether, according to her reports, a paragon of virtue. Except... Her eyes narrowed as she remembered the doctor's hesitation when she had asked if Gerard was married or involved with a particular woman.

'Not a particular woman, no...' The doctor had smiled carefully after a long moment of silence. 'But he is a young man in the prime of life; obviously there are stories...'

'Stories?' she had squeaked nervously, but the elderly man had not allowed himself to be drawn into a discussion about such an illustrious personage, parrying her questions adroitly until she had to give up gracefully. He had told her Gerard's parents had died many years before, that his sister was engaged to be married to a French Moroccan of impeccable breeding, and that if she accepted Gerard's invitation, which the doctor made clear he thought was an extremely generous and benevolent one, she would be treated with great respect and care as befitted the guest of such an important man. The phone call from Colette had clinched her indecision. Gerard's sister had sounded so bubbly and natural and genuinely concerned about her misfortune and anxious to help. It had all seemed cut and dried...until she had seen him again. Then all the doubts and fears returned with renewed vigour.

'You do not like me much, little one, do you?' It was a statement, not a question, and after one darting glance at the harsh profile she decided silence was definitely the best policy. There was nothing she could say, after all. She didn't like him; in fact everything about him grated on her like barbed wire even though she kept telling herself it was the height of ingratitude when he had been so kind. His height, the powerful masculine body, his arrogance and total domination of everything and everyone around him... It bothered her. Bothered her and frightened her and—— She shut off her thoughts abruptly. She didn't trust him. Not an inch. She didn't know why and probably there was no foundation for how she felt, but it was a fact.

She glanced again at his face and saw that the hard mouth was curved in a cynical, mocking smile. And that grated too.

'I will be interested to find out who you are, my sharp-clawed kitten,' he said softly after a few miles had passed in complete silence, the atmosphere tense and taut. 'I like honesty in people, men and women, and you are not short of that commodity.'

'You do?'

'I do.' She heard the thread of amusement in the dark seductive voice, and bit her lip tightly. 'I am clearly the lesser of two very real evils and it is a long time since I have been cast in such a role, especially by a woman.' The glittering gold eyes moved swiftly over her wary face before returning to the road. 'Especially such a beautiful woman.'

'You said you didn't find me attractive,' she retorted quickly in surprise before she had time to consider her words.

'I lied.' The deep voice was quite unrepentent.

As her stomach turned over in one flying leap she hunted for something to say, a casual remark that would defuse the sudden tension, but couldn't think of a thing, and as the miles continued to be eaten up by the beautiful car she forced herself to relax and concentrate on the

changing scene outside the car window. And it
was fascinating. Varied as Morocco was in its geography and climate, ranging from dry, gravelly
plains extending for hundreds of miles and bleak
shifting sand-dunes to rich tablelands in the
Middle Atlas Mountains that furnished grazing
for sheep and goats, the higher slopes covered in
oak, cedar and pine and rich in ski resorts for
the wealthy where rocky springs, lakes and ponds
abounded as well as streams well stocked with
trout, still nothing could be more varied than the
spectrum of people who inhabited the land.

Every town and city had its Moroccan and
European businessmen in traditional European
dress side by side with Berbers and Arabs in
flowing robes and wide, loose hoods, the women
veiled and dressed in sober grey and black. And
the transport... As Kit stared out of the window,
the odd sumptuous car rode alongside decrepit
taxis, wicked-eyed camels, horses, donkeys, bikes
and every other mode of transport known to
man. The buildings were piercingly white,
Moorish architecture showing its grace and
beauty in sunlit streets lined with orange trees...
She sank back against the upholstered seat with
a small sigh, her senses sated. She couldn't live
here; she must be on holiday—it was all too new
and exciting. Holiday? But she'd left because of
an argument, a ring...? She glanced down at
her ringless hands and her brow wrinkled and that
sick feeling of dread reared its head, before both
the image and emotion faded as quickly as they
had come.

'What is it?' She suddenly realised Gerard had been talking to her and she hadn't heard a word, and now saw they had left the confines of the town and were out on the boundary road. 'You have remembered something?'

'Not really.' She rubbed a damp hand over her brow as she shut her eyes for a brief moment. 'It was gone before I could make sense of it. I'm sorry, what did you say?'

'I wondered if you had ever seen goats climbing trees before,' he said drily. 'Over there, look.' As he brought the car to a standstill she peered where he was pointing, and saw a host of argan trees, their low spreading limbs covered with green leaves and small fruits that looked like olives, and then as her eyes rose upwards she was amazed to see several goats high in the branches nibbling away at the leaves and fruit, one or two of the sure-footed little creatures having ventured far out on the branches as they stretched for the tenderest morsels.

'They really are goats!' she breathed in surprise, her eyes stretched wide.

Gerard laughed softly, delighted with her astonishment. 'These trees are not found anywhere else in the world,' he said quietly as he started the engine again after several long minutes, 'and the goats adore the fruit. The seeds you see on the ground there——' he pointed to the mass of fruit seeds scattered under the trees '—are gathered up and washed and cracked and from the inner nut is drawn a fragrant oil used for cooking. Not that the goats care about that, of course.' He eyed her lazily before drawing on to the dusty road again.

The little incident had broken the tension for a time, but the very nearness of that big masculine body in the close confines of the car made her as jumpy as a cricket. Did he really find her attractive? she asked herself silently as the car purred on. That last look he'd given her, there had been something in the slumberous depths that had caused her lower stomach to tighten in immediate response, and she had hated herself for it, hated herself without understanding the reason why. But then there was nothing she *did* understand at the moment anyway, she told herself flatly. She was a mess.

They reached the small airfield where Gerard's private plane was kept amid a cloud of dust, and it wasn't until she was airborne, with Gerard at the controls, that she thought to ask about the location of Marrakesh. Everything had seemed so unreal, so nebulous, since she had woken up in the hospital that she still was finding it hard to convince herself that she wasn't in the grip of a dream . . . or a nightmare.

'Marrakesh?' Gerard's deep voice was thoughtful. 'Let me see. Well, it is the most African city of Morocco, at the foothills of the High Atlas Mountains due south of Casablanca. The region is dry but water has been piped down from the mountains into reservoirs, so a bath will be no problem.' He eyed her fleetingly, his expression searching and she flushed hotly. It was just as if he had undressed her.

'We have the normal old and new side by side,' he continued, after the twist of his mouth informed her he knew exactly what she was thinking. 'Modern agriculture, training schools and various industries as well as a camel market every Thursday that dates back into ancient history, and a fair in the great square of Djemaa-el-Fna that involves snake charmers, magicians, jugglers, acrobats and even the odd medicine man demonstrating miraculous cures in their bottles. I'll show you around once you are settled in; there are some wonderful medieval palaces and monuments——'

'No, there's no need for that.' She had interrupted him so abruptly that she hastened to qualify her refusal. 'I mean, I don't want to inconvenience you at all, Mr Dumont, you've been very kind and I'll be gone within a day or so——'

'Gerard.' Suddenly the handsome face was intimidatingly cold and harsh, the profile flinty. 'And please do not try to spare my feelings. Colette will do just as well as your guide.'

'I didn't mean——'

He interrupted her again, his voice dry. 'I know exactly what you meant; you neither like or trust me so let us leave it at that. I hope you will be reassured when you reach my home but, as you so graciously pointed out, it will be a matter of days until this matter resolves itself so your opinion of me is really of no importance to either of us.'

She deserved it. She knew she deserved it but nevertheless the icy autocratic tone made her see red. 'Look, I'm sorry,' she said tightly, her voice tense. 'If it's any consolation *I* don't understand why I'm acting like this, but when all's said and done I didn't ask to come with you, did I? Why did you insist——?'

'I am damned if I know,' he bit back angrily.

'Well, just turn the plane round and take me back to Casablanca——' she began furiously, only to stop abruptly as she realised the import of what she had just said. Casablanca? Why had she said Casablanca? The accident had happened on the streets of Essaouira, hadn't it?

'Casablanca,' Gerard repeated thoughtfully at her side, obviously catching the importance of her words too. 'I think we should perhaps ask the police to direct their enquiries more specifically in that city, yes?'

'I don't know.' She shook her head wearily, the spurt of rage dying as quickly as it had flared into life as she stared down at the white cotton trousers and neat coffee-coloured blouse that had been pressed and cleaned by the cheerful little nurse at the nursing home. Some time, in another life, she had actually chosen these things, walked into a shop and made the purchases of her own accord. *How could she not remember*?

'I will take care of it.' He spared her a quick glance, his face expressionless. 'And I do not intend to eat you alive, my thorny rose, but for the sake of my sanity, if not yours, could you please refrain from the cat-on-a-hot-tin-roof syndrome? My ego is beginning to feel a little fragile.'

'I'm sorry.' She stared down at her hands miserably.

'So you said.' The deep rich voice was cynically mocking again and immediately the guilt she had been feeling was replaced by hot anger. A fragile ego? Him? Not in a million years.

The fierce heat of the day was dying when they reached the huge strip of ground on the outskirts of Marrakesh which formed part of Gerard's estate. As he taxied the light plane into the hangar she saw a beautiful white Ferrari parked some distance away, its tinted windows and enormous side grilles proclaiming it a Testarossa. 'Your car?' She gestured resignedly towards the magnificent vehicle.

'My car,' he agreed gravely, his voice bland. 'Do you like it?'

'It's very nice.'

She heard a snort at her side and turned to see that he was surveying her with a dark frown, his eyes narrowed. 'Don't tell me,' he drawled slowly, the relaxed tone belying the sharpness in his eyes, 'for some reason you disapprove of the car.' It was a statement, not a question. 'Why do I get the feeling that if anyone else had owned it you would have given it the appreciation such functional beauty deserves?'

'I said it was very nice,' she protested carefully, aware of the truth in his words, 'but a car is just a car, isn't it? A grown-up child's toy?'

'A toy?' He shut his eyes briefly after killing the engine of the plane, and then opened them slowly, the narrowed slits gleaming gold. 'There is a six-year waiting list for this toy, as it happens.'

She hadn't noticed the middle-aged Arab standing to one side of the hangar but now, as Gerard jumped down from the plane and reached up to assist her, she saw the hangar doors being closed before the small man hurried across to them.

'Assad...' The two exchanged greetings and then Gerard turned to her, his face relaxed and smiling now. 'This is my great friend and man of all trades, Assad. You would not have noticed him at the time, but as chance would have it he was just entering my office building when you were attacked and saw it all,' Gerard continued quietly, 'not that it proved much help in the event. He speaks French, Spanish and Arabic but little English incidentally. None of my house staff does, unfortunately.'

'Oh.' She stared at them both feeling completely out of her depth, and as she turned away to glance again at the Ferrari she missed the softening of Gerard's mouth that indicated he was aware of just how she felt.

'The house is just a few hundred yards away but I asked Assad to bring the car in case you were tired. Shall we?' He indicated the car with a wave of his hand. 'Assad will see to the plane and follow shortly.'

She found, as she walked to the car, that she *was* tired, a deep exhaustion taking hold of her body and mind that made even the smallest response a superhuman effort. As Gerard held open the door she climbed slowly into the luxurious interior, her head pounding. 'Thank you.' She raised dull eyes to his and saw him frown slightly before he left to walk round the bonnet and slide in beside her.

'You need a warm bath and plenty of sleep,' he said levelly as he nosed the car out of the hangar and along a dry dust road towards a mass of trees in the distance. 'Both of which will prove no problem at Del Mahari. My home,' he added at her glance of enquiry.

'Del Mahari?' She let the foreign name slide over her lips. 'That sounds nice.'

'It means ''Racing Camel'',' he said expressionlessly, although she was sure there was a thread of amusement colouring the deep voice. 'My father enjoyed the sport, although I prefer to keep horses rather than camels. I find the latter singly unattractive creatures and more than a little bad-tempered, although that trait is not confined to camels, of course,' he added smoothly as he kept his eyes fixed ahead. She glanced at him warily, knowing it was a gibe at her but unable to respond to such an indirect insult. 'At the moment I have several beautifully trained horses of great speed and stamina who have mingled Arab and Berber strains in their blood line. Do you ride?'

The question was casual and she answered before she considered, the reply instinctive. 'Oh, yes, I love...' Her voice trailed away for a second before she recovered. 'Yes, I know I ride,' she said more firmly. 'I don't know how I know but I do.'

'Good.' They had reached the trees now which she saw were fruit trees, mainly orange, surrounding the outside of a rosy pink extremely high wall in which two huge iron gates were set standing open ready for the Ferrari to pass through, but Gerard stopped the car just before the gates and cut the engine slowly, turning to her and touching her face gently with one finger as he turned her face to his. 'Welcome to my home, little kitten,' he said softly, seconds before his warm, hard mouth captured hers.

CHAPTER THREE

IF SOMEONE had poured boiling water over her head Kit could not have reacted more violently. For a split-second, just an infinitesimal moment of time, she had frozen as his firm sensual mouth had captured hers, the smell and feel of him all-encompassing, and then she jerked away so savagely that her head ricocheted off the car window with a resounding bang that caused the air to vibrate.

'What on earth?' Gerard looked as shocked as she felt as he surveyed her beneath dark frowning brows. 'I was only kissing you, girl; what the hell did you think I intended?'

'I...' Her voice trailed away as she stared at him wide-eyed in the shadowed dusk, aware of the sweet odour of flowering jasmine being borne on the soft warm night air. 'I don't know, I'm sorry...' As her voice petered out again she took a deep breath as she tried to compose herself. 'But I didn't expect you to do that. I'm here as your guest, aren't I? I thought——'

'It was a kiss of welcome,' he ground out tightly. 'Nothing more, nothing less.' His eyes raked her face angrily.

'I'm sorry.' There didn't seem anything else to say and she was suddenly aware that she had made a terrible fool of herself.

'Then let us try it again?' It was the last thing she had expected him to say, and she stared at him with wide dove-grey eyes, the smudge of freckles across her nose standing out in sharp contrast to the pale creamy skin surrounding them. 'A kiss, nothing more,' he reassured softly as he leant forward again, his eyes liquid gold in the dim light. 'I won't hurt you.'

As he lightly stroked her sealed lips with his hard, sensual mouth she began to feel herself tremble, the sensations the gentle caress was producing warm and sweet to her shattered senses, and as he felt her helpless reaction the kiss deepened, his tongue invading the sanctuary of her mouth as she opened her lips to gasp at the heat spreading through her body. A kiss? This was a kiss? If she had ever been kissed like this before she would have remembered, she knew it.

One of his arms slid round her seat, his hand moving to the small of her back to urge her more intimately against his big frame, but he made no move to touch her beyond that, although she could feel the pounding of his heart against the solid wall of his chest. His lips left hers for a moment to wander languorously over her closed eyelids, her ears, her throat, before returning to her half-open mouth to plunder the soft interior yet again. And then he raised his head as he moved back into his own seat, and the departure was almost like a betrayal.

'As I said, welcome to my home,' he said softly as she opened dazed eyes to focus on the tawny brown gaze. 'I hope you will be happy here.'

He had started the engine before she could reply, and as they drove through the massive gates into the lush garden beyond she tried desperately to control the trembling that had taken hold of her limbs. This was a man she didn't like, didn't trust and barely knew, and she could react like that to his touch? What on earth was she? She didn't dare look at the big dark figure next to her, trying to focus her eyes and her thoughts on her surroundings and nothing else.

They appeared to be moving through an orchard, the wide winding drive snaking past olive, orange, almond and fig trees, and then the house was there in front of her, a magnificent white structure in traditional Moroccan design with delicate ornamentation and beautifully carved arches that looked as though they were covered in lace, so fine and intricate were the traceries on them.

Gerard drew the car to a halt in front of the massive arched front door studded in brass, which was immediately opened from within to reveal a small, slender woman of thirty or so who moved out on to the top step, her brown face wreathed in smiles and her body swathed in the Moroccan jellaba, a long loose robe of cotton. 'This is Assad's wife, Amina,' Gerard whispered quietly as he raised his hand in greeting. 'Assad's brother, Abou, also works here with his wife Halima and their family. Unfortunately Assad and Amina have no children, which has been a source of great grief to them, although Assad has resisted the temptation to take a second wife, which is quite permissable for him under Moslem law, especially if his first wife is barren.'

'Who says it's her that's at fault?' Kit asked quietly, annoyed at the inference. 'Couldn't it be Assad?'

'Quite possibly,' Gerard said drily by her side as he moved to open his door. 'But if you value your well-being do not even breathe such heresy within Assad's hearing.' He walked lazily round the car to open her door, helping her out of the low vehicle with a hand on the crook of her elbow. 'Moroccan men are extremely proud of their virility.'

'Not just Moroccan men,' she whispered back tightly. 'I think your whole sex can be incredibly unfair in this sort of situation. Couldn't you do something about it, help them in some way?'

'Not until Assad saw fit to mention the matter to me,' Gerard said coolly. 'It would be considered the height of impropriety for anyone other than he to raise such a delicate matter.'

'I think you men can be the most stupid creatures on the earth,' she murmured out of the side of her mouth as they began to walk up the gleaming stone steps towards Amina.

'That is what you think, is it?' The deep voice held a satirical, mocking note that made her want to kick him, hard. 'It will be a brave man indeed that takes you in hand, little kitten, but the rewards could be . . . interesting.'

Amina greeted them very prettily, although Kit didn't understand a word the diminutive Moroccan woman said, but the warmth in her brown face and sparkling eyes was welcome enough.

Gerard took her arm again as they passed through the front door and she found herself immediately descending two flights of large wide marble steps to pass out through another arch into a beautifully cool courtyard, shaded by banana trees, bougainvillaea vines and other flowering tropical plants flourishing in riotous colour and profusion amid the murmur of several whispering fountains.

'How gorgeous, how absolutely gorgeous.' She turned to him impulsively to find he was watching her with narrowed gold eyes, his face expressionless. 'What a beautiful home you have, Gerard.'

'I am most fortunate,' he agreed quietly after a long heart-stopping moment when his gaze remained fixed on her half-open mouth. 'I have apartments in Essaouira and Casablanca, which were a practical investment due to the amount of time I spend in the towns overseeing my businesses there, but this is the only place I consider home. Come, I will show you all of it and then we will have some refreshments that Amina has prepared before you retire.'

The rest of the winding, spreading house stretched and unfurled before her as she wandered round the high, gracious rooms on Gerard's arm. Several rooms had sofas and chaises-longues with low tables, desks and shelves fashioned beautifully in fine wood and inlaid with thin pieces of gold and silver and wood of a different

hue. Expensive books bound in Moroccan leather
and gold leaf lined several walls, ornamented
guns and daggers, trays of hammered brass and
copper and finely worked marble figurines were
scattered tastefully throughout the house.

On the lower level the floors were covered by
fine Persian carpets and on the first level, where
the bedrooms stretched almost into infinity each
with its own *en suite* bathroom, the floors were
of the finest polished wood with beautifully designed rugs scattered in each room.

By the time they returned to the large courtyard
the night sky was alive with tiny glittering stars
and the sweet, heavy perfume of flowering
jasmine and magnolia hung rich and intoxicating
in the still warm air. Amina was waiting for them
with a taller, slightly older woman, whom Gerard
introduced as Halima, Amina's sister-in-law. Like
Amina she had a sweet, gentle face and her
manner was graceful. Kit felt the two got on well
in spite of the difficulty that Amina's lack of a
family would undoubtedly cause between the two
couples.

'Eat a little; it will please them,' Gerard said
quietly as he noticed her somewhat bemused
glance at the low wide table filled with seemingly
hundreds of dishes of different food, as well as
bowls of ripe apricots, cherries, pears, plums, figs
and grapes. She felt so exhausted now that she
was working on automatic, eating a little fruit
and one heavily spiced sweet pastry and drinking
several tiny glasses of the very sweet green tea
flavoured with mint that the Moroccans rated so

highly, before leaning back in her chair and trying to force her eyelids not to close.

Nevertheless she must have fallen asleep, because the next thing she became aware of was being cradled in a pair of very strong masculine arms as she was carried upstairs. 'Gerard?' She opened dazed eyes to see his dark tanned face an inch or two from hers. 'I'm sorry, did I fall asleep? I can walk——'

'Be quiet.' His voice was soft and low. 'In two minutes you will be tucked up in bed and able to sleep as long as you like.'

If it was meant to reassure, it didn't, as she suddenly became aware of his hard body next to hers as he moved. The smell and feel of his alien maleness encompassed her, his almost menacing strength and power as he carried her up the stairs causing a wild, fluttering panic in her chest. Did he think *he* was going to tuck her into bed? she thought silently with a faint touch of hysteria, and *whose* bed—his?

'Colette went shopping for you this afternoon,' he continued steadily as they reached the landing and continued down the wide corridor to an open door halfway down. 'Unfortunately she had a dinner engagement with her future in-laws this evening and was unable to welcome you personally, but she will see you tomorrow.'

'Thank you...' She felt ridiculously vulnerable as he entered the room, a vision of the East in flowing wall drapes, large sunken bed and exquisitely delicate carved furniture.

He set her down carefully on a long low couch to one side of the bed and straightened to survey her with narrowed eyes. 'Can you manage without help?' he asked expressionlessly.

'Yes, of course,' she answered hastily, too hastily, and as her hand went protectively to the top button of her blouse she saw his mouth tighten.

'I wasn't going to suggest that I undress you,' he said with a cool smoothness that told her she had annoyed him. 'Amina would be only too pleased to help you.'

'I don't need anyone,' she answered quickly, her eyes flickering as he crossed his muscled arms over his broad chest, his face reflective.

'We all need someone.' He had deliberately taken her words out of context and they both knew it. 'You are not an island or a ship that sails alone over the sea of life——'

'I'm not a boarding vessel either.' She hadn't meant to say it, the words had just popped out of their own volition, but once said there was no taking them back and she stared at him aghast for a second as she waited to see his reaction.

'I am very tempted to do one of two things,' he said thoughtfully after a long silent moment when his eyes had taken on the consistency of splintered ice. 'One, in spite of your recent accident, is to take you over my knee and spank the hell out of that cute behind in the hope that the short, sharp shock treatment might knock some sense into the top part of your anatomy. The other...' He paused, his face hard. 'The other is to show you exactly what it would mean if I took you into my arms and decided to make real love to you.'

'You dare, you just dare,' she murmured desperately, terrified he would follow one of the threats through. 'You told me I was coming here as your guest, that you just regarded me as a fellow human being in need of help——'

'I told you before, I lied,' he said silkily, 'or at least it was partly a lie. You *are* here as my guest and you *are* a human being who needs help. You are also a very lovely and desirable young woman—surely it is not untoward of me to notice this?'

'There's noticing and noticing,' she said weakly.

'You mean I should not want you in my bed?' he asked with deceptive mildness. 'I am a normal thirty-five-year-old man, in case you had not noticed.' Oh, she'd noticed all right, she thought shakily—boy, had she noticed! 'Now while I certainly have never been promiscuous, neither have I been celibate since my youth.' He eyed her lazily. 'And no doubt, if you could remember, we would find that this air of innocence which I have to admit is so attractive is not a factual physical reality either.'

'Would we indeed?' she asked flatly as her pulse leapt. 'Well, I'll let you know when I know, shall I?' She was aiming at heavy sarcasm but he merely nodded his head sagely, his expression remote.

'If you like.'

'No, I don't actually.' She swung round on the couch and brought her feet to the floor, her knees tightly together and her hands in her lap. 'I don't like any of this conversation——'

'Why?' He interrupted her immediately, his eyes darkening. 'What has happened, that you cannot relate to a man except with hostility and distrust? You are young, lovely——'

'Look, please stop saying I'm lovely,' she said sharply. 'I might have lost my memory temporarily but I'm not stupid and I *have* looked in the mirror since I had that bang on the head. I'm passable, that's all, and you know it.'

'Passable?' His voice was soft now and very deep, and a trembling little shiver snaked down her spine although he hadn't moved an inch. 'Hair the colour and texture of red-brown silk, creamy skin that is as clear as fresh water, a mouth generous enough to drive a man wild, eyes like warm dusk——'

'Stop it.' The heat in her lower stomach forced the exclamation out of her mouth. 'Please, I don't want this.' She wasn't aware of the tortured pleading in her wide eyes or the tremulous curve of her mouth as she fought for control, but to the tall man watching her so closely, the body language said it all. Someone had hurt her, hurt her very badly, and in that moment he could cheerfully have committed murder if the man were there in front of him. His own body stirred fiercely, reminding him of the desire that had been paramount since almost the first moment of seeing her, and again he asked himself why.

It was true that she wasn't outrageously beautiful in the traditional sense: the tall slender body was as slim as a young boy's, her breasts small and firm against the material of the blouse she wore. Not the type he usually admired at all. And her hair, cut so short that it was almost severe, the lack of make-up, of any normal female adornment... No. To all intents and purposes she shouldn't move him at all and yet— And yet she did.

'Go to sleep now.' He turned on his heel abruptly, his face dark and closed, and strode towards the open door, pausing to turn on the threshold, his eyes veiled. 'And you can sleep in peace, no one will disturb you here. You understand?'

'Yes.' She stared back at him, her face pale against the rich reds and golds in which the room was decorated. 'I understand.'

And amazingly, in spite of all the doubts and fears and the heavy darkness that seemed to permeate even her sleep, she drifted into a thick deep slumber as soon as she settled herself among the luxurious silk sheets and tumbled pillows of the enormous sunken bed, sleeping through the night and far, far into the next day until Amina entered the shaded room later the following afternoon.

'Mademoiselle sleepy? Verrry sleepy?' Amina's heavily accented voice was soft and melodious as Kit opened vague dazed eyes as the small woman drew the fine drapes from the open window to reveal the shimmering blueness of the late afternoon sky. 'Now feast? Good, eh?'

'I'm sorry...' Kit was just staring at her non-plussed when a warm female chuckle from the open doorway brought her head swinging round.

'She wants you to eat something.' The small, finely boned woman standing on the threshold indicated the tray Amina had just picked up from a low table. 'Dinner won't be until much later. I'm Colette, by the way.'

So saying, Gerard's sister strode across the room and plumped down at the side of the bed on a thick Persian rug so that she was directly on an eyeline with Kit, who had struggled into a sitting position amid the rumpled sheets. 'That nightie all right? I didn't know what your taste would be, not having met you.' She grinned, a warm natural grin that showed lots of small white teeth.

'It's lovely.' Kit glanced down vacantly at the pale green lace. 'It was very good of you to go to so much trouble.'

'No trouble,' Colette said cheerily. 'Orders from the boss.' She grinned again and Kit couldn't help smiling back, thinking as she did so how different Colette was from her huge handsome brother. No more than five feet two, small and delicately made, she exuded an air of petite feminine attractiveness that went well with the tiny heart-shaped face, huge green eyes and mass of burnished copper hair. There was no trace of an accent in her voice either, Kit thought in surprise. Really, brother and sister couldn't be more different. 'How do you feel?' Colette eyed her consideringly.

'Much better for that sleep,' Kit answered quickly. 'It's very nice to meet you.'

'Nice to meet you,' Colette returned immediately, 'although you aren't at all what I imagined you to be.'

'No?' Kit found herself grinning unexpectedly at the note of surprise in the other girl's voice. 'You aren't what I thought either. You're not at all like your brother, are you?'

'Thank goodness!' Colette wrinkled a pert nose. 'I'll take that as a compliment! What woman wants to be six feet four and built like Tarzan anyway? Actually...' She paused for a second. 'We're half-brother and -sister. Gerard's mother died when he was very small and Dad met my mother three years later. She was an American,' she added as she took the tray for Amina who left them with a bob of her head, 'and constantly homesick. She used to spend half her time here with Dad, whom she loved like crazy, and half in America with her tribe of relations. I used to go with her of course, but Gerard never did. He preferred to stay at Del Mahari with Dad. It sounds like a weird kind of arrangement, I know, but it suited all of us. I honestly can't remember any of the family having a cross word when Mum and Dad were still alive.'

Kit wanted to reply to the casual confidence, she really did, but as Colette had finished speaking something had pierced her heart with such intensity that it was a physical pain. There

was something she had to remember, something
vital, but even as she sought for it it had vanished as Colette's voice broke into her mind
again, urgent this time.

'Are you all right? You look——'

'She looks as though she could do without your
chatter for a time.'

As both girls turned as one towards the deep
voice, Kit felt her heart stop for a stunned
moment and then rush on at a pace that took her
breath away. Gerard was standing in the doorway,
his golden-brown hair with its vibrant tawny
sheen blazing in a shaft of sunlight that turned
the narrowed eyes into slits of gold, and the big,
powerful body clothed in loose cotton trousers
and a thin, long-sleeved robe caught at the waist
with a belt of embroidered material. The front
of the tunic was slashed to the waist in a wide V,
showing the hard-muscled chest densely covered
by dark, curling body hair, and as Kit watched
him move into the room the sensual pull of the
man was so strong she could taste it. The Arab
clothes seemed made for him, the European
façade falling away as though by magic.

'You slept well?' The charming accent tugged
at her nerves and it was some seconds before she
could speak.

'Very well, thank you.' His feet were bare, she
noticed dazedly as he came to stand by the side
of the sunken bed before crouching down by her
side with a slight smile.

'Good. And Colette's chatter has not
tired you?'

'I've only been in here a couple of minutes,' his sister protested indignantly, with a scathing glance at her brother which the dark tanned face ignored completely.

'And now you are going to leave so our guest can eat her meal in peace.' The deep voice was silky smooth but neither of the two women missed the thread of steel underneath, and Kit was surprised to see Colette capitulate immediately, her only objection a slight grimace, and even more surprised at the flood of hot anger that the little by-play brought surging forth in *her* chest. He really was the most arrogant, high-handed——

'Don't frown.' As Colette left the room with a little wave of her hand and a cheerful smile she saw Gerard's eyes were tight on her face and tried to smooth out her expression quickly. 'And eat your meal; it is only a little cold meat and salad with a glass of wine.'

'You drink alcohol?' she asked slowly. 'But I thought——'

'I am French, not Moroccan,' he answered quietly, 'and not of the Moslem religion. I am in the fortunate position of being able to choose what suits me best out of two cultures—an enviable arrangement, do you not agree?' He was talking lightly, his attitude relaxed and easy, but for the life of her Kit couldn't respond. His nearness had tied her stomach into a giant knot and never had she been more acutely aware of her own body. The flimsy nightie that Colette had chosen left nothing to the imagination, and although the second she had heard his voice she had pulled one of the silk sheets high to her chin, she still felt helplessly exposed and curiously threatened. In his Western clothes he had been formidable but here, in his own surroundings and wearing what obviously suited him best, he had all the reassuring attributes of a prowling lion. She couldn't stay here, she really couldn't, and she should never have come...

'Dinner is at eight.' As he straightened she caught a whiff of something heady and again her heart pounded as though it were going to jump out of her body. Stop it, *stop it*. She shut her eyes tight for a second, furious with her weakness at what was only, after all, a chemical reaction to his overpowering maleness. He probably dressed like that on purpose, she thought balefully, as she watched him stride out of the room after a brief nod at her closed face, but no... Even as the thought took form she knew it was unfair. He was himself, that was all. And it was more than enough.

It took quite some time to force the food past the tension in her chest but she managed it at last, sipping the glass of light sparkling wine as she lay back against the rich silk pillows. What a room! She glanced round the exotic Eastern-style boudoir with something akin to wonder before padding across to the *en-suite* bathroom, with a swift nervous glance at the closed bedroom door before she ventured from the protection of the silk sheets.

After a long, cool shower she washed her hair under the flowing water before wrapping a thick bath-sheet tightly round her naked form and peering out into the bedroom beyond. What about clothes? Suddenly the practicalities of the situation she was in overwhelmed her. And make-up, creams, shoes...

The bathroom cabinet revealed a vast array of lotions and cosmetics as well as the more mundane essentials like toothpaste, tooth-brushes, all still in their packaging. Had Colette bought all this for her? She hoped not, she thought nervously as she made her way to the massive walk-in wardrobe at one end of the vast bedroom. This was embarrassing enough as it was. The wardrobe disclosed hanger upon hanger of European and Eastern clothes all roughly her size, with a large drawer of underwear, all lace and froth, at one side and several different pairs of shoes in sizes ranging from five to eight. She looked down at her slender feet thoughtfully. She didn't even know what size shoes she took, but she thought it was six. It was. The first pair of flat leather slip-ons she tried on fitted her perfectly.

By the time a huge gong rang through the house at exactly ten to eight, frightening the life out of her, she was dressed and ready to go downstairs and at least looking, if not feeling, in control. She had chosen an informal black dinner suit in thin silk, the large baggy trousers and thigh-length short-sleeved blouse a compromise between East and West, and apart from the vague thread of gold that featured intermittently in the material wore no other adornment, not even a trace of mascara. If anyone had told her she was trying to efface herself, to hide behind the severe colour, she would have denied it hotly and believed what she said.

Colette knocked on her door a moment after the last vibrations of the gong had died, taking her arm in a friendly hug as they walked down the massive curving stairs to the floor below. And Gerard was waiting.

She glanced at him nervously as he stood up, his big body uncoiling with sensuous grace from the low cushioned divan at one side of the huge hall, and as he walked towards them, the loose robes swirling about his hard muscled frame and his eyes narrowed and cool, she felt an immediate, and not unpleasant, rush of femininity in answer to his silent, powerful masculinity.

'Do not be nervous, it is just the three of us for dinner,' he said softly as he reached her side and, although it was meant as comfort, it did nothing to soothe her jangling nerves. She would have given the world to be oblivious to the sensations the big body clothed in sumptuous Arab raiment called forth from her own, but every muscle and sinew was alive and kicking. 'Have you eaten Moroccan style before?' he asked her quietly as he led the women into the dining-room, an arm round each of their waists.

'I don't think so.' She was concentrating very hard on putting one foot in front of the other

and ignoring the heat from his casual hand on
her skin.

'I find it more comfortable and conducive to
conversation than the European way,' Gerard
said lightly as he indicated one of the exquisitely
embroidered sofas scattered around an enormous
low table with the flick of a brown wrist. 'I hope
you have no objection to eating with your
fingers?' He raised an amused eyebrow at her
surprise. 'One uses the right hand, incidentally,
which is washed by Amina before the meal begins
and again afterwards; she would be most shocked
if you used the left.'

'Why?' Kit asked carefully as she seated herself
as gracefully as she could on one of the upholstered sofas.

'The left is used for more mundane duties,'
Gerard said blandly. 'In my father's time a thief
was sometimes sentenced to have his right hand
cut off which, besides branding him for life, kept
him from ever again eating with other people and
dipping into the communal dish. A cruel but most
effective punishment.'

She eyed him from under her lashes. 'You
aren't saying you approve of such barbarity?' she
asked with horrified revulsion.

'Of course Gerard wouldn't approve,' Colette
said easily as she flung herself down at her
brother's side. 'He's a real old softie under that
hard exterior.'

The dark eyebrows rose a fraction, but beyond
that enigmatic recognition Gerard made no

comment on Colette's statement which he obviously held in derisive disdain.

As Halima began bringing dish after dish to the large low table, Amina appeared with towels and a huge pottery basin, returning a moment later with a large receptacle similar to a kettle. As Kit held her right hand above the basin as Amina indicated, the small Moroccan woman poured a stream of soft, delicately scented water over it. 'It smells like roses,' Kit exclaimed in surprise to Gerard, who was watching her through slitted gold eyes, his expression unreadable.

'It is.' He smiled lazily. 'At the edge of the desert acres of rose bushes grow in fields of oases that stretch for nearly a hundred miles. When the roses bloom their petals are gathered in large baskets and carried off to a still to be boiled in water. In the still, the vapour that boils off is condensed into an oil called attar of roses, which is prized here for perfuming the ceremonial water. It pleases you?'

'Yes, of course.' She smiled nervously. There was a brooding intensity to the dark face that was quite unnerving. 'It's a lovely idea.'

'An ancient ritual,' he corrected gently, 'one of many that is most charming. I am not quite the savage you imagine.'

'I don't——'

But her protest was interrupted by Colette, who, quite oblivious to the undercurrents swirling about her, giggled light-heartedly at what she considered her brother's joke. 'You'll get used to him in time,' she laughed cheerfully, her small attractive face alight. 'Gerard, of all people, a savage!' She giggled again. 'I've never known anyone who knows as much about so many diverse topics as he does.'

'Ah, but that is head knowledge, Colette,' Gerard interrupted her coolly as Amina washed his hand, his gaze never leaving Kit's tight face for a moment. 'Nothing whatsoever to do with the inner man. We all have an element of the untamed lurking within, the beast that layers of civilisation cannot quite subdue. Is that not right, my English kitten?'

'You seem to know a lot about it,' she answered stiffly, 'and who am I to argue with someone who knows so much about everything?'

He opened his mouth to reply at the same moment as the telephone rang on a small table behind him. '*Là.*' He shook his head as Halima reached for it and picked up the receiver himself, listening intently for a few minutes before communicating in rapid Arabic with the person at the other end.

His face was closed and hard when he replaced the receiver at last, his eyes hooded and expressionless as they glanced across at Kit sitting quietly watching him. 'Who are you?' he said at last, echoing her words with a cold smile. 'It would seem you are a Miss Samantha Kittyn of London, England.' His gaze became piercing on her face, noting every flicker of expression. 'Or at least that is what the police have been told by your fiancé, a certain David Shore.'

CHAPTER FOUR

'WELL?' Gerard continued to hold Kit's eyes in a compelling stare. 'Does this information, as you say, ring any bells?'

'No.' She shook her head slowly, her face blank. 'Nothing at all.' *She was engaged? Engaged to be married?*

'I see.' She could have been imagining it, but just for a second she could have sworn it was relief mingled with satisfaction she saw mirrored in the glittering eyes. 'Perhaps this David is not the sort of man who makes a lasting impression?' The words were said so softly, with such a lack of expression, that for a moment the biting insult contained in the smooth voice didn't register, and by the time it did he had moved on detailing the essence of his conversation with the police inspector.

'After I telephoned the inspector in charge of your case today, the police concentrated their enquiries in Casablanca and it would seem almost immediately a report came to light. The Sabratha hotel were concerned this morning when one of their lone women guests, an Englishwoman, did not return as indicated the night before, and even more worried when the car she had hired was found in Essaouira by an enthusiastic police officer, to all appearances abandoned. When the

police checked your papers, which were fortunately in the hotel safe, all became clear. They
rang the address in England and spoke to your
flatmate and also her brother, the said David.'
The light brown eyes hardened. 'It would appear
he wishes to speak with you as soon as this is
possible.'

'Oh.' The effort it took to pull her gaze from
his was disturbing, *he* was disturbing, this whole
crazy drama was disturbing and she was right
bang-smack in the middle of it.

'However, Amina and Halima are waiting for
the meal to begin, so perhaps you could delay
the call for a short time?' he asked silkily,
although she knew, without questioning how,
that he had no intention of encouraging her to
phone David that night. Would he physically stop
her? She glanced at the tall, lean body clothed
in the flowing robes and, as her gaze travelled
upwards, met light stony eyes that were as hard
as nails. Perhaps, yes, perhaps, but it didn't
matter anyway; she had no intention of tele-
phoning a stranger in England and hearing
goodness knew what until she had had time to
collect her thoughts and decide what to ask.

At her acquiescent nod his eyes narrowed a
little as though he were trying to gauge what was
going on in her mind, but then he raised an auth-
oritative hand to the two Moroccan women and
the meal commenced.

As Amina and Halima placed in front of them
a huge dish of roast lamb surrounded by several
plates of small round loaves of delicious nutty

Arab bread, Gerard spoke quietly, his voice warm and relaxed now as he assumed the role of host again. 'It is customary to eat with the thumb and first two fingers of your right hand,' he said softly as he indicated for Colette to show her how, 'and as this is merely the first course of several, do not think you have to clear the dish.' He smiled slowly and, as before, her heart pounded at the difference it made to his autocratic, somewhat cold classical features. 'Amina and Halima will expect you to have a little of each course; they are delighted to have a guest that they can impress. The meat is so tender it will come away easily in the hand and it customary to have no plates unless you would like one?'

'No, no, this is fine,' she said hastily as she followed Colette's example and reached for a succulent piece of meat, finding the aroma irresistible. 'It's gorgeous.' She licked her greasy fingers appreciatively as she reached across for more, suddenly finding she was ravenously hungry.

When Amina arrived with the next course Kit's eyes turned automatically to Gerard and, as before, his gaze was trained on her face. 'This is a *pastilla*,' he said quietly, 'and Amina has spent many hours preparing it in your honour, so as you eat express your admiration. It consists of wafer-thin layers of flaky pastry filled with meat, almonds, hard boiled eggs, herbs and spices and will be very hot inside, so be careful.'

She nodded a dutiful response even as her heart began to thud violently in her chest. He looked so...foreign in the long loose robes of jade-green and black that clothed the big masculine body so carelessly, foreign and devastatingly, vitally male. Like a scene from the *Arabian Nights*! She shut her eyes briefly as she prayed for composure. But this was real life, not a play or film that she could walk away from, and she would want to walk away from this man, would need to. He was all-consuming, the antithesis of everything her instincts were telling her were right for her.

'Samantha?' She started at the name, her eyes opening wide as she looked into the gold depths of his. 'What is it?'

'I don't like that name.' She side-stepped his question intentionally. 'Samantha—I don't like it.'

'No?' He eyed her intently. 'Perhaps you had another name you were known by? Can you think what it is?'

She watched him over the rim of her glass as she took a long slow sip of wine, her eyes shuttered against the thoughts swirling in her mind, before shaking her head in the negative.

'I see.' He settled back against the low padded divan and bit into the *pastilla* in his hand, his teeth white and strong against the feather-light pastry, before fixing her with his gaze again. 'In that case, if I am not allowed to call you by the name we do know, perhaps, it would be in order to snap my fingers to get your attention?'

'Not if you expect me to respond,' she answered instantly, her hackles rising at the image his words conjured up. If he wanted a slave girl he could look elsewhere.

'Sam?' Colette entered the conversation, unaware of the subtle undercurrents. 'That's the normal abbreviation for Samantha, isn't it?'

'Not this Samantha.' Gerard's voice was a low growl. 'A woman should be called by a woman's name.'

'Well, that's a bit chauvinistic,' Kit said hotly as her eyes flashed from sister to brother. 'This is the 1990s in case you hadn't noticed. Women actually got the vote some years ago.'

'A retrograde step in my opinion,' Gerard said silkily as his eyes lingered on her hot cheeks. 'The feminist movement has a lot to answer for.'

'Why, you——' She stopped abruptly as Colette giggled at her side, and noticed the gold brown eyes surveying her so innocently were full of wicked amusement. 'You were joking,' she finished flatly, her eyes hostile even as she forced a smile.

'Was I?' His gaze never broke contact with hers as he spoke. 'Are you sure?' And now there was no amusement in the tawny depths, merely a deep searching intensity that seemed to look through into her soul. 'Do you *feel* who I am?'

'No.' She answered him in spite of herself, half mesmerised by the piercing quality of the narrowed eyes. 'I don't understand what you mean.'

'That is sad.' The room was very quiet now; even Colette seemed to realise her brother was saying more than the words held. 'To hurt someone is bad enough, but to take away their

basic judgement of others borders on wickedness. The Arabs have a saying that to know
oneself one must first learn to *feel* who others
are. That way you accept both the good and bad,
understand the imperfections so that there are no
damaging surprises later to mar a relationship. It
also enables one to pick out the one perfect jewel
and discard the rest.'

'It's not possible to do that,' she whispered
slowly.

'On the contrary.' There was no cynicism in
his face now, neither could it have been called
hard. 'The aura that is an essential part of each
one of us cannot be denied, but too many people,
especially in the Western world, look on the
outward appearance, trust the dubious sincerity
of mere words. The Arabs recognise that the inner
soul is far more discerning. But it takes time to
learn, to feel, and it is not easy; one can be hurt
in the process.'

'You're talking about instinct, sixth sense, call
it what you will,' she said tightly. 'That's all.
There's nothing mystical about that.'

'No, I am not.' He leaned forward slightly, his
body big and dark against the light cloth of the
divan. 'I am talking about feeling and being,
learning from every little incident that touches
our heart and drawing wisdom even from the
disasters. I am talking about gaining strength
inside, discarding bitterness and self-pity, looking
at everything through an inner light that exposes
the darkness and allows us to discern things as
they are so we have the choice of either accepting

or letting go. To gain the gift of *feeling* who others are should humble, not exalt, and in that process one finds oneself.'

'And if you don't like what you find?' she asked practically. 'I should think finding oneself is a dodgy business.'

He stared at her for a split-second before breaking into loud unrestrained laughter, his head thrown back and his mouth wide. It was infectious. She wasn't really sure what she was smiling at but she found herself smiling just the same. 'For such a bewildered little kitten you have very sharp claws,' he said after a few moments, when he could restrain his mirth. 'That will teach me to wax philosophical when I should be eating.'

As course after course came and went she found herself pondering his words. They had touched something very deep inside her and instinctively she had hidden behind humour because the alternative was too painful. Why? She searched her memory for something, anything, but the dark oasis was complete, allowing her mind rest and tranquillity from what had harmed it even as it kept its dark secret.

As Amina placed the last dish of sweetmeats on the table to join the bowls of cherries, peaches, grapes, oranges, bananas and dates already in place, Kit knew she couldn't eat another thing. 'That was wonderful, thank you.' She smiled up at Amina and Halima as she spoke, encompassing the food with a wave of her hand. 'It was all delicious.'

Gerard spoke swiftly in Arabic to the two women, who smiled back at her, bobbing their heads in delight at her appreciation before they left for the kitchen again.

'It is a little late to telephone England now,' Gerard said quietly as Amina washed their hands with the rose-scented water some minutes later before they rose from the divans. 'You agree?'

'I'll phone tomorrow.' She was very conscious of his great height as they walked through into the internal courtyard, the sensation both physically and mentally satisfying, although the little tremors that shivered down her limbs as he took her arm were anything but.

'In that case I would be most honoured to show you the gardens.' His voice was husky and deep, the slight accent giving a sensual lift to the words that set her pulses racing even as she chastised herself for her vulnerability where this man was concerned.

'I thought you said it was late,' she said carefully as Colette called goodnight from somewhere in the house, her voice light and carefree. Had she ever been like that? Kit asked herself painfully. Somehow she didn't think she had.

'Do not argue.' His voice was mild but firm. 'You have been asleep for most of the day and would not be able to sleep again so soon. A brisk walk in the cool of the night is just what you need.'

'How do you know what I need?' she answered obstinately as the old antagonism flared. He was so sure of himself, so terrifyingly sure. What did he expect of her? A brief little affair before she left, a quick titillation of his male ego? Some men had to know that they could have any woman they liked—perhaps he was like that? He couldn't be short of female companionship, that much was for sure looking the way he did. And she was no *femme fatale*. What could he possibly see in her beyond the thrill of the chase and ultimate conquest?

'Through here.' He led her through a delicate stucco arch constructed in a wall softly coloured with mosaic tiles of different hues, and she found herself walking down a long corridor at the perimeter of the extensive kitchens at the back of the house. Amina and Halima's voice could be heard within along with that of a man, probably Assad. Abou was rarely about and when he was seemed morose and withdrawn, quite different from his smiling brother who was clearly Gerard's close friend.

Gerard opened an iron gate set in a wall of criss-cross stone, and as they passed through into the gardens she was aware of the soft balmy blanket of sky above and the sweet perfume of warm vegetation below, of the tall, exotically clothed figure at her side, his robes flowing around him as he walked, and of her own stark vulnerability that suddenly gripped her throat in a stranglehold. What was she doing? What *was* she doing? It was as though a force stronger than herself was drawing her on. The gardens were lit by strategically placed lamps and for a few minutes she forgot her fears and she drank in the beauty all around her. A delicate stream with tiny waterfalls, bordered on either side by grass and flowers, meandered through lawns shaded by weeping willows, oaks and many other trees, exotic bougainvillaeas and hibiscus vying with the heady perfume of roses, honeysuckle and jasmine and the odd bower enclosed and hidden by thick, brilliant green ivy trained over latticed wood. There must have been two acres of land in all, but the gardens were set out in such a way that it seemed far, far more.

'My mother planted most of the trees herself.' They stopped under a spreading cedar tree, its vast trunk enclosed by a circular seat of wood, which Gerard indicated with a wave of his hand. 'Most Moroccan gardens are ornamental but she preferred a more relaxed environment.'

'It's absolutely lovely.' Kit sat gingerly on the very edge of the seat, her body as tense as a rod as he sat down beside her.

'Have you remembered anything at all?' They had sat in a silence that was anything but comfortable for several minutes before Gerard spoke again, and she had never been more aware of another human being in her life. The subtle but intoxicating fragrance that emanated from the dark tanned skin, the big muscled body and narrowed glittering eyes... He was like a creature of the night, dangerous, powerful and utterly at home in his natural habitat.

'Not really,' she answered jerkily.

'Have you tried——?'

'Of course I've tried,' she interrupted sharply, as she tried to banish the intimate atmosphere of sexual awareness with out and out hostility. 'I don't like being like this, for goodness' sake.'

'I was going to say have you tried loosening up a little?' The deep voice was cool and un-emotional, but as she glanced up into the impassive face she caught a little glimmer of reaction to her glance in the thickly lashed eyes moments before a curtain came down to hide their expression. He wanted her. The knowledge was a little jolt in her chest. Whatever the motive, that had been hot primitive desire in those tawny eyes.

'That's not exactly easy to do.' She drew her feet up on to the bench, clasping her knees close to her chest as she let her hair hang forward in a curtain over her flushed cheeks. 'I'm frightened.' Why she admitted that to him she didn't know; part of her wanted to remain cool and aloof but another part of her needed his hard masculine strength, his protection. Stupid, stupid, stupid, she told herself painfully. It was something far more basic than protection that was on his mind. She had to be alert, on her guard, every minute.

'Of course you are, I understand that,' he said softly. 'As I said, for a such a bewildered little kitten, you are being very brave.'

'No, you said I had sharp claws.' She tried for lightness but it didn't quite come off as her voice cracked slightly.

'It's the same thing.'

She knew he was going to kiss her and she also knew it was crazy, foolhardy, but she wanted him to. He terrified her, intimidated and threatened her in a way she didn't understand, but there was something stronger than all that turning her face up to meet his as his hand cupped her chin in a gentle hold. It was a deep, long, sensual kiss, and even as she felt her body respond the thought came that she wasn't ready for this. She struggled slightly as his arm enclosed her back, moving her intimately against him, but his body was like iron, immovable. He was very experienced. Even as the thought took hold she found herself relaxing in his embrace as his lips caressed her cheeks and ears, moving over her eyes with feather-like kisses that began a trembling deep inside she couldn't hide. And then he took her mouth again and she found her lips parting to allow him entry as her hands held on to the bulk of his hard muscled shoulders.

'You taste like honey.' The whisper brushed her skin with a million little sensations that were pure magic. 'So sweet, so very sweet.' She felt his warm hand on the skin under her top but was powerless to stop him, her breasts tightening and filling at his touch until she felt as though she would explode. He had told her during dinner that she was twenty-five years old, engaged to be married, and yet if she hadn't known better she would have sworn this was the first time she had been touched like this. As she felt the cool night air on her aching breasts she realised he had opened her top, his eyes feasting where his hands had wandered, and immediately a sense of shame and shock coupled with a deep ignominy at her lack of inches had her covering her body with her hands.

'Don't do that; you are beautiful.' Even as his voice spoke her mind repudiated the husky words. Beautiful? With her slender boyish body and small breasts? She shut her eyes against the ridicule and pity she felt she would see on his face. 'Kitten? Open your eyes.'

'No.' She tried to move away, to escape from the big body trapping hers, but he merely seized the opportunity to fit her more closely against him.

'What is it?' Her hands were trapped between her own body and the wall of his chest now, and she could feel coarse curling body hair where his tunic had fallen open baring his muscled torso. The sensation caused a raw panic as the reality of his masculinity pressed in on her, the knowledge of what he could do to her if he tried suddenly alarmingly real. 'What is wrong?'

'Please let me go.' She opened big tortured grey eyes to stare into the narrowed gold of his. 'Please.'

'There is no need to be ashamed of your body.' His voice was soft but with a steel thread of persistence that she recognised as inflexible. 'You are a very lovely young woman; this cannot all be so new to you.'

'Gerard...' She shook her head desperately like a tiny wild animal caught in a steel-jawed trap. 'Please.'

'Who has hurt you like this?' He relaxed his hold sufficiently for her to free her hands and button the blouse with shaking fingers, and then moved her chin to face him again, his touch gentle. 'I want you, kitten, you know that,' he said slowly, his voice thick and husky, 'but I can wait.'

'I'm——' Her voice cracked and she took a deep breath to try again, the feel of his arms round her making her shiver. 'I'm engaged to be married, *you said*.'

'But you are not married yet.' The light brown eyes narrowed and became hard. 'And whoever this David is, he has not made you happy or you would not be here now.'

'I'm here because of an accident,' she protested faintly as he stroked back the hair from her hot forehead, his eyes reflective.

'No, not the accident.' His face tightened. 'You have to face that, kitten. You are here because of something you want to forget, something that has hurt you so badly that your mind has taken refuge in the only way it knows how. If you were mine you would not have had to do this.'

'That's ridiculous.' The sheer arrogance of the statement sent a flood of welcome adrenaline into her limbs, quelling the humiliating shaking. 'How can you possibly say that?'

'Because of the way you react in my arms even as you are trying to fight me.' There was something almost menacing in the tanned features now. 'You want me although you are determined to deny us both. Is this not true?'

'I don't even know you!' she said in amazement. 'And I don't know what sort of women you are used to, but I don't fall into bed at the drop of a hat.'

'Who was talking about bed?' He moved her more closely against him, kissing the tip of her nose with warm lips. 'I am not a callow youth who has to prove himself by the act of possession. I thought we were getting to know each other a little, giving and receiving pleasure?' He stroked the side of her face with one finger, his touch tender. 'I have no intention of doing anything you do not like, kitten.'

'But——' As she began to speak he covered her lips with his own, kissing her long and hard as he enclosed her in the circle of his arms. Why did he have to be so good at this? she asked herself faintly as a river of hot smooth sensation flooded every nerve and sinew. Wonderfully, frighteningly good? How many women had he *had*, for crying out loud?

'Relax...' As his mouth moved to her throat and ears she felt her head go back to allow him greater access, her submission being met by a low growl in the base of his throat that thrilled and excited her, but he made no move to take the lovemaking any further than before and she sensed he wouldn't even as her hands fluttered in helpless protest as he touched her skin. He returned almost immediately to her mouth, kissing her for a long time, his lips and tongue teasing, provocative and sensual in turn until she began to think it was impossible to contain the emotions he was arousing. And then, quite suddenly, he stopped.

'What's wrong?' She opened dazed eyes to stare up into his face as he held her against him, his touch more restrictive than demanding now.

'I think that is enough getting to know each other for now,' he said gruffly, and as she caught the slight shake in his voice her eyes widened. He wasn't so much in control as he would have her believe, she thought, with a little thrill of excitement.

'It is?' The knowledge that she could arouse a man such as this was intoxicating.

'It is.' He eyed her drily. 'Unless you are prepared for me to lay you out on the grass and take you?' Her eyes dropped from his and he smiled sardonically. 'Exactly. So if we are presuming that discretion is the better part of valour, here endeth the first lesson.' As he leant across and adjusted her clothing with steady impersonal fingers before rising and drawing her up beside him, the sudden realisation that she had been playing with fire came hot and strong. The strength was all his, the sheer physical power totally in his court. If he had lost control... She glanced up into his face inches above her, noting the massive powerful shoulders and broad chest with a little shiver deep inside. She must have been crazy, mad—what was the matter with her, courting disaster like this? Was there some sort of drug in the air? And why was he bothering with her in the first place?

Because she was available? The answer came from deep within and hurt more than she could say. He was obviously a sensual, virile man well skilled in the arts of love. He must have women clamouring for his attention, beautiful sexy women who would know exactly how to please a man of the world like him. But he was here on his estate at the moment and she was the only woman around. He knew she would be leaving soon, that there would of necessity be no strings attached to a light affair with her even if she wasn't what he would normally choose. 'I prefer my women with a little more meat on their bones and definitely more submissive.' The words he had thrown at her a few days before came back with stark clarity. Oh, how could she have been such a fool?

She didn't speak again on the way back to the house, and fortunately he seemed lost in a world of his own, holding her hand loosely as they passed through the arch into the warm interior and only coming to himself as they reached the bottom of the long winding staircase. 'Kitten——'

She interrupted him harshly, the thoughts that had tormented her for the last few minutes making her painfully aware of her physical shortcomings. 'Don't call me that.'

'What?' The slight smile died on his lips as the narrowed gold eyes registered the naked hostility apparent in both her body and face.

'Kitten. I'm not your kitten or anyone else's,' she said tightly. 'Just because——' She stopped abruptly.

'Because?' Afterwards she realised she should have been warned by that silky smoothness in his voice but at the time it just hadn't registered on her angry mind.

'Because we exchanged a few kisses, you needn't think I'm ready to fall into your bed,' she said flatly.

'Fall into my bed?' He stood back a pace, crossing his arms as he did so and looking fleetingly like an imperious sultan faced with a rebellious slave, as the long Arab robes flowed round the powerful body and his tawny brown hair gleamed in the light from the oil lamp above his head. 'Is it not customary to wait to be asked?'

'I didn't mean——' She stopped abruptly. 'I wasn't *offering*,' she finished harshly.

'Good.' He eyed her with dispassionate coldness. 'Because you would have been turned down. I don't bed on the first date either.'

He had left her before she could retaliate, left her standing at the bottom of the ornately carved staircase as he disappeared into the labyrinth of a house without a backward glance.

CHAPTER FIVE

KIT slept very badly. Whether it was due to the fact that she had slept most of the day away or the molten anger that seethed in her chest like lava, or, and she had to admit to herself the last point was the most likely, the raging, over-powering sensations that Gerard's body had called forth from hers, she wasn't sure. Whatever, dawn was already touching the night sky with mauve-tipped fingers when at last she slept only to be awakened two hours later by a bright-faced Amina and a strong cup of coffee. '*Sbah el khir*?' At her dazed gaze the small Moroccan woman giggled with her hand over her mouth in apology. 'Is the good morning, yes? Go down now, *now*?'

'You want me to go downstairs?' Kit demon-strated the import of her words with a wave of her hands to which Amina responded with a vig-orous nod. '*Waha*, yes, yes. Down. You eat.'

Breakfast, at this time of the morning? She glanced at her watch wearily. It was only six o'clock. Did they always eat so early here?

When she walked into the dining-room ten minutes later after a hasty shower, her hair damp, it was to find Gerard sitting behind a newspaper at the end of the massive room with a small breakfast-table loaded with bowls of sliced fruit and small loaves of Arab bread and preserves in front of him. The whole scene was in such contrast to the Eastern atmosphere of the night before that she was lost for words as she joined him.

'Good morning.' The newspaper lowered at her approach and she saw the mode of dress had changed to a casual shirt and cotton trousers replacing the flowing robes of the day before, but in no way diminishing the raw sex appeal that oozed from the big frame as his eyes ran casually over her slender form, encased in her own clothes that Amina had washed and ironed and replaced in the wardrobe in her room. 'You'll need to change before we leave.'

'Leave?' Just for a minute she thought he was telling her she was being dispatched back to Casablanca that day, and the harsh jolt her heart gave unnerved her more than his words.

'It would seem in view of the developments of yesterday that your time in Marrakesh is limited,' he said impassively as Amina arrived with a pot of steaming coffee and a large jug of freshly squeezed orange juice. 'No doubt David will want you to join him as soon as possible.' The hard gold gaze was quite unreadable. 'In view of this I thought it would be advisable to show you a little of my country before you leave to return to your old life. This is acceptable to you? Of course, Colette would have been the perfect choice but she is otherwise engaged,' he continued smoothly, 'but no matter.'

'Oh, right . . .' It was too early and she had had too little sleep to enter into a battle of words and besides, she caught the thought abruptly but it had already taken form, she wanted a day with him.

He waited a moment for further comment and when none was forthcoming leant slightly forward, his male warmth seeming to encompass her air space although he was several inches from touching her. 'It would probably be better if you wore a long skirt and a blouse that covers all of your arms,' he said quietly. 'The Moslem religion expects this of its women, and although you are not bound by such things it would be considered an act of politeness, a respect of local customs.'

'Yes, of course.' She nodded stiffly. 'Would it be in order for me to phone England when I've eaten?'

'It is a little early, do you not think?' he said smoothly. 'We shall return in time for dinner tonight so perhaps it would be more... considerate to make the call then?'

She looked straight at him and held the cool shuttered gaze for a long moment before nodding again. 'All right.' Why didn't he want her to phone David? she asked herself silently as she helped herself to a bowl of freshly sliced watermelon. What possible reason could he have? She began to eat mechanically, her thoughts far away. Did he think the longer she was kept from outside influences the more chance he would have of seducing her? And just how long, exactly, did he intend her to stay here anyway? It had been meant as a refuge until her identity could be established, but surely that didn't apply any more?

'It has been very kind of you to let me stay here,' she began carefully as her thoughts prompted her to speak, 'but now we know who I am I don't want to impose on your hospitality any longer——'

'Rubbish.' The word was sharp and immediate and she blinked at him as he glared at her across the table. 'You have been *told* who you are but as far as I am concerned the situation has not altered. You are still unable to remember even the most elementary facts about your past life. For all we know this David could have ill-treated you, beaten you even; perhaps it is him you were running from.'

'I hardly think so.' She stared at him, surprised by the force of emotion in the dark face.

'You hardly think so.' He repeated her words with a bitingly cool mockery that brought immediate colour into her pale cheeks. 'And why do you hardly think so?'

'Because I don't think I'd put up with treatment like that from anyone,' she said hotly, her eyes flashing, 'least of all someone I'm engaged to.'

'Perhaps not.' He seemed to take a pull of air and almost force himself to speak moderately. 'But until you can speak from what you know and not from supposition, I think it advisable you remain here. The doctors assure me it is usually a matter of days in these cases when no physical injury is involved. It only needs one spark and you will be as before. Besides——' his face was expressionless now although the beautiful eyes were piercing on her face '—you hardly seem to be pining for this David.'

'I can't remember him, can I?' she answered sharply.

'Exactly.'

By the time they left the house nearly an hour later the dry sunny air was redolent with the scents of rosemary and jasmine and full of bird song from the fruit trees lining the drive, and as the powerful Ferrari passed through the gates on to the dusty road outside, the dominating minaret of the Koutoubia Mosque, 77 metres high, was clearly visible in the crystal-clear, startlingly blue sky.

As they took the main road to Taroudant out of Marrakesh, Kit was acutely aware of the big male body next to hers in the close confines of the car and quite unable to relax, alive to every slight movement of the capable brown hands on the steering-wheel, every small movement of his head as he checked traffic and negotiated man- oeuvres in the already considerable traffic.

They drove in silence for some time until after about half an hour had ticked by in uneasy quiet and the car had begun to climb in gentle spirals alongside the rushing torrent of icy water that made up the Ourika river, Gerard suddenly spoke. 'You are making me nervous.'

'What?' Her head spun to the handsome profile but he concentrated on the road ahead, his mouth slightly twisted at the note of surprise in her voice.

'I said you are making me nervous with this fidgety edginess and anxious face.' Now the clear gold-brown eyes did stroke her face fleetingly for one swift moment before returning to the windscreen. 'What is it you expect of me that you are so apprehensive, kitten?'

'I don't expect anything,' she answered weakly, the clean sensual smell of his aftershave registering on her taut nerves like fire.

'This is good.' He spared her another swift glance, his eyes narrowed and alive with mocking amusement. 'I was beginning to worry that I could not live up to your expectations as a—how you say—Casanova?'

'Oh, you . . .' Her voice trailed away as an adequate description failed her.

'I know, I am the savage, eh?' he asked with comfortable derision, his soft warm chuckle turning her limbs to melted jelly.

'I don't think you're a savage,' she answered carefully, trying to concentrate without success on the view out of the car window, its grandeur almost completely wasted on her as all her senses tuned in to his magnetic pull.

'No?' He was silent for a moment, his mouth serious when he spoke again. 'And what exactly *do* you think I am, my little English kitten, eh?'

'I'm not sure.' She glanced fleetingly at the hard profile and then turned her gaze back to safer subjects again. 'I think you're kind; you've been kind to me.'

'Kind?' If she had called him the devil incarnate he couldn't have been more furious, she reflected miserably, as the car swerved violently for a second before resuming its steady course.

'Old women are kind,' he said scathingly, running a hand through the tawny mane of his hair with a gesture that spoke of his outrage far more adequately than any words could have done.

'I didn't mean——' She stopped abruptly.

'Yes?' he asked intimidatingly.

'I didn't mean you weren't other things as well.' The air was suddenly prickly, charged with an electricity that sent small shivers flying down her spine.

'Such as?' he asked silkily, his voice soft.

'Well...' Hell's bells, this was *awful*, she thought helplessly as her cheeks became still hotter. What on earth did he expect her to say anyway? That she thought he was the most fantastic man she had ever seen? That one look from those amazing eyes and she was a trembling mess? She caught herself abruptly, surprised and alarmed at the way her mind was moving. 'I'm not going to tell you,' she said with sudden firmness. 'You're big-headed enough as it is.'

'I'm...?' The blank silence caused her breath to stop in her throat before he chuckled again a moment later. 'OK, you win that round, kitten.' She wasn't fooled by the apparent capitulation and sure enough a second later he spoke again, his voice deep and soft. 'But I take it I wouldn't have been too displeased by your summing-up?'

'You can take what you want,' she said tartly, regretting the import of her reply the second it left her lips.

'There's no answer to that.' She could hear dark amusement throbbing in the deep voice and would have loved to fire back with an appropriately scathing rejoinder, but her mind just refused to co-operate. 'Look, if I promise to behave would you at least try and enjoy yourself?' he asked a moment later, glancing at her hands clenched in tight fists on her lap. 'This is a wonderful spot and I would like you to appreciate it.'

'Yes, well...' She heard her voice with a definite feeling of self-disgust. What *did* she sound like! Moronic! 'Yes, all right,' she said more firmly. 'A truce?'

'A truce,' he agreed gravely, the slight quiver in the richly accented voice causing her to look at him suspiciously, but the tanned handsome face was quite expressionless and devoid of all humour.

As the car sped on, eating up the miles with careless disregard, she was entranced to see hanging on the almost vertical sides of the valley, tiny villages that were difficult to spot from any distance, being made of the same rich red earth as the valley itself, but were picturesque in the extreme.

'They look wildly romantic,' Gerard said quietly at her side, reading her mind accurately, 'but I have it on good authority they are murder to live in.'

'Are they?' She tried to picture the peaceful isolated life the villagers must lead. 'I wouldn't care.'

'With the right company, neither would I,' he said softly, a subtle inflexion in his voice bringing the colour surging into her face.

Why did he have to say things like that, she asked herself crossly, and, more to the point, why did she always have to respond on cue? She *knew* this was all a game, a momentary diversion out of his normal routine of business; why couldn't she at least pretend coolness? She was still seething quietly some time later, when the car passed through a little hamlet and came to a halt as the road petered to a finish in deference to the breathtaking majesty of the gorge.

'We walk from this point,' Gerard said comfortably as she looked at him expectantly. 'Amina has packed a picnic in the back of the car and we will eat shortly.'

'But...' She glanced round at the bottomless ravine and soaring peaks of the mountains above, suddenly feeling very tiny and very vulnerable. They could have been the only people in the world.

'No buts, my timid little kitten,' he said mockingly, laughing softly as she flashed him a furious glance of such venom that it rendered his description null and void. 'Here, you take the rug and I will bring the hamper, yes?'

They found a spot she was sure he had had specially made for a seduction scene, the grass a thick flowery carpet of hundreds of wild flowers

with an ancient cypress tree providing welcome
shade from the heat of the sun, although the soft
warm breeze kept the temperature comfortable.
As he spread the rug out under the green branches
she found that her stomach was clenched into a
giant knot, her nerves as tight as piano wire.
'Come and sit down,' he said mildly, his eyes
narrowed against the sun as he glanced up at her
standing rigid and still to one side of the blanket.
'What would you like to eat?'

'I——' She gestured with her hand abruptly as
she sank down on to the warm rug. 'Anything,
anything,' she said jerkily.

'Come here.' His voice was suddenly very low
and very tender as he stared into her troubled
face, and as she made no move to approach him
he rolled over to her, sitting up to face her as he
reached her side. 'I am not going to hurt you,
kitten,' he said patiently as he cupped her face
in his large brown hands. 'When are you going
to believe that? We are going to eat, maybe talk
a little, let the sun warm us and just enjoy the
moment. Now——' he smiled slowly '—you can
be mother.' He indicated the hamper with a lazy
wave of his hand. 'Wait on me, wench.'

They feasted on the hundred and one little
delicacies Amina had packed so carefully: tiny
mouthwatering pasties filled with ground meat,
chopped hard-boiled eggs, cheese and vegetables, small spiced lamb sausages, lemon
chicken dipped in melted brown sugar, succulent
prawns and tender lobster, fresh green salad,
nutty Arab rolls and freshly baked croissants,

besides every imaginable fruit Kit could think of and all washed down with a rich fruity red wine that tasted of honey and summer days.

'I'm going to burst.' Kit ran a lazy hand over the swell of her stomach. 'I couldn't eat another thing.' The good food and three large glassfuls of wine she had consumed had made her limbs like lead, and as Gerard moved close, turning her into his body so that her head was lying on his broad chest and her limbs were stretched along the length of his, she found she was powerless to resist.

'Go to sleep,' he said softly, kissing the top of her head as he settled her more comfortably against him, the feel of his hard muscled body producing a sensual warmth that was intoxicatingly good. 'You are tipsy.'

'Tipsy?' She tried for indignation but the emotion just wasn't there. What she wanted more than anything else was to have him make love to her. The thought should have shocked, but it merely tantalised and she realised he was right. She *was* tipsy. She giggled softly against the hard bulk of his chest. 'Did you do this on purpose?'

'Do what?' He moved her slightly to stare down into her flushed face. 'If you remember, my greedy little kitten, you poured the last two glasses of wine yourself.'

'So I did.' She giggled again. 'But you didn't stop me.'

'I'm no saint.' As he touched her mouth with his own, his big body turning to crouch over her, she gave herself up to the kiss with uninhibited pleasure, but after a long moment of his mouth devouring hers he moved back to his original position with a deep groan. 'Go to sleep, kitten.'

'Why?' She knew she was behaving badly but she didn't care. She was so tired of being frightened and lonely and defensive. She wanted... She wanted *him*.

'Because when I have you you will be fully *compos mentis*, my English siren, and you will want me with your mind as well as your body,' he said grimly.

'I do now,' she protested weakly, her head spinning.

'You think you do.' He raised himself on one elbow, and as her head rested on the thick grass she looked up into the tanned face above her but his features were a hazy golden shadow in the brilliance of the sun. 'But the wine has merely lowered the drawbridge temporarily; we cannot always rely on such a thing. This is how you should be, how you want to be, the real you, but you have to find that yourself with no outward stimulus and then, then you will be the woman you were meant to be.'

'But——' She stopped abruptly, her brow wrinkling. 'I'm going home soon, aren't I? There's David...'

'Damn David!' As she started at the savagery in his voice he caught her to him again, his voice soft. 'I am sorry, do not be afraid. But forget David for now, concentrate on me. I shall not let you go until you know yourself, kitten, however long that takes.' There was something in his voice she didn't understand, something she needed to comprehend. She stared up at him with huge drowning eyes, and he shook his head slowly as his mouth moved to take hers again. 'Dammit, but you are making this hard, so rich and ripe and honey-soft...' He was breathing hard now, his body rigid with control as he plundered her mouth with his, his tongue plunging and filling and tasting until she thought she would go mad with the sensations he was producing, his hands sliding over her body in an agony of hot desire as he held her to him, his arousal blatant and fierce against the softness of her thighs.

'Hell, woman!' As he wrenched his mouth from hers and rolled roughly from her she lay quivering and trembling, her body feverishly alive and aching with an alien need that made her aware of every part of her anatomy.

'Gerard——'

'No, don't, don't say a word,' he said harshly as he stood up in one violent movement and walked to stand some yards away, his hands palm down on a large boulder as he bent to take deep steady breaths, his back to her. 'You see? I have little control where you are concerned.'

They remained locked in a frozen tableau for long minutes until he straightened, walking back to the picnic hamper and taking a long hard pull of the iced water he had drunk after allowing himself just one glass of wine. 'It is getting late.' He glanced at his watch and then met her troubled stare with a purposefully blank face. 'I want to return in time for the entertainment in

Djemaa-el-Fna square, so perhaps we should leave now.'

'Gerard?' Her voice was a tiny whisper as the events of the last few minutes began to nullify the influence of the wine. 'What have I done wrong?'

'Nothing.' His voice was rueful with a dark amusement containing biting self-mockery. 'It is just a little disconcerting when one meets one's Waterloo, kitten.'

'I don't understand,' she said bewilderedly.

'That is probably just as well.' He eyed her grimly. 'But just trust me when I say it's time to leave, that's all.'

She must have slept on the way back, the lack of sleep the night before coupled with the relaxing effect of the wine producing a deep dreamless stupor from which she roused herself with difficulty as they drew into a side road approaching Djemaa-el-Fna square, the dusky half-light illuminated by flickering gas-lights which mellowed the ancient castellated ramparts around the old town.

'All right?' Gerard's voice was soft as he glanced at her and she sat up sharply in the seat as he stopped the car. As she met his veiled eyes the events of the afternoon came rushing back with humiliating clearness. She had thrown herself at him! Quite literally thrown herself at him. She wanted to close her eyes to blot out his face, but forced herself to answer in a normal voice that betrayed none of her inner agitation.

'Fine, thank you.' She smiled brightly. 'And you?'

'I also am fine,' he said quietly, his face deadpan. He indicated the street with a wave of his hand. 'Shall we?'

As they approached the square it was the noise and smells that registered first, the whole gigantic sideshow of snake-charmers, sword-swallowers, fire-eaters, musicians with painted fiddles and rattle snare drums, dancers, beggars, scribes sitting under umbrellas with the tools of their trade scattered around them, spellbinders, mystics, all too much to take in at first sight. Charcoal grills on which tiny fish sizzled were scattered among vendors peddling daggers, hashish pipes, Koranic texts and a hundred and one other items, not least violently coloured portraits of the royal family.

She was supremely grateful for Gerard's solid bulk at the side of her and his arm round her waist, his stamp of ownership welcome in the ever-flowing wave of humanity all around them. She glanced up at him under her eyelashes as they wandered through the crowds, wondering what he was thinking behind the impassive, slightly cynical face he presented to the world. Did the feel of her body next to his affect him as fiercely as it did her? He felt her glance and looked down, smiling lazily before letting his gaze rove over the crowd again over which he towered by a good few inches. She doubted it. She doubted it very much indeed.

By the time they had strolled through the *souks*, the entrance to which was in one corner of the square, watching the craftsmen at work gilding on leather and inlaying with enamel the sheaths of ornate silver daggers while others hammered out copper or smoothed cedar-wood, evening was being ushered in by the long wailing song of the *muezzins* calling the faithful to prayer. Many were answering the call, drifting away from the activity in the square for meditation in the mosques, and as Gerard led her back in the direction of the car the riot of colour, noise and bustle was beginning to die.

'I've had a wonderful day.' As he opened her door and she slid into the warm interior of the car, she smiled up at Gerard carefully.

'Good.' He rested both hands on the top of the vehicle as he bent to stare in at her, his eyes slanted. 'And you will inform your David of this when you call?'

'What?' As she met his gaze she saw the tawny eyes were very clear and very hard.

'I asked if you will tell your... fiancé how much you enjoyed this day.' He shut her door abruptly and moved round to join her in the car.

'Of course I will.' The few seconds had given her time to recover from the direct attack.

'And do you not think he will consider it strange that you are not missing him, that you have spent the day quite happily in another man's company?' He reached out and smoothed a strand of silky chestnut red hair from her cheek, his touch possessive. She forced herself not to flinch, to show no reaction at all as his skin touched hers.

'I don't see why he should.' She stared back at him, her face both defensive and vulnerable.

'No?' He shook his head slowly as he bent to brush her lips with his own before turning into his seat and starting the engine with a flick of his hand. 'Then you are either as naïve and untouched as I am beginning to think, or capable of a callousness that puts me to shame. If I had been foolish enough to let you leave my side I would have killed the first man who looked at you with desire in his heart.' His voice was so cool, so deliberate, that for a moment the impact of the statement didn't register on her mind, and when it did the tingling shiver that flickered down her spine left a trail of sensual warmth that sent the blood surging into her cheeks.

'That's ridiculous.' She fastened her seatbelt with shaking fingers and prayed for aplomb.

'No.' His voice was a low growl. 'That is——' He stopped abruptly and time ticked by for an endless second in breathless savagery. 'That is something quite different.' And then the powerful car sprang into life and as Gerard eased it into the crowded street she found she was still holding her breath in tense expectation.

They reached Del Mahari within minutes, and as Gerard led her into his beautiful book-lined study to make the call to England she prayed he would leave. He didn't. As he seated himself behind the massive cedar-wood desk and spoke to the operator, organising the call, she felt her knees grow weak and sank down into the seat he had indicated with a fearful heart. How would she feel when she heard this David's voice? A voice she must know very well?

'Here.' As Gerard passed the phone to her she took it with a trembling hand. 'It is ringing.'

'Hello? Emma speaking.' The bright voice seemed vaguely familiar but that was all.

'Emma?' She took a deep breath as Gerard picked up some papers from his desk and appeared to be engrossed in their contents. 'It's me. Samantha,' she added uncomfortably.

'Samantha!' The bright voice took on a note of incredulity. 'Since when did you call yourself that? Oh, sorry. . .' There was a clear moment of embarrassment. 'I forgot. Darling, how *are* you? We've all been worried to death here. Can you remember anything yet?'

'Not really.' Kit took a deep breath. 'Look, I know this might seem a strange question but what *do* I call myself, Emma?'

'Kit.' The disembodied voice at the other end of the phone answered immediately. 'You call yourself Kit. You hate Samantha.' There was a moment of awkward silence and then Emma's voice spoke again, her tone tentative. 'Look, Kit, there are a few things I ought to tell you; can you——?' The next second there was a noise almost as though the phone had been dropped and then a man's deep tones took over.

'Kit? It's David. I've practically lived here for the last twenty-four hours waiting for your call.'

'Have you?' The voice was almost a whine with a definite note of complaint in its depths, and it did nothing for her, nothing at all. She glanced across at Gerard, who was quite still behind the desk, his whole attention seemingly concentrated on the papers in front of him. She searched for something, anything, to say. 'How are you, David?'

'How am I?' Now the grievance became more clear. 'How the hell do you think I am, Kit? You disappear on holiday without letting any of us know where you're going and you ask me how I am?' There was the sound of a woman's voice in the background and when David spoke again his tone was more moderate, a note of concern forced into the peevishness. 'Anyway, enough of that. You still can't remember anything, then?'

'Not really.'

'Tough luck, old girl. What happened exactly?' As she explained the circumstances of the accident she waited for the inevitable question, and when it came she took a deep breath before answering.

'Yes, David, I'm still at the home of Gerard Dumont. He has been very kind.' The papers on the desk rustled abruptly but were immediately stilled.

'Oh, yeah?' There followed a pregnant pause. 'And how old is this Good Samaritan, anyway?'

'I really can't go into that now,' she said carefully. 'Perhaps next time I call.'

'Next time?' The snivelling content of his voice rang a bell, but not long enough for her to hold on to the image. 'Emma and I thought you'd be coming back now—there's no need to stay, is there? We've made it clear to the authorities we'll pay for your ticket home if your bag isn't found——'

'There's no need for that, David. Fortunately I'd left my passport and ticket and some other papers in the hotel safe. There couldn't have been much in my bag when it was taken. The police told Mr Dumont everything is in order.'

'Right. When are you coming home then?' he asked immediately.

'Soon.' She took a deep breath. 'I can't be more specific.'

'I miss you, Kit.' He had obviously decided to try another tack. 'I miss you badly, sweetheart. Are you missing me?' There was the sound of Emma's voice in the background and then he spoke again. 'Oh, sorry, silly question in the circumstances. Still, I am your fiancé, Kit. You do remember that much?'

'I suppose so.' Her head was beginning to thud; this was a hundred times worse than she had imagined.

'Then say you love me.' She met the request with a blank silence. 'Please, Kit, even if you can't remember, just say it for me.'

'I can't, David.' The refusal was wrenched out of her. 'But perhaps when I see you?'

'All right.' The word was sulky, and somehow the tone brought that flash of disturbing imagery again, prompting her next words.

'Why wasn't I wearing a ring, David?' There was absolute silence for a long moment at the other end of the phone and she thought for a second they had been disconnected. 'David? Are you there? Did I have a ring?'

'Yes.' His voice was smooth now, smooth and pleasant with the sort of artificial patience one used with a young child who was being unintentionally obtuse. 'But it's at the jeweller's, sweetheart; the stone had become a little loose.'

'Had it?' She wrinkled her forehead slowly as a picture flashed into her mind. It was a diamond ring, a beautiful diamond ring and she was handing it to someone... But the emotion that came with the image was one of disgust and rage, fury even. 'Was it a diamond solitaire?'

'That's it.' His voice was uneasy now and she wondered why.

'Well, this must be costing your Mr Dumont a fortune, Kit, I'd better let you go now.' There was a brief pause. 'I love you, sweetheart.'

'Yes, goodbye, David.' She couldn't, she just *couldn't* say she loved him back. 'I'll ring you with the flight arrangements as soon as I know them.'

She replaced the receiver slowly without looking at the big silent figure sitting at the desk, and turned to walk out of the room, her head whirling. She hadn't felt a thing beyond mild confusion when talking to that person and yet, if what he said was true and there was no reason why he should lie, she had promised to spend the rest of her life with him some time in the past.

She couldn't go on living like this, she just couldn't. There must be something the doctors could do?

'Well?' Gerard's tight cold voice stopped her in her tracks. 'What do they call you, anyway?'

'Kit.' She turned to face him, her eyes stormy at his abrasive tone. 'They call me Kit. Apparently I like it.'

He made a sound of acknowledgement in his throat as he stood up and walked towards her, his eyes narrowed on her pale face. 'It would seem my "kitten" is not too far removed from what you like after all?' She said nothing, sensing a thick, angry force vibrating from the taut body that was being held in check by an iron will. 'But of course it is not David who is calling you that, is it?' he said flatly as she continued to face him. 'That would obviously make a difference.'

'I suppose so.' She shrugged carefully, uncertain of how to react.

'You suppose so.' He nodded slowly. 'And the oh, so concerned, ever-attentive David? Has he explained why he was not on the first plane out here when he heard about your accident?'

'What?' She stared at him in confusion.

'Do not tell me the thought had not occurred to you?' he asked coolly.

'No, it hadn't.' The ring of honesty in her voice was so obviously genuine he had to believe her.

'You mean to tell me that this kind of lukewarm emotion that the man is displaying is satisfactory to you?' he asked, incredulously. 'I do not believe it.'

'I don't know about being satisfactory,' she said slowly as her brow wrinkled as she searched for words to explain what she was feeling. 'I think it's just that I've always been used to being on my own, sorting out my own problems.' She stared at him as the concept became a firm conviction. 'I don't expect anyone to take care of me,' she finished quietly, 'I don't think they ever have.'

'*Mon dieu*...' He took her wrists in a biting grip, his face suddenly dark with a fierce emotion he couldn't hide. 'You should expect it! Hell...' He shook her slightly, his eyes fiery. 'And you expect me to let you leave to go back to that? There is something wrong here, something very wrong.'

'I have David.' Why she said it she didn't know because it was the very worst thing possible.

'David?' The dark face was suddenly icy, thick brows lifting in insultingly cool contradiction. 'Oh, but of course, the English David.' In the split-second before his mouth came down hard on hers she felt pure fear, and then a rush of harsh pleasure drove every other emotion out of her mind. Kit was crushed against the hardness of his body as his mouth became more demanding, a low growling sound in his throat as he ravaged hers before returning to her open lips, his strong hands running over her body and leaving fire wherever they touched.

'And your David?' he asked harshly as he raised his head briefly, his eyes glittering. 'Do you think he can make you feel like this, respond to him like this?'

'I don't know,' she moaned softly as the hard driving pressure of his mouth sent her into a whirlwind of sensual pleasure.

'Well, I do.' He held her from him, his breathing ragged. 'You would not forget *me* so easily, kitten; you would not forget me at all.'

'I would——'

'Like hell,' he said softly, his eyes a brilliant unnerving gold and his mouth cruel. 'Like hell, kitten. I am not letting you go.'

As she wrenched herself from him and ran from the room she heard him say her name once before she reached the stairs, but continued her headlong dash until she reached the sanctuary of her room to fall breathless and shaking on to the bed.

What did he want from her? The thought mocked her as soon as it formed. She knew what he *wanted*! She flicked on the bedside lamp and padded across to the long full-length mirror on the other side of the room dazedly. But why? What was it that attracted him? She wasn't beautiful, she knew she wasn't beautiful, and the idea that he intended to enjoy a brief affair because she was available just didn't hold water the more she thought about it. She had seen how he drew every female eye today, seen it and hated it. He would have no problem in clicking his fingers and having every woman within a fifty mile radius come running!

It could only be that he thought she was playing hard to get, that he was enjoying the chase, the breaking down of her defences, she thought wearily. That had to be it. She crossed the room and flung herself on to the bed, her head pounding and her chest tight with unshed tears. And she hated him for it, she did. She ground her teeth in an agony of pain. *She did*.

She lay for long minutes in the shadowed cool room, determined not to cry, eventually rousing herself as a soft timid knock sounded at the closed door. She padded across and opened it without speaking to see Halima standing on the threshold, a loaded tray in her hands. 'You like eat here?' the Moroccan woman asked hesitantly. 'I bring, yes?'

'Thank you, Halima.' As Kit stood aside for the other woman to enter she flicked on the light switch at the side of the door to add to the dim light from the bedside lamp, and as Halima walked past her Kit couldn't stop a gasp of shock at the huge bruise marring all one side of Halima's pretty face. 'Halima?' She caught the woman's arm, causing her to turn to face her fully. 'What on earth have you done?'

'I no understand.' Halima's eyes dropped from hers to face the floor. 'You eat, yes?'

'Blow the food.' She took the tray quickly, placing it on the bed. 'Your face, Halima?' She touched her own cheek in explanation. 'What have you done?'

'I fall.' Still the other woman didn't raise her eyes. 'I go now.'

'You fell?' There was something wrong here. As the hairs on the back of Kit's neck rose in an eerie shiver she had the bizarre feeling she had been in this situation before, had the same conversation. 'How, where?'

'I no understand.' As Halima's soft brown eyes rose to look into hers Kit's heart pounded at the mute appeal in their liquid depths. Halima understood all right but there was something stopping her speaking. 'I go now.'

'Please, Halima.' Kit took her arm as she made to leave. 'How did this happen?' Halima didn't fall. The knowledge was uncanny but unmistakable and, as the thought solidified, Kit found herself beginning to tremble. She knew without a doubt Halima hadn't fallen. Someone had done this to her, hurt her, but how did Kit know that?

'I go.' This time Kit didn't stop her, but as the door closed she stood for a long time staring into space, icy little trickles of fear running up and down her spine. She had to remember, this was important. *She had to*. She drove her clenched fists against the side of her head in frustrated pain as her mind refused to give up its secret. This was the key to her amnesia here in her hand, but how did she find the door it fitted?

CHAPTER SIX

THE call for breakfast came at the sedate time of nine o'clock the next morning and Kit was amazed to find she had slept the night away. She hadn't expected to, she reflected ruefully as she luxuriated under the smooth warm flow of the shower, but the mental and physical exhaustion that had had her in its grip had acted as nature's sedative. Nevertheless, her stomach was churning unpleasantly when she walked nervously into the sunny breakfast-room only to find it empty. She reprimanded herself instantly for the thud of disappointment.

'Hi...' Colette joined her a moment later, the brilliant copper hair secured in a high ponytail on the top of her head and her small, slim body clothed in a loose flowing caftan. 'You were early birds yesterday.' The slanted green eyes rested briefly on Kit's warm face. 'Enjoy the day out?'

'Yes, thank you.' Kit aimed for a non-committal smile. 'Tiring, though.'

'I bet.' Colette nodded understandingly. 'Well, you're off the hook today. Gerard's already left for the new part of Marrakesh to sort out some business problems and he'll be away all day. He's told me to entertain you in his absence, if that's all right?' She helped herself to a huge bowlful of fruit as she chatted, her manner relaxed.

Obviously Gerard hadn't confided their difficulties to his sister, Kit thought warily, but then
he probably looked on her as a transient house
guest who would soon be gone after barely
causing a ripple in their well-ordered lives. That
being the case, why should he even bother to
mention her to Colette? The thought was incredibly depressing, but her concern for Halima,
which had been present since awakening, was
stronger, and now she seized the opportunity
while Colette was by herself to speak to her about
it.

'Colette?' She reached for the coffee-pot,
forcing herself to appear cool and relaxed.
'Halima had a big bruise on her face yesterday.
Do you know how it happened?'

'Did she?' Colette looked up in surprise. 'Well,
she was fine in the evening before you came back
although her youngest had been playing up a
little, stomach-ache I think. Perhaps she fell?'

'That's what she said.' Kit looked straight into
Colette's lovely green eyes. 'But I don't believe
her.'

'Don't you?' Colette's surprise deepened. 'Why
on earth not? Surely she wouldn't lie about
something like that? An accident is an accident,
after all.'

'If it was an accident,' Kit said grimly.

'What do you mean?' Colette straightened in
her seat, spoon poised midway to her mouth.
'Are you saying someone hurt her? But that's
ridiculous, who?'

'You say she was all right earlier?' Kit asked slowly.

'Absolutely fine.' Colette nodded positively. 'I had an early dinner, cold meat and salad as we didn't know what time you and Gerard would be back, and then Claude called to pick me up. She was fine then, absolutely fine.'

And then she had come home with Gerard. And they had argued. And he had been white with rage. But he wouldn't. He wouldn't, would he? She shook away the black thoughts, unable to face what she was thinking. 'Perhaps she did fall, then.' She forced a strained smile and reached for her cup. 'She must have.'

The two women spent the day in the shady comfort of the courtyard, alternating between spurts of conversation and long lazy silences. Colette was easy to be with, Kit discovered, the very antithesis of Gerard in fact, and she found herself warming to his sister with each hour that passed. The mood of relaxed serenity came to an abrupt end after a phone call to Colette towards evening time.

'That was Gerard.' Colette smiled as she walked back to the two sun-loungers set under the dappled shade of a huge African fern. 'He had lunch with Claude apparently, and has offered to take us all out tonight. We're to be ready for seven.'

'Oh.' Kit stared at her as a little thrill of apprehension reared its head. Was it coincidence that Gerard had had lunch with Colette's fiancé or did he think that by inviting the other two along she would find it impossible to refuse to accompany him? 'Does he often lunch with Claude?'

'Fairly often,' Colette said blithely as she settled herself comfortably on the warm lounger. 'They do a lot of business together; it was through Gerard that I met Claude.'

'I see.' So this could well be a business angle and nothing to do with her at all. She shook herself mentally for letting her imagination run away with her. She should have known she wasn't that important to him after all.

'Gerard asked if you'd remembered anything. You haven't, have you?' The lovely green eyes glanced her way as Kit shook her head slowly.

'No, not really, just the odd thought that comes and goes.'

'Right.' Colette nodded as she settled herself back and shut her eyes. 'Well, ten more minutes and then I guess we'd better get ready. The restaurant Gerard mentioned is an old Moorish palace and there's a good floor show. It's mainly for the tourists of course, but the folk dancing and music is excellent and Gerard thought you might like it.'

Colette meant nothing by it, Kit knew that, but somehow the other girl's words emphasised her fleeting, transitory influence in their lives more than anything else could have done. She *was* just a tourist after all, she told herself bleakly, and an incompetent if not downright pathetic one at that. What would have happened to her if Gerard hadn't stepped in and taken over as he had? She felt a little trickle of icy foreboding run down her spine in spite of the warmth of the day. And what would happen to her now he had?

She found it difficult consciously to titivate her appearance as she got ready for dinner later that evening. Somehow making the best of herself didn't come naturally at all and she wondered why, applying just a light touch of brown eye-shadow on her eyelids and a touch of mascara on the long thick lashes that shaded her eyes, and then feeling distinctly uneasy at the effect as her eyes widened and darkened, turning into lu-minous black pools. She was just thinking about washing the make-up off and keeping her skin bare of all embellishment as usual when Colette entered the room after a cursory knock.

'Nearly ready?' The other girl was stunning in a black catsuit of raw silk that showed her lithe, neat body off to perfection, the copper hair loose and flowing in soft curls and waves to her shoulders and her eyes outlined in a vivid green that should have looked outragreous and didn't. 'Aren't you going to wear any make-up?'

'I have.' Kit motioned to her eyes awkwardly. 'But I think I'll wash it off, it doesn't suit me.'

'Rubbish.' Just for a second the likeness to Gerard was overwhelming. 'You could get away with heaps more with that short bob, it em-phasises your marvellous bone-structure and lovely eyes, but you don't make the most of them. Here...' She took a make-up brush from the dressing-table and dipped it in a pot of pearly powder carefully. 'Just the barest touch across

your cheekbones to highlight them.' She stood
back to admire the effect, her eyes narrowed.
'And a little more eyeshadow with just a touch
underneath your eyes too. Try this lipstick—I
think dark plum is your colour.'

Before Kit could object to the new face staring
back at her, a disturbingly beautiful face,
Colette's eyes moved to the dress Kit had chosen
for the evening that was lying across the bed, a
subdued little number in pale grey cotton with
long sleeves and a modest neckline. 'You aren't
going to wear that?' The other girl's eyes were
frankly horrified.

'Isn't it right for where we're going?' Kit asked
anxiously.

'No way.' Colette dismissed the dress with a
disgusted wave of her hand. 'That's fine for lunch
in town but this is an evening out, for goodness'
sake. I know just the thing!' She reappeared from
the walk-in wardrobe a moment later with a short
crimson cocktail dress in crushed velvet, the dark
wine material throwing Kit's bare neck and arms
into pale relief as Colette held the dress against
her chest briefly. 'That's your colour, that's definitely your colour,' she said slowly, her voice satisfied. 'Look what it does to your hair. I never
knew it had so much red in it.'

'Look, I don't think——'

Colette waved her objections away without
even speaking as she handed Kit the dress. 'Put
it on.' As Kit hesitated Colette glanced at her
watch. 'We're late, Kit, put it *on*.'

'But——'

'No buts.' Colette's eyes narrowed again when the sleeveless dress was in place, the rounded neck wonderfully flattering against Kit's flawless creamy skin. 'You want something ... I know.' She raced out of the room only to return thirty seconds later with a long pair of lacy gold earrings in her hand. 'Take those studs out of your ears and put these on,' she said commandingly before stepping back, her head on one side, to admire the overall effect. 'You look stunning.' She shook her head slowly. 'Gerard's going to blow a fuse.'

'Colette!' But Kit was laughing, a sudden feeling of recklessness pervading her whole system. She'd be gone from this place soon and would never see him again. Maybe, just maybe, he might remember her as she looked now if he ever thought about her at all? And somehow, although she knew it was crazy, pointless, it was suddenly desperately important that he did think of her now and again.

'Come on.' Colette took her arm firmly as they left the bedroom as though sensing her nervousness. 'Claude's waiting downstairs. Gerard got delayed with some important business deal but he's home now and will be down shortly.'

He was down already. Both men were sitting waiting in the huge hall as the two women descended the stairs, and as Gerard glanced up and saw her the expression on his handsome face stopped Kit's heart. She glanced away from the naked wonder, the hot and hungry desire that had lit the cold aristocratic face from within, with a feeling of panic gripping her throat. She shouldn't have dressed up, shouldn't have let Colette experiment like this. She didn't want to attract him, she didn't want him to want her, she didn't...

'Kit.' She raised her eyes helplessly to the brilliant gold of his. 'You have taken my breath away.' He wasn't smiling. 'You look quite beautiful.'

'She was going to wear an old grey thing.' Colette was prattling away at her side as Claude moved forward waiting to be introduced, but Gerard seemed blind and deaf to anyone else, his eyes fixed on her hot face as he moved to take her arm in his. 'But that looks so much better, don't you think?' She nudged Gerard sharply as he still didn't speak. 'Are you going to introduce Claude to Kit, then?'

'Of course.' Suddenly the fire was banked down as he noticed the frantic thudding of her pulse against the creamy smoothness of her skin, the alarm she was trying to hide. 'How remiss of me.'

It took the taxi fifteen minutes to reach the restaurant where Gerard had booked the meal and for the whole time Kit was as tense as a bowstring. Gerard was devastatingly cool and enigmatic in an expertly cut light grey suit which, when teamed with the old gold silk shirt and tie he wore so casually, seemed to accentuate the broad shoulders and hard-planed muscled body until she could hardly breathe. She glanced at him under her eyelashes as they passed through

an open gate into an avenue of orange trees, ger-
aniums and datura towards a massive building in
the distance. The air of authority, of command,
was starkly clear even when as now he was relaxed and informal, and it unnerved her. She took
a long deep hidden breath. More than a little.
She didn't like his strength and power and arrogant masculinity, she found it threatening. She
blinked as the cool gaze turned to her, trying to
veil her eyes from that razor-sharp male mind.

'You are very thoughtful.' The light, easy tone
would have sounded mildly teasing to anyone
else, but there was something burning deep in the
light brown gaze that told her he had sensed her
animosity and was annoyed by it.

'Not really.' She turned her gaze out of the
window, glad of the other two's presence in the
car. 'Is this the restaurant?' she asked carefully,
her voice bland.

'Yes.' As the taxi stopped at the foot of high
marbled steps and they alighted into the warm,
fragrant night air, Gerard took her arm, slipping
it through his before she could object. 'You're
with me.' His voice was very low and soft in her
ear. 'Whether you like it or not, OK?'

'I don't know what you mean.' She tried to
swing round to face him but his arm tightened
like steel, forcing her to remain at his side.

'You know exactly what I mean,' he said, still
in the same low voice. 'He is in England and I
am here and I'm damned if I will play second
fiddle tonight. You are with me, Kit. Reconcile
yourself to the fact.' There was a coldness in his

voice that chilled her blood, but the next moment
the other two had joined them and they walked
up the steps as an apparently relaxed and ani-
mated foursome, although his grip on her arm
felt as though it was crushing her bones.

The old palace was in Andalusian style, built
round a patio crowded with fountains and plants,
and once through the door they walked along a
passageway lined with ancient wooden doors
behind which the noise and activity suggested the
interiors had been made into one gigantic kitchen.
The actual restaurant was on the first floor in
what had obviously been the main reception-
room in years gone by, its mellowed walls lined
with weapons below cedar-wood lintels carved
with Kufic script and a pine-cone design, and
although the vast room was already nearly full
the whole atmosphere was one of relaxed bene-
volence and airy space. One panel at the far end
of the room was hung with Berber carpets from
the Middle and High Atlas mountains, the pre-
dominant colours of dark red and gold giving
life and brightness to balance the other, more
sombre, walls. The main central part of the huge
wall that overlooked the plant-filled patio was a
line of delicate stucco arches, the upper portions
open to the air and light and the bottom patterned glass, and it was to a table in this prime
position that Gerard led them, the waiter bobbing
along at his side.

'Would you like me to order for you?' Gerard
asked quietly a moment or two later as she stared

nonplussed at the menu written in several languages, not one of which was English.

'Please.' She looked up to smile her thanks but saw he was looking elsewhere, the gold gaze trained on a party of eight or more people who had just entered the restaurant at the far end of the room. Almost as though his presence drew her glance, one woman, a little taller and certainly more extravagantly beautiful than the rest, turned her dark head their way, the lovely almond-shaped eyes widening and brightening as she caught sight of Gerard. She raised one slim arm in acknowledgement of Gerard's nod before following the others to a table on the other side of the room, turning her head once or twice more in their direction before she was finally seated.

'Some friends of ours,' Gerard explained briefly as his narrowed eyes returned abruptly to Kit's purposely blank face. She was saved the necessity of a reply by Colette waving to the group in her turn before turning and giving Kit a little breakdown on each one.

'And the woman in the green dress is Zita,' Colette finished quietly as her gaze rested on the siren who had waved to Gerard. 'She'll probably come over in a minute.'

'Guaranteed.' Claude's voice was dry. Gerard said nothing, his eyes veiled and distant as they met hers. Kit didn't ask why, she had the feeling she already knew.

Sure enough, within five minutes Zita arrived at their table and with a sinking heart Kit saw the other woman was even more beautiful close

to. Black almond-shaped eyes set in a pearly
smooth skin, full red lips that reposed in an inviting pout, long sleek black hair coiled into an
elegant braid on the top of her head... She really
was something. And her figure! High full breasts,
tiny waist and the longest legs Kit had ever seen
off a racehorse. 'Gerard...' The perfect lips
smiled alluringly. '*Comment vas-tu?*' And she
spoke French. Kit almost shut her eyes in desperation. She should have known.

'I am fine, Zita.' Gerard and Claude had stood
up at her approach and he now indicated Kit with
a wave of his hand. 'This is Kit, who is staying
at Del Mahari at the moment. Kit, meet Zita.'

'How do you do?' Even as Kit spoke she knew
the relationship between them. The way Zita's
smooth slender hand rested possessively on
Gerard's arm, the faintly whimsical twist to the
beautiful mouth, the way her body inclined just
the slightest towards his... The body language
said it all. They had been, or were, intimate.
There could be no doubt about it.

'This is nice, that you stay with Gerard? You
are on the holiday perhaps?' The words were
polite and spoken in a husky, heavily accented
voice that was pure magic to any man within
earshot.

'Yes.' Kit found she could smile quite naturally and talk easily even as her mind func-
tioned on a different plane altogether. It was
almost as though she was used to saying one thing
and thinking another. 'But I'll be leaving shortly.'

'This is sad.' Zita didn't look sad, Kit thought tightly. In fact the black eyes had lit up at the knowledge. 'You maybe come back again?'

'I doubt it.' As the other woman nodded graciously and turned to speak briefly with Colette and Claude before weaving her way back through the tables, Kit found her hands were clenched into tight fists under the table and forced herself to ease her fingers loose, stroking the tightness out of her knuckles slowly.

'She's very beautiful.' She spoke to the table generally but it was Colette who replied, Gerard sitting in silence, his narrowed eyes watching her every expression.

'Yes, brains as well as beauty too. She's a doctor, a good one I understand.'

'Oh, yes?' Don't react, don't show any feeling at all, she told herself grimly as her stomach turned over. 'Have you known her long?' she asked calmly.

'We grew up together.' Now it was Gerard who spoke. 'Her parents were great friends of mine.' He smiled a cool smile. 'I understand we were inseparable until school age. Zita was sent away to a private school in Switzerland and then university, after which she carved out a first-class career.'

As the waiter appeared at their table the talk turned to food but, although Kit continued to chat and socialise normally, inside she felt raw. And she had thought her pathetic little display tonight would make him remember her? Her mouth twisted bitterly. With women like that

around? She was a fool, such a fool. Why hadn't
she dressed as she had wanted to tonight? At least
then she wouldn't be feeling quite so much like
a fish out of water.

The meal was delicious, course after course including Morocco's national dish, *couscous*,
moistened by a thin piquant sauce that was quite
mouth-watering, but Kit could have been eating
sawdust for all it registered on her taste-buds. She
was aware of each movement Zita made, every
time she glanced over in their direction, her black
eyes languorous and warm as they lingered on
Gerard's face in profile to her. Gerard seemed
oblivious of the other woman's attention as he
chatted lazily, his dry wit and cynical repartee
drawing many a chuckle from Claude and
laughter from the women, although Kit had never
felt less like laughing. And he knew she was
acting. She glanced at him once as she smiled
dutifully at some pleasantry. The gold eyes were
icy.

The floor show began as they were eating
dessert and Kit had to admit it was breathtaking,
from the beautifully dressed folk dancers in their
robes of gold and red to the acrobats who whirled
and twisted in an incredibly small space without
putting a foot wrong. She tried to concentrate,
reminding herself that soon all this would be a
distant memory, but the sense of outrage and hurt
was growing stronger although she was at a loss
to understand why. She had no right to feel anything at all where he was concerned. She was engaged to be married, for goodness' sake, and his

liaisons were his own affair. He wasn't flirting
with Zita, in fact after that first acknowledgement he hadn't glanced at her once, so there was
no justification for this bitterness that was filling
her mouth with bile. But it didn't help. All the
cold logic didn't help.

They sat drinking the thick black coffee the
Moroccans favoured as the floor show finished
and the space was cleared for dancing. A small
band of three musicians appeared to one side of
the floor, and almost the moment they began
playing Zita and a tall dark-haired man who was
obviously her partner for the evening made their
way across the room to their side. He was very
handsome, Kit noted dispassionately as the two
drew near, tall, muscular, with the sort of Eastern
good looks that sent European women wild.

'I would like you to meet Salem.' Zita was
speaking directly to Gerard as she stood with her
hand slipped casually through the other man's
arm. 'He's a consultant at the hospital.'

She wants him to be jealous, Kit thought
numbly. It was obvious, so obvious that as Kit
turned slightly and caught Claude's eye he winked
very slowly and then shrugged, his eyes wicked.
She smiled back in return, betraying none of the
emotion that was twisting her insides into a coiled
spring, and watched Gerard as he rose to shake
hands gravely with the other man, his face
pleasant but reserved. As they all began to chat
generally, Zita somehow managed to be leaning
lightly against Gerard's shoulder, her high full
breasts pressed against his body and a few inches

of space between her and Salem now. If Salem
noticed the manoeuvre he didn't seem to mind
and after a few, and to Kit excruciatingly long,
minutes had crept by he surprised her by leaning
forward and taking her hand in his.

'Kit? This is a very unusual name.' He smiled,
showing strong white teeth. 'Would you care to
dance?'

'What a good idea.' Zita's swift response had
Kit thinking all this was pre-arranged. 'You dance
with me, Gerard, yes?'

'Kit has not been well; I don't think——'

She interrupted Gerard's voice with her own,
hurt pride making her eyes brilliant as she rose.
Let him dance with Zita, let him do anything he
wanted to! She didn't care, she did *not* care.

'I'd love to.' As Salem's hand centred in the
small of her back and they began to walk to the
dance floor she was conscious of the other two
following them a step or two behind, hearing
Zita's low throaty giggle with a tightening of every
muscle in her body.

One or two other couples had already taken
the floor, and as they reached the small raised
area the tempo of music changed from a lively
beat sound to a soft dreamy ballad. Salem was
very circumspect, holding her close but not too
close and engaging in conversation as they drifted
round. In any other circumstances she might have
been bowled over by him, she reflected silently
as she smiled up into his undeniably handsome
face, but with Zita draped over Gerard like some
sort of fur collar just a yard or two away the only

emotion she was feeling was one of pure undiluted rage. Zita's dress was cut just low enough to show off her ample bosom to its full advantage while still remaining in the bounds of propriety, and her smooth brown arms were linked round Gerard's neck in a way that reaffirmed all Kit's earlier suspicions. They knew each other well, very well.

'Have you known Gerard long?' Salem was still valiantly trying to pretend that the situation was normal, but as her eyes left the other couple and returned to his she saw his own had darkened, whether with anger or hurt she wasn't sure.

'No, just a week or so.' She forced a polite smile to her stiff lips as Zita's throaty giggle snaked back to them again. 'Have you known Zita long?'

'Too long.' The answer wasn't quite what she expected, and as she raised enquiring eyebrows he smiled with more than a touch of bitterness. 'I've always been around, you know? Like the little puppy accepting crumbs from the rich man's table? I think tonight was the first time I understood why I have been allowed into her bed but not her heart.'

His frankness left her struggling for an appropriate reply, and as he glanced down into her troubled face his own softened slightly, a wry smile touching the corners of his hard firm mouth. 'I am sorry, English Kit, that was not fair. The problem is mine and not yours. I think your Gerard is very fond of you.'

'Do you?' She raised disbelieving eyebrows and now it was her face that was bitter. 'Let's put it this way: if you could have me or Zita, would there be any contest?'

He stopped dead, staring at her for endless seconds before drawing her more closely against him, his chin resting in the soft silk of her hair. She caught sight of Gerard's face for one moment and the expression darkening his countenance brought momentary, if acrid, satisfaction. 'Yes, there would,' he said softly, 'and your Gerard is no fool. You do not trust him?'

'Trust him?' She drew back slightly and rested her hands on his broad chest as she stared up into the hard male face. Zita was a fool. This was a good man. 'No, I don't suppose I do.' She shook her head slightly as the ballad finished. 'Could we go back to our table? I need to powder my nose.'

'Of course.' As they passed the other couple Zita had pulled Gerard's head down to meet hers as she whispered something in his ear, and the hot acid rage that flooded Kit's system enabled her to march through the tables and collect her bag from under her seat on legs that were rock-steady. She was out of the massive arched doorway at the opposite end of the room to the entrance before Colette could offer to join her, but rather than enter the ladies' powder-room at one side of the winding iron staircase she ran down the narrow steps and out into the dimly lit patio they had overlooked from their table during dinner, where one or two couples were sitting quietly enjoying an after-dinner drink in the un-usually beautiful surroundings.

She found a quiet spot and sank down on to a convenient, beautifully carved stone seat beside a sparkling fountain, her thoughts in turmoil. She had to be quiet and think. She needed——

'Kit?' She heard Gerard's cool voice with a feeling of doom. She didn't want to talk to him now when she was angry and hurt and working purely on emotion. She needed to get control of herself, probe why Zita's behaviour had upset her so badly. 'Is anything wrong?'

'Wrong?' She smiled brightly, her voice brittle. 'Why should there be anything wrong, Gerard?'

'That is what I am asking you.' He sat down beside her, stretching his long legs out in front of him and leaning back against the stone seat with a hard sigh. 'Why have you come out here?'

'Because I wanted to.' The rage was taking over now, which was the last thing she wanted, but he was so damn cool, so aloof, so detached. 'I wasn't aware I had to ask your permission.'

'Then that was your first mistake.' The arrogant audacity brought her head snapping up to meet his, her eyes glittering with fury. 'I am responsible for your welfare and you are not . . . well at the moment.'

'I am perfectly well.' She glared at him angrily. 'If you mean I can't remember anything, then say so.'

'All right.' His voice was sharper now. 'That is exactly what I mean. I made myself accountable for your safety and until you are yourself——'

'Myself?' she hissed savagely with a bitter little laugh. 'I wouldn't recognise what "myself" is if it rose up and bit me! But a temporary loss of memory doesn't make me a complete idiot into the bargain.'

'Meaning?' he asked coldly, his voice dry.

'Meaning you and Florence Nightingale in there,' she bit back tightly. 'I would have thought even you would have more sensitivity than to bring me here knowing she'd be around. What are you looking for anyway, a harem?'

'Even me?' He ignored the rest of the accusation as his mouth thinned and the gold-brown eyes narrowed into dark slits.

'Yes, even you.' She was facing him now, half turned on the seat with her body bent slightly forward as though she were preparing to pounce. 'Deny it. Deny you've slept with her.'

'Why would I do a thing like that?' In contrast to her flushed face and burning rage he was icy cool, a veritable block of stone.

'You have, then, you admit it?' She felt the blood in her veins run cold.

'It's not something I have to "admit",' he said with frosty contempt. 'Zita and I were more than friends once, a long time ago, but it is in the past and no concern of yours. Nothing can be gained from pursuing this conversation, so I suggest we return to the others and, just to set the record straight, I had no idea Zita and Salem would be here tonight.'

'Really!' The word was tantamount to calling him a liar, and now he gripped her arm tightly as he jerked her to her feet, his eyes murderous.

'Yes, really. Now if you are finished we will return.'

'Let go of me, Gerard,' she hissed quietly, her voice trembling with outrage. 'I won't be man-handled by you. You might get away with it with those unfortunate enough to have to put up with it, like Halima, but not——'

'I beg your pardon?' She realised too late what the little demon of jealousy had led her to. How could she have said that? she thought in stunned terror, the look on his face draining her anger and leaving her barely able to stand. 'Explain yourself.'

'I didn't mean...' Her voice faded as she searched desperately for a way of escape, but there was none.

'Colette told me of your conversation this morning,' he said icily as he slowly, and very pointedly, removed his hand from her arm. 'Do I take it you have decided that I am the per-petrator of Halima's misfortune?'

There was nothing she could say. She didn't believe it, not really, but the words had been a weapon that she had used to deadly effect and she wished with all her heart that she could have revoked them. It had been cruel and vicious and she was disgusted with herself, but seeing him with Zita like that had done something to her she would never have believed. But that was no excuse. She could offer him no excuse. She stared

at him dumbly, her eyes enormous in the
whiteness of her face.

'Right at this moment I would like to whip you
to within an inch of your life,' he said brutally,
his voice harsh and his face bitter, 'but that would
only give credibility to the low opinion you have
of me. For what it's worth, I have never raised
a hand in anger to any woman in my life and
quite honestly I do not care if you believe that
or not.' He drew himself up and away from her
as though she were untouchable. 'And no doubt
you do not.' Dark angry colour had flared across
the high cheekbones, the tawny brown hair and
gold eyes alive and glowing from the muted light
overhead that threw the contours of his face into
savage shadow. 'Hell . . .' His eyes raked her fer-
ociously like a furious wild animal about to
strike. 'What the hell am I bothering for,
anyway? I don't need this.'

'Gerard, I'm sorry. I didn't mean——'

He cut off her voice with a savage gesture of
his hand, his eyes glittering with fire. 'You are
sorry? *Sorry*?' He gave a harsh bark of a laugh
that caused her to flinch. 'Till when? Till the next
time? Do you think I am not aware that every
time I reach for you you cower away like a
frightened doe? Every time I look at you those
big grey eyes are wary and afraid with something
approaching hate darkening their depths——'

'No!' She shook her head desperately. 'I don't
hate you.'

'Yes, you do.' He nodded wearily. 'The more
so because of this attraction between us that you

do not like but cannot control. There is something in me that you cannot tolerate, Kit, you know it.' She stared at him dumbly, shocked by his perceptiveness. 'You imagine that I can illtreat Halima, behave like some sort of monster in private and then put on another face for the world. That is it, isn't it, Kit? You do not trust me at all. Well? Do you?' She couldn't answer, her head whirling and her stomach churning as she tried to formulate the confused darkness inside her. She didn't feel like that about him and yet . . . and yet she did. It was almost as though something was warning her, threatening her every time she was with him and yet she wanted, needed, to be with him too. It was crazy, mad. If she couldn't explain it to herself, how could she possibly expect him to understand?

'I thought I could make you understand if you came to Del Mahari, that with time you would see——' He stopped abruptly.

'See?' she asked brokenly.

'It doesn't matter.' He stared at her bitterly. 'This revulsion, hate that you have for me is too deep, too fierce.'

'You want me to leave?' She forced the words out through the blockage in her throat and it was only as she spoke that she realised how much she wanted to stay, and the depth of her desire was frightening. 'I can go tomorrow.'

'You will stay until I return to Casablanca in a week's time,' he said icily and as he withdrew from her both in body and spirit she realised he had misunderstood her words, that he had thought she was asking to go.

This wasn't about Zita. As she continued to sit in the quiet of the beautiful surroundings, the lap of water from the fountain murmuring in the softness, she struggled to make some sense of the torment. Zita had merely been the catalyst in letting the poison out, but the results had been devastating. He was finished with her, the cold emptiness in those narrow gold eyes had said it all. She might be leaving in a week's time but as far as he was concerned the farewells had already been said.

CHAPTER SEVEN

THE rest of the evening and the drive back to Del Mahari was an unmitigated nightmare from which there was no awakening. Once back at the house Kit disappeared to her room after a cursory goodnight to a clearly troubled Colette and her icily silent brother, reliving the whole disastrous night over and over again in her mind as she prepared for bed until she thought she would go mad.

Zita's party had left shortly after her return to the restaurant to go on to a party of one of the hospital staff, to which Zita had invited them and Gerard had grimly refused. For the remainder of the evening she and Gerard had sat in a sharp splintered silence watching Colette and Claude wound round each other on the dance floor. She had made one attempt to talk to him and had been rebuffed so savagely that she hadn't tried again.

After an hour of tossing and turning and ranting and raving against herself, him and the whole of life in general, she acknowledged defeat and decided to creep downstairs in search of a hot drink. She knew where the kitchen was, although as yet she had not entered it, but with the rest of the household asleep she decided that a mug of warm milk and a quiet seat in the cool of the shadowed courtyard were just what her bruised mind needed. She couldn't stay in her room alone for one more minute anyway; the goblins of fear and panic and regret were going to send her hysterical if she didn't break their vicious circle.

Pulling a light robe over her wafer-thin nightie, she opened the door warily, peering out into the silent landing beyond for a moment before treading quietly across the stained wooden floor and walking to the top of the stairs. The house was eerily unfamiliar in the grey gloom of the night, but such was her despair and hopelessness that she could have been confronted by the devil himself and not turned a hair. The ache in her chest was a physical pain that took her breath away, compounded of so many emotions that she would have found it impossible to name just one.

On reaching the ground floor she found the kitchen without difficulty and made herself a warm drink from the cartons of goat's milk in the massive, sparkling clean refrigerator. Before she left, she glanced round the enormous immaculate room which was filled with every modern convenience known to man. He was wealthy, enormously, fabulously wealthy and handsome, successful, intelligent into the bargain. She supposed she ought to feel flattered that he had noticed her at all in the biological sense even if it was as a temporary diversion, but she didn't. She felt crushed and wretched and more alone than she had ever dreamt it was possible to feel.

'You are *not* going to cry,' she told herself fiercely as the rush of tears at the back of her lids made her eyes sting. 'You are going to get over this, find out who you really are and start living the rest of your life. This was just a temporary refuge, he told you that.' She brushed across her eyes angrily with the back of her hand. And this fiancé in England. No one could *make* her marry him if she didn't want to, and she was suddenly absolutely sure she didn't. The knowledge relaxed something deep in her being. Just hearing that petulant male voice on the telephone had told her that.

She had just padded silently down the steps into the courtyard, making for a low wooden bench seat built in a circular design round one of the largest fountains, when a slight movement on the periphery of her vision brought her heart thudding into her mouth. She froze, moving silently into the shadows as she peered through the semi-gloom of the warm tropical night, acutely aware of her lack of clothing.

'Convince me I am not as drunk as I would like to be and you are not an apparition.' Gerard's voice didn't sound at all intoxicated. In fact it sounded lazy, sardonic and full of a derisive cool mockery that seared into her tissues like fire considering the circumstances. How dared he be so in control, so off-hand, so damn *imperturbable* when she was falling apart? None of this had really affected him at all. He wasn't real, he just wasn't real.

'I didn't think anyone would still be up,' she
said tightly without moving, pulling the robe
more firmly over her breasts with her free hand.

'Oh, I am up, Kit. I am definitely up.' He rose
from the very seat she had been making for and,
as her eyes adjusted to the darkness, she saw a
bottle of whisky on the floor, half full, with an
empty glass beside it. 'Won't you join me?' He
waved one hand in an expansive gesture that
made her realise he had changed since they had
returned and was dressed in the Arab clothes of
that first night. She stood hesitating, half hidden
under the protection of an overhanging palm,
only to jump violently as his voice stabbed
through the air like a knife, all pretence of non-
chalance gone. 'I am not going to rape you,
woman; there is no need to look at me like that.'
He reached her side with a few swift steps and
she found she was quite unable to move although
every instinct urged flight. 'You obviously came
out here to sit,' he said grimly, 'so sit.' There was
no way her legs were going to carry her over to
the seat he had just vacated, so rather than in-
flame him still more she sank down on to a small
stone wall enclosing a mass of sweet smelling
roses, their perfume heavy in the still night air.

'Do you still want me, Kit, physically I mean?'
he asked after a full minute had ticked away in
painful scrutiny. He was standing looking down
at her from his great height, legs slightly apart
and hands on hips for all the world like some
powerful sheikh safe in the protection of his own
little world where his authority and influence were

law. 'You wanted me that day in the mountains, do you remember?'

Did she remember? She prayed that the extent of her wanting wasn't written on her face. 'I don't think this is going to get us anywhere——'

He laughed harshly, sitting down on the wall next to her so the warm spicy male smell of him enveloped her and his thigh was pressed close to hers. She could feel herself begin to tremble as her pulse began jumping like a yo-yo. He was different tonight somehow; it was as though a brake that had always been applied before had suddenly been lifted. 'Well, the softly-softly approach sure as hell didn't win any bouquets, did it?' The bleak, cynical tone of voice hurt her and she turned to look at him to find his eyes narrowed on her face. She tried to veil her gaze but it was too late, she found herself melting into the rich golden brown that circled jet-black centres over which his heavy, thick black lashes curled in an almost feminine display. But there was nothing else feminine about the hard ruthless face staring back at her so arrogantly, it was pure male and infinitely threatening. 'Well?' His square jaw was set ominously. 'You have not answered my question?'

'I . . .' She felt mesmerised by the sensual aura reaching out to entrap her. His eyes were hungry, leaving her in no doubt as to what he wanted, his mouth twisted with an intense craving that found an answering echo in herself. 'Leave me alone——'

'Answer me.' His accent was very pronounced, his voice deep and husky. 'Tell me you do not want me, that you feel nothing when I hold you in my arms, and I will not touch you again, I swear it.'

She could feel the very air around them, each tiny particle thick and heavy with expectation, and somewhere in the undergrowth a tiny cricket sent its unmistakable sound into the night. The electric excitement that was causing her blood to sing through her veins also sent shivers of fear flickering down her spine. He was so big and dark, so alien in his flowing Arab clothes that sat on the muscled frame in a way that sent hot desire coursing through her body until her legs felt weak. How could she feel so attracted and so threatened at the same time? It was as though she were two different people in the same skin, or maybe... The thought froze her breath. Maybe her intuition, her sixth sense, cut through all the layers of civilisation and the guise he showed to the world and recognised something evil underneath?

'I don't want you.' The words were a soft sigh on the perfumed air and they both knew she was lying.

As one powerful arm moved behind her back the other hand lifted her chin imperiously to meet his mouth, but instead of the harsh invasion she was expecting his lips were soothing and light, stroking her mouth and tasting her slowly as he drew her more closely against him. As the kiss deepened and his tongue began to explore the sweet hidden recesses of her mouth, the raw desire that had hit her so savagely before returned with renewed vigour. She forgot she was almost naked, more so as the robe fell open as she arched and moved against him, she forgot everything but the shattering sensation of being in his arms and having him make love to her.

The hand under her chin moved up into her hair, his fingers threading the red silk tightly as he drew her head back for further penetration, and now his tongue was a hungry invasion causing the delicate nerves near the surface of her skin to burn hotly as they became suffused with blood.

His free hand began to move sensuously over her velvet skin, softly, carefully at first and then, as he felt her complete submission, his touch became more intimate until she moaned completely, completely lost in this her first sexual experience. His tongue flicked lower to her throat, detouring to her ears for long breathtaking moments before continuing its descent, his breathing accelerating sharply as he felt her helpless trembling.

She wound her fingers into the crisp richness of his hair, its texture rough and virile under her searching hands, and then he moved to cover her mouth in another sweet, hungry kiss that was unbelievably sensitive for such a big, arrogant giant of a man. And it was the tenderness that was her undoing. As he swept her on with him to each new embrace, each new intimacy, she lost the power of rational thought. The world and every-

thing in it consisted of Gerard's touch on her
skin, his mouth on hers, the feel and smell of
him enveloping her very spirit.

'Come...' As he swept her up in his arms and
began to walk with her the dizzy, intoxicating
effect of his lovemaking was temporarily cur-
tailed. He had passed through the graceful arch
and was walking up the stairs before she could
control her breathing enough to speak, and then
her voice was a weak whisper against the hardness
of his body.

'Gerard?' The narrowed gold eyes glanced
down at her, a fire in their depths that caused
her heart to pound. 'What are you doing?'

'We will be more comfortable in my room.' He
smiled down at her, kissing the tip of her nose
as he spoke although she had caught the shak-
iness in his voice. 'I want this to be slow and
perfect, I do not want anything to spoil it. I want
to kiss every inch of that satin-smooth skin until
you beg for fulfilment. I want it to be right.'

'Gerard——'

'I want you, Kit, but it is more than that, do
you understand me?' He stopped at the top of
the stairs as he gazed hard into her liquid grey
eyes.

'But Zita? And the others...' Cold reason
began to quell the fire and soon the trickle was
an icy flood. 'I'm not like that, Gerard. I can't
just make love with you and then walk away.'
She began to struggle panic-stricken in his arms
and he held her close for one more moment

before letting her feet touch the ground while still keeping her in the circle of his arms.

'Listen to what I am saying to you——'

'No!' She tried to shrink from him but the steely arms were too strong. 'You said that day on the mountains that I would have to want you with my mind as well as my body, and I don't. I don't, do you hear!'

'Why not?' His face had changed, the tender light in his eyes being replaced with a fiery anger that was blazingly hot. 'What the hell do you see when you look at me, anyway?'

What did she see? She stared at him aghast. She saw a man that she wanted without rhyme or reason in the emotion. She saw a man who had unlimited power over both her mind and body and had only to click his fingers for her to fall at his feet. She saw someone who terrified her senseless. Her eyes mirrored both her horrified self-awareness and her shock of the full knowledge of it, but as he searched her face he read only the fear, disgust and blind panic.

'If I walk away from you now it is the finish, *vous comprenez*?' He let go of her and stepped back a pace, the robes swirling round his hard form as he folded his arms and surveyed her with eyes that were as cold as ice, his burnished hair gleaming in the light from the oil lamp left burning halfway down the landing. 'Do you understand me, Kit? I will never reach out to you again. I have stood all I'm going to take and so the decision is yours. I will not carry you into my bed kicking and screaming, dammit——'

'Gerard——'

'No, I will not have this "Gerard, Gerard",' he ground out savagely, his face proud and aloof. 'I want a woman in my bed, not a spoiled child who changes with the wind.'

Her eyes were the wounded eyes of a hunted animal and, as she tried to speak and failed, something pierced his heart and caused a constriction in his chest that made it impossible to breathe. How dared she affect him like this, reduce him to this and still look at him like that? Couldn't she see what she was doing to him? What she had been doing to him since the first damn moment he had laid eyes on her? 'Well?' He didn't know what was driving him on to smash even the remote chance he had of making her trust him a little, let him into that closed mind, but at this last rebuff something had snapped. 'What is it to be?' He watched her drag her eyes from his face and turn slowly, her shoulders stooped like an old, old woman, and as she walked down the landing and into her room, shutting the door quietly, he wondered what he had ever done to suffer agony as he was feeling now.

As the next few days crept by in some sort of terrible normality, Kit found she could just survive if she kept her mind in an empty vacuum. Gerard disappeared into his study every day immediately after breakfast to re-emerge in the evening in time for dinner, his face stony and closed and his body tense. Meal-times were something to be endured, the atmosphere so fraught that she couldn't eat a thing and her nerves stretched to breaking point after an hour in Gerard's grim company. Poor Colette, after the first day, had retreated into a bewildered but polite silence after Gerard had snapped so fiercely at her that her face had gone white with pain and outrage. She clearly didn't understand what was happening but just as clearly wasn't going to get involved, and Kit couldn't blame her. Gerard as he was now was enough to deter anything and anyone.

On the morning of the day she was due to return to Casablanca Kit woke early before it was light and lay for hours watching the sun rise, her mind dull and aching. Gerard had informed her the night before in a terse, short statement that they would be leaving shortly after breakfast, and as Colette was away with Claude's family for the day she had already said her goodbyes to Gerard's sister, who had been quite tearful.

As her mind began to stir itself and begin the torturous cross-examination that she had to stop a hundred times a day, she flung the covers back quickly, diving into the shower and washing her hair before dressing quickly in her own clothes and deciding on a slow walk round the gardens before breakfast. She had to do something to maintain the numbness she had forced her mind into over the last few days, she couldn't break down now.

It was still very early and the air was soft and warm, carrying a faint promise of the heat of the day in its perfumed depths as she crept quietly out of the sleeping house and into the fragrant beauty of the gardens. She wandered for over an hour in the delicately landscaped surroundings, sitting for some time in an exquisitely fashioned bower under the shade of an almond tree watching a host of small birds wash and brush up in a large bird-bath, fighting and squabbling as they pushed for the best position like a group of naughty schoolchildren.

Soon she would be in Casablanca, probably only stopping overnight if a flight home could be arranged for the next day. Home? The word pierced the numbness with brutal clarity. Where and what was home? Who was David, Emma...? When would she *remember* ...? She jumped up as the same old pattern reared itself. She wouldn't think of this now, couldn't, not when the parting from Gerard still had to be faced and overcome. As she walked towards the house she glanced at her watch and realised breakfast would soon be ready, her footsteps quickening as she reached the path near the servants' quarters that led past the kitchen and into the side of the house.

The first piercing cry brought her to a dead stop with her hand clutched to her throat as she listened to the sound being cut off in mid-stream. What or who was that? She stood frozen to the spot, unable to move, as her ears strained to catch more cries. There was absolute silence for a few seconds and then a child's voice began to whimper shrilly, the sound something between a cry and a moan, but with a blood-curdling familiarity that brought the fine body hairs all over her skin standing on end. Then a woman's voice began to wail loudly, joined a moment later by another female shouting, and within seconds the uproar was added to by a man's voice ranting and raving in Arabic, his tone harsh and full of furious anger.

As Kit glanced desperately up and down the deserted pathway wondering if she should venture into the door facing her and interfere in something that was definitely not her business, she was almost knocked off her feet by Amina, who emerged from the arched doorway like a bullet out of a gun. The small Moroccan woman clutched at her arm, her face desperate. '*Min-fadlik, minfadlik.*' She gestured into the interior pleadingly as the noise rose.

'Amina?' Kit shook her gently, her face white. 'What is it? I don't understand. Is someone hurt?'

'Please, you come.' Such was Amina's agitation that she was trying to drag Kit towards the open door. 'Come, come now.'

'Amina?' Kit heard Gerard's voice with a feeling of overwhelming relief as the two women turned to see him emerge from the far interior of the house with Assad, obviously having enjoyed an early morning ride. 'Amina, *shnoo hada*?' At the sight of Gerard and her husband Amina burst into noisy sobbing, the flood of Arabic that passed her lips interspersed with a wailing cry that was echoed by the other voice inside the house which she presumed was

Halima's. By the time Gerard reached them his
face was black with rage and, after physically
placing Amina in Assad's arms with a muttered
command in Arabic that Kit didn't understand,
he strode past her and into the noise inside, his
eyes glittering with unholy fire. A moment or two
after he disappeared the noise was cut off as
though by a knife and then he reappeared in the
doorway with one of Halima's children in his
arms, a little girl of about five. As Amina's hands
reached instinctively for her niece and he placed
the whimpering child into her arms, Kit was
shocked to see Gerard's knuckles on his right
hand were bruised and bleeding as though he had
been in a fight.

'Gerard——?'

'Just a moment.' He spared her a swift glance
before conversing with Assad and Amina in their
native tongue for some moments, gesturing as he
finished towards their quarters, to which they
promptly disappeared with their little bundle.

'Gerard?' She touched his arm tentatively, her
face white, and as he turned to face her saw his
face was contorted with a bitter rage that was
frightening.

'The man is an animal.' He shook his head
slowly, raking back his mass of tawny brown hair
from his forehead and leaving a smear of blood
from his bleeding knuckles on the brown skin.
'This time he has gone too far.'

'An animal?' she asked weakly.

'How a creature like Abou can father numerous offspring and yet Assad and Amina are

childless beats me,' he continued with savage bitterness, his mouth twisted with anger. 'Well, I warned him the last time I wouldn't stand for any more; this is on his own head. I have shamed him no more than he has shamed himself.'

'Gerard, are you saying that Abou beats his family?' Kit asked faintly as she felt the present begin to recede and a terrible blackness grip her soul. 'Is that it?'

'Of course that's it,' Gerard answered irritably as his eyes searched the empty doorway, an ominous silence from within. 'I would not have the man within a thousand miles of here except for the fact that by employing him his family comes under my protection and Assad and Amina are on hand too. It is unbelievable that Assad came from the same womb that housed that savage.' As his eyes moved back to her they narrowed with alarm at her glazed eyes and chalk-white face. 'Come, do not be so upset. A drink will calm...'

Colin. Her stepfather Colin. As her memory returned in a flood of nausea she knew why the sound of Halima's child's screams had shocked her so. They were her screams, her cries, her hurt. For ten long years she had lived in the fear of one man, her mother's second husband. Her own father had died when she was five years old and within months her mother had married again, to a man who was obsessed by his big, voluptuous wife whose selfish, fleshly nature was in perfect harmony with his own lecherous desires. From the first moment Kit had set eyes on him she had feared and loathed him, her hate only being equalled by his for this scrap of puny humanity who took some of his wife's attention from himself. At first her mother had tried to protect her from the beatings, the neglect, the mental cruelty, but the erotic, lascivious world he had introduced her to was too much of a pull and soon she was submissive to every word he said. The gut-wrenching fear and dread that had accompanied every second of Kit's waking hours for years returned in its full horror.

He had been a tall, handsome giant of a man with a synthetic charm that could be turned on at the drop of a hat and his dominating, sensual, arrogant nature had apparently found no fault in her mother whom he had loved to the exclusion of everything and everyone else. The days and weeks and months of time spent locked in her room had been preferable to the spasmodic beatings incurred for any little minor fall from grace, but it was the mental cruelty that had hurt the most. The subtle, and not so subtle, mockery of her thin, boyish shape, the constant ridicule and searing contempt that had marked her childhood and teenage years had left their damage.

When Colin and her mother had been killed in a car accident just after her sixteenth birthday they had left her extremely well off financially and an emotional cripple. Masterful men, especially if they were good-looking, she found quite repellent, preferring males who had no power to touch either her heart or her intellect. She had to be in charge, absolutely and un-

equivocally, physically and emotionally. That
part of it she had never understood till now, she
realised numbly. But as the handful of boyfriends that she had had before David flashed
across her mind, she saw they were all from the
same mould, easily led, happy to take second
place, content with the odd chaste kiss and
making no demands on her in any way. And she
had gone out of her way to make sure she didn't
attract the more masculine type of male—the
severe hairstyle, lack of make-up, subdued
colours... She raised her eyes to Gerard's concerned face. And it had worked. Until now.

'Kitten?' The use of the endearment after days
of a formal and cold Kit sent hot panic shooting
through every nerve. 'You have remembered,
have you not?' He swore softly as he took in her
enormous pain-filled eyes and white mouth.
'What is it? What has made you look like this?'

His movement to take her into his arms was
one of pure compassion with no sexual under-
tones at all, but as his flesh touched hers she leapt
backwards with such revulsion that his blood ran
cold. 'Don't touch me.' Her mind was struggling
to accept the enormity of what it had been trying
to forget as well as the knowledge that with this
man, and with only this man, she had let down
the defences. She had allowed him to touch her
because she had been unable to fight the attraction that was in every square inch of that big
male body, she had allowed him to disturb her,
to subdue and subjugate, *she had allowed him
into her head*. 'Don't you ever touch me again.'

'You are ill.' Her eyes were dilated, the veins on her forehead standing out in stark contrast to the ghastly pallor of her skin, but as he reached for her again she almost snarled her warning.

'Stay away.' She backed from him in much the same way as one would retreat from a ferocious wild animal. 'You disgust me, do you hear?' As his face turned white, something painful pierced her heart but she forced herself to go on. She had given him too much power; if he but knew, he had it all. What could she do? *What could she do*? She loved him. She had committed herself to the very thing that would destroy her if she didn't tear it out by its roots. 'I never want to see you again.'

And then she ran, blindly and with her heart bursting, until she reached the sanctuary of her room where she collapsed on the floor to lie panting and stunned by the enormity of the confrontation until it was time to walk out of his life forever. And it had to be forever. Her flesh crept as she allowed herself to recall little separate instances from her childhood that had been devastating at the time. Colin had taught her to think of herself as both unlovely and unlovable, discouraging any friends that she might have had and insisting on a rigid regime that had him snarling like a dog if she so much as took a step out of place. She had been petrified most of the time, a fact that still had the power to make her curl up with shame.

And when David had betrayed her...? She took the incident out of the back of her mind and placed it squarely in the light. She had been horrified and upset and disgusted but—— She paused as she forced herself to face the truth. It hadn't touched the part of her she had kept for herself. In a strange kind of way she had hardly expected anything better of him. So why had she allowed herself to become his fiancée in the first place? The answer was stark and clear and brutally ugly. Because he would never be able to have any power over her, she hadn't loved him.

She sat up abruptly and wrapped her arms round her legs, her eyes staring blindly ahead. She had chosen him simply because she didn't love him, because there would never be any danger of her loving him; she could always be in control of her emotions and his influence over her.

And Gerard? Gerard was different. Dangerously, menacingly different. She had survived the years with her stepfather as much because of her hate for him as her will to escape his authority over her and make a new life for herself when she was older. She had vowed he would not break her, that the ultimate victory would be hers. But Gerard could shatter that new life, destroy her peace of mind for evermore if she was foolish enough to let him. Love was stronger than hate, she had always known it really; that was why she had avoided it all her adult life. And love was a luxury she dared not allow herself. The final price might be too high, it could destroy her. Because if he ever got tired of her, rejected her after she had opened up her heart and her body to him, she would not survive it. And how, looking as she did, being the sort of person she was, could it end any other way?

She didn't realise until much later that Colin had won after all.

CHAPTER EIGHT

THE journey to Casablanca forever remained a blur in Kit's mind. She was to recall in later days snatches featuring Gerard, his mouth taut with pain and his eyes stony, dealing with the endless formalities and settling her into her hotel, but at the time the emotional vacuum that had followed the storm of emotion held until the moment he left her at the hotel.

'Kitten?' They were standing in the reception area of the hotel lobby, Gerard having acquired her key for her from the receptionist. She had no luggage and had firmly refused his offer to see her to her room. 'You must tell me what is wrong. Is it David? Did he hurt you in some way?'

As though the name were a magic key she suddenly saw her avenue of escape. He wanted her, physically he wanted her very much, he had made that perfectly plain, and being the sort of man he was he might pursue her if she didn't finish this thing in a way he would understand. 'David?' She forced herself to look up into his face, the first time she had consciously looked at him since the moment her memory had returned, and was shocked to the core by the surge of feeling that flooded her system as she took in his strained face and worried eyes. She loved him, how she loved him. She wanted to wipe away that look

of concern in the gold eyes, smooth out the lines
at the side of his mouth and eyes—— She caught
herself abruptly. This was forbidden territory and
dangerously, criminally treacherous. 'Of course
David hasn't hurt me; we're engaged to be
married, aren't we?'

'Exactly.' His eyes held hers tightly. 'Something is strangling you and he seems the obvious
solution.'

'I'm fine.' She shook back a lock of hair from
her face, vitally aware that he had been careful
not to touch her since the episode with Halima's
child, and forced herself to continue. 'And I can
assure you I am not worried by David in any
sense.' The ring of truth in her words convinced
him and the frown that was marring his brow
deepened. How could she be worried by a creep
like David? she asked herself desperately.
Compared to Gerard he was a mere boy. 'I just
want to get back to him now,' she continued
bleakly as her stomach clenched at the lie. 'See
him, hold him—you know how it is.'

'How it is?' He echoed her words in such a
mild tone that she was fooled until she glanced
up into his face again.

'And you should be pleased,' she continued
wildly. 'You can get back to the sort of woman
you prefer now. Women like Zita, voluptuous,
sexy, real women——'

'To hell with this.' He took her arm in an iron
grip that was intensely painful and almost
dragged her into the small deserted coffee lounge
at the side of reception, forcing her into a seat

with scant regard for her feelings in the matter. 'Sit down, shut up and do not move,' he ground out angrily through clenched teeth, his eyes blazing.

Strangely the show of strength, of brute force, did not intimidate her at all, it was almost a relief. He was running true to form like all his type, like Colin. He wanted her and that was all that mattered, this animal desire that had to be sated.

'Don't try to bully me, Gerard,' she said coldly. 'It won't work.'

'Bully you?' He stared at her, his face incredulous. 'Is that what you think I'm doing? Can't you see even now?' He shook his head slowly, his eyes searching her strained face for something, anything.

'Of course that's what you're doing,' she said bleakly, 'what all your type do. At least David——'

'David?' He spat the name into her face with terrifying bitterness. 'Do not hold this David up to me as some sort of hero or I shall not be responsible for my actions. If your fiancé is such a model of virtue, why the hell did he let you travel alone to a foreign country knowing you could not speak a word of the language? Answer me that? And he must have known that something had happened that had terrified you?'

'It's not like that——' She caught herself abruptly. She couldn't explain, either about the circumstances of her coming to Morocco or about her childhood and Colin. No, definitely not that. She had never been able to speak of it to anyone, feeling in some strange, totally illogical way that part of it was her fault. If she had been prettier, nicer, more lovable——

'The hell it isn't.' He reached out and shook her angrily. 'If you were mine I would protect you with my life, not set you up for pot-shots from every Romeo who might try his luck.'

'You have no idea what you are talking about.' His touch, even in these circumstances, had started off a chain reaction in her body that spoke more eloquently than words of how dangerous this man was to her self-control.

'Maybe.' He eyed her grimly. 'And why is that? Because you will not talk to me, *really* talk to me. I know no more about you now than when we first met. *Mon dieu*——' he raked his hair in that gesture she was beginning to know '—can you not see that you are being monstrously unfair to both of us?'

'There is no "us".'

'Oh, yes, there is,' he corrected softly, his eyes as hard as flint. 'There is very definitely an us, kitten, whether you like it or not. Do you want me to prove it to you?' Before she had any idea of his intention he had taken her mouth in a hard, cruel kiss that burnt into her flesh like fire, his lips grindingly hard against hers, his arms rigid bands around her body. She tried to fight him, for long seconds she really tried, and then she melted into his embrace helplessly as his lips worked their sensual magic. When he finally let her go he was breathing heavily, his eyes glittering hotly. 'Well?' His voice was arrogant and she didn't have the experience to recognise the desperate uncertainty it was concealing. 'Can you deny what is between us?'

You are talking about sex, she told him silently as she touched her bruised swollen lips with the tip of a finger. Animal lust, biological attraction, call it what you will. I have seen what that does. There has to be more than that.

'Goodbye, Gerard.' She left the coffee lounge expecting he would follow, call her, something, but it wasn't until she had reached the lift and the doors had closed that she realised she had just said goodbye to him in the final sense.

On reaching her room she found it was all as she had left it, her own clothes neatly packed away in the mirrored sliding wardrobe, her shoes neatly arranged below. Ordered and controlled and safe. Just as she ran her life. She heard the sound of a little animal whimpering and it was a few moments before she realised, with a sickening lurch of panic, that it was her own voice. This wouldn't do. She stared into the dressing-table mirror and tried to wipe the desperation from her eyes. She was in charge of her own life now and managing OK. She would never give that life, the one she had clawed for herself out of the dregs of heartache and suffering, over to a man like him. However much she loved him. And she did. She stared back at the familiar face in the mirror, glad it was her own again. She did love him so much. What was she going to do? She lay back on the bed and hunted for the release of tears but they wouldn't come. What *was* she going to do? How was she going to get through the rest of her life?

Morning came, as it inevitably did, but Kit had not slept at all. At first light she packed her suitcases and then showered and washed her hair, ringing down to Reception to check they had a note of her request for a taxi at ten. Her flight wasn't leaving until two but she just wanted to get to the anonymity of the airport where, surrounded by hundreds of people, she could really be alone.

The thought of breakfast was repugnant but she went down to the dining-room just the same. She hadn't eaten properly for days now and that, coupled with all the emotional stress, was beginning to make her feel distinctly odd.

She had just forced the last piece of toast down, helped on its way by a strong cup of black coffee, when the screech of burning tyres outside the large plate-glass window made her turn and look through the clear glass. Gerard's Ferrari had just negotiated an emergency stop in a clear no-parking zone which he totally ignored as he leapt out of the car and ran up the hotel steps without even locking the door.

'No...' She shut her eyes as she whispered out loud. She couldn't face him again, this was unbearable. As she glanced desperately round the half-full room she considered, for a split-second, disappearing into the ladies' cloakroom and staying there until he had gone, but immediately the futility of the idea dawned on her. She could hardly incarcerate herself there all day, and even if she escaped into the city eventually she would be forced back to the hotel. Knowing him as she did, he would simply wait until she returned and her luggage, money, even her passport were locked in her room. She took a deep breath and stood up on unsteady legs. From the look on his face this wasn't going to be pleasant.

He wasn't in the lobby and she rang for the lift, hoping against hope she could get to her room before he found her and at least avoid making a fool of herself in public. In those torturous years of childhood and adolescence she had become very adept at hiding her feelings and maintaining a poker face however bruised, physically or mentally, she might be. But somehow, somehow with Gerard that skill learnt so painfully was quite useless.

As the lift doors opened and he stood in front of her, the blood throbbed in her ears so violently that she thought she was going to faint. He obviously thought so too, moving forward quickly and taking her arm in a firm hold as he drew her inside the lift and pressed the button for her floor, ignoring with regal and uncharacteristic rudeness the two businessmen hurrying towards them.

'Good morning, kitten.' He didn't look down at her as he spoke, keeping his eyes on the closed door as the lift took them swiftly upwards, his hand still tight on her arm as though he was afraid she would run if he let go.

'What are you doing here?' she asked faintly through numb lips. The sight, the feel, the smell of him was making her heart pound so jerkily it actually hurt.

'In a moment.' As the lift stopped and the doors slid open they moved into the thickly carpeted corridor and towards her room at the far end before the full reality of it all hit Kit. Then she stopped abruptly, twisting in his hold as she stared straight up into his dark face, her eyes defiant.

'I'm not moving another step and there is no way you are coming in my room,' she stated flatly.

'Rubbish,' he said calmly, bending down and lifting her into his arms to the startled gasp of a middle-aged couple just leaving their room. '*Bonjour*.' He nodded at them grimly as he strode past, walking the length of the corridor and depositing her outside her room with a determined flourish. 'Do I have to search your bag for your key or are you going to be sensible and open the door yourself?' She stared at him warily as her trembling fingers reached inside her handbag and found the cold metal. In spite of the apparent calm dignity he was furiously angry, she knew it. The narrowed gold gaze glanced down at her, his eyes as cold as ice, and she knew she was right.

She tried twice to open the door but her shaking fingers couldn't insert the key in the lock, and at the third try he took the key from her with a hand that was rock-steady and opened the door at once. 'In.' His voice brooked no argument.

She preceded him into the sunlit room and nerved herself to turn and face him.

'Well?' She had aimed at defiance but her voice sounded more pleading than anything else. That fact alone brought her chin up high. She had had years of grovelling to a madman and had vowed long ago she would never be in that position again.

'Why did you let me believe that you were engaged to be married to David?' he asked with deadly reasonableness.

'What?'

'You heard me!' As she shrank back at the low growl, he physically shook himself, taking a deep breath before he spoke again, his voice back in the even moderate tone. 'You broke off your engagement before you even came to Morocco. Now you might have forgotten that at the beginning but not after yesterday. You remembered the whole caboodle yesterday. So——' he eyed her menacingly '—I repeat my question. Why did you let me think you were still committed to someone else?'

'How did you find out?' she whispered slowly. There was no point in denying it. He knew.

'Your little flatmate was worried she hadn't heard from you since big brother talked to you last,' he said with icy sarcasm. 'She was worried he had upset you. She phoned to say that she was disgusted with the way he has handled your... indisposition and couldn't go along with his lies and deceit. It was a most interesting conversation.' The lethal gaze darkened ruthlessly.

'Most informative. Well?' He took a step towards her and she nerved herself not to retreat. 'I want an explanation.'

'It was easier to let you think I was still involved with David,' she said painfully.

'Easier!' Dark colour flared across the high cheekbones turning his eyes into golden points of light. 'Who the hell was it easier for—you? I've suffered the torments of the damned imagining you going back to him.'

'Don't be silly.' Now she did take a step backwards but more so that she didn't fling herself into his arms than anything else. 'We've only known each other a couple of weeks; there's nothing between us.'

'Do not try that line again,' he said bitterly. 'You know how I feel about you, dammit; everyone else does. I've been through hell trying to adjust my more carnal inclinations to the fact that you were looking towards me for protection, for refuge. That you were ill, frightened. I tried to tread carefully, show you my home, my family, build up your trust, but everything I did seemed to force us further apart and all the time I thought you were being faithful to David. Hell!' He swallowed tightly. 'How you must have laughed.'

'It's not like that,' she whispered desperately.

'Then what *is* it like?' he snarled furiously. 'Tell me, open that beautiful lying mouth and tell me. Why did you break off your engagement?'

'Didn't Emma tell you?' she asked painfully.

'No, she wouldn't.' He gestured angrily with his hand. 'She said he had let you down in some way but that you would tell me if you wanted me to know.'

'I found him in bed with someone else,' she said flatly, hearing his sharp intake of breath as she lowered her head so that her hair shielded her hot cheeks.

'The fool.' She felt him make a move towards her and then stop. 'And that's what you were trying to forget? But all men aren't like that, kitten, don't you see——?'

'That's not it! David's not it!' The words exploded out of her like bullets and then she was absolutely still, her eyes fixed on the floor.

'Kitten, you can't just walk out of my life,' he said softly after a full minute had passed. 'You must realise that. I knew the instant I saw you you were mine——'

'Don't say that.' She raised shocked eyes to his. 'This thing, it's just an attraction between us, like you feel for lots of women. It doesn't mean anything; Zita would do just as well——'

'Stop it.' His voice was steely now and full of authority. 'I want you, kitten, but not just for a day or a week or a year. I want you as my wife, as *mine*, do you hear? I want to share every new morning with you, be there with you at night——'

'No!' If he had suggested a gross obscenity she couldn't have reacted more violently. 'You don't really care like that, you're lying.' Her voice was wild, her eyes desperate. 'Admit it——'

'You don't want me to love you, do you?' His voice was quiet now and threaded with incredulity. 'That is what has frightened you all along, is it not? You sensed this feeling between us just as I did and it scares you to death. Why?'

She shook her head helplessly but he moved to her side in one angry stride and grasped her upper arms tightly, shaking her slightly in his rage. 'Oh, no, no more of that. Damn you, you *will* tell me, Kit. I have no intention of letting you go, and to hell with these secrets. I don't care what you've done, what you've been before you met me——'

'It's nothing like that.' She was as white as a sheet. 'But the sort of love you say is between us is dangerous, cruel and dangerous. I know.'

'How can you?' He stood back a pace, his eyes stony. 'You haven't given it a chance so how can you possibly judge? I have known many women in my life, I admit it, but not one of them has touched my soul until you. You are my other half, Kit, like it or not. It would have been easy to let myself drift into a comfortable relationship, marriage, more than once before now but I knew that essential element was missing. I just didn't know what it was until I met you.' The words that he spoke so sincerely were like a funeral bell tolling in her mind.

'I don't want you to love me like that,' she said wildly. 'Don't you see? A love like that leaves no room for anyone else, the world narrows down to two people and how the strongest can make

the other feel. And I wouldn't be able to stand
up to you, I'd become just like her.'

'Her?' he said quietly. 'Kitten, we are not
talking about the same thing——'

'No, we aren't,' she agreed sadly, the bleakness
in her face stilling his breath. And then she told
him, her voice flat and expressionless as she de-
tailed the years of humiliation and bitter torment,
the constant fear that was with her day and night
and the dread of hearing her stepfather's footsteps, his voice. She had known no hope, no joy,
no peace in her life until they both were dead,
and that all in the name of love...

'That was not love, kitten.' His voice was infinitely tender, his face full of such compassion
and concern that she wanted to run from the
feeling that was bursting forth inside her. She
thought she had seen him in all his moods but
this gentleness was a thing apart. 'If your stepfather had truly loved your mother it would have
encompassed you too. Love is not something that
detracts, it is like the amoeba, it divides only to
grow and multiply. It is a good thing this Colin
is dead.' Now something blazed briefly at the
back of his eyes, swiftly veiled. 'After what you
have told me he would not have remained long
in this world.'

'You couldn't have done anything.' As she had
first finished speaking he had moved to take her
in his arms but she had avoided his touch sharply,
and now he made the same gesture which she
again eluded with a twist of her body as she
walked across the room. 'No one would have be-

lieved you. I tried time and time again but he was
so charming you see, so likeable.'

'I would not have wasted time on words.' There
was something in his voice that told her he was
deadly serious, and again his very arrogance, his
strength, his total confidence in himself sent an
icy shiver snaking down her spine. These were
the qualities that had hurt her as a child; what
made him different from Colin? Everything, her
heart sang out in reply. Probably very little, her
head countered immediately. 'You have not told
these things to anyone before?' he asked softly.

'There was no one to tell,' she answered simply.

'David?'

'David!' She laughed shrilly and then caught
herself tightly. It would take very little to make
her hysterical and she couldn't let go now. 'No,
I couldn't have told him,' she said more quietly.
'David, all my other boyfriends, they were
just...friends. You know?' She turned to look
at him and saw his face was strained and tense,
his eyes concentrated on her face. 'I didn't want
more than that,' she said flatly. 'Even with David,
believe it or not.'

'And now?' The room was very still, the only
sound the low hum of the air-conditioning, and
for a moment time seemed suspended as he held
her gaze.

'I'm sorry.' The words were dragged out of the
depths of her. 'I can't...'

'You can,' he said fiercely.

'No.' She shook her head blindly. 'I don't even
know you——'

He reached her side, drawing her into his arms
even as she struggled against him. 'You only need
to know what is between us,' he said thickly, his
mouth meeting hers in a scorching kiss that
burned her flesh. 'That is all that matters...' She
put her hands on his strong upper arms intending
to push him away but somehow, somehow her
arms slid up round his neck, her fingers lost in
his hair as his mouth continued to plunder hers.
She loved him, she loved him so much...

His lips roamed over her face, stroking gently
against her closed eyelids, her forehead, her
throat. His arousal was fierce against the softness
of her body and her own inner thighs were
aching, throbbing, with a primitive need that she
couldn't hide. As he drew her down on to the
soft thick carpet she was hardly aware of what
she was doing, all the emotional turmoil and
physical strain of the last few weeks culminating
in a need to be cherished, desired, wanted. His
breathing was harsh and ragged as he ran his
hands over her slender body, his lips caressing
the rapid pulse at her throat before continuing
lower as he crouched over her. Tiny tremors
began to shake her limbs as sensation after sensation washed across her body in an ever-
increasing momentum, his experienced touch
working a subtle magic against which she was
helpless. She had never known it could be like
this, she thought dazedly. She wasn't herself any
more, the person she had known for twenty-five
years, he had transformed her—— The thought
broke through the sensual warm haze like a thun-

derbolt and she surprised them both as she shot upwards, scrambling away from him in an undignified retreat to sit panting a few feet away, her eyes wild.

'Kitten?' As he saw the panic in her frightened face he could have kicked himself for going too fast. What was the matter with him? he asked himself savagely. She had just told him she had been through hell on earth for ten years of her life and he was going about things like a bull in a china shop. He swore silently. 'What we feel for each other is natural——'

'But that is how *they* were,' she breathed slowly with horrified revulsion as she struggled to her feet. 'He only ever wanted to look at her, be with her, touch her——'

'He was sick.' Gerard's voice was harsh as he cut into the memories. 'You know yourself he was sick. He didn't love your mother, he was obsessed by her. There is a world of difference between the two.'

'Is there?' She stared at him white-faced. 'But how do I know that what I feel for you is love and not obsession? And how do you know?' It wasn't quite the way he had imagined her declaring her feelings for him, but at that moment he was happy to take anything he could get.

'Darling——'

'No.' She faced him stony-eyed. 'You make me feel vulnerable, helpless, exposed——'

'As you do me.' He made no attempt to touch her now. 'It works both ways, this love.'

'Please leave, Gerard.' He straightened slowly, his body stiffening.

'You do not mean that.'

'I mean it.' She walked past him and opened the door. 'I do.'

He knew he could have her. He glanced at her mouth, trembling a little underneath the bravery, at her eyes, haunted and dark, her mouth still bruised and swollen from their lovemaking. Yes. He could have her. But at what cost to them both and especially her fragile equilibrium?

He walked past her and out of the door.

CHAPTER NINE

'I'M SORRY, David, there is really no chance we could get back together again.' As Kit looked at the tall, attractive man in front of her she wondered how on earth she could ever have considered spending the rest of her life with him. The fair, boyish good looks did absolutely nothing for her and when added to the weak, soft mouth and insipid blue eyes... She hid an instinctive shudder. He was nothing like Gerard, nothing at all. Her stomach turned over violently and she resolutely blanked the name.

'I don't blame you,' Emma said vehemently at her side, earning a black scowl from her brother which she returned with sisterly fierceness. 'The thing with Virginia was bad enough, but to lead Kit on like that when you knew she was ill and vulnerable, to pretend——'

'Shut up, Em.' Had his voice always had that faint whine in it? Kit asked herself in surprise. Probably. Very probably.

She had been back in England for a few hours, arriving unannounced at the flat to find Emma all alone and touchingly pleased to see her. David had arrived within the hour for dinner, something he had always been in the habit of doing even before they were engaged, and when he had immediately started to reproach her for not letting him know of her intended arrival she had made

it quite clear exactly where he stood. He took it
surprisingly well, partly because he knew her well
enough to know there was no possibility of her
changing her mind and also, and, more to the
point, because Emma had made it absolutely
plain that she was backing Kit one hundred per
cent, both with regard to the business the three
of them owned and also in a more personal sense.
Emma's loyalty had surprised and touched Kit;
she hadn't realised how much the other girl cared
about her and the knowledge was balm to her
sore heart.

David had just left, without dinner, when the
phone rang as she was having a bath, forcing
herself to relax her aching muscles in the foamy
warm water as Emma prepared their meal. She
heard her friend answer the phone, speak for a
few minutes and then replace the receiver. 'Kit?'
Emma called through the partly-open bathroom
door. 'That was Gerard. He wanted to make sure
you had got home safely.'

'Did he?' She sat bolt upright in the bath,
slopping a great wave of water on to the floor,
and took a long deep breath to calm her racing
heart before she spoke again. 'Fulfilling the last
of his host duties, I should think.'

'Umm...' Emma's voice was thoughtful. 'Are
you saying the guy isn't interested in you?'

'Not really.' Kit closed her eyes tightly. She
didn't need this right now. 'Ships that pass in the
night and all that.'

Emma snorted loudly. 'And pigs might fly.'
After that meaningful comment Emma left her

in peace and from the sounds in the tiny kitchen continued preparing their steak and salad.

He had phoned. The desolation and sick darkness that had been with her ever since leaving Morocco lifted fractionally. What exactly had he said to Emma? She was out of the bath and into silk pyjamas and a loose towelling robe within seconds, padding through to the kitchen in bare feet as she rubbed her wet hair with a towel.

'Did Gerard leave a message?' she asked casually as she poured them both a glass of chilled white wine and then sat on the edge of the kitchen table watching Emma expertly toss a green salad.

'The ship that passed in the night?' Emma asked drily, as she prepared the two juicy steaks sizzling under the grill. 'No.' She darted a quick look at Kit's carefully blank face. 'He just asked if you were home, how you were, that sort of thing.'

'Oh.' The darkness was back again fierce and strong. She should have known and she couldn't blame him really. He had wanted to know that his duties were discharged, that his commitment was over. She still couldn't believe that he had let her go like that—it went against everything she had learned about his dominant, assertive, hard personality—but perhaps in the end he had decided enough was enough? She flinched inwardly. She was a mess, emotionally and mentally. Perhaps he hadn't wanted a complication like her in his life? And if he had forced himself on her? The thought quickened her breath as she recognised that within a few minutes it wouldn't have been rape. But she would have hated him, and herself, afterwards. But he couldn't have known that, she argued weakly. Could he?

'Kit, what's wrong?' She came out of the reverie to find Emma in front of her, her friend's round face troubled. 'I don't want to pry, I know you are a very private person, but we have been friends for years now and if I can help?' And somehow, unbelievably, she found herself telling another human being of the trauma of those first years within twenty-four hours of first mentioning it to Gerard. It was as though the telling of it to him, and his understanding, compassion and complete lack of censure, had opened an avenue of healing she wouldn't have believed possible. And then she told Emma about Gerard, all of it, and as her voice finally trailed to a halt she found Emma was surveying her through frankly incredulous eyes.

'And you let him go?' her friend squeaked in amazement. 'Kit, they don't come gift-wrapped like that very often. Don't let Colin and your mother continue to ruin your life, for goodness' sake. Ring Gerard, do something!'

'I can't.' Kit shook her head slowly. 'I really can't, Emma. I can't explain but I've got a hell of a lot to work through before I'm fit for myself, let alone anyone else.'

'But that means you've lost him,' Emma said weakly.

'I know.' Kit shut her eyes as the desolation grew. 'I can't bear it.' But there was nothing else she could do.

The next few days were a nightmare of struggling to do her share of the work in their tiny business after sleepless nights, forcing herself to eat although even the thought of food was sickening, and generally going through the motions of life while screaming inside. All she could think of was Gerard and the fact that she had thrown away the only chance of happiness she would ever know, and yet... She forced herself to confront the truth. If he were in front of her, right now, she would chicken out again. She knew it.

She rose, dull-eyed and exhausted, on the fourth morning of her return to England to find a small package on the hall table. 'Postman delivered it a minute ago,' Emma informed her casually as she disappeared into the bathroom for a shower, her nonchalant tone belying the look of intense interest that accompanied it. 'Postmark's Morocco...' The bathroom door shut with a martyrish click.

She looked at the bold black writing that covered the small parcel and her nerves jumped. It was his writing. She knew instinctively. She opened the package very carefully.

'To my darling kitten,' and in brackets, 'I can call you that because you cannot tell me not to, being thousands of miles away. I love you, I will always love you. Wear this sometimes and think of me.' Enclosed was a narrow gold bracelet inlaid with tiny diamonds set in the shape of hearts. She sank down on the hall carpet, the bracelet still in her hand, and cried as though her heart would break.

Flowers arrived the next day, five beautiful red roses, the dew still fresh on their perfect leaves, and again an accompanying note. 'A rose for every day we have been apart. Think of me.'

The next day it was a raw silk scarf, similar to one she had admired on Colette, the message on the card tender and romantic and funny. And the following day a tiny kitten, fashioned exquisitely out of crystal. 'I adore you, my sweet love, never doubt it for a minute.' And so it went on. On the days that a gift didn't arrive a letter would, and she grew to look forward to these more than anything else in life.

The tenor of the letters changed from day to day as he wrote describing his life at work, at Del Mahari, his morning rides, his aspirations for the future, his regrets for the past. 'He's courting me,' Kit realised with a little catch in her breath, three weeks after the first gift had arrived. 'All those miles away and he's courting me.'

'Of course he is.' Emma sighed enviously as she glanced at the tiny water-colour of Del Mahari that had arrived in the morning post signed by the artist himself, G. Dumont. 'I told you, Kit, they don't come gift-wrapped like him too often, certainly not round here.' She glanced out of the window at the driving rain that shrouded the morning with its icy spray. 'The first of November. I bet it's a lot warmer where he is.'

Kit nodded bleakly. Anywhere would be warmer if he was there.

In the third week of November, when the post didn't arrive before she went to work one

morning, she felt utterly bereft. Perhaps he was
tired of this one-sided courtship? Perhaps yesterday's letter was the last one she would ever
have from him? She made more mistakes in one
morning than she had made in the whole of her
working life, and after she had snapped at Emma
and David for the umpteenth time she went home
in her lunch hour telling herself she needed an
hour away from the business. The indescribable
rush of relief that flooded her senses as she saw
the thick envelope with that familiar writing lying
on the mat informed her that she had been lying
to herself. In more ways then one. He wasn't a
fierce, passionate stranger any longer, he had
opened up his heart and his soul to her, trusting
her with the very essence of himself. So what was
she going to do about it?

The phone call came a few nights later. She had
been lying curled in front of the fire, alone for
once, reading through a few of his letters. He
had sent her a huge fluffy brown teddy-bear that
morning with reproachful honey-gold eyes. 'He
can keep you warm at night until we can arrange
a more satisfactory substitute. Think of me.'

Think of me? She had done nothing else. He
filled her days, her nights, her dreams and slowly,
subtly, had filled the void in her past, but her
sheer dependence on his strength, his consistency, scared her to death. He wasn't like
Colin, she could accept that now, but she couldn't
bring herself to make that step of faith, to trust
him as he obviously demanded she do.

As the phone rang she picked it up automatically, her mind a thousand miles away, and then froze, her heart pounding as his deep rich voice echoed down the line. 'Hello? Could I speak to Kit, please?' The rush of tears into her eyes was blinding and still she couldn't speak. She loved him, she needed him, she didn't know how she was going to get through the rest of her life without him—— 'Kit? Is that you?' he asked softly after a few tense moments had ticked by.

'Yes.' He would never know the effort it cost her to speak. She was shaking so much she could barely hold the phone.

'How are you?' he asked slowly after another long pause.

'Better.' This was awful. Speak to him, say something, she told herself frantically. Thank him for all the gifts, the cards, but most of all the letters, those wonderful, funny, romantic, sexy, thoughtful letters——

'Good.' She heard him take a hard breath and then he spoke again, his voice soft. 'I have some news for you,' he said quietly, 'something I thought you would like to share. Amina is expecting a little one.'

'She is?' In spite of her turmoil she knew a moment's deep joy. 'That's wonderful, but how did it happen——?' She stopped abruptly as she realised what a stupid thing she had just said. 'I mean——'

'I think I know what you mean,' he said steadily, but she caught the throb of amusement he was trying to hide and flushed hotly. 'I took your advice as it happens, talking to Assad, and once a minor problem was cleared it was all systems go. She is only just pregnant but——' he smiled down the phone '—nevertheless very definitely so.'

'That's wonderful,' she repeated, her voice weak.

'You see it is possible to love someone more than life itself and still care about others?' he said softly. 'Love should beget love, kitten, a stone dropped in the pond of life producing endless ripples. You care about Amina and Assad as do I; that does not threaten or diminish what we feel for each other.'

'Gerard——'

'Listen to me,' he said urgently. 'I am not like Colin and you are not like your mother. *Our* children will be living products of our love to be cherished and protected and cared for, do you understand me?'

'Our children?' It was happening too fast, much too fast, she thought as she raised a hand to her throat, her face stricken.

'I am going to ask you one thing, Kit.' His voice was tense now, a note of harshness in its depths. 'Do you see me in your future at all? I know what you've had to go through, what you are still going through, but I need to know that much. I can show you that we're made for each other, wonderfully compatible in bed and out, I can teach you to trust me, to believe in compassion, tenderness, all the normal things you've missed out on, but only if you allow me in.' There was a blank pause and she heard him swear softly into the stillness. 'Dammit, I need something to hang on to, kitten. It might not be fair but it's what I need. I shouldn't be asking you this, I should be maintaining the strong, silent macho approach while I deluge you with flowers and gifts and love-letters——'

'Don't, Gerard.' Somehow he had managed to sound supremely arrogant and childishly humble at the same time, and it was a dangerous combination. She couldn't think when his voice was stroking over her nerves like thick cream. He was asking her to throw away the safety barriers that had been in place for all of her adult life. If he did love her, and still she could hardly believe that a man like him could feel such a powerful emotion for someone like her, but if he did, how could she love him back as he would expect to be loved when she was such an emotional coward? She bit her lip till it drew blood. She was afraid, of commitment, of belonging, of life and love... With all those inhibitions so firmly entrenched she would destroy them both.

'Is that your answer?' His voice was cold now but she didn't realise it was rigid self-control that was making it that way. She couldn't answer him, couldn't speak the death knell to the future, and so she put down the phone without saying a word. 'Like the coward you are,' she whispered silently into the empty room. 'Colin was right, you don't deserve to be loved. You aren't worth anything.'

There were many times over the ensuing days when she thought she wouldn't get through, but somehow she did. All around her Christmas preparations were in full force but she was untouched by it all, a tall slender automaton mechanically going through the motions. She knew Emma was worried about her and tried to reassure her friend now and again, but even that was a perfunctory response and not one from the heart. Her heart was dead. It had begun to die that first morning when it had waited in vain for his letter, and the morning after that, and after that, until she had accepted the inevitable. There would be no more letters.

Emma and David were going home to their parents' house in Hertfordshire for Christmas and, although Emma tried to persuade her to join them right up until the moment she left on Christmas Eve morning, Kit remained adamant. She wanted a quiet Christmas, she assured her friend brightly. A good rest to recharge her batteries. They both knew it was a downright lie but Emma eventually bowed to a will stronger than her own and left, after obtaining a promise from Kit that she would phone her every morning until she got back. 'Just to let me know you're OK,' she said with transparent concern as she lugged her suitcase down the stairs.

'I'm not going to do anything silly, you know, Em.' Kit smiled wryly in spite of her misery. 'I'm a fighter at heart.'

'Are you indeed?' Emma looked up at her from the open doorway into the street as Kit paused on the last step of the stairs. 'Well, you had the knock-out blow a couple of weeks ago so I still want that phone call.'

The small flat seemed desperately empty when she walked back in after waving Emma goodbye.

She cast a desultory eye over some outline sketches she had been working on at home for a new idea in beachwear but couldn't face them, switched the TV on to find rosy-cheeked children singing carols and general good-will to all men on all channels and switched it off again, and eventually curled up in a chair with a book in which she hadn't the faintest interest.

'You are lucky,' she told herself out loud after reading the same page several times and throwing the book down in disgust. The design business was really beginning to take off and the order book was full, David was reconciled to the change in their relationship and the three of them worked exceptionally well together, she was healthy, young, with no financial worries... She bowed her head into her arms and wept and wept...

After a morning of moping around the flat and indulging in morbid self-pity she got thoroughly angry with herself and went for a brisk walk in Hyde Park for most of the afternoon, returning at dusk to a tea of muffins and blueberry jam. She had reconciled herself to the fact that this Christmas had to be endured but the New Year would be better...wouldn't it?

After a long hot bath she settled down on the settee in silk pyjamas and a warm fluffy dressing-gown, deciding she might as well be comfortable in her misery, glancing round the small room, festive with Christmas cards and a tiny tree that Emma had bought, with heavy eyes and an ache in her chest that was a physical reality. She missed him, unbelievably, desperately so. But it was better this way. She would make him miserable with all her baggage from the past, her insecurities, anxieties, her inability to believe and trust in him. This way he could find someone else. Her heart thudded jarringly but she forced herself to think rationally. He had probably found someone else already or maybe Zita was helping him cope with rejection? Whatever, there had been no letters, no contact since that painful phone call, so he had clearly washed his hands of her once and for all. For the first time she admitted to herself how desperately she had needed a short note, a little card, anything to tell her he was thinking of her this Christmas. But there had been nothing. She bit her lip but the tears were already falling and within seconds were a veritable, scalding hot river.

The doorbell brought her head snapping up in horror. Who on earth...? She waited, rubbing her wet eyes with the back of her hand and sniffing helplessly. It rang again, more stridently this time and then again and again. 'Oh, hell.' They weren't going to leave. She caught sight of herself in the tiny hall mirror just before she opened the door, and shut her eyes briefly at the sight. She had never been able to cry prettily at the best of times and this was *not* the best of times.

'Hi.' As the door opened on its chain and she peered warily through the crack she knew for certain her mind had cracked at last. He couldn't be standing there, not really. She wanted him so much, needed him so much that her subconscious had dragged him up to torment her.

'Kitten?' The big dark figure in its black over-coat moved slightly and she leapt back as though it had burnt her, shutting the door with shaking hands. He *was* here. It was him. And what did she look like? She lay back against the door as her heart pounded and the blood sang in her ears. She didn't believe this. As she slid the chain off and opened the door she stood back a pace staring up into his dear, dear face.

'I didn't think you were going to let me in for a minute there.' He smiled but it didn't reach his eyes, and she noticed his mouth was white with strain, his face tense. 'I take it I *can* come in?'

She couldn't speak, her breath was strangled in her throat, but she stood aside waving him in as her eyes devoured him. As he passed, her senses reeled at the familiar smell of his after-shave, the height and breadth of the big body, the tawny brown hair and darkly tanned skin. He was so good-looking, so dangerously good-looking. What on earth did he want with her?

'Kitten?' He turned as she shut the door and tried another smile which had no more success than the first. He was nervous! She stared at him in amazement as the thought crystallised. He couldn't be... but he was. 'I know you are here by yourself and I don't want you spending Christmas alone,' he said softly, his eyes stroking over her damp flushed face and swollen pink-rimmed eyes and narrowing sharply. 'Have you been crying?' This time his voice was more like the old Gerard, direct and compelling and de-manding a reply.

'A bit,' she answered shakily as she rubbed at her nose again, desperately trying to brush her hair back from her sticky face. 'I look a mess——'

'You look beautiful.' His voice was gruff and choked with emotion. 'You could never look anything else to me.'

'Gerard——'

'I know, I know.' He raised his hand in an abrupt acknowledgement of her voice as he swung round to face the window, his back rigid. 'I haven't come here to bully you, kitten, please believe that. I know you need time and I can see that I was trying too hard, not giving you time to think or sort out what you want. It was all me, me, me, wasn't it?' He shook his head slowly, still with his back turned to her. 'I was overwhelming you when you needed desperately to be able to step back a pace and evaluate both the past and present and get it all straight in your head. It was just that I thought I might lose you.' His voice broke but he recovered instantly. 'I thought that when you had sorted it all out I might not feature in your plans and so I was trying to force the pace. I didn't realise it until I phoned you. I'd been trying to reassure you, you see, show you what I am inside, how I think, feel——'

'Gerard.' This time her voice caught him and he turned to face her, his eyes desperate.

'Don't say it, kitten.'

'Say what?' she asked shakily, stunned by the pain and misery in his face.

'Goodbye.'

'Goodbye?' What was he talking about?

'I need you.' He lifted his hands and then let them fall back by his side as his eyes searched hers across the room. 'I need you more than I've ever needed anyone in my life. You *are* my life.' He shook his head savagely. 'I know you are the one who has been hurt, who needs someone strong to lean on, to protect you, but dammit, I'm falling apart inside. I eat you, think you, breathe you, sleep you. You feature in every little thing I do, every thought I think. I can't go on like this——' He stopped abruptly. 'Hell, Kit, I didn't mean to say——' He stopped again.

He needed *her*? Not Gerard, she thought as her stunned eyes searched his face. But it was true. As she held the beautiful gold-brown gaze she saw he was hurting too, that a pain as deep as any she had felt had marked his face. How could she not have understood? she asked herself brokenly as tears began to run in rivulets down her face. How could she have kept them apart for a minute? He needed her, wanted her, *her*. When he looked at her he didn't see someone unworthy, unlovable. He didn't see her as she saw herself, as she had been taught to see herself all through her childhood. *He loved her.* 'You need me?' Her lips formed the words but they were a light breath on the air. 'You really need me?' she asked more strongly, as a joy more piercing than any pain melted the fear and hurt.

'So much.' He was watching her, his eyes searching her face, unsure of her reaction. 'But I can wait, I can be patient——'

'I can't.' And still he hesitated, unable to believe what she was telling him.

'I want you as my wife, kitten,' he said slowly. 'I want you to join yourself with me. I want you to trust me, to understand that I'm there for you no matter what, but I know it will be hard for you. I can wait for physical love, if that's what you want, however long——'

'How long does a special licence take?' she asked softly as the tears still continued to fall.

'A special licence?' And then, at last, he was at her side gathering her into his arms and smothering her face with kisses as he groaned her name against her lips.

'I love you, I love you,' she said over and over again so that he would know, *really* know.

'And I love you.' He raised his head briefly to look down into her red, sticky, tear-streaked face. 'I always will.'

'I know,' she said quietly, lifting her hand to his hard tanned cheek, and it came to her in a blinding flash of relief that she *did* know. Finally. She would never doubt the depth of his understanding, his compassion, again. As Emma had said, they didn't come gift-wrapped like him too often and she wanted this gift, oh, she did.

'Why the Mona Lisa smile?' he asked softly as he looked down at her, a wealth of love in his eyes, and as she told him he gave a grin that was pure wickedness. 'I like your Emma,' he said with satisfied male arrogance. 'It's only her encouragement that gave me the hope to think I still had any chance at all.'

'You've been talking to Emma?' she asked in surprise.

'Of course.' He hugged her close to him, taking her mouth in a long hard passionate kiss that made her toes curl, before burying his face in the soft silky skin of her neck with a smothered groan. 'I could eat you alive,' he muttered gruffly. 'I don't know if this cosy Christmas is going to be such a good thing after all. I might be a gibbering idiot at the end of it. Restraint might be good for my soul but there are certain other parts of my anatomy that aren't controlled so easily.' He kissed her again, his hands warm and dangerously sensual as they moved beneath the silk of her pyjamas to the swell of her breasts. She shuddered at his touch and he stopped instantly, looking down at her as he drew away.

'It's all right, I know all this is new to you, don't be frightened.'

'I'm not *frightened*,' she said softly, feeling bereft as the warmth of his body left hers and more than a little put out.

'You aren't?' he asked delightedly, enchanted by her candour.

She shook her head slowly, her eyes slumberous. 'I think it's time I unwrapped that package,' she said softly. 'I've waited too long for this particular gift as it is.' And all he could do was agree.

Emma Goldrick was born and raised in Puerto Rico, where she met and married her husband Bob, a career military man. Thirty years and four children later they retired and took up nursing and teaching. Goldrick hobbies include grandchildren, flower gardens, reading and travel.

In 1980 they turned to collaborative writing. After sixty years of living in over half the world, and a full year of studying the Mills & Boon® style, their first submission was accepted in 1983. Since then, they have written over forty books between them, which have been published worldwide.

Sadly, in 1996, Bob Goldrick passed away. Emma continues to write in his memory.

DAUGHTER OF THE SEA
by
EMMA GOLDRICK

CHAPTER ONE

SHE struggled to open her right eye. The other was swollen shut. A vague male figure stood by the bed. She blinked, trying to bring it into focus.

'*Iorana oe*,' he said in a deep soothing baritone. The Polynesian words flowed melodically. She tried to repeat them, forming them deep in her parched throat, in the way he had sounded them 'Yorahna ohe?' He chuckled.

'What does that mean,' she croaked. He came closer to the bedside.

'*Iorana oe*,' he repeated. 'It means hello, goodbye, greetings.'

'Oh,' she sighed, disappointed.

'It also means *live happily*,' he added with another chuckle.

'Ever after?' she pleaded.

'Yes, if you like,' he said sympathetically. 'Live happily ever after.'

Her body stopped shivering for just a moment, and a feeling of peace welled over her. But her eyelid was too heavy. It blinked, closed, and she fell down into the maw of terror again.

The great waves which pounded and rolled the tiny rubber raft bounced her up and down, smashing her into the tiny case of stores in the bow until she was bruised and battered. Until she gave up the unequal fight, and withdrew into herself, coiling up in a foetal ball and letting the ocean do its will. At first she cried, clutched herself there in the darkness. She could see nothing. As she stepped aboard the little craft, her father had struggled to set up the tiny tent-like roof that kept the raft from foundering under the hammer blows of

5

wind and rain. And then the deck had dipped under
water, and the raft had floated free. She was still able to
think, back then. She struggled to raise one corner of
the tent and scream into the wind. But her father could
not hear. It was the money again. He had pushed her
into the liferaft and had gone back into the cabin for
the briefcase that held the money. And then he and the
yacht had swung in one direction, the raft in the
other, and the wild typhoon had blotted out the world.

She was too good a sailor to believe that it was the
end for both of them. They had come too close to the
rocky shore of Moorea, and the yacht had bounced off
the rocks at Itihau Point. So that gave them two ways
to drift. Around the point itself, under the pressure of
the wind, and on to the little beaches of Itihau. Or out
into the equatorial current, and up the chain of islands
to wherever wind and sea would take them.

All that was in the first night, as wind and current
battled for the tiny inflatable raft. She had laughed and
cried and prayed and sang until her body had no
strength to do more. And then she had withdrawn into
the hidden corners of her mind, where no storms could
follow. So she knew nothing, actually, of the next day,
or the one that followed, when the great winds blew
themselves out. And, as a sort of after-thought, tossed
the little craft so high that it cleared the reef at Te
Tuahine.

Gentler winds propelled the little orange raft across
the lagoon and beached on the black sand just under
the eastern point, where Mona Atau stood guard over
the entrance to Pakua Bay.

It might have rested undiscovered into the heat of the
tropical sun, if Sam Apuka had not drunk too much
beer at the festival. Not *kaava*, the local fermented
coconut drink, but imported beer, carried all the way
from Tahiti in bottle. Although the *kaava*, on top of all
that beer, might have been a factor. In any event, just

before sunrise, Sam rolled off his sleeping mat, wandered out into the moonlight, and took care of his problem.

The moonlight was the trap. At forty, Sam Apuka knew the value of moonlight, the lure of hip-swinging *vahine*, the sound of the slack-string guitar. He kicked his toes in the sand and wandered up the beach, wondering if his head would ever stop pounding.

The orange brilliance caught his attention. Eagerly he turned his attention to it. A new phenomenon in this tiny island world always drew a crowd. Sam knew what it was. After all, had he not worked for five years for CEP, the *Centre d'Experimentations du Pacifique?* That was before he caught *fiu*, of course.

It took only a minute for his gnarled hands to unfasten the ropes and throw back the cover. And by that time he had gathered a crowd. Two other men, pale bronze shadows in the moonlight, peering over his shoulder.

'What you got there, Sam?' one of them asked in the delightful mixture of French, Polynesian, and English that served this last island outpost of French Polynesia. '*Aue*, look at that. That some beautiful *vahine*, b'lieve me, brother!' The three of them stared down at the contents of the rubber raft. One magnificently lovely girl, her long blonde hair hanging in wet strings around her oval face. She was curled up in the foetal position, knees up against her capacious breasts, hands wrapped around her legs. She might be five-foot-four, perhaps. Her eyes were closed, and dried salt cemented her eyelids together. She hardly appeared to be breathing. She wore a bright orange lifejacket strapped loosely around her torso, and nothing else.

'Man, that some *vahine* you got there!'

'I ain't got her,' Sam Apuka told him sternly. There was a need to speak sharply to the young men. The old ways were almost gone. The young grew up with no reverence. 'And she no *vahine*. Look at that hair. *Mon Dieu!* That one a *popa'a*—a European. *Te Tamahine Tanqora*. Daughter of the Sea, that who she is. Come on, you two. We carry her up to the Big House.'

She woke for the second time. The room was plain but cheerful. Bamboo framed it, and pandasu leaves, woven in strips, shielded the walls. There was a gap at the bottom and top of each wall, to let the breeze blow through. Sunlight was flashing at her. Three huge bamboo chairs barely cluttered the room. She was lying in a bed. Wide, comfortable—also of bamboo. Her hair clustered around her face, fresh-washed, smelling of coconut oil. But her lips were dry, thickened by salt rime, and her throat was parched.

'Now I sit up and look around,' she mumbled to herself, 'and somebody comes in and I say "Where am I," and he says, "Are you Rose Lambert?" And I say, "Yes, I'm Rose," and he says "Where's your Papa, Rose Lambert? We know all about both of you. And if we can't get him we've got you. I arrest you for embezzlement, woman." And I say—holy murder, I can't say any of that!'

There was a stirring at the side of the bed. She turned her head. A little girl nestled in one of the big bamboo chairs. Eight years old, perhaps—nine? Her adult teeth crowded her tiny mouth. Straight golden hair, knitted up into two pigtails, a gingham dress sat lightly on her shoulders, and fell to about mid-thigh. Obviously too small for her. She looked like a little elf who had been too long in some man's care.

Not a native girl. Not hardly. A peaches-and-cream complexion, highlighted by a line of tiny freckles that ran across one cheek, up the bridge of her nose, and out on to the other.

'Hello.' The child was cuddling a teddy bear, almost bigger than she. Well-scuffed, with one eye missing.

'Hello?'

'You been sleeping for a long time, did you know? It's the day after tomorrow already.'

'The day after tomorrow?'

'Well, the day before yesterday was the day you came, and then yesterday, and now is the day after, and all you've done is sleep.' Was there some accusation there? Rose struggled to clear the cobwebs. Obviously conversation was a desperate thing in this household! It might be better to go on the offensive.

'I like to sleep,' she said firmly. The little girl thought it over carefully.

'My name's Josie,' she contributed.

And there I am, caught in a dilemna, she told herself. Even with a child I can't make conversation. Make up a name? And then forget it the first chance, and put my foot in the soup? I need something simple!

'My name's Josie,' the child repeated, just a little bit louder. 'You haven't got deaf, have you?'

'No, I'm not deaf. That's a nice name. Does it stand for Josephina?'

'No, it just stands for Josie. I ain't supposed to ask you what your name is.'

'Oh? Did someone tell you that?'

'Yup. Daddy says it's supposed to be some kind of test. What is your name?'

'Josie, I hope you won't be angry with me—but I just don't remember.' And that's it, she told herself. The simplest form of lie. Don't ask me any questions, because I don't remember *anything*. No selective memories that can trip me up. I'll go all that way. Amnesia, isn't that what people get when they've been in shock? That's me. Forty-eight hours in a liferaft, and I've got amnesia. And that's a story I can stick to through hell and high water!

'You don't remember your own name! Daddy, did you hear that?'

'Hear what, love?' He had come in so quietly she would not have known he was there, had not his daughter looked up. She must be his daughter. I wonder where his wife can be!

'I said my name was Josie and she said she can't remember *her* name. Ain't that funny?'

'Isn't, baby—not ain't. And no, it isn't funny. Didn't we say something about that?'

'You mean about I shouldn't ask? Well, I——'

'Hey, no additional dialogue, pest. Scoot out of here. Out!'

'But Daddy! She's a girl, and I ain't seen no girl this——'

'Not right now. pet. Our—lady is just recovering. Scoot.'

'Okay, meany. Shall I tell Miri to bring the meal?'

Rose watched the pair of them as they jousted. There was a deep affection there, betrayed by the look in their eyes, by the casual touching that spoke myriad messages, by the tilt of their heads as they talked. Two people who loved each other. Just the way Papa and I love each other!

The little girl is a beauty, and will grow into something more, Rose thought. The man—well, he's not exactly ugly, but he's far from handsome. There's a deep scar on his neck, behind his ear. And furrows down each side of his face. 'Worry lines,' her mother called them. His ears were rather small for such a large head, and his chin sported a vertical cleft of note. Brown hair, brown eyes. No, not handsome, but still rather—imposing? It was hard to read his expression. A man who kept his own secrets. He smiled at her.

'Do you want to get up?'

'I—I can't. I don't have any clothes.' And neither does he! He's wearing tight blue shorts, frayed at the legs, barely enough to cover the law. What law? A woman had come into the room. A Polynesian, carrying a jug of some liquid. She looked to be in her early twenties. She wore a brilliant red and yellow *pareau* draped around her hips. It fell to just above her ankles. And all the delightfully female rest of her was left on view!

'We can get you a *pareau*,' he continued. 'Like the one Miri is wearing. One size fits all.' There seemed to be a bubble of laughter in his voice. At least Rose chose to interpret it that way.

'If that's what she's wearing, I need considerably more than that,' she sighed. 'I don't seem to remember what I normally wear, but I'm sure it's more than that!'

'You don't remember anything at all?' That's what is sparking his interest, she noted. He's got that hawk-look on his face. There's something about my fake amnesia that interests him tremendously. What *is* it?

'No,' she returned vaguely. 'Nothing at all.' And as she watched him from under the fringe of her long eyelashes she would have sworn that he was relieved to hear it. He came over to the bed.

'Drink this.' He offered a glass of something cool. 'As soon as we restore your body fluids you'll feel better. There doesn't seem to be anything broken, although you have a number of bruises.'

She sipped eagerly at the glass. Orange juice. And something else, something unknown to her. 'Papaya juice,' he chuckled. There was a crackle of noise from some other room in the house. A radio!

'I have to run,' he said, and did. The girl called Miri came over and chattered at her in an odd mixture of Polynesian, French, and English. They wanted her out of the bed. She managed to fade their words into the background, and concentrate. The voice on the radio was speaking rapid-fire French, somewhat beyond her Louisiana *patois*. But she caught the gist of it. It was a call from the police on Tahiti, being relayed through the adjacent island of Maupiti. In the middle of the next

sentence somebody turned something down, or closed a
door, for the rest of the conversation was lost.

Oh God, she thought. The storm has gone, and it's
clean-up time. Where is Jules François Lambert, who
stole from the Banque Pacifique? Or his missing
daughter, Rose. Where! The police would appreciate
information in order to make an arrest? Oh God!

Supporting hands helped her to her feet. She forced
her muscles to move her, across the room, where the
little girl brushed the curtains aside, out into a long cool
corridor angled so that the trade winds blew eternally
down its length, and down three doors to the bathroom.
It's what I do most every day, she told herself
hysterically. Walk naked down the hall, held up by a
tiny girl in a too-short dress, and a lovely *vahine*
wearing next to nothing!

The bathroom was more than she expected. A tin
shower-stall, open to the sky for one thing, and a
complicated chain affair attached to a huge barrel
poised overhead. A rather large enamel hand basin,
with a plastic pipe coming out its bottom, and no taps.
Of course, she sighed. All the water has to be carried.
And then, the height of luxury, a Scandinavian
chemical toilet! Not bad, considering.

Her two escorts propelled her into the shower, and
one of them pulled the handle attached to the chain.
The water that spurted gloriously over her was lukewarm, clear, clean. She wallowed in it, enjoying its cool
touch, its massaging action on her sore shoulder muscles.
The water ran for about three minutes, and then stopped.

'Damn,' she muttered under her breath. There was
the melodius sound of laughter from the room behind
her. She turned around. The little girl, Josie, had gone,
and in her place were two more Polynesian beauties,
younger than Miri, and equally under-dressed. They
might have been twins—despite the fact that such a
thing is considered terribly unlucky! The two newcomers

chattered like a pair of magpies, and then stopped and
giggled again. Miri gave some command. One of the
smaller girls stepped out of her pareau and joined Rose
in the shower. In a moment she was being soaped
vigorously from head to foot.

'Moera and Leaha,' Miri called. 'They have no
English. They are surprised that you are white all over,
no? They never see such a thing before. They say you
are plenty woman. The men will be mad for you, you
understand!'

Not me, Rose thought grimly. I'm not joining the
lust-parade on this damn island! All three of the
Polynesians giggled again. Wondering, Rose looked
down at herself. Her pale white skin was turning blush-
red in some very embarrassing places. Damn! she
muttered under her breath. The soaping was over. Miri
pulled the handle of the chain again, and the water
gushed as before, exactly three minutes, no more. She
had always had a furtive hatred of her own slightly
over-stated curves. Especially in the French society,
where 'slender' and 'sleek' equated to beauty. Under the
urging of Moera, she stepped out of the shower and
into a huge warm towel. Both Miri and Leaha began a
gentle massage, drying her off. They hissed in sympathy
at the great black bruises on her shoulders, giggled as
they dried her long blonde hair, holding its strands up
beside their own raven-darkness for comparison.

When she was thoroughly dried they led her out back
to the bedroom and gave her her first lesson in the use
of the all-encompassing sheet of cloth that made a
skirt, or, when folded differently, a sarong. One of the
cloths they showed her was heavy, the other two very
light. Colours splashed wildly in all of them. Miri had
left them to go back to the kitchen. By dint of sign-
language Rose asked the other two girls about the
differences. Both giggled. 'This *tapa*,' Moera told her,
pointing to the heavier material. 'Hard to make.' She

made a movement indicating the pounding of fibres. 'This one,' she pointed to the lighter cloth, 'This Bir ming Ham.' And both of them seemed convulsed in giggles again. Rose shook her head, and no longer tried to repress her own smile.

The first *pareau* demonstration was a complete failure. They draped the cloth just above her hips, letting it fall gracefully to her ankles. It looked wonderfully sexy, but when she peered into the little wall-mirror, all she could see was her breasts, standing proudly unsupported. 'Too much,' she sighed, and tried her sign-language again.

The sarong was just a little better. Tied over her breasts, with both shoulders bare, it dropped to just below her knees. But the knot bothered her. She had often worn bath towels in this manner, and could not easily forget how little force it took to disengage them. Finally, against the objections of the pair, she devised a draping that went over her shoulder, much like a Roman toga, with the bottom falling half-way down her thighs. She smiled her thanks to the two girls. They left the room, looking too sombre to be true. She offered a grateful word in her Louisiana French. Moera looked back at her, shook her head, and said *'Aita e pe'ape'a.'* He came into the room as they went out.

She pirouetted to demonstrate her mastery of the fashion. 'Good,' he chuckled. 'But you won't get away with it. Everyone will laugh, you know.'

'No, I don't know,' she snapped. 'What did Moera say when she went out?'

'Aita e pe'ape'a?' he repeated. 'Loosely translated, it means "it ain't no big thing".'

'And why will everybody laugh?'

'Because you've got the customs backward,' he laughed. Tears actually formed in his eyes. 'You cover your breasts. In the outer islands the old customs still hold. If you've got 'em, show 'em!'

'Well—I don't intend to be a peepshow,' she snapped at him. Her legs were growing shaky. She felt behind her for a chair, and dropped into it. He could sense that she was disturbed, and grew solemn. 'But that's only half of it,' he sighed. 'In Tahiti you show the breasts, but never—never—never—do you show the inside of the thighs above the knee. To be frank, my dear, you are now indecently dressed!'

'Damn you all!' The tears came too readily. She struggled to pull down the hem of the *pareau*, with little success.

'Hey,' he offered soothingly. 'You've done well so far. Keep your chin up, my dear. We trying to get liquids into you, not out. Hungry?'

For some stupid reason he sounded so reasonable that the tears dried up. She dabbed at her eyes with her knuckles. He whipped a huge white handkerchief out of the pocket of his disreputable shorts. 'Always carry one for stray weeping women,' he intoned.

She snatched at it, more to hide her expression than to dry her eyes. Do you really, she thought. Altogether too well trained, aren't you. Where's your wife, I wonder? 'I guess I must be hungry,' she stammered. 'I guess I could eat a little bit.'

'That's the way,' he returned. 'A little now, a little later. In a couple of days you'll be completely well. How long were you in that raft?'

Her mind snapped to attention. Trick question number one gets simple answer number one! 'I don't remember any raft,' she said cautiously. 'Was I in a raft?'

'No, not to my knowledge.' He answered quickly, as if trying to cover up some *faux pas*. 'I was thinking of something else. You can't remember a thing?'

'Not a thing. Do you know who I am?'

'Yes.' Nothing more than that. No embellishments. It's like talking to a stone, she told herself fiercely. But before she could rephrase her question, Miri came in with a tray.

'Sit over here,' he directed, arranging a small stool adjacent to a rickety table. The native girl balanced the tray gracefully while he cleared the mess of papers and books, then set it down. 'Help yourself,' he commanded.

The food was set out on wooden platters. There were no utensils. Nothing seemed familiar, everything smelled good. He watched, smiling, and then began to identify things.

'Fish here,' he pointed to one corner of the platter, where little squares of white meat were piled up. 'And sauce over there. Dip the fish in the sauce and have at it.'

'What kind of fish?' She was busy at the work. The little cubes were hard to handle, but the sauce was spicy, tasty. She essayed five or six pieces, then stopped to lick her fingers.

'Bonito,' he told her. 'We live off the sea. The Bonito run in the channel between our island and Maupiti. Like it?'

'It's delicious,' she chuckled, digging in for another piece. 'How is it cooked?'

'Cooked? It's not,' he returned. Her hand stopped in mid-motion. His eyes lit up in glee.

'Some joke,' she snapped at him. 'Raw fish? What's this?'

This was a concoction that looked like fried potatoes. 'Breadfruit,' he told her. 'Fried in coconut oil. It has no real flavour of its own, but it's highly nutritional. Give it a try.'

She did. It had a bread-like taste, crunchy, with some pleasant flavouring which she could not identify. He filled her glass with a thin white liquid. 'And this?' she enquired.

'Coconut milk,' he said. 'We've run out of powdered milk, and there's no dairy business on the island. If you get thirsty for real milk, we'll fly over to Papeete one day.'

Like hell we will, she shouted to herself. Fly over to Papeete? Back out of the frying pan and into the jail. You don't catch me that quickly, Mister whoever you are! And while I'm on that subject: 'You never did tell me your name,' she pouted.

'Name? Oh, *my* name. It's Gendron. Giles Gendron. Pretty soon you'll know it as well as your own.' He was trying to make a joke out of it. And amnesiacs probably never see the humour of things like that, she told herself. It took but a second to concoct a dismal face.

'Or probably forget as quickly as I have my own,' she returned. He had the grace to blush.

'I'm sorry,' he apologised. 'I keep forgetting. Have you had enough for now?'

'I—I think I have,' she stuttered, 'but there's still this —this grey paste on the plate. What's that?'

He bent over her shoulder to look. 'Well, I'll be darned. The kitchen help is putting on the dog for you, my dear. That's *poi*. It's a special paste made from taro roots. Very popular. Hardly ever lasts past the kitchen door, it's so good. Taste it with two fingers. Like this.' He demonstrated, twirling two fingers together in the mixture, pulling them out, and hastily shoving them into his mouth.

'You have to move fast. Good *poi* is thick enough not to drip away, but just barely.'

She gave it a successful try. 'And that's good *poi*?'

'It is if you like it. *Poi* is an acquired taste.'

'I like it.'

'Well, don't let it go to your head,' he laughed, coming over to her stool to stand close behind her. 'It might help if you stretch your legs a bit.' He offered an arm. She struggled to her feet, but dizziness assailed her, whirling her off balance, weak kneed. He snatched her up before she fell, and slipped her back into her bed. She managed a weak 'thank you' before her eyes closed.

For two more days they plied her with food and drink, and then he was back again. 'Now we walk,' he commanded. Her legs moved stiffly, and her upper calves complained, but she moved—out of the bedroom, into the hall.

'Bedrooms to the right. Three of them.' He gestured. 'So they get the morning sun. On this side, the dining room, my workroom. That back alley leads to the kitchen. It's a separate building.'

He led her through a double set of screen doors, and out on to a broad veranda that completely surrounded the house. 'This is the place where we do most of our living,' he said.

She sank thankfully into a lounge chair which he pulled up for her, and looked around. 'It—it catches my breath,' she said happily, and gave him her best smile. She was looking east, into the morning sun. The house was situated on a rise of ground, about five hundred feet from the end of a narrow bay. A pair of mountains, twins they looked to be, guarded either side of the bay. A long gleaming white beach in the shape of a huge V spread beside the green water. The bay opened on to a reef-sheltered lagoon. A half-mile out a narrow channel cut through the reef, and into the deep blue of the pacific waves, smashing in white fury on the coral. At the near end of the bay a small stream poured down from the mountain behind them. To her right, two more mountains blocked the view to the west.

'*Pakuo*,' he pointed. 'That's the bay. The river is called *Papetahemaitai*—if you've breath enough to say it, that is. The mountains guarding the mouth of the bay are Mona Aui, and Mona Atau. The pair to your westward are what give the island its name. *Te Tuahine*. The Sisters.'

'And the one behind the house?' She had swung herself out over the rail of the veranda, looking up at the towering broken peak behind them.

'I can't tell you that,' he laughed. 'That's Pele's mountain. The Goddess of the Volcano, you know. There's a secret name that only the *tahu'a* knows. But everybody else, they just pretend there's no mountain there. We're all Christians here. Nobody believes in the old gods, that's for sure. Nevertheless, nobody goes up Pele's mountain except the old priest—the *tahu'a*. And all that on an island two miles across and eight deep.'

It was too much for her to absorb. She was still tired. Her bones racked and ached. A brace of coconut palms stood sentry in front of the house. Generals of the coconut army, she mused. Down behind the beach a whole army of them stood, while in the wetlands at the delta of the river, bamboo shoots swayed in the breeze. A tiny paradise, the mountains, the beaches, the wild growth of papaya, breadfruit, banana. And flowers beyond description, birds of brilliant colour. All marvellous.

'It seems like paradise,' she sighed.

She could hear the shouting of children at play from just around the curve of the bay. A cluster of thatched huts marked a village in the distance. The breeze was laden with gardenia, vanilla, lemon, oranges. 'All perfect,' she told him.

'And yet—not really,' he returned. 'Up until thirty-five years ago nobody lived here. There was no entrance into the lagoon. Te Tuahine has the one thing most pacific islands lack—water. But there was no way to get at it. And then the French government took over Murumura—at the other end of this island chain—as a test site for their nuclear weapons. The people here were re-settled from Murumura. It cost a fortune to blast a passage through the reef, and here you see the results.'

'And you? What brought you here?'

It was the wrong question. She could see the tiny muscles at the side of his mouth flicker, and a curtain came down over his face. She wished desperately that she might recall the question, but she wanted to know so badly. 'Should I not have asked that?' she pleaded. He seemed to be staring into the distance, watching the frigate birds making their way back from the deep ocean.

'Oh, it's a legitimate question,' he sighed.

'For which you don't have a legitimate answer?'

He smiled over at her. 'Dead hit,' he chuckled. She relaxed against the back of her chair, returning his smile. Things seemed to be so much—nicer—when he smiled. It was almost as if he had daemons to dispell, and was human after all.

He seemed to be ready to say something else, when a huge Polynesian man came up the side of the hill, evidently using a set of stairs she could not see. He was a big man by birth, she noticed. And he carried a few extra pounds around the stomach, which bulged out of his tattered tan shorts. His feet were bare, a big straw hat perched on top of his jet black hair, and all the rest of him was sun-bronzed. Gendron got up and went to the edge of the porch. '*Iorana oe.*' He offered. 'I hear you got the sickness, Sam. You came home to get better?'

Big white teeth flashed at them both. 'You know it,' Sam roared. 'Five years I work. Good pay. Carry the loads, drive the truck, keep the accounts. Hey, I do pretty good for a Kanaka boy, no?'

'Until you catch *fiu*, huh?'

'Just so. Until I catch *fiu*.' The Polynesian struggled up on to the porch and dropped uninvited into one of the bamboo chairs. It complained under his weight.

'You've been sick, Mr—Sam?' Rose felt the need to say something. He didn't *look* sick. Who could be sick in Paradise? 'Is it something infectious?' Both men roared in laughter. She could feel the blush spreading across her face.

'I didn't think it was all *that* funny,' she said coldly.

'Of course not,' Gendron comforted her. 'We beg your pardon. It's the disease that's funny, not anything you said. *Fiu* is the disease of boredom. When a Polynesian has had enough of doing some one thing, then he gets *fiu*—he walks off and leaves it all behind him. Mr Apuka has been working with the French nuclear organisation, the CEP. And now he's come home. That was some party the other night, Sam.'

'*Aue*,' the big man grinned at him. 'Too bad you don't come, Giles, we stay five, maybe six, hours on the beach. Plenty of roast pig, plenty of fish, plenty of beer. And then we dance—lord how we dance. I don't go home until all the beer is gone. And how you feel, little lady? You have a rough time.'

'I—I feel all right,' she stammered. 'Mr—Giles—has taken good care of me—and the girls too, of course. But I—I just don't remember anything!' There, she thought fiercely. Get your excuses in early and then let them chew on that! But Sam seemed not the least bit surprised. He nodded, flashed that broad smile, and turned to Giles.

'That liferaft,' he suggested. 'Young Fatara. He thinks to marry, you know. He comes to me today. He got his hut, but he lose his boat in the storm, no? So what you think we give him the raft, he can use it to fish in the lagoon, at least. Nice young man.'

'Good idea,' Giles returned. Rose was facing away from him as he spoke, but his tone drew her eyes back to his face. He was making some sort of signal to Apuka—some wiggling of the fingers, arching of the eyebrows. Now what, she asked herself? Does he feel some sort of guilt, giving away my raft like that. She was about to make a comment when a thought suddenly struck her. Amnesiacs certainly wouldn't recall the existence of a rubber raft! Even though they had ridden one of them for days on end! She ducked her head and looked back out to sea again.

'Mr Apuka,' she asked softly. 'Are you the chief in this area?'

'Me?' He laughed, every portion of his body shaking. 'No more chiefs,' he finally gasped. 'The *Ali'i* all gone, lady. No more *mana*, no more nobles—all gone. And pretty soon all the Polynesians go *pau*. Too many Chinese, too many Malay, too many French. And now, too many tourists. Pretty soon we are like Hawaii— everybody *tamarii afa*. Mixed breeds. Is not bad, you understand. The most beautiful vahines must have some *Tinito* blood. *Nehenehe*, them. All beautiful.'

'And you don't mind?'

'*Aue*, lady, everybody minds, but nobody does nothing. Only the *tahu'a*—the priest—only the *tahu'a* cries in the mountain.'

'The old religion still lives in places?'

Sam chuckled at her ignorance. 'The first white man comes to stay on the island is British missionary,' he said. 'Before the French. Long before. We all belong Church of England. You come to church sometime and you see. Hey, I gotta go. *Parahi*.'

She watched him go, feeling the strangeness of what she had seen and heard. It brought her back to her own problems. She needed to know much—so very much—before this Paradise could be a refuge. Sooner or later the police would come. Native police, of course. Tahiti was now self-governing, with its own elected officials, and France controlled only its external relations.

'I need to know,' she told him. 'I need to know who I am, where I am, and what's going on. I need to know. Desperately.' She sank back in her chair and gave thanks for her training in dramatics. 'And why all this looks familiar.'

'You don't remember a thing?'

'Nothing!' He seemed to be assessing her again. And then he took his decision.

'We came here three years ago,' he said. 'I'm a writer. This is a good place for writing. Josie takes school lessons by correspondence. There's a place in Maryland that specializes in educating overseas Americans. I don't want to tell you much more. I talked by radio to a doctor in Tahiti yesterday. He tells me that your memory will come back on its own, and that prodding you will cause harm.'

'But I *have* to know at least who I am. You *do* know, don't you?'

'Oh yes, I know all about you,' he laughed. He leaned across the wicker table that separated them and tilted her head up. She was compelled to look into those dark blue eyes. It was like seeing a new world through a keyhole. There were flecks of gold in those depths, and a gleam—almost of desperation. Oh no, she screamed at herself. He can't really know—can he? Was he calling the police on that radio? Telling them that he knew where Rose Lambert was hiding? No! She almost screamed the denial aloud, but barely managed to restrain it.

He was fumbling with her right hand. She looked down, terror-stricken, to watch. He was slipping a wide gold ring on to the third finger of her left hand.

'You left it in the bathroom,' he said softly. His eyes were glued to hers. 'You're my wife—Josie's mother.'

CHAPTER TWO

SHE managed to get back to her room just after sundown. The long afternoon had worn down her feeble reserves. It had been a light dinner. Smoked fish, *mahimahi*, Miri insisted, although it looked a lot like tuna. A salad of sweet mango accompanied it, garnished with nuts, and a sprinkling of grated coconut. Tea was served.

'It's one of our major difficulties,' Giles told her as she cradled the warm cup in her hand. 'Coffee is too expensive. We have it for a week or two after the supply boat comes in, and then it's back to tea. Tea is not only cheaper, but easier to come by. Wine is almost impossible. Beer somewhat less so. But we do have plenty of water, and that's something you can't say about most Pacific islands. None of the atolls in our chain have underground water. And even Maupiti, our neighbouring island, lives entirely from rain-water. Nice in the wet season; not so nice in the dry.'

And then he had taken her arm and gently escorted her to her room. There was a sort of caress in his voice as he turned her around at the door, kissed her gently, and walked away down the hall. She was alone for the first time that day.

What in the world is he up to? She threw herself down on the bed wearily, determined to reason it all out. I'm a faker. He thinks I have amnesia—I hope. That's *my* game. But what the devil is *his* game? He must surely believe the story I gave him, otherwise he would hardly dare to try that one on. 'You're my wife!' Indeed! Have I come across some sex-starved Crusoe? It hardly seems possible.

The place swarms with good-looking native girls—

24

and I'll bet a dime to a doughnut that he wouldn't have to whistle up a storm to get one of them into his bed!

And then the little girl. Josie Gendron, no less. Why, the child looks more like me than she does like him! But he *says* he's her father, and she seems to agree. Or is he the con man *par excellence*, who not only has the child believing that she's his, but now wants to convince me that I'm his wife? Walk softly, Rosie, she sighed to herself. If only Papa were here—just to listen to me tell it. Would he ever get a laugh!

Poor Papa. I *have* to believe that he escaped the wreck. We've always been so close. There's always been a bond between us, no matter what the distance—and I *know* it's not broken. I can feel it still! Lord, keep Papa safe. And with that thought she fell into a deep and troubled sleep. Which was just as well for her state of mind, for she missed the entire conference in the kitchen.

'Look, it's the only way,' Giles said to the group. He was still in his tattered shorts, but had thrown on a light cotton T-shirt against the cool of the night. He ran a worried hand through his thatch of hair. Sam Apuka was there, along with Miri, the other two Polynesian girls, and little Josie. 'She doesn't remember a thing. It's not an uncommon happening. There's no identification on her or on the raft. All we have to do is keep her confused for a few days—a week at most. Somebody is pressuring the Tahiti government to take action. And the police judiciary mean to send an inspector to see for himself.'

'You think they would have forgotten, no?' Sam stretched himself and yawned. 'Me, I need a good night of sleep. How come they don't forget? It all happen three—four years ago.'

'Because my former wife has sworn to a charge of kidnapping,' Giles said disgustedly. 'My own child, and they charged me with kidnapping.'

'But you didn't kidnap me,' Josie pleaded. 'I asked you to come and get me. Don't that count?'

'No,' her father sighed. 'You're a minor. The court gave you into your mother's custody after the divorce.'

'Crazy, these Americans,' Sam said. 'She don't want the kid, no? How come she keeps trying to track you down?'

'So I couldn't have her,' Gendron replied bitterly. 'Just so I couldn't have her.' His fingers clutched into fists as he pounded on the table-top. Hold your temper down, he ordered himself. Blowing your top, that's what got you into this damn mess. Be diplomatic! But his heart and mind could not agree.

'So you kidnap your own kid, and you run to Samoa, but that's too close to American law, and you come to Te Tuahine? How come.'

'Because the French-Tahitian law isn't all that easy on extradition, damn it. There's a lot more respect for the child's rights in these islands!'

'Ah, but now she knows you are somewhere in French Polynesia? How come she know that?'

'Private detectives,' Gendron snorted. 'I pay her plenty of alimony. She uses it to hire detectives. And to support that no-goodnik she's living with.' The bile rose in his throat at the thought. I should have killed the bastard, he told himself.

'Aha. She lives with another man? How come they don't get married? Then the kid have a mother and father. That's the best.'

'How come they don't get married?' There was a sharp cynical snap to his voice. 'Because if she marries again she loses all the alimony. What else? She likes the sound of money. And a bird in the hand is worth two in the bush?'

'Huh?' Sam chuckled. 'What bird we talkin' about?'

'The money bird,' Miri interrupted. 'What is past makes no difference. Giles is here. Josie is here. Now we need to keep them here.'

'Okay, okay. I just try to understand.' Sam shifted his not inconsiderable weight in his chair. 'Just tryin' to understand. And I don't need no *vahine* to explain. Was a time when everybody knows his place. Those were the good times!'

'Are you that old?' Miri was laughing at him with her eyes, but trying her best to look respectful. And not succeeding.

'Someday,' Sam threatened, 'you gonna meet a real *tane*—a real man—who set you straight. You see!'

'Not you, old man. Not you!' Miri was laughing, and Moera quickly joined her. Apuka glared at them both, and then joined in. Polynesians love to laugh, even at themselves.

'So why not give the child back to her mother,' Sam asked, when the gale had passed. 'Any girl better off with her mother. Always.'

'Not always,' Giles interrupted grimly. 'Not always.'

'I don't wanna go back,' Josie said. 'I *won't* go back! That man—he kept touching me. I told my mother, but she just laughed. Said it was just in fun. I didn't think so. He likes to hurt people. So I called my Dad. And he came and got me, and they had a terrible fight. I ain't gonna go back. No way!'

'Well,' Sam said reflectively, '*popa'a* ways very funny. I never understand at all. Better here on the island. All the children belong to all the people, always. Nobody hurts children. Never! So what we do now?'

'The way I figure it,' Giles said softly, so softly that they all seemed to cling together conspiratorially, 'We convince this little lady that she's Josie's mother. We really get her to believe it. So when the inspector arrives, he finds me and my child—and my wife all perfectly happy together. We'll have to shuffle a few truths, of course. Josie—you're only six years old, remember.'

'But I'm nine—almost ten, Daddy.'

'We're playing a game, Josie. An important game. You are six years old. This little lady is your mother. You were born here on the island. Can you fix the church records, Sam?'

'Sure. Easy. Nobody keeps record all the time. Just once in a while, when somebody feel like it, then we enter everything we can remember. Births, deaths, weddings, typhoons, like that.'

'Fine. And you, Miri, you tell the rest of the women. Everybody must be told. Don't miss a soul.'

'Ah—Giles.' Sam had a sudden afterthought. 'It ain't gonna work if we don't tell the *tahu'a*. And for sure he have to go up the mountain, to tell Pele. No doubt about that.'

'Oh God! I'd forgotten him!' Giles threw back his head in disgust, ran his fingers through his hair in a nervous reaction, and returned to the debate. 'We *have* to tell him. That crazy old priest and his volcano goddess? Surely you can control him?'

'Hey,' Sam rumbled. 'The old religion is gone, no? But the old habits, they ain't gone. We tell the *tahu'a*. He goes up the mountain and tells Pele—and then everything goes okay!'

'I don't know about that, Sam. He and I have had some pretty tough arguments.' For just an instant Giles felt the cold hand of defeat resting on his shoulders. But whatever was to be done, had to be done here. They had run too fast, Josie and he. There was just no place else to run. It *had* to work. This little woman was the key to success— a gift from God, so to speak. It *had* to work. 'Okay,' he sighed. 'I'll tell the *tahu'a*. Now, how about everybody to bed and get some *tooto*. We all have a lot to do tomorrow.'

He watched them all go. He was tired, mentally tired. His daughter slipped a hand in his, and they laughed as they watched Miri and Sam leave together. Despite their arguments, and a fifteen year difference in age, the two were attracted to each other.

His daughter tugged him out on to the veranda. There was a half-moon, low and silvery in the sky, lighting a path across the calm Pacific. The stars seemed close enough to touch. Sirius, Tahiti's own navigational star, stood quietly overhead. The only sound was the lulling sigh of the waves touching gently on the beach. A heavy musk of vanilla, hibiscus, orange, and ocean salt came down the wind. It rattled the paper-thin leaves of the bougainvillaea. The faint sound of voices drifted up to them from the village. Happy voices.

'You think we can fool them all?' Josie asked. 'All of them?'

'We can if we try, love.' He ruffled her skein of soft golden hair. 'You don't want to go back to New York, and I don't want to lose you. All we have to do is convince this woman. And both of us have to work hard at it. Can we?'

'I—I don't know, Daddy. I'll try. What's her name?'

'Lord, I'd forgotten that,' he sighed. 'I'll think of something.'

'And she can't tell us, can she?'

'It is a mess, isn't it,' he chuckled, picking the little girl up and cuddling her close to him. 'Why do we two always seem to get into these stupid messes? Come on now—you're up late for a six-year-old.'

'Daddy! I'm—oh, it's the game, isn't it. I hafta remember. Yes, I'm up late for a six-year-old. Are you gonna tuck me in and tell me a story?'

'I surely am, baby. All about the little girl who was eaten by the *tiaporo* because she forgot her lines.'

'You're just making that up,' the little girl laughed. 'Devils don't eat little girls. Only boys!'

'Okay, okay smarty. Off to bed with you.'

He followed her down the corridor to the bathroom in the far back of the house, and then to her bedroom, squeezed in between his own and that of their guest. What the devil is the woman's name? We have to call her something—something that won't upset her.

'When do we start the play?' Josie whispered to him after he had shushed her, pointing a finger next door. 'Tomorrow?'

'I suppose so, sweetheart,' he murmured, tucking the single sheet over her slight form. Her night gown is too small for her, he mused. Everything is too small for her. I just can't seem to find the time to see to everything. And I just can't see her running around like the native kids. What am I, some kind of inverted snob? He sat beside the girl's bed, holding her hand, until her steady breathing demonstrated that she had dropped off to sleep. He disentangled her fingers from his own, lay the tiny arm down on top of the sheet, and tiptoed out.

Start the play tomorrow? He paused by the doorway where the castaway girl lay. The almost-transparent curtain blew in the wind. She was muttering something in her sleep. He brushed the curtain aside, and went in. The moon, shining brilliantly through the two windows, provided plenty of light. She was tossing and turning on the bed, the words she muttered too indistinct to make sense. He moved closer to the bed and bent over the tossing form. The sheet had slipped completely off her shoulders, and she was sleeping nude. He gasped as the silver moon painted the fullness of her breasts, the tiny waist, the burgeoning hips. He leaned closer. 'Papa! Papa! It's me, Rose!' There were tears streaking her cheek.

Oh Lord, he thought, what now? She was shaking, quivering, and instead of inspiring pity she stirred him erotically. 'Damn,' he whispered under his breath. 'Another minute and she'll wake up the house!' It was only an excuse, but he seized on it avidly, discarding his shorts and climbing into the wide bed with her. As his arms came around her she seemed to welcome them, moving close to him, cuddling her forehead on his neck, so that the fragrance of her hair filled his nostrils.

The weight of her breast fell on his chest. He sucked in a startled breath, and then, unable to control himself, let his hand drift down until it cupped the soft fullness of her. A rush of feelings swept over him, feelings he had not experienced in years. Lust and nostalgia, he told himself grimly, but his fingers climbed the mountain of desire, and her bronze tip stiffened under his questing touch.

She had fallen into a turbulent dream. The tiny yacht was almost standing on beams end as the force of the typhoon toyed with it, forced it closer in on the rocky shore of Moorea, where the great stone fangs reached out to them. She had been sleeping nude. She snatched at her life jacket and ran. A thunderous crash upended her world and sent her sliding the length of the small cabin and out into the open cockpit. 'Papa! Papa!' she yelled into the wind. 'It's me, Rose!'

The strong warm arms came around her, cradling her safe from the ravening ocean. She snuggled in closer. There had been many a close scrape for them, she and her father, and in every case his fertile mind had brought them through safely. There was no need to fear. Until suddenly a huge hand trailed fingers down her shoulder and took up the weight of her heavy breast!

Her eyes snapped open. The wild night at sea disappeared. Silver moonlight painted a bamboo room in a bamboo house, and the warmth of a very male body squeezed close up against her. Her mind fumbled, having trouble sorting reality from dream. And the hand that held her breast in thrall squeezed gently.

She had only one hand free. The other was trapped between their two bodies. That free hand came around, fist clenched, and smashed into the shadowed face. 'What the hell,' he muttered, startled. But his grip relaxed. She rolled away from him like an enraged cat, spitting her anger as she landed on the floor on hands and knees, and then scrambled up to wedge herself protectively into a corner of the room.

'What the devil do you think you're doing,' she hissed at him. 'Get out of here you—you——'

'Husband,' he supplied affably. 'I'm your husband, Rose. What else?' He sat up in the bed, his back against the headboard, the sheet crumpled down to his waist. 'Surely you don't think that we found Josie in a bush?'

She was startled into frozen silence. Oh my God. The 'husband' routine! He thinks that I believe that? But if I tell him the honest truth I'll be blowing my own cover. Selective amnesia is too much for me to struggle with. It was all or nothing. Damn the man! Taking full advantage of me, isn't he. What a rotten arrogant—

'Rose?' And he knows my name? Another part of the crazy game that he's trying to play? Well, I really have no choice, do I! That jail in Papeete is the worst I've ever seen. I couldn't possibly survive for a day locked up in that place!

'I- maybe,' she sighed. 'You say so. I—I don't remember. I just don't remember—Giles. You can't— you just can't jump into my bed and think that I'll welcome you just can't do that! How can I know for sure that you're my husband, when I don't even remember you?'

He stirred against the headboard, putting his face into shadows. 'Believe me, Rose,' he said softly. 'How would I know your name otherwise? Or that you have a mole on your right buttock. How?'

'I don't know,' she answered despondently. Her mind ran at full speed. How does he know? The mole, of course, because he had his hand- oh, Lord, this is too impossible to be happening! Why don't I just give up and tell him the truth? Or why don't I fight back? Why should he have it the easy way? I just can't give up to *him*. It would only take him ten minutes to discover that I'm just another stupid virgin. Damn the man!

Why don't I remember him? What would a real amnesiac feel about—and the idea struck her full in the face.

She grappled behind her on the chair for her *pareau*, winding it around her in sarong fashion, and then returned to the attack. 'Why don't I remember you, Giles,' she asked softly, almost whispering. 'Is it because I don't want to remember you? Why do I have all these bruises, all these cuts? Is that why I don't want to remember you? Because you did all this to me? Beat me up, did you? Is that how you get your kicks? Why else would your wife not want to remember you? Giles?'

He swung himself up off the bed in one swift motion, a dark shadow now, with the moon over-swept by high clouds. She tried to back away from him, but his hands trapped her shoulders. She winced as they closed on her bruises, but it was too dark for him to see her face. His hands shook her gently.

'No, damn it, I didn't lay a finger on you,' he snapped. 'It was—well, I can't tell you what happened. And you *are* my wife!' The bitterness, the dark threat behind the words, sent a shiver down her spine.

'Daddy?' The little voice from next door broke in on them. 'Daddy? Is something wrong?'

'No, baby,' he reassured. 'I was just talking with your mother.'

'Oh? Mommy? You didn't come to say good night to me, Mommy!'

'Well?' he hissed at her. 'Doubt me all you want, but the little girl believes—and she needs you! So you don't remember me—or anything else, for that matter. But Josie loves you, and I won't have anything done to upset her- -not anything, do you hear?'

'I—I——" She was at a loss for words. She who had the gift of gab from the Irish half of her family. Not a word could she get out. It wasn't just the man. A consummate con man he was, but the little girl was in as deeply as he! How in the world can a girl that age play me up like this?

'Well?' His lips were inches from her ear. The sibilant sound rattled around inside her head, adding to her confusion.

'All right,' she whispered. 'I'll try to do what I can—with the girl, mind you. Not with you! I don't want you near me, you understand? Not until I remember!' And that will be a cold day in Hell, she assured herself.

'Just don't forget,' he returned. 'Play it up.'

'I'll do my best,' she whispered. And then, a little more loudly, 'I'll come now, Josie. I must have fallen asleep too early.' Then, back to the whisper, 'Turn me loose, you——'

'Loving husband,' he interjected. 'Come on, we'll both go and say good night to the child.' One of his hands came around and patted her in a proprietary manner on her bottom. She flinched away from him, and started towards the door, outraged.

'You never used to be so hard to hold,' he chuckled, as he followed her into the corridor and down to the next room. Like hell I wasn't, she swore at him under her breath. Like hell I wasn't! But the cold image of the jail in Papeete flashed into her mind. She forced the rest of her feelings into a dark corner of her mind, fixed a smile on her face, and went in to say good night to her *daughter*.

He stood back from the bed while the two of them exchanged a hug and a kiss, and only came up to the bed after Rose had carefully rearranged the pillows, straightened out the sheets, and planted another kiss on the little girl's forehead.

'Don't forget to kiss Daddy!' Heaven protect us, he thought, she's padding her part. If she over-does the whole affair—oh Lord. Although it looks as if we have Miss Rose—Mrs Rose—in a spot she can't wiggle out of! Now, give us a couple of days to spread the word around the island, and let the inspector come and do his worst!

'Daddy?'

'What, baby?'

'You didn't kiss Mommy.'

'Oh. You mean now?'

'Of course now. I can't sleep if you don't.'

The child had the bit in her teeth, he thought. Shakespeare could have used a kid like this! And she wasn't going to give up until it was done her way.

Warily his hands spanned Rose's waist and turned her to face him. She had her head bowed. The long silky hair hid her expression as she stood passively under his hands. Come on, co-operate, he wished at her. She might have sensed the message. Her face turned up towards his, just as the moon escaped the clutches of the clouds and sprayed the room with silver again. A quiet oval face, a beautiful complexion. A Mona Lisa smile on those full lips. Oh well, in for a dollar, he told himself. Make it look good!

He stooped to her, lightly touching his lips to hers. Warm, moist lips, slightly parted. Make it long enough to be effective, he warned himself. And then suddenly the tip of her tongue touched his, the warmth evaporated into boiling cauldrons of wild feeling that sent streaks of flame up and down his spine. His arms tightened around her involuntarily, as he pressed closer to taste the sweet fire of her. Her breasts, hardly hidden under the thin cotton of the *pareau*, flattened against the muscles of his chest. He pulled her even closer. Her arms arched up around his neck. The room disappeared, faded into the background as he gasped for breath, then plunged into the maelstrom again. He shifted his target, nibbling on the tip of her ear. She moaned, scraped sharp nails down his shoulder blade and then suddenly seemed to recover, struggling to push him away.

He released her reluctantly. Her hands flashed immediately to the slipping knot of her pareau. And then, as if she were completely exhausted, she leaned forward against him, and almost slipped to the floor. He swept her up in his arms.

'Wow!' the little girl said.

'Wow is right,' he gasped, still short of breath. 'Go to sleep you little monster. *Tooto maitai*. Sleep well.'

'Is Mommy asleep?'

'I don't think so, love, but almost.'

'Did I do well, Daddy?'

'You did fine, baby. Go to sleep now. I have to carry Mommy back to her own bed. And you be sure to be quiet. She needs her rest.'

Yes, I surely do, Rose warned herself. Keep the eyes closed. Get your pulse-rate back to normal. You're an amnesiac. You don't remember anything. Especially you don't ever remember being kissed like *that* before! Feel the strength of those arms! You'd think I weighed only as much as his daughter. Keep those eyes closed! You're asleep, remember? If he kisses you like that again you're a lost soul, Rose Lambert!

'Rose?' He cuddled her closer, urging a response. She fought with all her willpower to deny it. Carefully, gently, he stretched her out on her bed, pulled the sheet over her, and dropped a feather of a kiss on her forehead.

'*Iorana*,' he whispered in her ear.

I wonder what that means, she asked herself as she heard his footsteps fading into the distance. He told me once, and I've really forgotten. I wonder what that means?

CHAPTER THREE

THE sun came up in a violent mood, sparking reds and blues and yellows off the clouds to the east of the island. One moment it was pitch dark. In another there was a line of green light along the horizon. Then for about fifteen minutes the skies were rampant with colour. And then the sun vaulted up, and the tropical day had begun. She leaned carefully against one of the bamboo posts that held up the roof of the veranda. For the first time since coming ashore on the island she felt—not entirely well, perhaps—but comfortable enough to make do for herself.

She had been wakened by the raucous clamour of the frigate birds as they headed seaward for their first meal of the day. Behind them the herring gulls were lined up to dive-bomb the lagoon. In the palm grove just in front of the house a pair of Golden Plover were disputing housing rights with a pure-white tern. The scene from her window had drawn her irresistibly. She swept up her *pareau*, knotted it carefully over her breasts, made sure that it fell decorously to her knees, and padded barefoot out of the house. She stood there at the steps and breathed deeply, loving the clean wet smell of the ocean, clear and unpolluted, as it no longer was on Tahiti, the Big Island.

The early-morning sounds of nature filled her ears, and so she was startled when a small hand slipped into hers. 'Mamma?' She looked down at the tousled blonde head, the too-short night gown, the big smile.

'Good morning Josie. Did you sleep well?'

The child was having difficulty, thinking in English, trying to express herself in French, with an occasional

37

Polynesian word thrown in. 'I slept well, Mamma. Did you have breakfast?'

'Not yet, love. I didn't want to wake anybody up.'

'You wouldn't of,' the little girl teased. 'Except for Daddy, that is. He likes to work in the night time, and he don't never get up in the morning. Moera is already in the kitchen, getting the breakfast ready. But now it's *vahines'* time at the beach. Come and swim?'

'I—I can't, Josie. I don't have a bathing suit.'

'But nobody wears a bathing suit, Mommy. Only girls can come to the beach until an hour after sunrise. It's the custom. And you always used to come swimming with me!'

There it goes again, Rose chided herself. Always. As if she and I had known each other all our lives. 'Always?' she teased.

'Well, always before you got sick. Please?'

'I——' but the look in those eyes, so much like her father's, could not be denied. Come on, Rose, she told herself. You heard the child. You and all the rest of the women on this crazy island go skinny-dipping every morning, right? You remember, Rose, don't you? And just for a moment it seemed all so real that she laughed.

Holding hands, they scrambled down the steps carved in the hill below the house. Simple steps, dug in shallow succession, walled with logs, that allowed them to set foot directly on the sparkling white sand of the beach. As Josie had said, across the river on the other side of the bay, several *pareau*-clad figures were running to the water. Watch, she commanded herself. Get it right the first time.

Across the bay the women barely hesitated, dropping their gaily-printed *pareaux* on the sand, and plunging into the quiet waters of the bay. And when in Rome, she asked herself? Josie had already slipped out of her tiny gown and was knee deep in the inviting water. Rose stood in the sand for an indecisive moment, shifting her weight from one foot to the other against the rising heat of the beach. And why do I have to be born the only prude in the family, she sighed. Her fingers climbed to the knot at her breast, paused there as she looked anxiously around, and the cloth fell to her feet.

She was off like a startled fawn, splashing out to thigh depth, then diving forward in a shallow racing dive, eager to get under the water. And not because it's cool and clean and inviting, she snapped to herself. Her head broke the surface almost half-way across this narrowest portion of the bay. Two sleek bronze forms ghosted by her in the other direction. One of the women raised her head just long enough for the traditional *'Iorana oe*,' before the dark head disappeared again. Rose floated lazily in place. 'Crazy language,' she muttered to herself. 'One phrase seems to mean everything. But I like what *he* said better. Live happily ever after!' She rolled over on her stomach, circling until she spotted Josie's little head plugging doggedly after her. Rose shook the water out of her eyes, porpoise-dived again, and glided back to enjoy the girl's company.

They raced and played and floated for another twenty minutes before the sound of a conch-shell trumpet disturbed the air. Almost immediately the *vahines* in the water streaked for shore, and were gone.

'We hafta go,' Josie shrieked at her, giggling. 'Now it's the men's turn. Hurry up, Mommy. It's *tapuu* to watch the men!'

'I'll bet it is,' Rose returned sarcastically. And I certainly won't, she told herself. But her head turned almost against her will, to snatch another look across the bay. And she was giggling as much as the little girl as she followed her around the head of the bay, struggling into her wet *pareau* as they went. Their new path skirted the marshes at the mouth of the little river, and then turned uphill.

'And where in the devil are we going now,' she finally gasped, as their way took them into the bamboo groves, and out of sight both of the house on the hill and the village by the sea.

'You'll see,' Josie teased. As indeed she did. Their final turn took them through heavy growth and out on to an earthen dam that created a pool of fresh water behind it.

The little girl, who was carrying her only garment in her hand, dropped it on the dam and jumped into the pool. 'I can't go all day with that salt on me,' she called back. 'Come on in. You'll be surprised.'

So I'll be surprised, Rose told herself almost hysterically. That's all I've been since the moment I landed on this island. Surprised, that is. Nobody wears any shirts, but everyone has something up their sleeves! Oh well. Once again her fingers struggled with the knot in her *pareau*, and the flimsy garment fell to the ground. The water looked deep enough, up to the level of Josie's neck, but it was too risky, this diving into unknown waters. So instead of diving she stepped off the edge of the dam, and promptly received her surprise. In the middle of the tropics, where the sun averaged ninety degrees or more on a normal day, the water bubbling merrily through the little pool was as cold as ice!

'Why you little monster!' she yelled as soon as she regained her breath. 'You're my daughter? What kind of a way is that to treat your mother? I'll get you for this, you little——' And the ensuing chase, punctuated by laughter, was more than enough to give them both a thorough fresh-water rinse. They both stumbled out of the pool a few minutes later, and stretched themselves out on the top of the dam, panting.

And now's the time, Rose thought. The child is diverted. She won't be thinking carefully. I've got her in the right situation. She leaned closer to the shivering form. 'My, what big teeth you have,' she said. 'Are you really my daughter, Josie?'

But the girl was as elusive as quicksilver. 'Yes, of course I am,' she laughed. Both hands were behind her back, and there were crossed fingers on both.

They wasted minutes letting the sun dry them off. It didn't require a great deal of time. And it's not really wasted, Rose assured herself. Time is different here in the islands. There are long hours, and short hours. Only the stupid clock requires discipline and order. So finally they dressed, and wandered back hand-in-hand to the stairs that led up to the house. They stopped a quarter of the way up. An old man was coming down. As soon as she saw who it was Josie ducked behind the older woman and clutched at her for support.

'It's him,' the girl whispered. 'It's the *tahu'a*!' She didn't sound afraid of the old man—just cautious.

And he was an *old* man. Older than any Polynesian Rose had seen in her short three weeks in the islands. His face was over-run with wrinkles, his short hair was white, and tattoos covered both shoulders. He walked with the aid of a bamboo stick, but his proud body bent not an inch. A loin cloth and a little leather pouch strung around his neck on a leather thong was his complete attire. In his eighties, Rose thought, but look at the posture, the dignity of him! She stepped aside to give him room, feeling the absurd need to curtsey as he went by.

The old man noticed her instinctive gesture, smiled, and stopped. His cold steel eyes ran up and down her. There was a start—almost a look of surprise, as he examined her long blonde hair. His eyes shifted to the child's. When he spoke, his French was clumsy, as if it were something he had learned long ago, and never put to use.

'*Aue*,' he exclaimed softly. 'Apuka was right. *Te Tamahine a Tangora!*' He drew in his breath sibilantly through his teeth, and then, to Rose's amazement, switched to a very pedantic English. 'The Daughter of Tangora! Apuka was right!' Rose struggled with her breathing. Something about the old man left her unable to breathe regularly. And then he was gone, ambling down the stairs, leaning on his bamboo staff, muttering something under his breath.

'And what in the world was that all about,' Rose inquired as they resumed their climb.

'Don't ask me,' the suddenly subdued Josie returned. 'You can't expect a six year old kid to know everything!'

'Six years old? Come on, kid. Stop pulling my leg. You've got all your adult teeth.'

'So—so Papa says I'm—pre-something.'

'Precocious. I'll just bet you are, little miss. But I love you just the same.' And strangely enough, she told herself as they climbed on to the veranda, I think I mean it!

When they wandered into the dining room the breakfast table was set, and he was there. Somewhere behind them, in the cookhouse, a constant giggle accompanied the preparation of the meal.

'Ah, there you are,' he said as he got up. The little girl ran to him and hugged him. Then he stretched both hands out to Rose, pulled her to him, and kissed her forehead gently. 'Good morning love,' he offered softly.

'Good morning to you.'

She backed off warily, bumped into a chair, and slumped into it. Somehow or another this man was just too much. Someone to be feared. She could feel a little quiver of—fear—course down her spine. She folded her hands on the edge of the table and tried to look the prim prude that she knew she was.

Josie broke the ice. She scrambled up into her own chair, her tongue going a mile a minute, recounting everything. And I do mean everything, Rose reminded herself. Is there no way to turn her off?

'And your mother actually went swimming without her clothes?' The phrase penetrated her daze, and turned her blush-red.

'Of course,' his daughter returned as she dug into the tea and *firifiri,* the Tahitian equivalent of doughnuts. 'Everybody does. There's a lot of her, Daddy—ah, you know that anyways, don't you? She swims like a fish, and jiggles when she runs! I'm gonna be like her when I grow up!'

'Josie,' Rose snapped at her. 'That's not the kind of thing to talk about at the breakfast table!'

'Well, I'd really love to see her swim,' he laughed, heightening her confusion.

'You know you can't,' his daughter stated firmly. 'It's *tapuu.* You know that!'

'Yes, I guess I'll have to take your word for it then,' he laughed.

She tried desperately to find something to change the subject. *Firifiri,* of course. 'I'm surprised that we don't have croissants for breakfast,' she offered. 'In——' And you're about to give the whole game away, she shrieked at herself. She fumbled for an innocuous ending. 'I just thought that croissants were the French breakfast,' she stammered.

They both stared at her. 'You remember something?' he prodded.

'No,' she sighed. 'Just croissants, that's all.'

'Ah.' He seemed vastly relieved as he leaned back in his chair. It creaked as his weight changed. 'Yes. Of course. Croissants are the usual breakfast of the French. And you can get them in Tahiti, but not out here. Flour doesn't keep very well in the tropics. We *have* croissants, you know. For a couple of weeks after the quarterly supply boat comes in, we have a great many nice things.'

'The supply boat?' Again that quiver of alarm ran up her spine. A regular supply boat! Then there *was* communication between this speck in the Pacific and its neighbours. And sooner or later news would flow down that communications link!

'Yes,' he repeated. 'Four times a year, from Tahiti. We buy staples, and they take away our copra. Whenever anyone around here is willing to work at it, of course.'

'Oh!' They could both hear the tension in her voice. He decided to probe.

'In fact, it's due next week some time.' He offered the news casually, off-hand, but his eyes were glued to her face. She did her best to school her features. Her hair helped. As she ducked her head it swung around her face and hid her—for the moment—from his searching gaze. 'It will bring a surprise,' he continued. She ducked her head again. Oh God, not another surprise, she begged to herself.

'A police inspector is going to fly out to Maupiti, and the boat will bring him over,' he continued.

He didn't have to be a close observer to catch her reaction. Her head snapped up, the long strands of silky hair swirling around her throat. She was suddenly pale -completely white. Her eyeballs rolled up under their lids. She pushed her chair back from the table, upsetting the bowl in front of her, and staggered backwards.

He sat immobilised for just a moment, and then as she tottered, he was up beside her, just in time to catch her as she collapsed into his arms.

'I think your mother has fainted, baby,' he said quietly. 'Too much excitement, too soon.' He stood there with Rose in his arms, her fair hair tumbling over his shoulder, the sweet clean smell of her clogging his nostrils, sending those same quivering sensations up his arm, down his spine, that he had experienced the previous night. Dear God, he thought, can it really be just abstention? Look at her almost an angel, with all her muscles relaxed, and that permanent look of fear hidden behind closed eyelids. I wonder who she really is. I wonder what the devil she's so afraid of? If I didn't need her so badly, I'd try to find . . .

'You just gonna stand there, Daddy?' The little girl came over to his side and took one of Rose's drooping hands in her own. 'She's nice,' Josie whispered. 'I—I wish we could keep her for always. Daddy?'

'I'm going to take her into her room,' he snapped, using anger to suppress this other haunting feeling which he could not identify. 'See if Miri is in. We need some—oh, I don't know. There's a little vial of smelling salts in the first-aid kit. Ask Miri to bring it in, please.'

'You're not mad at me, are you?' Josie was trembling. 'I know I didn't do no good this morning. She don't believe I'm six years old. I told her you said I was a *precious* child——'

'Precocious,' he interrupted. 'No, I'm not mad at you, baby. At myself, yes—but not you. Hurry up!'

He hurried down the hall with his burden, but at her bedside, was reluctant to put her down. The feeling of warmth as he held her close was the most pleasure he had experienced in many a day. Josie's right, he told himself. She's a whole lot of woman. Firm, yet soft. Curved the way Botticelli liked to paint them, warm and round. As I like them. Let's face it—as all red-blooded American men like them. Why did she faint? She looked well enough beforehand. Tired, perhaps, from the swimming? One minute lively and lovely, and then—bingo—she's out like a light.

Something to do with what I said? What the devil did I say? The supply boat is coming. How would that bother her. Unless? Unless there were others with her out there in the ocean. Somebody she loves—somebody dear to her, lost in that same storm. And she's afraid to find out whether it's true or not? And that's what is causing the amnesia? She's afraid to find out! She

thinks the supply boat will bring in news of the wreck. I
guess it must have been a wreck. And she doesn't want
to know, so she's got amnesia! It all fits, just the way
the doctor described it on the radio! Poor kid. Poor
lovely beautiful kid!

He could hear the noise as multiple feet hurried down
the hall. Carefully he stretched her out on top of the
sheet, re-arranging the fall of her *pareau* at her knees to
cover those beautiful thighs.

It took another fifteen minutes to coax her back out
of the darkness. She came gently back, keeping her eyes
closed until the last moment, and then gently feathering
her lashes. He was her first sighting. She flinched away
from him in the bed, and a cold hardness flashed across
his face. Josie crowded in front of him, to be rewarded
by a weak smile, all she could muster at the moment.

'Mommy? Are you all right?' The little girl threw
both arms around Rose's neck and hugged her close.

'I'm all right,' she managed to get out. 'I'm all right. I
think—maybe I just need something to eat, or
something.'

'I'll get it right away,' Josie said. 'I'll make some fresh
tea, and——'

'I'll make the tea,' Miri interrupted. Both of them
hurried off on the same errand, leaving her alone in the
room with him. He could hardly fail to notice that she
edged over to the other side of the bed and struggled to
get up.

'No,' he commanded, brooding over her. There was
no warmth in his voice, and she missed that. She
stopped, half off the bed, one foot on the floor. 'Stay in
bed,' he insisted. 'For the rest of the day at least. Was it
something you remembered?'

'No, I—I don't think so,' she sighed. It was getting
harder and harder to maintain her cover-story. Harder
and harder to stop herself from reaching out to him,
confiding in him. And only her fears held her back.

Carefully she settled back in the bed, and once again he reached over gently and re-arranged the bottom of her *pareau*. The hard bitter look on his face gradually faded, to be replaced by—something. She was unable to put a name to it.

He started to say something to her, and then halted. Josie bounced into the room carrying a wicker tray. 'Breakfast—again,' the little girl announced with a giggle. 'I—could you sit up, and I could put the tray across your lap?'

He was around the bed before she could answer, piling pillows behind her, and then gently lifting her up to a sitting position. One of his arms accidentally brushed across her breasts. Tendrils of pleasure shot up into her mind. There was total recall of the night before. She caught her breath, then bit down hard on her lower lip to keep control. He hardly seemed to notice.

She managed a smile. Josie moved in close, and set the tray down across her lap with all the aplomb of a professional waiter. And then Miri was back, carrying a pot of fresh hot tea, and a puzzled look on her face. 'Tea is hot,' she offered, pouring a cup and setting the pot down on the bedside table. Rose flashed her a smile and picked up the cup in both hands, treasuring it as she sipped. Miri turned to Giles.

'He come back,' she said. 'We could talk outside, no?'

He followed her out into the hall. 'Who came back?'

'He came back,' the girl repeated. 'Almost impossible, no? He change his mind. The *tahu'a*.'

'Just like that? I thought he was going to have a fit when I mentioned the subject to him. What happened?'

'I don't know for truth. Is very involved. You know he would never answer a question from a *vahine*. He talk and talk and talk. Now, let me see I can get it right—he say, he receive a message from Tangora. Well, you know, he is an old man, and maybe not right in the head, *comprenez*.'

'Hey, all I know is that if he helps, everybody helps. And if he doesn't help, nobody helps. What message did he get?'

'He say Tangora say, "Help my daughter." That's all. So he comes to say he helps!'

'Good lord. I don't understand what's going on. Who the devil is Tangora?'

'The great sea-god. From the old religion. You know!'

'No, I guess I don't,' Giles sighed. 'I haven't had the time to meet all the old gods. Help my daughter?'

Miri waved a hand towards the bedroom. 'That is what Sam Apuka said. When he saw her in the— when—oh dear.' She giggled nervously, and tugged him away from the door and down the hall. Nervous giggles overtook her. She cupped her face in her hands and struggled to recover. 'Sam say when he first see her, the waves whisper something to him. *Ionei mea te Tamahine Tangora*. He swears he heard it. He tells it all over village. I think too much beer, big head. What you think?'

'What do I think? Lord, how can I think anything. What does that mean, what Sam said?'

'It mean, "Here is the daughter of the Sea-God." Sam swears all true. He go fishing with the *tahu'a* this morning, and he tell him. Crazy. Nobody b'lieve that kind of thing no more. All *haeire atu*—all that go away, long time ago. What you think?'

'Well it's beyond me' he sighed. 'But whatever, if he's willing to help, everything is set for next week. All we've got to do is keep Rose happy, and we're home safe. And in the meantime I've got to get some work done.'

They both walked slowly back into her bedroom. She was feasting daintily on a mango, laughing as Josie entertained her with tumbling exercises. The little girl stopped when he came in, and took his hand, tugging him towards the bed.

'With the ship coming next week,' he said, 'I've got

to get back to work. I promised to send in the next three chapters by this boat, and agents are devil-worshippers.'

'I'll look after Mommy,' Josie immediately volunteered.

'And I also,' Miri added. 'The kitchen work can wait.'

So there seemed to be nothing left for him to do. He waved them all a half-salute and started for the door.

'Daddy!' Josie stamped her little foot. She sounded considerably aggravated at him. Her head was jerking, trying to convey a message.

'Oh!' A broad smile flashed across his face. He came closer to the bed, leaned down, and caressed Rose's forehead with his lips. Just a feather-touch. Her teacup rattled in her hand, until finally she managed to get it back to the tray. She folded her hands to hide the shaking.

'Hen-pecked, that's what I am,' he complained jovially as he left the room. Yes, and what does that make me, Rose asked herself desperately. If I didn't know for sure that he's trying to con me, I'd—well, I don't know what I would do but I'd do something! If he didn't scare me so much, I—oh damn!

Miri was busy clearing a place for a chair right next to the bed. The Polynesian girl was laughing, flashing her beautiful white teeth as if she knew what it was all about. And I wish *I* did, Rose told herself. There's something about Miri today, though, that—well, she wasn't like this yesterday. I'll think what it is in a minute. But right now there's Josie—and that awful dress she's wearing. She looks as if she's being dressed by the Abbot of a monastery, or something. My daughter! I'll give her *my daughter* until it comes out her ears. And his too.

'Josie? Why is that dress so short? Every time you move I can see your underpants.'

'I—' the little girl had been caught unawares. 'I—all

my dresses are short,' she said defensively. 'My daddy likes them that way!'

'Then something must be done about it,' Rose said determinedly. 'What you need is some shorts, and a few blouses. Easy things to make. Do we have a sewing machine in the house?'

'*Ea*' Miri tendered. 'Yes. An old Singer pedal machine. You know to make such a machine go?'

'You bet,' she responded agressively. 'Among other things. Or you could wear a *pareau*, Josie?'

'My Daddy won't let me,' the girl sighed. 'He says I'm not to run around naked like the other kids. I'm supposed to be somebody. I don't know who.'

'My husband's a snob,' Rose chuckled. 'And I didn't know.'

'But you know so very little,' Miri giggled. 'Except sewing machines. That you remember! Some things come back, no? First croissants, and now sewing machines.'

'I—ah—well, I didn't really remember.' Rose struggled to cover the mistake. 'It just *seems* that I think of sewing machines as something that——' Oh lord, shut up, she told herself, the more you fumble around, the worse it gets! And there's a policeman coming next week. To get you, Rosie Lambert, what else. I wonder if he'll have a picture of me on a 'wanted' poster? Rose Lambert, jailbird! Come on, Rose, there's no use glooming about it. When he gets here, that'll be a different story. In the meantime, live!

'And until I'm able to throw a thing or two together, Josie,' she continued, 'you'll put away all that nonsense, and wear a *pareau*. Miri, could you find something?'

'Plenty *pareaux*,' the Polynesian woman cautioned, 'but the girl is right. Mr Gendron, he will, how you say, blow the stack off?'

'Not to worry,' Rosa chuckled. 'I'm the mother, no?'

She added the little ending in bravado. Okay, let him rant and rave. If he's invented a mother for his child, he'll have to put up with her strong character and firm ideas—or he'll blow the works on whatever scheme it is that *he's* working on!

Josie was laughing hysterically, rocking back and forth on her heels. Look at that, Rose told herself. Even the kid knows what's going on, and me, I don't know from beans. 'You don't like the idea?' she asked.

'Oh, I love it. I really do.' There were tears running down the little cheeks. Happy tears. Her feelings were too much for her battered French, so the child switched over to English. 'We ain't had so much fun in years, and I like it a lot,' she teased. 'Only you gotta train Daddy better. Oh, I'm so glad you came—I—I mean, it's wonderful to have my mother back again!' A clock chimed in the hall. Ten o'clock. I think I've put in a sixteen hour day already, and it's only ten in the morning, Rose sighed to herself.

'I gotta go. I hafta study for two hours every morning,' the little girl said. Her eyes pleaded for a day off, but Rose was not about to fall into *that* trap so early in the game.

'Then get on with it,' she commanded gently. 'And be sure to bring your papers in here this afternoon so I can check them.'

She earned a smile—a broad happy smile—and the child ran for the door.

'She never walks anywhere?' Miri turned back to her at the question. 'Every time I've seen her she's always running,' Rose explained.

'All children the same,' the Polynesian returned. 'Childhood filled with many joys. If she walks slow, she will miss something. I go find her two, three *pareaux*.'

'Come back afterwards,' Rose pleaded. 'I need to talk to *someone*. I feel as if I were on a merry-go-round that keeps going faster at each turn.'

'Merry-go-round? *Me fifi roa.* I don't understand?'

'Forget it.' She waved a thank you hand. 'Hurry back. You can put off some of the work, can't you?'

Miri looked at her with her soul in her eyes, lovingly. 'In the islands there is always time for people,' she said softly. 'You rest. I come at once, no?'

She was as good as her word. Not ten minutes later she moved gracefully through the doorway with a second pot of tea. 'I can use that,' Rose laughed, wishing that she knew the secret of that graceful walk. 'Now. Set a spell, as they say back home in my country. And tell me something. Anything. You and Mr Apuka?'

The other woman smiled at her as she settled into the chair. 'You read faces, no? Yes. Me and Sam. We are friends for years, when I am a child. Then he goes away five years, you know. That is the island sadness. All the young men, they want work. They go away and work for the CEP, for the Fisheries, for anybody. And then when they finish they like too much the cities, and the entertainment. They go Tahiti, live around Papeete. Think it is the best life, you know—and they never come back. But Sam, he comes back. And last night he knows I am child no longer, and we think as before, you understand, so I move my mat to his house. And maybe, when the Priest comes by on the supply boat—oh, not next week, the one after that—maybe we get married. That part is not so important, you understand.'

'I'm not sure that I do,' Rose laughed. 'But it's what *you* think that's important. I read Margaret Meade's book about Samoa, of course.'

'Ah see!' Miri chortled. 'You remember more! Too bad not something else. I know about Margarete Meade. I go to school in Bora Bora, and we study. Her book is nice for *popa'a*, but——'

'But?'

'But not exactly true. One thing she does not

understand. Our people wish to make their friends happy, so we tell them what they want to hear. Happens all the time. Suppose we go walk, you and me, and we see a bird. You say, look, is *Nono Anu* bird. I look. Is not *Nono Anu*, is *Ute Ute Anu*. But you want it to be *Nono Anu*—and to say you are wrong makes you unhappy. Bird, he don't care what to call him. Me, I don't care what to call him so long he don't eat me. So I say, oh yes, is *Nono Anu*. You understand?'

'I suppose I do,' Rose returned. 'But it's confusing to a stranger. You'll have to put up with my ignorance for a while, I'm afraid.'

'You no stranger,' Miri said seriously. 'You *Te Tamahine*. That's plenty. You one of us.'

'I wish I could be,' Rose sighed. 'You are all so free. I wish I could be that way. I wish I could even wear a *pareau* the way you do. But I don't have the nerve. You are so free.'

'Hah!' Miri laughed so hard the tears welled. 'We not free, not at all. You look, but do not see. We live by custom. Everything has custom. We say the old ways are gone, but on the small islands they are still here, hiding behind mask, no? The old *tapuus* still run. What happens to *vahine* who stays to watch the men swim? Pele comes out of her mountain, that's what, and punish that fool. You better b'lieve it. And you better not wear *pareau* like I do.'

'Well why not, for goodness sakes?'

'Because, what you think—you get all over sunburn. Then you no good for your man at all, huh? I do something like that myself, Sam, he gives me a good knock, no?'

'Okay, I give up,' Rose giggled. 'So find me some cloth, and I'll make Josie and I both some skirts and some blouses.'

'I bring the machine this afternoon,' Miri promised. 'Now, what else you want to talk about?'

I want to talk about him, Rose told herself desperately. My—my husband. 'How long has Mr Gendron—how long have we been here on the island,' she asked cautiously, not knowing whether Miri was a part of the conspiracy or not.

'Oh——' the island girl was fumbling for words. Rose's heart sank. Not another one, she prayed desperately. 'The child—you know—she is born here on *Te Tuahine,* but I am not here at that time. And then he come back three years ago? Yes, three years. He is a friend of Mr Maravais, the man who builds this Big House. He buys everything, that Giles. Whole island belongs to him now. And he writes. Locks door in study, hang red sign in hall. Only room in house with a door. He says to me, he says—Hey, Miri, you tell all *kanaka* boy anybody comes to my room when red sign hangs out, gets plenty trouble, b'lieve me. So then he stays six months, and then he goes off. We don't see him for long time. But then when he comes, he brings child.'

'Just the child?'

'*Aue,* now. What have I said. No, no. He brings you and the child.'

'Two years ago?'

'Pretty close. We measure time better by supply boats coming, not by years.'

And that makes one more, Rose thought sadly. They're all in it. Everybody in the house! Two years ago Papa and I were living high on the hog in Monaco. That was one of our good years. The last one, come to think of it. But—come on, Rosie. Why let it get you down? Pull up your socks and get things moving. That's what Papa always said. You've been just a little loose with the truth yourself, haven't you dearie? Papa. Where can he be? I know he's not dead. I can still feel that bond between us. He's not dead—he's just— somewhere else. And now? Giles has some plan, some programme. And he needs me for a wife. Complete with a long background and history. So I just can't be Rose Lambert, can I? When the policeman comes, if he doesn't have a picture, why here I'll be. Mrs Giles Gendron, complete with husband and child, all who've known me since Caesar was a pup! All I've got to do is keep my cool and agree with everything they tell me. Well, most everything. And there's only a week to wait.

'Thank you, Miri,' she sighed. 'I feel—just a little bit tired. I'd like to rest for a while. Do you mind?'

It was true. Her eyes were heavy. And the weak smile she mustered was enough to convince the native girl. Miri watched the eyelids slowly drop, heard the sigh of relaxation as all the limbs fell loose. '*Iorana oe*,' she whispered over the sleeping blonde beauty, and flowed gracefully out of the room.

Rose slept through the lunch, and through the silent afternoon, when even the birds seemed to take the time to rest. He came with the child to look in from the doorway, but nothing disturbed her deep and quiet sleep. No nightmares, no memories, no pains. To all intents her brain was turned off, and her body relaxed in a jumble of loose limbs that brought a smile to his face. He came back twice during the afternoon and night. Once he re-arranged her *pareau*, smoothing it down over her lovely legs. The second time he brought a damp cloth and wiped away the beads of perspiration from her forehead. She noticed neither appearance, nor noted the length of time he stood by the bed brooding over her, a strangely warm smile on his face. The night passed, and it was morning again.

CHAPTER FOUR

SHE lay on the beach in the late afternoon and stretched, squirming against the soft whiteness of the sand like a cat. The little teddy which she had sewn up for herself in place of a bathing suit, was just enough cloth to be decent as long as it was dry. Wet, it was of no more use as a cover than a fistful of cobwebs. Her wrap-around skirt, brought along to meet the Polynesian requirements for modesty, was rolled up under her head as a pillow.

She suppressed a giggle as she looked down at her *daughter*, beside her. Here they were, two *popa'a*, dressed mother-and-daughter style in the same cut and colour of outfit, the result of the several long hours Rose had spent over the ancient sewing machine. Out of the thousands of bolts of *pareau*-cloth on the island, and there seemed to be at least twenty miles of the stuff, she had concocted for them both several sets of wrap-around skirts and sleeveless blouses, and a round half-dozen of the head-to-toe Missionary dresses, the *muumuu*. Not exactly high fashion, to be sure, but the best her needle could provide. There had been no help from the island women. They all looked at it as an exercise in foolishness. Pleasant foolishness, but . . .

'Now, if I only had some decent underwear,' she sighed.

'You mean like silk and lace and all that stuff?' Josie giggled.

'Like silk and lace,' she returned, pushing up the brim of her big straw hat to get a better look. They had established a close rapport, she and this little girl who claimed to be her daughter. And perhaps more than a rapport, perhaps more than just a liking. Which may be only over-compensation, Rose warned herself. To make up for the fact that that father of hers scares me to death! Every time I look around quickly, there he is, staring at me. As if I were the next dish to be served!

She settled back again, hands clasped behind her head, hat pulled forward to shade her face. At that angle only the narrow line of surf smashing at the reef was within her sights. The whole world seemed to be at peace. And look at me! It was, what—Monday night when I came ashore. I don't remember Tuesday at all. Wednesday I met both the Gendrons, and came down with amnesia. Thursday he told me they were my 'family'. Friday I seemed to have slept through a day, somewhere. Saturday we walked around and kept out of each other's way. He and I, I mean. Sunday I went to the church service. Sam Apuka led the service. I didn't understand a word of what he was saying—but wasn't the singing marvellous? It almost seemed spontaneous, interrupting the homily when the spirit moved, first one voice, then a dozen, then the entire congregation. And what could have a nicer sound than '*Rock of Ages*' sung to a hula beat!

Monday. What did I do on Monday. I sewed, mostly. The *tahu'a* came by and we had one of those conversations where he went away happily, and I hadn't the slightest idea what he was talking about. And here it is Tuesday. The ship comes tomorrow. Or should I say the police come tomorrow. Looking for Rose Lambert, of course. Which gives me just twenty-four hours to practise up on being Rose Gendron, wife, mother—and Lord help me, what else? Lover? I haven't done too well in that line so far—and I've got to do better! 'You hear me, Rose?'

'What did you say?' Josie was up on one elbow, staring at her. Her tiny body glittered from the applications of coconut oil her father had insisted on.

'Nothing. I was talking to myself. I find it very

important to see if I agree with myself!' The little girl's eyes sparkled at her, proof that the affection was not all one-sided. And then, because Rose's mind was squirreling around with her own million problems, it slipped. 'Didn't your other mother ever do that?'

'She didn't make no funny—ohhhh!' The little hands went up to cover her mouth, and a look of astonished reproach swept over the elfin face. The eyes turned stormy. 'You made me say that! You made me!' The child jumped to her feet, indignation showing in every angle of her body. Indignation, and something else. Fear? Rose struggled to sitting position, an apology on the tip of her tongue. But by that time the girl was already several yards down the beach, running and crying at the same time.

Now you've damn well done it, she scolded herself as she let her muscles relax and collapsed back on to the sand. Now you've really blown the whole thing! What kind of a stupid amnesiac are you, Rose Lambert? Do you have some sort of death wish or something? The day before the boat is due in, the one with the cop on board, you have to shoot off your mouth and blow everything! And now the poor little kid will run to her dear daddy. God, I wonder what *he'll* do! Wearily, disgusted with herself, she readjusted the straw hat over her face and closed her eyes. There really wasn't anything else to do. Was there, Rose? No place to run, is there?

No place to run. No place to—what was it he had said. 'Nobody ever goes up there. If it has a name, only the *tahu'a* knows what it is. Everybody else just pretends that there's no mountain up there.' Pele's mountain! Her eyes snapped open. What about that! If the police were coming on the supply boat, you could presume they would have to leave with that same boat. How else? So all I have to do, she reasoned, is to sit tight, pretend I'm a loving wife, and then as soon as word comes about the boat, I disappear up into the mountain that isn't there! I'll need food—no, I guess I won't. There are plenty of orange and breadfruit trees and—oh Lord, everything up there. And plenty of water. All I have to do is go, right? C'mon, girl!

She hustled herself to her feet, picked up her odds and ends, and started back towards the house. It was a long walk. For some reason the two of them had ventured all the way down the bay to a point that looked out into the ocean, just under the peak of Mona Aui. She had been attracted by the colour. Down here just a few feet from where they had stopped, the sand was all black, a reminder of the island's volcanic past.

Across from her somewhere in the village, she could hear the soft sound of Polynesian music as a group of ukeleles strummed, and a slack-string guitar picked out one of the haunting island melodies. The music wandered across the water just as the first of the outrigger canoes moved in to the bay from the lagoon, with the day's catch. Each note seemed to fall out of the air fully-rounded, like some perfectly shaped rain drop. She smiled at her own romanticism, shook her hair to free it of the loose sand, and hurried up the stairs to the Big House.

'Hi!' He was standing on the veranda as she made it up the last of the stairs, head down. Now's the time, she told herself. Pour it on. You catch flies with honey, not with vinegar!

'Hi yourself.' She put a smile into the phrase, walked directly to him, and gave him an enthusiastic hug. He was so startled that for a moment he had trouble juggling the drink he held in his hand. And then he reacted. His free hand came around her shoulders, pressing her into his chest gently but firmly. She turned her head aside to lay her cheek against him.

The hair on his chest was a light brown, almost the colour of his well-tanned skin. Soft, not wiry as she had expected. For just a moment she overcame her fears, her tensions, and relaxed against him. She could hear and feel the soft bubble of laughter that ran up from his lungs. Mr and Mrs Giles Gendron, she mused. The whole thing seemed so startlingly real. She squeezed herself against him, then whirled away, accepting the drink he offered. It was something and scotch. Tall, cool, refreshing. She sipped avidly at it, then accepted the hand he offered. He towed her around to the side of the house, where several lounge chairs waited. She sank into one of them, breathing a huge sigh of relief.

'Busy day?' He toasted her with his glass.

'Mm,' she answered. 'Yes and no. We walked too far. All the way down to the black sand.' She gestured in the general direction of Mona Aui.

'Josie came home all upset,' he stated. And if you're waiting for me to explain it will be a mighty cold day on *Te Tuahine*, she promised under her breath.

'Did you ask her why?'

'No,' he admitted. 'She ducked out of the way. That kid is getting to be a typical woman. I like the bathing suits you made. And the outfits. I just hate to see my only daughter grow up like a native kid.'

'I'm married to a snob?'

'No,' he protested, and then slightly crestfallen, 'Well, maybe yes. Is that wrong?'

'I don't know,' she sighed. 'I just don't remember whether I think that's bad or good.'

'You still don't remember a thing?'

'Nothing.' And then she had another thought. Maybe I shouldn't make it all that easy for him. There's some reason why he doesn't want me to remember. Maybe if I turn the screw, I might get him to tell me what's going on. 'I keep having this dream,' she said softly. 'I keep dreaming that I'm in a liferaft, and it's pitching and tossing—and that's all.'

'That's all you remember?'

'About the dream? Yes, that's all.' Keep your voice low, she commanded herself. Be a little bemused. 'Yes,' she repeated, savouring the words, 'that's all. Just the liferaft.'

'Something subconcious,' he offered, taking another pull at his glass. 'You saw the little raft down on the beach and it was so out of the ordinary that you remembered it.'

Thank you, Dr Freud, she muttered under her breath. The opportunity to give him another dig was too good to be passed up. 'Maybe I should tell the Inspector about it when he arrives tomorrow?'

'Oh, I wouldn't do that!' He almost dropped his glass in his hurry to reassure her. 'A dream like that has nothing of interest to the police. No, certainly don't bother him with something like that!'

'Well—all right.' She could taste the excitement. It was like baiting a bear. Half the thrill came from knowing that he could unpredictably strike back. But he owes me one more shot, she promised herself. At her demure best she looked him straight in the eye. 'But won't he ask where the liferaft came from? It's so unusual.'

'Not all that unusual,' he returned. 'Besides, the Inspector will be late getting in tomorrow, and I doubt if he'll notice a little thing like a liferaft. You seem different tonight.'

'Different?'

'I don't know if that's the exact word, but you're more relaxed. Almost as if you had—accepted the situation.'

'Accepted? That's a strange word to use.'

'I—yes,' he stammered. 'Perhaps I should have said becoming more adjusted to things. I'm not very clever with words.'

'But you make your living—our living—with words!'

'Ah, but that's different. There are two different languages, you know. The written one and the spoken one. And besides, when I'm at work my characters do exactly what I tell them, and never never ever talk back.'

'Hardly ever?' His eyes flashed at her as she ducked her head in disgust. If you plan to make this situation last, Rose Lambert, she lectured herself, you'll have to stop quoting Gilbert and Sullivan. This man is no dunce. Hardly ever, indeed! Fool! Divert him, quickly. Fight. Argue! 'Is that what Josie and I are supposed to do,' she asked sweetly. 'Never talk back and do exactly what we're told?'

'More or less.' He was laughing at her, those big dark eyes sparkling out a challenge—one she dare not accept. She gulped the rest of her drink, folded her hands demurely in her lap, and leaned back against the softness of the chair. That predatory look was forming around the edges of his mouth. His lips were slightly parted, showing magnificent teeth. Lord, I've got to get away from him! She found herself shivering. She brushed her hair forward around her face, stood up out of the lounge chair, and mumbled at him. 'I've got to check up on Josie.' She was gone before his 'what did you say,' caught up with her.

The child was not in the house. Following the twinge of her intuition, she slipped her feet into a pair of rubber thong slippers, and went down the hill to the fresh-water pool behind the dam. She could hear the sound of argument as she came closer, but only the child was there when finally Rose wove her way through the stands of bamboo and out on to the banked edge of the pool.

'Josie?' The girl had seen her, but turned her back defiantly, pretending to be watching something up near the caved in top of Pele's mountain. Rose hesitated for a moment, and then walked over and dropped a hand on the child's shoulder. 'Josie,' she repeated, doing her best to keep her voice at a soft persuasive pitch. 'I'm sorry if I made you feel bad. I would never do that intentionally. Please?'

The child wheeled around and grabbed at her as if she were the last refuge in the world. The tears began just as her little head buried itself between Rose's breasts. 'I *want* you to be my mother,' the child sobbed. 'I *want* you—for always!'

Rose caressed the silky blonde hair, made soothing noises, held the slender body close. 'Forever's a long long time,' she sighed.

'But that's what I want,' Josie sobbed. 'You're—nice. So very nice. You do nice things, and you say nice things, and it's fun to be with you, and you're so—so soft and I like to cuddle up with you, and—and I can trust you, that's what. You don't make kid-talk at me, and—well—I just need you to be my mother!'

'But I *am* your mother, Josie. At least that's what your daddy said.'

The tears slowed, came to a stop, and were properly terminated by a couple of wild sniffs. 'You know that's not true, don't you,' the little girl accused.

Once again the whirlwind rattled through Rose's brain. You know that's not true! Of course you know. But there's a world of difference between knowing something secretly in your heart, and coming out plain and outspoken with it. I *need* you to be my mother? How many times had Rose herself wanted to say something like that to the multitude of women her father had brought home after her mother died. I *need* you! That was the operative word. And I can trust you, that's what!

Her hand automatically stroked the girl's glistening hair. 'Yes, I knew that,' she answered softly. 'I don't know why your daddy said what he did. I knew it wasn't true, but he must have had some reason for saying so. But all that isn't important. Not any more. We start from today, shall we? If you really need me, Josie, I'll be your mother for as long and as well as I'm

able. I can't make any promises about being a
wonderful mother, you understand, because I don't
have any mothering practice. And I can't promise it will
last forever, because only God knows what's around the
corner for either of us. But I *will* try, if that's what you
want.'

The hug became ecstasy. 'It is. That's just what I
want—Mommy. Oh, I love you so!' And because that
was an expression she hadn't heard a great deal of
lately, Rose Lambert had difficulty stifling the tears
that threatened to break loose. They strolled back up to
the house, arm in arm, the girl's chatter bouncing off
the close-knit growth that hemmed the path, frightening
a flamboyant big-billed toucan who was busy building in
the bush. So much so that the bird haunted them the
rest of the way up the path, screaming raucous insults
at them as only a toucan can.

'Don't mention this to your father,' Rose prompted,
as they stopped at the foot of the stairs. 'He might not
quite understand. Just between us girls?' Josie looked a
trifle doubtful, and then gave in.

'You betcha! *Oui! Ea!*' And having been reassured in
all three languages, the pair of them tumbled up the
stairs to answer the call of the dinner bell that hung
next to the hibachi charcoal grates in the kitchen.

Dinner was a lovely meal. He had managed to
squeeze in a whole chapter of the new book, and it was
running well. To be honest about it, it was running
away from him. None of the characters were following
the plot line. He found it hard not to laugh when he
met Rose's eye over the steamed Bonito, the fried
breadfruit, the sweet pau-paus. And my characters
never talk back? Lord, how pompous can you get.
Look at her sitting there in the long *muumuu* she had
made for herself. The missionaries had designed the
gown so that every woman looked like a sack. Rose
looked like a million dollars. Of course it wasn't black,

the colour the women wore on Moorea. How could it be when there was only the brilliant *pareau* cloth to work with! Magnificent. Her pale oval face was accumulating a tan, just the right colour-contrast to set off her hair. And those deep green eyes, like a cat, always watching! She laughed at one of Josie's little jokes. All of her laughed, and the *muumuu* clung close to her exciting breasts, and shook with glee. He could hardly unpin his eyes. He had completely lost track of the conversation.

'Toucans?' he asked, when prodded.

'Yes. We saw a whole flight of them. How in the world did they get here?'

'You mean how did a short-range South American bird arrive here in the Pacific islands?' So I'm stalling, he told himself. How else am I going to make some sense out of what's going on. Look at the two of them. They really *could* be mother and daughter. 'Well, I'm not an ornithologist,' he commented. 'All I really know is what I've heard from Sam and the *tahu'a*. When he's talking to me, that is. The long range birds like the frigate—I don't know where they came from originally, but they're on most of the islands. They can navigate at will, over great distances. And the herring gulls. They island-hop. The plover is a migratory bird. You only see them here at certain times, when they get ready to enter the Pacific fly-ways. About the long-tailed cuckoo, I haven't any idea. They're just here. And please don't ask me how any of them find directions.'

'Like the navigators in the great canoes, Daddy?'

'Well, no, not exactly, love. And all the great canoes are gone. I doubt if anyone in the Society Islands today knows how to make a great canoe. I read an article once about a man in Samoa who conducts schools, and builds canoes. But he's the only one left, I'm afraid. No, men navigated a little differently than the birds. They used the stars, the wind, water patterns, birds in flight, clouds, anything. You know that all the big islands have a cloud that hangs over them? We have one, Tahiti has one—all the islands. Distinctive clouds that you can see for miles at sea. And of course Sirius rises and sets exactly on the latitude of Tahiti. So if you sail at night, and want to go to Tahiti, you only need to keep Sirius directly overhead. Next question?'

'Well, you didn't answer the first one,' Rose commented. 'About the toucans? Or does that long speech indicate that you don't know about toucans? They came in the war canoes, perhaps?'

'Don't be a wiseacre,' he laughed. 'Toucans are the easiest answer in the world. Like a great deal of the life on these islands, the Toucans were brought in by man. To be specific, Sam Apuka's father brought six pairs of them in from South America not more than twenty years ago. Their only enemies are palm-rats and kids who want them as pets. Any other questions, children?'

She kicked his ankle under the table. It seemed the sort of thing any self-respecting wife would do in the face of such blatant chauvinism. It hurt her toe more than it did his ankle. Miri, bringing in a bowl of fruit for dessert, tch-tched when she saw the action. Polynesian girls never strike their men—even when they need it!

Josie needed no coaxing to get her to bed. It had been a hard day indeed for the little girl. She clutched at Rose's fingers while her father read her a bedtime story, one of the scarey kind that she really liked, from an inexhaustible book. At least it seemed to have no end, this magic book. It also had several pages missing. And sometimes he held it upside down as he read. But the same story was never heard twice, and no one else could ever find the right page and a favourite story, no matter how hard they tried. Unless it could be that his fertile imagination was making them all up as he went along? At least Josie accused him of doing so, and he felt the need to make a blanket denial.

He always judged the story-endings to a nicety, waiting until the child's eyes began to blink before the tale roared into some drastic and logical climax. And then he would close the book and watch as his daughter slipped over the reef into slumberland.

He could feel the stirring of a breeze on the back of his neck as he completed the tale. Just enough to flutter the small hairs, nothing more. It came loaded with the base odour of burning charcoal, the sharp ginger smell of the frangipani, the penetrating sharpness of vanilla. Both of his women seemed to be dreaming. Josie, her eyes completely shut, cuddled on her right side facing her mother—Lord, how easy it is to think that way— her mother. Rose, leaning back against the bamboo chair, her eyes half-closed, a smile playing at the corners of her mouth. She was still holding the baby's hand.

He felt that stirring within him again. Not just lust, playing at his loins, but something—something more. Some faint regret, some remorse. If only we had met ten years ago! But that couldn't be, his practical mind told him. Ten years ago she must have been a child, hardly Josie's age. Is that what's wrong with me? Middle-age regrets? Crying out to youth to be sustained? But his romantic mind was not willing to give up the dream. Hell, the girl is—what—twenty? To my thirty-five? What's wrong with that? After I get free of all this mess, we'll—The child stirred, breaking his chain of thought. Rose gently disengaged her hand and stood up. He followed her out of the room, around the house to the open veranda where talk would not disturb the sleeper.

'Another drink?' he offered.

'Yes, but no alcohol,' she decided. He helped her into one of the lounge chairs and went over to the table where drinkables were kept. 'Orange juice?'

'Yes, that's fine.'

He poured her a tall cool glass from the evaporative cooler, then fixed himself a double shot of Scotch. After serving her, he carried his small glass over to the edge of the veranda and looked up. High above him the scattered stars wheeled in train, the Southern Cross high in the sky. A three-quarter moon trailed fingers of silver across the tiny waves running beyond the reef. The roar of the sovereign sea played counterpoint to all the other noises of the night.

He came back to her chair. The roof of the veranda kept her face in a half-light. He felt the urge to reach down, to tilt her chin up into the moonlight, to—but he fought off the urge. It was always there, damn it. The need to touch her! Damn! He squeezed his glass and tossed off the remainder of its contents.

'You know a lot about the islands, don't you,' she queried softly. Even her voice gave him a strange sensation. It was a soft husky contralto that climbed up to a squeak when she was excited.

'Some,' he returned. 'I've always had this thing about the South Seas. Read everything I could when I was a kid. I came out here for two years—two *wanderjahren*—after I finished at Ohio State. The university, not the prison.'

'I never thought otherwise,' she giggled. 'You're altogether too—too slippery—to get penned up in the pen.' The moment the words were out she regretted them. Poor choice –slippery!

He turned away from her to cover his surprise. A beautiful nature, a magnificent body, and a tongue as sharp as a rapier. Well, if you let a word or two turn you off, you deserve everything you get, he lectured himself. And went back to the topic at hand.

'So I and a couple of my friends put together all our money and bought a schooner, and went into the copra trade. Two years it took us, to go broke and to discover that there were a million ways to live better than hauling copra. But we got a good education out of it, and my first book was based on my experiences. And you?' He threw the question in as a teaser, and got back the answer he deserved.

'Who me? As far as I know I've never been in the copra trade, nor sailed a schooner anywhere. Although I suppose I must have read my share of South Sea island romances. I'm sorry, Giles, but I still just don't remember. I really try—but I don't remember. Was that recently when you did all that?'

'Ah—no.' He was caught short by her smooth transition to another subject. 'No, that was some years ago. Back when I was your age.' He had finally manoeuvered her into the moonlight, and now he searched her face for a response or a rejection. For any sign at all, to tell the truth. 'I'm thirty-five, you know.'

'Do I know,' she asked hesitantly. 'I—that really doesn't seem to be very old to me. I'm only—lord, I don't even know how old I am. But thirty-five isn't very old—at least I don't think so!'

And then she was back in the shadows, and he hadn't seen a single sign for or against. Just the words. But they were enough to go on. Thirty-five isn't very old—and by Harry I feel younger already. It's almost as if she just stamped a visa on my passport; a permit to enter youth again!

Now then, the aircraft will land at Maupiti about noontime with the packages and the policeman. The supply boat will sail almost immediately. It will take them six hours to get here, at flank speed. Which is just as the tide is making. The best time in the world to come through the reef. If only I can keep her sweet until then!

And that's what is confusing all my thinking. I don't dare to trust my emotions. What I feel for her has to be balanced against what I feel about her. She's the queen-

pin of my little play. The play either works, or Josie and
I go down the drain. But if it *does* work—I swear it,
Rose whoever you are, I'll devote all my energy and all
my time and all my money—if it comes to that—to find
out what *your* problem is. To find out just what it is that
you're so busy forgetting!

'You're very quiet,' she probed.

'Just thinking. There's a dance over at the village
tonight. Care to walk down that way?'

'A *tamure?*'

'Where in the world did you learn that word?'

'I—I don't know. It just came to me. Will it be a *tamure?*'

'No, no—nothing like that. Just a little get-together.
The *tamure* is only for some big celebration, and it's a
wild time, lady. A lot of tourists come looking as if they
expect a Hawaiian hula. Huh! They go away with red
faces every time. The *tamure* is wild—but wild. It's a
real fertility dance. And if that's what they were having,
I wouldn't have invited you to go!'

'Well,' she giggled. 'I learn something new about you
every day. First, you admit to being a snob, and now
it's obvious you're some sort of prude to boot!'

It was all true, but it hurt to hear her say so. He
turned away again, staring down the bay to where a
bonfire had just been lit. And I'm learning something
about me every day too, he told himself cynically.
Things I never knew before. Is this why Helen and I
couldn't stay married? It startled him when Rose
ghosted up beside him, leaned a shapely thigh against
his, and put her small hand on his bare arm. 'I didn't
mean to upset you,' she offered contritely.

Instantly that spark was back. Not just the words,
but the touch, the warmth of her, and the sweet smell.
There was no perfume on the island, save that of the
flowers, no soaps save what the islanders made from the
coconut. Nevertheless she smelled—enticing, sexy,
earthy, clean, honest—all the words fitted.

'It's not important,' he gruffed, finding it necessary to clear his throat. 'Would you like to go down?'

'I don't think so,' she sighed. No matter what he said, the words had a coolness about them which had not been there before. 'Couldn't we just sit and talk?'

'If you like.' He guided her back to the lounge chairs, pulled two of them close together. He helped her re-settle herself before he dropped down on to the adjacent chair.

After a moment of silence, she asked, 'The boat comes tomorrow?'

'Yes. Late tomorrow afternoon. Around six or seven perhaps, depending on the weather.'

'It will be a big event, I suppose?'

'Hey, considering that it only comes four times a year, yes, I guess you could call it a big event. We re-stock our staples, get in a few luxuries.'

'I never see anybody working. What do they use for money?'

'Copra,' he laughed. 'Always the copra. They could get rich from it if it didn't smell so bad. The entire village has managed to put together—oh, five tons of copra since the last ship came. They'll load that up, haggle about it until dawn, and then not stir another finger until close to the next boat time.'

'And then?'

'It depends on what they think they need. If they want a great deal, things will hum around here. If not, they'll make a stab at it, and quit.'

'Is it hard, making copra?'

He reached over and picked up her hand. 'Why you really don't know anything, do you! Copra is dried coconut. They take it over behind Mount Atau to avoid the smell, crack the nuts, and leave it in the sun to dry.'

'You sound as if you don't quite approve.'

'That's not true, Rose. It's their way of life, out here on the outer islands. In Tahiti they all live by the clock, punch time cards, obey traffic lights. Out here they live as they want to. No, I approve all right. Not everybody in the world should be stuck with their noses to grindstones. To tell the truth, maybe I'm sorry for myself, not for them. They live the good life, and I envy them. Even if my Calvinist upbringing won't allow me to emulate them.'

She changed the subject. 'There's a shooting star. Do you make a wish?'

'Silly. You only wish on the "first star I see tonight." And I already did that.'

'Really? What did you wish for?'

'Oh no, lady. If I tell, I don't get my wish.'

'Then how in the world can anyone know if you got your wish?'

'Easy,' he whispered. He leaned over her chair, trapping her within his arms, pulling her over towards him. He was prepared for a struggle, and wrath to follow, but nothing happened. She seemed almost to flow across the space between them, a frictionless being, and suddenly he could feel the soft moist warmth of her lips under his as he gently kissed her. He had been planning this for the past three hours. Planning for the moment when he would offer her just a touch—the tiniest touch—of himself.

But as soon as the contact was made, all his plans went up in smoke. There was that spark again, that static spark that seemed to leap between them, crackling as it struck where their lips were joined. And it seemed to affect her as well as himself. Instead of struggling against him, she squirmed closer, arms threading themselves around his neck, pulling him closer into the trap that was her soft body.

He went willingly, all sense of proportion lost in the dazzling feeling that blinded, deafened, and turned him into a raw pulsing mass of emotion. He pressed harder, until her lips opened to him, inviting his penetration.

His hands swarmed up and down her back, up and down her sides, defeated by the folds of the capacious *muumuu*, but still relishing the softness, the warmth. She was moaning in his ear, moaning something he could not quite understand. And then suddenly she stiffened in his arms, and the contact was broken.

In a fragment of a second her hands came down to his chest, beating on him, forcing him away. He tried to recapture the warmth by holding on. Her hands beat a tattoo against his chest, against his cheeks, but to no avail. And then she began to shiver. He felt it instantly. All up and down her spine she was shaking. Something wet fell on to his bare chest. Something salty wet. He continued to search for what they had lost, but there was no hope of finding it. She was sobbing now, tearing sobs that wracked her frame. He took two deep breaths to settle himself, and then slowly pushed her away, keeping control of her by hands which clutched her shoulders.

'What is it?' he whispered. 'What?'

'I'm afraid,' she sobbed, almost collapsing in his hands.

'Afraid of me?' He had never even *thought* the idea before, never mind voiced it. A woman who is afraid of me? What sort of monster does she think I am, for God's sake! What kind—and yet there she is, shaking and shivering as if I were Gargantua, and she the virgin in my clutches. My God! Deep inside his stomach revolted, forcing bile up into his throat as his hands shook slightly, and released her. She fell back on to the chair, still sobbing. He struggled to his feet, looked down at her huddled form, and then around the horizon as if to see if he were still grounded in reality.

'Well, I certainly didn't mean to frighten you,' he growled bitterly. He was trying to hide his damaged male ego, and not quite succeeding. 'I didn't realise that I was that much poison. Good night!'

He stormed down off the veranda and plunged on to

the trail that led to the beach. She sat up and swung her legs off the lounger, trying to stem the flow of tears with her knuckles. He was outlined against the lights across the way as he started down the stairs to the beach. Gradually he sank below the level of the top step, and was out of sight.

She forced herself to her feet and went over to the edge of the veranda, resting against one of the bamboo pillars that supported the roof. The tears slowed, and finally stopped.

'And now look what you've done, Rosie Lambert,' she sighed. 'Call him back? No, don't. Things are bad enough as they are. Let it go—until after the police have left. And then, if everything works out and I don't get arrested, then I'll tell him. Tell him that it's me I'm scared of, not him. I've never felt this way before. Never! Lord knows what I would have let him do tonight—what I would have helped him do—if it had gone on for another two minutes!'

'Mommy? A sleepy figure in a long flowing nightgown peered around the doorjamb and came out into the moonlight. 'I thought I heard you cryin'. Was you cryin'?'

'Yes, love.' She held out a hand and the child came up to be enveloped in a hug.

'And you was talking to yourself. That's a bad sign.'

'So you say.' She tickled under the little chin, just enough to bring a giggle. 'Mothers talk to themselves all the time, didn't you know that? It's a lot easier than trying to explain to Daddys what life is all about. Back to bed, ragamuffin. Scoot!'

CHAPTER FIVE

THE ship came up to the reef at six o'clock, almost an hour before sunset, when the tide was almost at its highest. They watched it from the veranda, Giles, Josie, and herself. The little girl was on pins and needles, anxious to go. Most of the villagers had already headed for the rickety dock near the mouth of Pakuo Bay, where the sloping shoulder of Mona Atau provided protection from the trade winds.

'There's no hurry,' he said. 'Relax. And for goodness sakes, finish your dinner.' There was a snap in his voice. She had never heard him speak to his daughter like that before. 'They still have their boats out,' he added.

'What in the world are they doing?' Rose wanted to appear uninterested, but couldn't. The ancient freighter had come to a halt, and two small boats were out ahead of it, doing something over the narrow entrance to the reef.

'They're sounding the channel,' he told her grimly. 'It's an artificial channel, you remember ... Oh Lord, I'm sorry. I didn't mean that. The channel was blasted out of the reef about twenty years ago. Before that time this harbour just wasn't accessible.'

'So what has that to do with now?'

'Well, the government treated the reef as if it were made out of granite. Something you could blast a hole through, and sit back to enjoy. Only granite is dead stone, while coral is alive. The reef has been gradually rebuilding itself. So whenever the ships come in they sound the channel to see how deep it is.'

'Daddy, I don't like fried plantain. I don't!'

'Oh come on now,' her father snapped. 'You've eaten

it for years, and there's no reason why you can't eat it tonight!'

The girl returned sullenly to her plate. Not knowing quite what to say, Rose stared down at the manoeuvering ship. The little boats had just scuttled back to the freighter, and water was boiling at her stern as the old double-stacked ship made all possible steam, and dashed for the harbour.

'She's coming in,' she exclaimed in alarm. The scene looked somewhat like the end of a Hollywood chariot race. The battered old ship kicked up a froth at her bow, scattered the cloud of tiny outrigger canoes that had gone out to meet her, and celebrated her success by a triple blast on her whistle. Rose could see the steam shooting up before she heard the sound. She started to count immediately. 'One thousand one, one thousand two, one thousand three——' and the sound arrived. It was surprisingly deep-throated for such a tired old ship.

'Who taught you that?' He leaned over the table, his lips almost at her ear.

'Why—why I don't know,' she said soberly, trying to avoid contact with him. That little chill ran up her spine again. This amnesiac business isn't as easy as I thought, she told herself. And with just one slip, he—well, I've no idea *what* he would do, and that's the problem. 'Did I do something wrong?'

'No. That's a fine way to measure distance. Sound travels so much slower than light does. And the ship is about three miles away, right?' His cool hawk eyes were on her, ready to pounce at the slightest mistake.

'If you say so,' she sighed.

'I wanna go see the ship,' Josie muttered. 'I really wanna go!'

'Stop nagging,' her father barked. 'We'll go when your mother is ready to go.'

'Oh, please—don't wait for me. It's almost two miles

down there, and two to come back. I'd rather not go all that way. Can't I just wait quietly here, and you and Josie go to enjoy the fun?' It was hard to keep her voice level. Her thoughts were rattling around, ricocheting off each other in their haste to get her attention. This has to be the time, she told herself. While they go down, I can just—just disappear.

'We-ell,' he drawled. 'Yes, it's quite a walk, and you've been busy all day. Okay. You rest and enjoy yourself, and I'll make the sacrifice. Are you sure you can walk that far, Josie?'

'C'mon, Daddy. What an excuse. You know darn well you want to be there, and they'll start unloading tonight, and you'll want to see all the things they bring, and——'

'Okay, okay.' He threw up his hands in defeat. 'Henpecked, that's what I am.'

'Oh, Daddy, that's cornball stuff. I'm ready.'

Rose laughed at them both. It seemed all too easy. What would a mother say now? She reached out and trapped the child's shoulder. 'Whoa up, young lady,' she admonished. 'It will be cold before you come back. Take a shawl to wear. And for goodness sakes, go to the bathroom first.'

They started out fifteen minutes later, laughing as they went. She watched them as they disappeared step-by-step, over her horizon and out of sight. The laughter came floating back on the cool twilight air long after their heads had dropped from sight. Miri came out to clear the table.

'You don't go, *madame?* It is all excitement. You don't go with your man?'

'No, I don't go,' Rose laughed. 'But you do, Miri. You go with *your* man. I'll clean up these things.'

'But, I——'

'Shoo. Go. *Viti viti.*'

'Okay, I go,' the island girl giggled. 'But is the wrong

word. *Viti viti* mean fast. Go fast. Word should be *quickly*. You say *haapeepee!*'

'So I will—*haapeepee!*' Her accent was so terrible that Miri gurgled, but fled down the steps just the same. She turned and waved before she disappeared. Rose returned the wave and laughed at herself. She had been taking daily lessons in the Tahitian dialect of Polynesian. 'And every vowel must be pronounced,' she lectured herself as she followed the movements on the beach across the bay. The little freighter was now making a very cautious approach to the rickety pier. The sun was low on the hills behind her, the mountains of Pele. And it was time for her to go.

Carefully she cleared the table and carried everything back to the kitchen. It took but a moment to scrub and rinse everything under the stream of cool water pouring out of the bamboo pipes. One last look, longingly, around the house. Through his cluttered workroom where papers and books and dust struggled for command, through his bedroom where his clothes were scattered, and then quickly out of the house.

An hour later she had reached a little clearing above the house, and was completely exhausted. She had walked the other mountains earlier. Tuahine, Mona Aui, Mona Atau. They all were girded by neat well-tended paths, so that one had the impression of wandering through a garden. But not here. Pele's Mountain had many trails, but all were overgrown, hardly more than indentations in the tropical growth. The same orange groves breadfruit trees, vanilla bushes, mangoes all flourished here, but in untouched wild growth. Her every step had been a torture.

Shoes were something she had hardly needed at the Big House, or at the beach. The mountain had frightened her. She borrowed a pair of Miri's rubber Japanese sandals, consisting of a hard sole and a thong which fit between her big toe and its neighbour, to hold them on. In addition to being strange to her, they were a size too big. Her soles were chafed, and the thong was rubbing a blister into being between her toes.

The machete was a total disaster. She had seen it hanging by the kitchen door, and snatched it up at the last minute. The natives used the big knife to cut their way through underbrush. In their hands the blade had swung gracefully and easily. But doing it for herself, she quickly discovered was like trying to decapitate a rattlesnake with a pen knife. Nothing went right. Either she swung the blade too lightly and it bounced off everything, or she swung too hard, and the blade threatened to cut her foot off. In total frustration she started to hurl the heavy knife off the side of the mountain, sloping steeply down behind her. But then she thought again. She had no idea what sorts of wild life might be running free up here. Even the Garden of Eden had snakes, didn't it?

So all in all, when she broke free of the underbrush and came out into the little clearing it was like some gift from the gods. Behind and below here were the trees through which she had been forcing her way. Ahead of her was a sharp deep chasm, looking out on to Pakuo bay. She straggled over to the edge and made herself comfortable on a pile of warm stones. The heat startled her, and then her slow mind reasoned it out. The sun had heated the rocks all day; now it was almost gone. It wasn't the stones that were warm, but the air that was too cold! She stretched herself out flat to absorb some of the warmth while she caught her breath. The cold fingers of the high-altitude breeze toyed with the perspiration on her brow. She shivered.

'So you told Josie to take a shawl,' she told herself sarcastically. 'So where's yours? Idiot! What you need is a mother to look after you!' Or a father, she added silently, or a—husband?

She sat up and wrapped her arms around herself, staring down and out to sea. The mouth of the bay was in shadows. Torches appeared, some stationary, some moving. It made a pretty picture as the quick and silent tropical night fell. She sat there, unmoving, thinking.

Here in this high place she could intuitively feel her father's presence. She *knew* he was alive. Somewhere, somehow, he had come through the storm. She just *knew* it. It was not an unusual feeling. She had for so long been a partner in his life that there was a bond between them. A bond that could not be snapped by distance, condition, or time. And the bond was still tight, still tugging at her, connecting her through the unknown night to her father. She clasped her hands behind her neck and lay back on the flat of the stones, smiling.

Time passed. Unmeasurable time. The dog-star was plodding downhill into the west. The moon threatened to rise in the distant east, over towards Tahiti, and down below she could hear conch-shell trumpets sounding. She sat up to look. At the pier flares guided a line of workers going back and forth like worker ants. But there were other flares out in the night. Up along the heights of Mona Atau, across the ridge between the Two Sisters. Sets of widely spaced lights, they flickered and wove patterns, as if the whole village was moving in the night.

A trembling fear locked on to her spirits. They were searching for her! The police authority had called out the whole village to find her! Desperation drove. She stumbled to her feet, flexed her stiff muscles, and forced them to take her farther up the mountain, deep into the dark jungle again, and then finally, out on to the lava lip where nothing grew.

She was looking down again, directly into the crater of the volcano where, in some distant past, Pele's mountain had blown her top off and sent molten lava

streaming down toward the bay below. The cavity was
in darkness. The moon was not yet high enough to dig a
path into the crater area. Give it a few minutes more,
she told herself. Just a few minutes, and there'll be light.
She was shaking again, but not from the cold. She
slumped down on to the crumbling lava bed, wrapping
her arms around herself to stay the shaking that was
tearing her to pieces. She turned around to look back in
the direction from which she had come.

Below her, very far away now, the flares were light-
points at the dock area. A fading fire twinkled here and
there in the village. The mountains were dark. She
could not see the Big House, hidden from her under the
curve of the mountains. One lonely tear trickled down
her cheek.

By now the moon had topped the jagged edge of the
crater, lighting paths, casting shadows. Rose took a
deep breath. Her leg muscles almost refused her
command to move. A well-marked trail wound its way
down into the open maw. She plunged ahead,
staggering carelessly. The rubber sandals slipped on the
crumpling lava rock. Slip and you're dead, you poor
fool! In one careless minute you can be off the edge!
Down into that—she stopped and steadied herself
against a rock outcropping. The silver fingers of the
moon had touched the surface of the crater, where
glittering silver-painted water gleamed at her, roiled
slightly by a tiny breeze. There was a lake in the crater,
and not many yards below her!

She struggled with her breathing, trying to steady her
nerves. A few more yards. Only a few. She stepped
carefully, testing the path with her foot before
entrusting her weight to it. Down, and farther down.
And the trail ended. She was on a flat plateau that
served as the shore of this miracle lake, and near at
hand, to her right, the mouth of a huge cave opened.
She groped for it, found a great flat rock at its mouth,

and dropped down on it, moaning her relief. Her feet contacted something in the shadows, and displaced it. It fell to the sand at the foot of the rock with a dull thud.

The slight breeze that blew over her was warmer, much warmer than she had felt on the outer lip of the mountain. And she was tired, desperately tired. She coiled herself up on the rock, opened her ears to the gentle lapping of wavelets in the lake, and closed her eyes.

Visions flashed across her inner eyelids. Black and white images. Her father, waving, a cheerful grin on his too-handsome face, but safe. Little Josie, staring directly at her, her mouth twisted in agony, screaming 'Please don't leave me, Mommy!' And then Giles. His deep-furrowed face marked with concerns, problems—searching—for what? Her mind had no answer but she clung to this last image as if it were a life line. What worried Giles? What was it about the coming of the police that *he* was concerned about? Why did he insist that she was his wife, that Josie was her natural daughter? Why was it, when he was so remote, so cool, she was afraid of him? The puzzle was too deep for her tired mind. She gave up the struggle.

She slept fitfully until it grew suddenly warmer, and then she slept soundly. When she awoke she was in deep shadow. The sun was up, but not high enough to light the crater. There was a robe thrown over her. An old ceremonial robe, plaited with feathers. And a little distance away, an old man, squatting by a tiny fire. The *tahu'a*. He was roasting something on a stick. She sat up. The movement caught his eye. He smiled, got up, and came over to her with the stick.

'*Tamahine?*' He came around the flat stone platform on which she rested, but did not touch it. 'You eat?' He offered her the roast. She held up both hands in a repulsing gesture. Her few weeks on Tahiti had taught her that no mere *vahine* ate in front of a *tahu'a*—but then, he knew that, didn't he? Then why did he offer?

He smiled, showing a mouthful of perfect teeth. 'No *tapuus* here,' he chuckled. 'This is Pele's place. Here only is a man and a woman, and this foolish plover. Eat.' He stripped a section of meat from the roast and nibbled on it, all the while extending the stick to her. Trembling, she followed suit. The meat, rich in juices, trickled down her throat and revived her. The old man squatted down in front of the rock and dissected the remainder of the bird.

'The man,' he offered, after considerable gnawing. 'He fears for you. All over the island they search, but nobody would come up here. You heard Pele call, no?' He gestured towards the rock. There was enough light for Rose to see where she was. It was not really a rock, but rather a carefully assembled stone platform, with stones intricately cut to notch into each other. She scrambled off on to the sand, dragging the feather cape behind her.

'Oh Lord,' she sighed. 'It's a *maere*? A Sacred Platform?'

The old man laughed and nodded. 'Built for Pele. This is her place.' He waved a hand around the circle of the crater. 'She called and you came, no?'

'I—I don't know,' Rose stammered. 'Nobody called. Nobody believes in that stuff any more. I just didn't—I couldn't—my husband, he——'

'The man? He is not your husband. Not yet.' The old man spoke softly, every word flowing like a liquid. 'And of course. Nobody believes. That is all—what you Americans call—mumbo jumbo! Eat.'

'You know that he——'

'I know,' the old man laughed. 'The real business of a *tahu'a* is to know things. Everything. The man wrestles with his own terrible problem, and you wrestle with your own terrible problem—but you do *not* know—you are sent here because of Pele's terrible problem. And when you and he solve Pele's problem, you also solve your own!'

'Nonsense! That's all—what you said. Mumbo jumbo.' He doesn't know anything, she told herself fiercely. Not anything. He's only an old man. A doddering old man! Him and his crazy goddesses! He was smiling sympathetically at her, almost as if he could read her mind.

'Just an old man,' he chuckled. 'Just dreams, no?'

'I—I——' She struggled for some soft explanation that would not hurt, and found none. It didn't seem to bother the old man. He settled himself into a more comfortable position, and offered her the rest of the roast. Without thinking about it, she accepted. He wiped his fingers clean in the sand.

'I am old,' he mused. 'When I was young there were great times, *Tamahine*. There was the great war, no? Americans came to Bora Bora. Thousands of them. They brought books, radios, dreams, airplanes, electricity, babies. I saw it all. And then they went home, and the islands were empty of them. They took their generators, their airplanes, their God, but not their children. We wanted the children.

'Then I went to Papeete, Honolulu, Samoa. Everywhere the *popa'a* touched, the Polynesian ways died. So at last I came here to Tuahine. Pele no longer thunders, and Tangora no longer raises the waves, they say. But since we only have our dreams, why should I not cling to them, no?'

'I—you really believe in the old religion?' she stammered.

'Believe? Perhaps. Why not? Pele lives. Tangora lives. She no longer screams for the blood of sacrifice; he no longer rules the war canoes. We have all come to our elder days, Pele and I. But many of the old habits are left. Did you know that if a *vahine* sleeps on Pele's *maere* that all her dreams will be true?' He looked up at her with a very sharp eye. She ducked her head to hide the blushes. In the moments before she had awakened she had dreamed again. Strange dreams, that sent her writhing in her sleep, moaning. Dreams about Giles Gendron. Dreams about—Lord, *that* could never come true! She shook herself to regain control, and the old man laughed. She dug her teeth into the remainder of the roast and tore it from the stick.

'The man—he wants you,' the *tahu'a* said. He got to his feet and brushed himself down.

'For some scheme,' she snapped back at him through a mouth half-filled with meat. 'He doesn't *want* me. He *needs* me. There's a difference. And I don't know why he needs me.' The last sentence came out wistfully.

'Old men learn some things ' he said solemnly. 'He wants you. Walk carefully *Tamahine*. You have an errand to do. I go down to tell them you are safe. You will come?'

'When the boat leaves,' she answered. 'I—when the boat leaves.'

'When the boat leaves.' He nodded as if the explanation were very clear to him. And then he turned away and plodded up the path, into the bright sunlight, and out of sight. She sat back, remembering the glint of of sunlight on his pure white hair.

'Fortune-telling,' she told herself forcefully. 'Nothing but fortune-telling. Hah!' But she could not repress the uneasy feeling that came to her. All my dreams will come true? Dad is alive and well? Josie will cry over me? Giles will drive me mad in his bed? Stuff!

But it was worth a thought at that, she told herself, as she walked around to the front of Pele's *maere*. It was worth a thought. I'm twenty years old, going on one hundred. I've been my father's nursemaid since mother died. Seven years, with hardly a chance to meet a—some young people. I've been so busy being my father's shadow that I haven't had a chance to be me. Why, I don't even know who *me* is!

It was at that point that her swinging foot touched the little stone figure lying in the sand. And somehow or another she remembered. The little statue had been standing at the front lip of the *maere* when she sprawled down on it during the night, and her foot had knocked it off into the sand. She bent over and picked up the little figure. Hardly more than a foot long, the soft stone had been given the likeness of a crouching woman, her hands clasped around her knees, her huge breasts protruding. Where the face should be was a worn blank. It looked to be a thousand years old. A *tiki*! She smiled at the idea, just as the sun's rays penetrated the crater wall and sparkled over her and her new find.

A real *tiki*! She had heard enough in her few weeks in Papeete to recognise it as one of the symbols of the Old Religion. Dedicated to some minor goddess, she told herself. Ancient. Valueless. The islands were full of little *tiki*s. But this one's mine! She cuddled it in her arms and started back out of the crater.

It was easier going than it had been coming. The paths seemed to be better marked going downhill. Within the hour she was back at the little outcropping where she had stopped to rest the night before. She crept quietly back to the edge of the cliff and looked down. The village was sleepily quiet. The dock was empty. Out some distance beyond the reef she could see a pillar of smoke that marked the position of the old freighter.

'And that settles that,' she told her little world, with a vast sigh of relief. 'The boat's gone, and the policeman with it, so that does it!' She held up her little statue to let it see the sight. Now I *am* being a fool, she chided herself as she started down towards the Big House. Playing with dolls, no less! Nevertheless she cradled the little stone figure in the shelter of her arm, and was singing as she stumbled out of the last clump of trees above the house.

'My God, woman, where the hell have you been!' Giles grabbed her by both arms and swung her around, back into the trees. He almost jarred her little *tiki* out of her arms.

'Don't do that,' she snapped. 'You're hurting me!'

'Hurting you? You don't know what hurting means. Not yet, you don't,' he snarled. 'It took me half the night to get Inspector Tihoni to bed. And if it hadn't been for that damn *tahu'a* I don't know what kind of a story I would have concocted.'

'You're good at stories,' she hissed at him. 'Let go of me!'

His hands dropped to his sides. 'Okay, okay.' His face was pale, his eyes haunted. 'I've got a lot riding on this visit. The *tahu'a* said you were up in the mountain, tracing some ancient stone work. It sounded good. The Inspector bought it. Stick to it.'

'I'm sure you could have thought of something better!' She put all of her disdain into the statement. 'I was communing with Pele, or something like that?'

'Damn,' he muttered.

'What?'

'That's what the *tahu'a* said. His exact words. You were communing with Pele. Did you really meet that old fake up on the mountain?'

'If you mean the *tahu'a*, yes. He may be old, but he's not a fake. And we talked. Now that I think of it, his story made a hell of a lot more sense than the line you've been feeding me!'

He grabbed at her elbow this time. 'Just what in hell do you mean by that smart remark,' he snapped. Her jaw fell open. She had never in the world intended to make such a statement. The policeman might have gone with the freighter, but all ships had radios!

'I—I didn't mean anything, really,' she sighed. 'I'm tired. It was cold up on that mountain. I'm hungry.'

'Well, I should hope so,' he growled. 'Into the house.

And remember who the devil you are, Mrs Gendron!'
He took her arm again, a shade more gently than
before, and hurried her the last few steps to the house.
She stumbled a couple of times, and the thong of her
sandals rubbed against yesterday's bruises and blisters.
He left her on the veranda.

'Get yourself a shower and get cleaned up,' he said
coldly. 'I'll be in the dining room.'

I'll be in the dining room! She mimicked under her
breath. The colossal nerve of the man. Snap to, female.
Here are your marching orders! Oh Lord, I wish I were
six-feet-five and could beat him up the way he deserves!
But it was only wishing. She hurried down the corridor
and into her room. There were strange things strewn
around the room. Packages, and men's clothing. She
shook her head to clear it. Sleeping on the stone *maere*
had not been all that restful. My brain must be addled,
she sighed to herself. Maybe I *am* Mrs Gendron. Maybe
my amnesia is real? Nonsense!

She fumbled around in the confusion and managed
to find herself something to wear. A *pareau*, a pair of
soft slippers. She set the stone *tiki* down on the bedside
table, picked up her chosen clothing, and hurried off to
the bathroom. Hurry, one side of her brain told her. He
said hurry! Why, the other side of her brain queried.
Just because that—that arrogant man said so? Hah! It
required a great deal of determination, but she slowed
down. Why is it so hard, she asked herself. Why?
Because I'm afraid of that man? Lord, what's come
over me lately. Rose Lambert was never ever afraid of
anything or anybody—well, almost never. Her lip
twitched in laughter. Almost never. She ducked into the
bathroom, shed her dirty clothes, and went into the
shower stall.

The warmth of the water was comforting. It was not
sun-hot as it would be later in the day, but it was warm
enough. She lathered extravagantly in the coconut-oil

soap, rubbing vigorously, singing. A voice sounded from just outside the shower curtain.

'Mamma?' There were volatile tears in the voice. Rose reached over and flipped the curtain back. There were tears in the eyes, too. Big round ripe tears, dropping one after the other from those lovely little eyes. Josie.

'What is it, love?' It was impossible to hide the affection in her husky contralto voice, and she really didn't want to. Her hands kept up their rhythmic massage, moving large globules of soapsuds around on her body, but her mind was engrossed in the scene before her. The dreams. My Papa is alive, Josie is crying over me, and *he* wants me! 'Josie?'

'I——' The little girl leaned against the steel frame of the shower. 'I couldn't find you. You didn't sleep in bed, and I thought you was gone away on the boat! I couldn't find you, and Daddy was so mad he just yelled at me, and I thought I—Mamma?'

There was only one way to answer that appeal. Rose held out both soap-splattered arms, and the child ran into them, soap and all. The little head buried itself just under her breasts, and the salt tears ran down across her abdomen. They clung to each other like a couple of castaways on a raft. Until the little girl sputtered and began to laugh.

'I think I got soap in my mouth,' she spouted. 'I'm all over soap!' But the tears had stopped, and there was a glitter of happiness in those wide eyes.

'Might as well not waste it,' Rose laughed. 'Here, slip out of that dress and we'll both rinse off together.' Small fingers hastened, and in a moment they were both nude. Rose flicked the shower curtain shut. 'Ready?' she asked.

'Ready,' Josie giggled. 'Only I think I'll hug you some more?'

'Of course, love.' With one of her hands entangled in

the girl's hair, Rose used the other to pull on the chain controlling the shower. Rinse water poured over them. They did a crazy little dance around the shower stall, and sang a silly song Rose remembered from her own childhood. And when the three-minute spray halted they were both glowing.

'We have to get some more bigger towels,' she told her daughter as they struggled with the little hand-towels that hung on the rack. My daughter! That's really how I think of her, isn't it. My daughter. Too bad that she comes as a package with that—that man. We could be very happy together, Josie and her mother!

'Daddy said he was ordering——' The little girl stopped her wagging tongue by plastering both hands across her mouth.

'Daddy said?'

'Daddy said keep my mouth shut,' the little girl answered, chagrined. 'And I almost gave the whole thing away, didn't I? I ain't very good at this secret business.'

'Me neither,' Rose giggled. 'Turn around here now while I dry your hair. You haven't been shampooing enough lately. You've still got sand in the base of your hair. Tch.'

'Tch? What does that mean?'

'It means, little love, that as I look you over more carefully, I can see that your mother doesn't take care of you well enough. And it also means that you're a long way from being six years old. Just look at you!'

'Is it bad, the way I look? I gotta be six. At least for three more days I gotta be six!'

Rose shook her head, laughing. 'No, love. It all looks very nice. Very nice indeed. But if you have to play six years old for another three days we'd better keep you covered up. Me too, for that matter. Suppose you run and get each of us one of those *muumuu*'s that I made. The red and green and gold ones. And I think you'd better hurry. I suspect your father is angry with me, and he's waiting!'

'Mommy?' When I get bigger will I look like you?'

'Well, perhaps not entirely, love. God puts growing orders—a genetic code we call it—in each of us when we're born. I guess you'll still look somewhat like me. We have the same colour hair, the same eyes, you know.'

'I didn't mean like that. I mean, like, you're all curvy and soft, and like that. Will I?'

'Ah. I can't tell that, love. *My* mother was all slender and *chic*, and look how I turned out. I'm too—well, there's too much of me.'

'Daddy don't think so.'

'Daddy doesn't?'

'Nope. Yesterday I was teasing him, and I said, boy, have we got us a lot of Mommy there! And he said yes—isn't it wonderful That's what he said.'

'Hey, that's enough of *that* talk. Scoot.' Rose turned the girl around and gave her bottom a tap in the right direction. 'Hurry up.' The girl scooted, missing the flashing blush that spread from Rose's oval face all over her delightfully curved body.

Dressed demurely in all-covering loose *muumuus*, the two delayed just a moment in Rose's bedroom while she displayed her new find. 'That's cute,' Josie said. 'You can't hardly see nothin', and yet it looks like—well, I don't know what it looks like. What is it?'

'It's a *tiki*,' she explained. 'In the old days Polynesians used them to mark their temples, to stand in for their gods, and things like that.'

'That ain't no god,' Josie commented solemnly. 'No way!'

'Perhaps not,' Rose offered. 'She's definitely a female, isn't she. You like it?' The child nodded. 'I'm going to keep it here in my room. I'm not sure your father will approve of the idea, but I'm going to anyway.'

'We better go have breakfast,' the girl reminded her. 'Why don't you bring it with you and show them.'

'Them?' Rose was busy wrapping the little statue up in a *pareau*, covering it from head to foot.

'Yeah. We got company for breakfast. You missed everything. Where was you?'

'I—I went up the mountain,' Rose offered softly. 'Come on, let's go see just how angry your father is!' She scooped up the offered hand in one of hers, and used the other to pick up the packaged statue. They both skipped as they went down the hall. At least they did until Rose's feet reminded her of their poor condition. There was nobody in the dining room.

'*Iorana*,' Miri sang out from the kitchen. 'They decide to eat on the veranda. You like eggs for breakfast?'

'Eggs? Where in the world did we get eggs?'

'The boat comes, of course. Powdered eggs, you understand, but they make nice scrambled?'

'You bet,' Rose called back. 'Anything!'

The two of them wheeled around, went out the front door to the shady side of the porch, and came to a dead halt. Giles was standing there beside the laden table making small talk with a massive Polynesian man. He was dressed in the lightweight uniform of the Island police.

'I——' Rose struggled to run, but the little girl's hand anchored her. Giles was talking with his hands, the typical method of island cross-language conversations. A look in the policeman's eyes caught his attention, and he turned.

'Ah! Rose!' He came over to her, taking her hand from Josie's, and towing her over to the table. 'Rose,' he offered the introduction, 'this is Inspector Tihoni from Tahiti. My wife Rose, and this is my daughter Josie.'

The big man rose and sported a smile all over his bronze face. '*Madame*.' It was a cultural shock she was not prepared for, hearing the almost-perfect French coming from this almost-perfect Polynesian giant. And then English, equally as good. 'We heard that *Madame* is interested in the old ways, no?'

Rose shrugged her shoulders helplessly. Now it comes, she told herself bitterly. 'Are you Rose Lambert,' he would say next. 'You're under arrest for having a father who steals money, Rose Lambert!'

'I—I,' she stammered, and got no further.

'Sit down, Mommy.' Josie was holding a chair for her. She offered a weak smile of thanks and sank down into it. Come on, her brain nagged at her. Go on the offensive. If he hasn't the time to say 'Are you Rose Lambert,' he'll never be able to arrest me!

'My mommy's been sick.' Josie stepped close to her side and gave the policeman a fierce protective look. 'You gotta be careful when you talk with her. You make her cry and I'll——' Two little fists were raised threateningly. Rose gulped for breath, and quelled the mutiny by sweeping Josie up into her lap.

'Yes,' she said, her words pouring out as if a dam had burst. 'We—my daughter and I—we're interested in the old ways. This is my daughter.' She pulled Josie closer, bending the little face down beside her own. Establish an identity, her mind screamed at her. Quickly!

'And that, of course, is what I came to find out,' the police officer offered in a friendly manner. Startled, Rose leaned back away from him, her face turning pale. *That's* what he came all this way to find out? Why?

'In Papeete there is some doubt, you will understand, about whose daughter she is. The American Consul is most insistent that we find out. And now of course, my eyes tell me. She is certainly your daughter, no? The hair, the eyes, the smile. Of course!' He beamed at them all.

Gendron beamed back at him, then came over and

rested an arm on Rose's shoulder. 'Perfect,' he said. 'Perfect.'

Not willing still to let the officer get those fatal words in, Rose babbled on. 'We—I—last night, I found something on the mountain,' she rattled, putting the wrapped package on the table in front of her. 'And I thought—I knew I—well, I brought it down because it shouldn't be lying up there on the side of the mountain, and——' While her tongue wagged on her brain began to function. He came about Josie? But it's all right because Josie is my daughter? What's going on here? What in the world is . . .

Miri interrupted. She carried out a loaded tray that smelled like heaven. Ham and eggs, Rose's nose told her. How long has it been since I had ham and eggs. And—good Lord—bread!

'Flour. Also from the boat,' the Polynesian girl whispered in her ear. 'While it lasts, we have bread!'

'*Iorana!*' Another voice with the Polynesian greeting. Rose looked down, off the porch. The *tahu'a* stood there, proud in the crown of his white hair, his *pareau* slung gracefully at his hips. 'So you came, *Tamahine*. Good. Everything will be!'

That was all he said. Everything will be! Rose lifted her dazed eyes to Giles. This whole conversation had long since run far over her head. Her *husband* was looking back at her. Not like a hawk about to strike. More like a—a lover? A warm cheerfulness had erased the worry furrows on his face, and had left him almost—almost handsome. The corner of his mouth was twitching, as if he were fighting off laughter. Quickly she swivelled to the policeman. His solemn eyes were following her fingers, which were slow unwrapping the *tiki*.

He's such a big man, she thought, some of her fear returning. He'll just grab me by the scruff of the neck and drag me down to the—'Oh Lord, the ship has sailed.'

'Until the day after tomorrow,' the Inspector offered. 'There is one more stop in the chain of islands, you know. *Motu One*. But I have no reason to go to that island, so I wait here. It stops here on the way back.'

And then he'll do it, her mind rattled on. Then he'll do it! Do they put manacles on woman prisoners? Why am I so frightened of him? First it was Giles I was afraid of, and now it's the policeman. He's so big. He's AUTHORITY! He'll just—and she stared at the policeman, in shock. Her fingers had finally unveiled the little statue.

Inspector Tihoni's eyes shifted, flared, and a look of surprise flashed across his face. He pushed back his chair and backed away from the table to the very edge of the veranda. Giles looked at him with astonishment. The old *tahu'a* cackled. The big burly policeman pointed a heavy finger at the little statue.

'*Sacré Bleu!* Pele!' he half-shouted. He took one more step backward, and fell off the end of the veranda.

CHAPTER SIX

THE old *tahu'a* was laughing as he helped the Inspector back on to his feet. 'On no,' he said. 'Nobody in the islands believe in the old gods. Nobody. That is correct, Inspector?'

'Of course. No one believes in such superstitions. We are a modern people.' The policeman was having trouble with the collar of his uniform. It might have been too tight. Well, at least *something's* making him turn all mottled red, Rose told herself.

'Then this—this statue of Pele is just an old superstition?'

'Just so,' the inspector told her. 'It—surprised me, nothing more.' Just the same, when he resumed his seat at the table he made sure he was as far from the ugly little *tiki* as he could get.

'There is a mistake,' the *tahu'a* said. He was staring straight at Rose, as if trying to impress something of great importance on her mind. 'This is not a statue, *Tamahine*. This is Pele herself. You brought Pele down from the mountain.' He smiled as if it were a good joke—that only the two of them could share. Inspector Tihoni seemed to turn pale, and Moera, who had come out on to the veranda with another platter just in time to hear his words, dropped the entire load, screamed, and ran back to the kitchen. No amount of coaxing would bring her back.

'I think I'd better put her away,' Rose sighed, and instantly lectured herself. Don't you have enough troubles of your own, she snarled. Why do you let this—this witch doctor convince you that—put *her* away. Now he's got *you* believing it! She appealed to

96

Giles silently. He nodded his approval, and gave her a quirky little grin. She tried out a tentative return smile, and felt rather pleased because it seemed to work. She scooped up the *pareau* in which Pele had originally been wrapped, and made up another package.

'Josie,' she said softly, 'take this into Mamma's room and set it on the table please. And come right back to this wonderful breakfast!'

The *tahu'a* watched the little girl run into the house with her burden. He laughed, a very satisfied laugh. The Inspector watched too, and gave a huge sigh of relief when she disappeared down the hall.

'And now breakfast,' Rose said firmly. 'What can I serve you?' She offered first to the old Polynesian. It seemed only proper. He represented the oldest authority. He made a small selection among the fruits, accepted the coffee, and had two of the deliciously light croissants that the girls had produced. The other men made their selections, and by the time Josie came back all were eating.

The little girl slipped into the chair beside Rose, offered a big smile, and began with her ham and eggs. Rose wrinkled her nose at her, tapped gently at the elbows on the table, and dug in for herself. After a satisfactory time the police officer cleared his throat, brought out a notebook, and looked around expectantly.

'It will require a report,' he stated, and then sighed. 'Everything requires a report. Now then—the little girl is named?'

'Excuse me.' It's gone far enough, Rose told herself. Another minute of this and I'll go right through the roof. I *have* to know what the devil is going on!

The Inspector paused, notebook open, pen ready, and waited for her to continue.

'I——' she stuttered. A deep breath steadied her nerves. 'Why? Why must there be a report. What do you want to—what's going on here! What! For God's sake, somebody tell me before 1 lose my mind!'

'Ah!' The policeman capped his pen and seemed to find something terribly. important to examine on the table top. After a moment he lifted his head again. '*Madame* has been sick, no?'

'My wife sustained a head injury,' Giles interrupted nervously. 'Sometimes she—forgets. And we didn't want to worry her, so I didn't tell her about—anything,'

'But I have to know,' Rose demanded fiercely. 'I can't—you have to tell me!'

'Yes.' The Inspector had decided on his next course of action. 'I am come, *Madame* Gendron, because we receive from the United States, through Paris, you understand, a most formal complaint. There is a charge of to kidnap. A child has been stolen in New York, from the home of her mother. A terrible thing, no?' He took another sip at his coffee cup, considering his next few words. 'There is a—a break in the home——'

'A broken home,' Giles interjected. His face had turned to stone, his voice the same.

'*Merci*. The broken home, of course. There is the divorce, no? And the court has said to the mother, take the child. But—well—this terrible charge from the Americans say that the father have come to this house in New York, have committed breakage to enter, assault, battery, and have kidnap this child. So will the Police in Tahiti please to investigate this *Monsieur* Giles Gendron to see if he has taken this child. Now——' He uncapped his pen again, took one more tug at the coffee cup. 'This little girl, her name is?'

'Josie,' Rose offered, very tentatively. She had *heard* the explanation, but had not reasoned it out.

'Josie Rose Gendron,' the child recited. Rose gulped quickly and flashed a look at Giles. He returned one of injured innocence. The Inspector wrote busily in his book.

'And her age is?'

'Six!' All three of them spoke in unison. 'I'm six years old,' the child repeated.

'And the mother's name?'

'Rose,' she told him, fighting against the weight of a pair of suddenly-heavy eyelids. 'Rose Harriet—Gendron.'

The Inspector scribbled diligently. 'And the child was born where?'

'San Francisco,' Rose sighed, having no real idea what the truth might be.

'Portland, Oregon,' Josie hurried to get in.

'Right here,' Giles growled, doing his best to out-shout everybody. 'Right her on Te Tuahine.'

'There is some—disagreement?'

'Not at all,' Giles insisted. 'I told you about my wife's—small illness. The child was born here. Monsieur Apuka can show you the records.'

'Yes, of course. Right here.' For some reason Rose felt she had to support the claim, but her mind was in a complete whirl. Not only was she receiving more—facts—than she cared to know, but she was also beginning to tire.

'Ah.' More scribbling in the Inspector's book, and then he closed it and carefully put his pen away in his pocket. 'And so obviously then, it is not possible that this child could be ten years old, by the name of Caroline, eh?'

Josie started to say something, and her father pressed his leg against hers under the table. All three of the *Gendrons* presented a united front, smiling at the policeman. 'No, of course not,' Giles said very conclusively.

'And this other child,' the Inspector mused. 'You are not concerned that this other child of yours is missing?'

'Of course I am!'

Rose settled back in her chair, and waited to see how

the scheming conniver would work his way out of *this*
little corner. 'But I don't know what I can do about it,'
Giles continued. 'I don't have any money. My former
wife gets it all in alimony payments. Are you *sure* this
isn't something that she arranged?'

The policeman laughed. '*Cherchez la femme*—in fact,
two of them?' He raised an eyebrow, and chuckled.
'No, monsieur, we do not know such a thing, nor can
we find out. It is a matter for the Americans. We act
here only out of—friendship—with them. They say,
look in Tahiti for a ten year old girl stolen from her
mother. And instead we find a happy family, a father, a
mother, and a six year old girl. The government of
Tahiti will do nothing to disturb a happy family, you
understand!' He thumped the table to make his point.

And by this time some of the data was beginning to
make sense in Rose's tired mind. Why—why that
dirty—that rat! She turned to stare at Giles. Waves of
anger pulsed at her throat, flushing her face. He could
see it all. That's what he's using me for, she screamed to
herself. I'm just trying to avoid a little—unpleasant-
ness—about fifty thousand embezzled francs. *He's*
wanted for kidnapping! And making me into a
surrogate mother just to support his dirty underhanded
conniving . . . Ahh!

The policeman came for *him*, not for me. And Giles
took one look at the poor little amnesiac, and set me up
in the middle of a kidnapping charge! Lord, what a naïve
little lamb I've been. Damn the man! Her two small
hands balled into fists. She placed them carefully on the
edge of the table behind her plate, wishing she had the
nerve to thump and rant and rattle. Josie snuggled a
little closer, and used her own hands to cover her
'mother's'. The warmth of the little body against her
side partially restored her control. That, and the little
wandering truth that managed to surface on top of all
her anger. You *could* rant and rave and rattle, little

Miss Lambert, if only you hadn't been so damn busy trying to con *him* at the same time!

'So,' the policeman continued. 'That settles that little problem. Now, I have a hundred boring things to do. I must check the register of births and deaths and marriages, and make a health inspection of the copra gathering, and all the other things a government wishes to know, *ehe*? And perhaps, since I am empowered, we might celebrate a few civil marriages. Who knows?' He stood up, all the magnificence of his Polynesian forebears outlined in a French police uniform. 'Isn't it strange,' he mused, looking over at Rose. 'Twice in two weeks I deal with a case where a woman is named Rose Harriet.'

'Twice?' she asked weakly. Don't ask, her conscience barked at her. Stupid woman, don't ask! You not only don't want to know, but you don't even want him to think about it!

'That's quite a coincidence,' Giles said, rising with his guest. 'Another Rose Harriet?'

'Just so,' the policeman nodded. 'Hard to believe, no? Rose Harriet Lambert. A very involved case. Arson, embezzlement, storms at sea, an important witness, shipwrecks, and Rose Lambert is missing. Oh well, it is hoped that she will turn up, but—the ocean is very big, and the islands very small.' He waved a hand to them and, in company with the *tahu'a*, started down towards the beach and the village.

Everything is coming unstuck, Rose sighed to herself. Just for a moment there, I thought I was home free. Just for a moment. But no, I had to be stupid enough to give him my right name. Where else in all the Pacific would there be a young blonde named Rose Harriet. Stupid, stupid, stupid! But what did he say? *Arson* and embezzlement? What in the world does that have to do with anything. And how come he said Rose Lambert was missing? Because they've found Papa?

It was all too much. One weary hand pushed her plate aside, the other made a little nest on the table, and her head came down into it. Before the Inspector had disappeared from sight she was fast asleep, drawn deep into the cavern where fears could not follow her.

'She's fallen asleep,' Josie whispered when they turned back from watching their departing guests. 'Just like that, she's fallen asleep!' To Josie, falling asleep was a complicated endeavour, requiring squirming, story-reading, a doll to squeeze, and a bed on which to sprawl. It wasn't something one did while sitting at the breakfast table!

'Yes,' her father said softly. 'The poor girl is exhausted! All night up on the mountain, and then all this.' He put an arm around his daughter and squeezed her. 'But she did royally well for us, didn't she? I don't think we have any more reason to worry about your mother chasing us. At least not for a year or two.'

'Rose *is* my mother,' the little girl snapped at him. 'Her. That one right there. I don't got no other mother. And I don't want no other mother!'

'Hey, baby.' He cuddled her closer, but over her shining head he was looking at the sleeping woman. Something was touching his heart. There's a whole lot of woman there, he told himself. A lot of loving and care, and—my God, what a figure! Is it only because I've not seen a white woman in two years?

'We hafta keep Rose!' His daughter had backed away from him, and her beautiful green eyes were demanding a pledge. One that he was not sure he could make or keep. 'We *hafta*!' For just a second he felt the same way. Yes, we *do* have to keep her! But he set the thought aside.

'She's not a toy or a pet,' he said solemnly. 'She's very—nice. But probably she has people of her own, and a place to go to. Hey, precious, for all we know she may be married and have children of her own.'

'But if she didn't, Daddy? Could we keep her?'

He withdrew into a typical parental defence. 'Ask me again later,' he said. 'Right now we've got to get your mother to bed. You run ahead and open things up while I carry her inside.'

She stirred when he slipped his arms under her knees and lifted her off the chair. Her head lolled back against his shoulder, and she snuggled down under his chin. She was no light weight, but he had expected that. A whole lot of woman, a pocket Venus! That ancient male stirring ran up through his blood. Damning himself, he let his upper arm shift slightly, until his massive hand cupped the softness of her breast. She moved slightly, closer to him, and smiled in her sleep. It was too much to ask, that his hand move away, he told himself. Too damn much to ask. As he carried her down the hall, that hand flexed against the firm softness of her, and the stirrings ran riot in him, even as he lectured himself about taking advantage of her.

His daughter was standing beside the stripped bed, holding one finger over her lips in a shushing motion. He got a grip on himself and lowered the woman to the bed. One gentle hand slipped off her sandals, the other moved to the hem of her *muumuu* before common sense intervened.

'Go ask Miri to come and undress your mother,' he ordered gruffly. The girl nodded and vanished. Isn't that strange, he asked himself. She's as stubborn a spoiled little minx as you might ask for, but tell her to do something for her *mother* and she's away like a shot!

He stared down at the face of the woman on the bed. Sleep had stolen away all her defences. She lay there in a seductive sprawl, a lovely smile on her face, her hair scattered in disarray across the pillow. Unable to control himself, he let his hand wander through the golden silk, spreading it out carefully, combing it with stiff fingers. She stirred again and the smile disappeared. He snatched his hand back, and then, driven, bent over and kissed her full on the lips. Miri came into the room as he did so.

'*Aue*,' the island girl whispered. 'I thought there is a mistake. Why you want *me* to undress your wife. You will do that for yourself? *Nehenehe*, that one.'

'Yes, she *is* beautiful,' he sighed, moving away. 'But you'd better undress her, Miri. I have to get back to work!'

'Strange, you *popa'ae*,' the girl chuckled. 'A beautiful *vahine* of your own, and you have to go back to work?'

He worked hard all afternoon, until the sun slanted in the windows, and he knew it was close to five o'clock. He looked around at the scattering of pages on the desk, the table, and the floor. It had been a fruitful afternoon. All his juices were flowing. As they have to be, he reminded himself. Helen cleaned us out, and we've spent the advance from this book already. It *has* to be a best seller. We need the money! And this one ought to do it. High adventure, high sex, an exotic background—Lord, I can almost taste the movie rights! He was smiling as he turned off his little machine and covered it.

He left the papers still strewn around the room. That was his little fetish. He would straighten them all out tomorrow, before he started off at the keyboard again. That overnight 'seasoning' was what brought him all his luck. And that's what a successful writer needs. Perception, language, and luck! He was smiling as he stepped out into the hall.

A breeze from the north was blowing into her room, sending the drapes at the doorway billowing out into the corridor. He stopped and looked in. She was sprawled out on her back, outlined under the thin sheet that almost covered her. Her hair surrounded her head like a halo. The sheet followed her form lovingly, sagging between her wide-spread legs and outlining her hips and thighs in all their fullness. She half-turned in her sleep, and the cover fell away from one full ivory breast. The bronze tip captured his whole attention. Immediately he could feel that surge of impatient maleness coursing through his blood. He could not free his eyes from that roseate nub, standing there on the peak of its alabaster mountain, challenging him. His feet carried him across the room. He moved like a sleepwalker, unable to control his own passions. Across the room, to the side of the bed.

He dropped to his knees, inches away from temptation. She moaned slightly in her sleep, and moved. That one perfect breast quivered slightly, and was still. His mind commanded him to go—to get up and run before he spoiled everything. You need this woman's co-operation, he hammered at himself. You need her to complete the deception. And now you know something more about her too. There couldn't possibly be two women in the islands named Rose Harriet. So that makes you Rose Harriet Lambert, little lovely, with all the police on the lookout for you! Get up and leave, his mind yelled at him.

Little woman, hah! His eyes were feeling a peculiar strain. His hands actually moved to help him push himself up and away. But they moved only an inch or two, coming to rest on the edge of the mattress. And instead it was his head that moved. It bent forward slowly, until his lips surrounded the beautiful bud that faced him. Surrounded and gently tasted with his rough tongue until the softness hardened and thrust at him. He looked up at her. Her eyes had snapped open, filled with—what?

She was caught up in those milliseconds between sleep and awakening, when the rapid eye movement indicated a dream in progress. It was a wild screaming dream, filled with enormities—and Giles. The two of them, intertwined in hot passion, clinging to each other, naked, striving each to arouse the other. Until suddenly he touched her breast with his lips, and the dream shattered. It left her bereft, unsatiated, awake. And staring at him.

'What—what are you doing!' Trembling words at first, words seeking a re-entry into the dream world. Words looking for completion. And then anger, as her mind sorted out the scene in front of her. He was doing just what she had dreamed—and in her dream she had cried for more, even more. But the dream was shattered, and she was slowly rousing to rage. Not because of what he was actually doing, but rather because of what he had failed to do in her dream!

He mis-read the situation entirely, hunkering back on his heels and letting a mask slip over his face. The hawk mask. The predatory hawk. She gathered the sheet around her for protection, and slid as far away from him as the bed would allow.

'You have no right!' She stamped the words out one at a time, coldly, arraying them like little soldiers marching to battle.

'No,' he sighed. 'I—there aren't any excuses. I looked in to see if you were all right, and I saw you. That's something no ordinary man could resist. And that's all I am. An ordinary man. I suppose you would like me to say I'm sorry?'

'Not if you don't mean it.' She tried to encapsulate the words in ice, but failed. There was a tremor in her voice that she could not control. There was something about this troubled man that was growing on her. Some subtle thing she could not understand. Not grand passion. Not love. Just some indefinable—something.

'Well,' he sighed, struggling to his fee, 'then there's no use saying it, because I don't feel the least bit sorry, and I suspect I'd do it again the next chance I get!'

'Well, don't hold your breath waiting,' she snapped

at him. The dream had truly dissolved and things had returned to normal. She was still a refugee on a tiny island, afraid for her own safety and for her father's, locked into this man's schemes until the inspector left. And the last thing in the world you need, she told herself, is to fall into some crazy entanglement with this—arrogant man! How could it be possible that he fathered a lovely child like Josie? All of a sudden I feel a great deal of sympathy for his former wife, whoever she is!

His question came out of the clear blue sky. 'How old are you, Rose?'

'Twenty,' she snapped back at him, without giving it a thought.

'Ah! You do remember something!'

Oh Lord, shut your stupid mouth, she yelled at herself. Shut your stupid mouth!

'So you do remember something,' he insisted.

'Yes,' she said angrily, and defied him to pry another word out of her.

'So tell me what you remember.'

'I remember that I'm twenty,' she returned defiantly. And let me see you make something out of that, Mr Gendron!

He waited for a moment, hoping for some amplification. She sat up in the bed, holding the sheet up to her neck, defying him. 'All right,' he sighed. 'At least that's something.' He lifted a wrist to check his watch. 'Only twenty minutes until dinner time,' he commented. 'You'd better get dressed. This is our last performance with the Inspector. The ship will dock at seven tonight, and leave at four in the morning.'

She managed to be early, in fact. A girl whose wardrobe consists of three *muumuus*, four *pareaux*, and four sets of wrap-around skirts hardly finds a problem in dressing for dinner. For this night she chose another *muumuu*. When she walked out on to the veranda he was waiting for her with a tall cool glass in hand. He passed her the drink and slipped an arm around her waist.

'Look down there.' He gestured with his free hand. A few feet below the house Josie and Inspector Tihoni were deep in conference, *tête-à-tête*. The big man was sitting on a large tree stump. The little girl stood in front of him, her hands clasped behind her back. Even at this distance Rose and Giles could see that she had her fingers crossed. When the dinner gong rang the pair came slowly up the walk, seemignly content with their world. The Inspector smiled at them and walked by.

'I need to clean up,' he said. 'The records are somewhat dusty. Would you believe that the official papers have not been audited in fourteen years?' He hummed a little song as he went down the corridor towards the bathroom.

'What did he want,' Giles asked quickly.

'Nothin'.' The little girl gave her father a hug. 'He asked me was I happy here with you and Mommy. So I told her sure I was. Who wouldn't be, I said. And then he said, you know, I have a family of my own. Six daughters, I have. And I said, that's nice. And then he said again about was I happy here, and I said of course I was, and wouldn't wanna live no place else 'cept with you and Dad.' A little hand stole out and trapped Rose's in a death grip. Rose squeezed a return promise that they both understood without words.

'Well what do you know,' Giles mused. 'Still suspicious. Troops, we need to put on a good show tonight, so we can send him off in a happy mood. Right?'

'Right,' Josie chimed in. 'Mommy? Right?'

'Oh—of course. Right.'

It didn't turn out to be a difficult problem. Sam Apuka appeared as an added guest, and Miri joined them at the table. The conversation was world-wide, and then localised.

'Yes,' Sam answered the Inspector's question. 'We grow here on Te Tuahine. Now we are eighty three people. Forty-four children and thirty-nine adults. The life is good. But we worry about the reef, you know. When France has need of us they blast a hole in the reef. It costs much money. Now Tahiti governs itself. Where comes the money to blast again? Already the reef grows, no? Even the local freighter, he worries to come in. What becomes of us when the reef closes?'

They all sat and stared at each other. Change the subject, Rose commanded herself. Be a real hostess. Turn them into some other line of thought. Quick! She took a deep breath, dived off the deep end, and —'Miri, when are you and Sam going to get married?'

Every adult at the table turned to stare at her. Miri turned her head away and giggled nervously—the sort of giggle that denotes embarrassment all around the Pacific basin. Somebody kicked Rose in the ankle under the table. It became stunningly obvious to her that she had managed to get both feet in her mouth with one sentence!

'Perhaps I could explain,' the Inspector offered. Since nobody else made an offer, Rose turned to him in desperation. His face was awash in strange expressions, as if he were carefully marshalling all the right words before he spoke.

'It is still the custom of the outer islands as in the old days,' the policeman started out cautiously. 'People marry to raise families, and boy children are most necessary, you understand.'

Feeling utterly stupid, Rose nodded her head.

'And so you must see that a man who wishes to raise a family would want to be—er—sure that he would have boy children, no?'

'It—it sounds plausible,' she stammered, wondering how deeply the basic Polynesian sex lecture was going to go. 'But there is a catch in it?'

'A delightful expression. Catch in it! American?' She nodded. 'So it is the custom that a girl should be able to demonstrate that—er—she can—ah—provide boy children before the marriage is arranged. You understand?'

'What!' All her beliefs were outraged, and she could not hold back. 'You mean to tell me that Miri has to——' Giles was signalling to her, gesturing to where Josie sat at the foot of the table, her little ears perked up so as not to miss a word. Oh Lord, Rose sighed to herself. Oh Lord! She struggled to regain control over her face, and sank back in her chair. The silence around her broke as everybody tried to introduce a new subject, all at the same time. Rose let it all wash over her. But she could not leave it lie; she had to worry the bone just one more time. 'Everybody knows,' she muttered under her breath, 'that the male determines the sex of the child!' Which earned her another warning kick on her ankle!

The dinner party broke up at nine o'clock. Josie was yawning madly, as was the Inspector. Sam and Miri seemed to be eating each other up with their eyes, and soon they made their excuses and went off to the village. In the distance they heard conch-shell trumpets announcing that the old supply ship had returned.

'That Apuka is a fine man,' the Inspector said as he rose from the table. 'He'll make a fine headman here. And you, Mr Gendron, Mrs Gendron——' he seemed to hesitate between the two names. 'You add something to the island. I will file a negative report about this case of kidnapping. There is clearly no truth in it. All the papers will be filed in our headquarters in Papeete. And by this time next year nobody will be able to find it, not even for the most inquisitive of American Consuls. So I say good night. In the early morning I go quietly, not to waken you. I wish you many sons.' He waved to them all and went off down the hall.

Giles put his arm around her waist. He's been doing

a lot of that lately, Rose thought. And it's not too unenjoyable, either. And then Josie came around from the other side of the table and butted her head into Rose's side.

'Tired, love?' she asked. The little girl nodded wearily.

'Did we do a good job, Daddy?' the child asked.

'Remarkably good,' he said softly. 'It couldn't be better. Just a few more hours now, and we'll all be away free and clear.' Rose noticed the inflection. *We'll all be*— as if they shared a conspiracy together. But it did sound— nice. Just a few more hours, and it would no longer be important what the Inspector remembered about Rose Harriet Lambert. She wrapped an arm around the pair standing on either side of her. It's really not difficult at all to think of myself as Rose Gendron! I'll think about his little con game tomorrow. When the sounds of the policeman moving around from bathroom to bedroom had stilled, she squeezed Josie's hand.

'First it's bed for you, love,' she whispered, 'And then me. Come on. You can shower in the morning.' The little attentions, the settling down, the little story, all filled a half-hour. When Josie was finally asleep Rose stood up and stretched. Lord, it had been a strange day, among strange people. What a crazy mix-up! She walked down to her own room, fumbling in the dark for the shorty nightgown she had made for herself. The moon was late in rising, and the tropical darkness had settled on everything. Moving around the bedroom she stumbled a couple of times. Those darn packages, she swore under her breath. I forgot to ask anybody about them, and they're all over the room! But in the end she managed to finish her own toilette, and tumbled into bed.

I'm beginning to live in this bed, she thought. I spent most of the morning here, part of the afternoon, and now here I go again. I don't think I can sleep, but I can suddenly she was shaken out of her musings. Somebody had brushed the drapes aside at her door and had come into her room. 'Who is it,' she hissed, wary of waking the little girl next door.

'It's me,' he answered softly. 'Where the devil is my— damn, did they have to put all those packages in the middle of the floor!'

'Shh,' she retorted. 'Josie's asleep. What in the world are you doing in my room?' She could hear by the noise that he had found his way across the cluttered floor, and had settled into the chair by the bed. 'Well?'

'Well what?' One of his shoes clumped as it landed on the floor.

'What are you doing!' She could feel panic rising, blocking her throat.

'I'm getting undressed. What the devil do you think I'm doing?'

'You can't undress here. You must be out of your ever-loving mind! Get out of here. Go back to your own room!'

'Think!' he snorted. The other shoe dropped to the floor.

"Think?' she hissed. 'If you don't get out of here I'm going to scream the house down!'

'Go ahead,' he said under his breath. There seemed to be two or three other words involved there, but Rose decided that she just didn't want to hear them.

'Why—why are you doing this to me,' she sighed. The tears edged closer to her eyelashes. 'Why did you——'

'Think,' he repeated. 'We've got three bedrooms. Josie has one, the Inspector has one, and that leaves this one to be shared between my wife and I. My wife certainly won't mind sharing a room with me, will she?'

'What kind of logic is that,' she snarled at him. 'I told you before I didn't want you to lay a hand on me until——'

'Oh just shut up and move over, Rose,' he snapped. 'The bed is wide enough for four of us to sleep here. There's no way of avoiding this. Mr and Mrs Gendron spent a quiet night in the connubial nest, and the Inspector goes home to Tahiti without a care in the world, right?' The bed sank and rocked as he stretched out beside her. It was too dark to see what he was wearing, and she was driven by a need to know. She stretched out one tentative finger in his general direction. Somehow he sensed it was coming, and seized it in one of his big paws. She tried to pull away, but he moved her hand inexorably forward, until the fingertip touched his upper thigh. Nothing, her finger signalled. That's what he wears in bed. Nothing!

'For heaven's sake,' he muttered into her ear. 'I don't plan any great rape scenes, Rose. Close your eyes, there's a good girl, and let's see if at least one of us can get some sleep before morning.'

She snatched her finger away. Its tip was burning, burning. She moved it to her mouth and sucked on it, trying to control her panic. He shifted in the bed a couple of times, rocking her, sending shivers up her spine. In all her life she had never shared a bed with anyone, never mind a full-grown virile male! And how come you think about him that way, Rose, her conscience asked. A full-grown virile male, indeed! She held her breath so she could listen to his. He seemed to be exhaling more slowly, as if he were asleep. She extended her finger again—just to be sure he was asleep, of course. He was much closer. Too much closer! Her finger touched gently on his chest, felt the warmth of it, and the pulsing life within. Damn! She pulled the finger back, turned on her side with her back to him, and did her best to compose herself. It wasn't easy. Counting sheep didn't help. But counting *tiki* statues did. Row after row of little stone statues she counted, manoeuvred, re-arranged. They all looked like Pele. He wants you. That's what her dream on Pele's *maere* had told her. He wants you. Eventually, if you count high enough, you discover that he wants you. How much higher do I have to count before he *gets* me? And with that thought wrapped around her she dozed off.

Sometime late in the night, long after the Inspector had stolen quietly away to the ship, a rain storm swept down on the island, cleaning the air and adding depth to the perfume of the night flowers. In typical tropical style it poured an inch of rain down in an hour. The huge drops battered at the corrugated roof of the house, and the crescendo of smashing bashing water startled Rose into half-wakefulness. Instinctively she recoiled and found herself hard up against his frame. He reacted. Two arms came around her, pulling her closer. There was an instantaneous feeling of— protection, comfort. She relaxed against him, halfway back in her dream, enjoying the soothing motion of his hand on her stomach.

'I——' she started to say.

'Don't talk,' he whispered in her ear. 'Don't talk. I know. Everything's all right.' There was a hypnotic spell in that deep voice of his. He continued talking, saying nothing, and gradually she fell under the spell of it all. When his hand moved upward from her stomach to the mound of her breast it all seemed—proper. She made no protest. But when he walked his fingers up to the roseate tip of that lovely mountain the world seemed to jump all around her. For the first time in her life she felt a wicked response, a driving flaming spark that ignited all the passions that a woman possesses. He's my husband, she told herself fiercely. He's my husband. And knowing the lie, it was still excuse enough to overcome her doubts. She gasped and turned towards him, opening her eyes for the first time.

He loomed over her, a huge dark shadow in a darker

room. She could feel the strength of him, the maleness of him, as he moved closer. His lips brushed hers. A tender touch, warm, moist, pleasant. And then they returned, at the same time that his hand stroked her silken flank. The pressure of his lips became more urgent, more demanding. She started to say something, and his tongue slipped past her guard. And her world blew up!

She snatched at him madly, winding her arms around his bare shoulders, pressing herself hard to conform to his contours. He tantalised her mouth for an endless time, and then slipped away from her lips, nibbled at her ear, the softness of her throat. And then he moved down to where her swollen breasts waited to receive him. She squirmed against him frantically, not knowing what else to do. Her fingernails left marks on his back, red striations that matched the fever in her brain. Someone was moaning in a soft contralto voice.

He fumbled briefly with her nightgown, then one of his huge hands seized it at the neckline and tore it straight down. She had the crazy urge to get closer to him, to feel the hardness of him all over her soft skin. Wildly she struggled to free her arms from the remnants of her gown. His hands played havoc with her, running up and down her back, across her buttocks, down her thighs. He broke her stranglehold around his neck, turning her over flat on her back. His hands moved again, down the little mound of her stomach, into the area where no one had ever been before. She could feel the scream of pleasure building up in her as he caressed just the right spots. 'Giles,' she whispered fiercely at him. 'Do it! Do it now!'

There was no time for thought no room for conversation, no place for explanation. Do it, her mind kept screaming. Do it now! He rolled over on top of her. She welcomed his weight, as her tensions mounted higher and higher. He brushed her legs apart and poised himself, gone beyond control beyond stopping. She pulled and tugged at him, urging him closer, into the final union. And the pain struck her. Slight, transitory, but a warning none the less.

It was enough to bring her back to reality. Her whole mind and body froze in position, interrupting the delicious rhythm that had sent her into mindless ecstasy. 'No,' she muttered, and then louder, 'No!'

He was too far gone to stop, although he recognised that his partner was no longer with him. In one wild surge he reached his peak, and collapsed on top of her. And it was only then that he recognised the meaning of the frail barrier he had destroyed. She lay there beneath him, trembling, suddenly cold. Tears ran down her cheeks.

'Rose?' Half doubtfully, half apologetic.

'Damn you! Damn you! You had no right!' Her voice was a fierce hissing whisper, filled with all the remorse of years. The pain had quickly disappeared, but the memory of it hung over her head. 'You had no right,' she hissed at him.

'I thought you gave me the right, Rose,' he returned hoarsely, unbelieving. 'You came to me, I didn't come to you! I thought that was what you wanted.'

'Well you thought wrong, damn you! I didn't invite you to rape me. It was the storm. It—it frightened me!'

Her mind struggled, seeking an excuse for herself. He had no right! The storm—and—I could have stopped him! Why didn't I? I've never had any trouble stopping all the other grapplers. Was it because he told me I was his wife? He almost had me believing it! He *did* have me believing it. It has to be *his* fault. I couldn't stand it if it were *my* fault. I'd just—just break up in little pieces. All those years. Saving myself for this? It *has* to be his fault. Who could have expected that it would hurt so much? My God, what has he done to me!

Her hands pushed ineffectively at him, until finally he roused and rolled to the edge of the bed. What in God's name have I done to her, he thought. Not only a sweet lovable kid, but a virgin to boot. I've really done it this time. But I—I thought that was what she wanted! Why am I trying to excuse myself now! Why didn't she find it as good as I did?

'I'm—terribly sorry, Rose,' he whispered. 'I didn't mean it to happen. It was just—one of those things. I really thought you wanted it!'

'Yes,' she hissed at him. 'Just one of those things. A one-night stand. I hope you enjoyed yourself, because *I* certainly didn't. God, what have you done to me!'

'I didn't realise—I just couldn't stop, Rose. What can I do to make you see how sorry I am. I'll do anything!'

'I'll bet you will.' Her voice was as cold as an Arctic mountaintop. She drew away from him, sitting up against the headboard on the far side of the bed. 'I was your wife, you said. And Josie was my daughter. Sure! What other lies did you tell me?' It isn't true, her conscience complained. You know it isn't true!

'I'll do anything, Rose. Ask me anything.' She could hear the agony in his voice, and it pleased her to know he was suffering.

'Fine,' she grated between her teeth. 'Make me a virgin again.'

He snatched at his shirt and shorts and stomped out to the veranda, snarling both at himself and at her. 'I don't do miracles,' he muttered, banging his fist into the bamboo pillar of the veranda.

Straight ahead of him, to the east, the sun was a thin line of light against the horizon. The sea breeze blew in at him, laden with fresh-washed air. In the distance gulls were diving inside the reef. Near at hand the wind rustled through the paper-thin leaves of the bougainvillaea. Behind him, through the window he could hear her softly weeping. 'I'm a cross between Hitler and Attilia the Hun,' he muttered as he searched his pockets for a cigarette. The weight that his conscience saddled on him was heavier than any burden he had ever carried in his life.

CHAPTER SEVEN

SHE sat in the dim corner of her bedroom for half the morning, huddled in a chair near the window, completely covered from head to toe in the largest *muumuu* she could find. Time after time she tried to think logically, and was unable to do so. Time after time she relived those few minutes in the night that had so completely changed her life. 'If only I had stopped him,' she muttered to herself. I could have stopped him. Couldn't I? I never meant it to be this way. I always dreamed of—a man who loved me. There was no love last night, not on either side. Animals, both of us. But it was his fault. If he hadn't lied and cheated, if he hadn't forced himself into my bed, none of it would have happened. So it *is* his fault. Damn the man!

Miri brushed the door drapes aside and came in, stopping suddenly when she saw Rose huddled in the corner. *'Aue.'* she exclaimed softly. 'I think you are at the beach, Mrs. I come back later and——'

'No,' Rose sighed. 'Go ahead with whatever you have to do.'

'You don't even open the presents?'

'What presents?'

'Here.' Miri pointed to the half dozen packages littering the room. 'You don't even open? He spends many days to look in catalogue. Look here.' She picked up one of the smaller bundles and opened it, laying its contents out on the bed. 'There. What you think?'

It was an exciting collection of European clothing. Everything from day dresses, slips, underwear, daring bikinis. Miri hugged one of the sheer little blouses to her cheek. 'Lovely,' she chanted. 'You like?'

119

'No, I don't like,' Rose snapped. 'Get them out of here. All of them. Right now, Miri. Get them out of here!' Her voice rose to a crescendo of loathing that could be heard throughout the house.

'You no like? I——'

'Get them out of here,' she snarled. 'Now!'

The other woman stared at her with wide eyes, and then began to collect the packages in her arms. 'You think he will——'

'I don't give a damn what he will,' Rose shouted. The Polynesian girl shrugged her shoulders and went out with her arms loaded. A few minutes later Giles tapped on the doorframe and walked in. One all-encompassing look was all he needed.

'You're acting like a child,' he said gruffly. 'The clothes were ordered a week ago. You——'

'I don't want anything from you,' she told him through clenched teeth. 'I don't want *anything* from you. All I want is to get out of here. And if you ever touch me again, so help me God I'll kill you!'

'So, you're convinced it was all my fault, are you? You had nothing to do with it?'

'Yes,' she snarled at him. 'Get out of here. Surely I can have some place to myself. I don't think I've ever hated a man as much as I hate you. Get out of here!'

'Be honest with yourself. It wasn't rape, you know.'

'It was,' she shrilled at him. 'Lies and deceit, and then brute force. Oh it was rape all right. I was your wife, remember? Mother of your daughter? Hah!' She wrapped her arms around herself and rocked back and forth miserably in the chair.

'All right,' he sighed. 'And now we have to talk about what happens next. After we're married, I thought we would——'

'Married,' she screamed, and struggled to her feet, threatening him with both fists. Now what the hell, he asked himself. Thank God I sent Josie off to the village with Miri!

'After last night, the least I can do is marry you,' he offered stiffly. 'After all, you might very well be pregnant, you know. It seems the only sensible thing to do, for us to get married.'

'Sensible!' she screamed.

'Yes, sensible,' he said, struggling to keep calm. It's like talking to a volcano, he told himself as he watched her shake and shiver in her rage. 'I need a wife, and you need a husband. Especially if you should be pregnant. Under the circumstances, I——'

She had simmered down, but only slightly. 'I wouldn't marry you if you were the last man on earth,' she shouted, pounding out the rhythm of each word by thumping a fist into her open palm. 'You are undoubtedly the most arrogant, arrant man I've ever known. Do you really think I would let you take over my life after what you did to me last night?'

He lost control. 'Well, I'm not all that keen about marrying you, either,' he snapped. 'But we have to. As it happens——'

'Forget it,' she interrupted. 'It's not going to happen, damn you. And as for being pregnant, I thought it was the island custom to see if I could produce a boy before you offered marriage! Damn all you men. Now you let me tell you something, Mr Know-It-All Gendron. The only thing I want from you is a way off this island. And quickly.'

He stared at her, non-plussed. It had taken a whole morning of musing for him to come up with the idea of marriage. And here she was turning it down in anger, insulted. A perfectly legitimate offer that an awful lot of women would grab at!

'I could make you a very good husband,' he told her self-righteously.

'You haven't proven it yet,' she snarled back at him. 'It takes two to tango. You're already a one-time loser.

Why wouldn't Helen want to keep you on? Because you're such a good husband? Hah!'

'That's hitting below the belt,' he objected.

'I just hope so,' she snapped at him. 'This is supposed to be a serious discussion. I don't have time for little jokes, like *Rose is going to marry Giles*. Now, how soon can I get off this island?'

He leaned back in his chair, fumbling around in his mind. No matter how he added it up, it still came out the same way. She *had* to marry him. And it wasn't only the matter of easing my own conscience. Josie is the main problem. I have to do something about Josie, and quickly. Why didn't I notice that the child is growing up? She acts more and more like a native girl every day, and her English is so bad that—wow. She needs a mother, that one. One whom she respects, and even—loves? Rose Harriet just fits the bill. And then there's me. But his usually facile mind refused to wrestle with *that* problem.

He fingered the newspaper clipping in the pocket of his shorts. The one he had cut out of the newspapers that arrived with the supply boat. She needs us as badly as we need her. Now why in hell can't she *see* that! What we—all three of us—need is time. Time enough for Josie to settle down. Time enough for me to paper over that massive mistake I made last night. Hey, as far as she's concerned, I'm the good guys. So I'm not in love with her—relationships have been built without love by many a couple. I'll do it. After you've been accused of rape, blackmail is hardly a terrible crime!

'I'm afraid that's impossible,' he told her. 'There's no way off this island until the next supply boat comes. That will be, oh let me see now—three months from now. December. Close on Christmas, I suppose.' And try that one on for size, little lady! He watched the sudden flare in her eyes.

'You mean I have to wait around here for three months?' Her face reflected her astonishment.

'Three months? Never!'

'I thought you never said never,' he chuckled. 'But that's correct. Three months until the next boat. You could swim, of course. Maupiti is just six miles over that way.' He waved to the north. 'Now that's civilization. They have air service to Tahiti three times a week. Most weeks, that is.'

'Six miles? That's not very far. I'll bet I could get one of the fishermen to take me over there.'

'No you don't, Rose Gendron. Don't get the villagers mixed up in our problems!'

'I'm not Rose Gendron, damn you. I'm not your wife. I never was your wife, was I! You proved that last night, you—you monster. I hope the Inspector comes back so I can tell him about you and your daughter!'

'That's blackmail, Rose. Out and out blackmail!'

'And you deserve it. Every bit of it!'

He stood up, towering over her. He's doing that on purpose, she told herself. Trying to intimidate me. Monster!

'You seem to recall a great deal these days, Rose,' he said amiably. 'You're twenty, you're not my wife, you hate me—what else do you remember, Rose?'

She was too angry to control her tongue. 'Everything!' she snarled at him.

'Everything?' He cocked one eyebrow at her.

'Yes, damn you,' she shouted at him. 'You thought you were so damn smart, didn't you? Play the little lady for a sucker? Hah! Let me tell you something, you conniving—you—you. I never did have amnesia. Not at all! So there!'

It was all out before she could stop herself. And then, shivering with anger, she had to stand there while he bent over almost double, laughing until the tears came to his eyes. Just once, she thought—just once I'd like to be a man. I'd beat him up something fierce! I'd 'Why are you laughing?'

'Rose, that's funny,' he gurgled. 'While we were busy conning you, you were busy conning us! Now that's funny!'

'Well I don't see the humour of it,' she said coldly. 'I was scared half to death.'

'And you know what makes it even funnier,' he chuckled. 'The rape scene. So it was rape because I told you you were my wife. Naughty naughty, Rose!' He shook an admonitory finger at her and broke out in uninhibited laughter again. She stamped her little foot in anger, unable to free herself from the sudden cold fear that struck her.

'Sit down, Rose.' He forced her into a chair. She perched nervously on its edge, her back straight, feet flat on the floor, heels together. Her fingers nervously wrestled with each other in her lap.

'So tell me about Rose Lambert,' he said softly.

'I don't remember any Rose Lambert,' she muttered.

'Then you've got a very strange memory,' he snorted. 'Look at this.' The crumpled paper he handed her was from the front page of the Papeete newspaper. She unfolded it and stared.

HAVE YOU SEEN THIS WOMAN, the headline said. Beneath it was a distorted picture of Rose Lambert, on her fourteenth birthday, with her hair in two pigtails, and her undeveloped face almost unrecognisable. It's the picture Papa always carried in his wallet, she told herself. So they *must* have Papa. Or perhaps just his wallet? She brushed the thought aside, and read on.

'Police in the islands are searching for ROSE HARRIET LAMBERT, the daughter of one of the principles in the investigation of the fire and embezzlement at the Banque de Pacifique early in September. During that crime two million francs in gold, currency, and securities were stolen, and the building torched to hide the evidence. Miss Lambert was last seen aboard the yacht *Southwinds*, during the typhoon of September 7th. Miss Lambert stands five feet four inches, with long blonde hair and green eyes. A reward is offered for information.'

She handed it back to him, on the defensive. The slight breeze that sometimes wanders through in the heat of mid-morning wrestled with her hair, blowing it into a clever mask across her features. 'No, I don't remember any Rose Lambert,' she muttered.

He laughed again. A short barking laugh, with a triumphant ring to it. 'Despite all the sudden truths,' he said, 'you and I have a great need of each other. I need someone to look after Josie for the next three months. Someone who can love her and teach her how to be a woman. If you agree to do that, I guarantee to get you out of the islands—to anywhere. Samoa, New Zealand, the States. Anywhere. And along with that I can promise you a stake to start life over again. What do you say to that?'

'What the devil did you suppose I would say,' she shouted at him. 'No! I intend to find some way off this island, and the sooner the better!'

'Why now that's too bad,' he mourned, plainly not meaning it. He leaned over closer to her and, in a conspiratorial whisper said, 'Just remember, the first minute that I find you gone from the island, Rose, I will radio the Police that Rose Lambert is on her way to Maupiti. There's a reward, Rose! And think what sort of welcome you'll get when you come ashore!'

'Why you—you——' She was entirely out of words bad enough to be used on him, and he was laughing again. She took six deep breaths and fought to control her temper. 'That's pure blackmail,' she squeaked at him. 'Blackmail!'

'Isn't it though,' he laughed. 'Bargain?'

She jumped up, and immediately regretted the move. He was much closer. And somehow much bigger. She clenched both fists so tightly that her nails bit into the palms of her hands. She shook and trembled in her anger, and her fists wavered. But it was thought, not anger that she required to elude his trap, she told herself. She walked away from him, stamping her feet down hard to steady her nerves. Up and down the restricted space she stomped. He moved back out of the way and let her pace.

It was fear of the unknown that held her in thrall. What has happened to Papa? If the police have *him*, why would they want me? Any step I take, any word I speak, might harm poor Papa. Information. I've got to get more information. *Somebody* knows! The Inspector certainly, but he's gone. There has to be some other source of news. And until I get more information I have to—to give in to this—monster. I have to! Mind made up, she ground to a halt in front of him.

She stared at the third button on his shirt, refusing to meet his eyes. Her hands were clasped behind her back. He needn't know *everything* I think, she told herself fiercely.

'All right,' she grumbled. 'It's a bargain.'

'And very graciously said,' he chuckled. 'So, for three more months you will be Mrs Rose Gendron, and will instil some discipline in my daughter, and teach her how to grow up.'

'Hey, wait. I didn't agree to be any Mrs Gendron. That's not in the cards.'

'All or nothing, Rose,' he said solemnly. 'All or nothing.'

'Oh—I—damn you. You'd better not touch me, do you hear!'

'I hear, love. And I swear I won't ever touch you— damn, there's that word again. I swear that I won't hardly ever touch you, except for when you ask me to.'

'And *that* will be a cold day in summer,' she huffed.

'And I'll expect you to dress up to the name,' he

continued, 'so you will accept the clothes I bought for you. Right?'

'Damn you,' she muttered, and turned away. There's a difference between accepting and wearing, she told herself.

'Hey, that's no way for a lady to talk,' he added. 'Here comes your daughter. Switch heads, Rose darling. You are now officially my wife again.'

'Damn you,' she muttered again. It was all the words she could muster.

Josie was all chatter that night. Miri had taken her through the village, re-introducing her to the children, presenting her to the elders.

'And that boy Terri,' she chattered. 'He's my age, or something, and he has his own outrigger canoe, Mommy. He took me out on the bay and we fished. I didn't catch nothin', but he said that was okay, 'cause girls aren't supposed to fish anyways—that's man's work.'

And that is the first link in your set of chains, Rose whispered under her breath as she scrubbed the little girl's back under the shower. The first step is to convince you that men can do things better than women, and that's the beginning of female subjugation. Damn men!

'What did you say, Mommy?'

'Nothing. Nothing, dear. You got a good burn on your shoulders. The next time you go out for the day you must remember to put some sunscreen on.'

'How come? Terri don't wear none.'

'No, and he doesn't have your European skin either, love. You just remember that.'

'Why?'

Rose laughed at herself. A sudden flashback had pictured her in the bathroom with *her* mother, having the same sort of argument. 'Because I said so, that's why.' And waited for the argument that never came.

'Oh.' Josie said. And that was the end of that subject.

She went tiredly to bed, but still had something on her mind. 'What Daddy bought you. Are you going to wear that stuff?'

'I don't know, love. Maybe we can make it into something for you to wear. We'll make a lady out of you yet!'

'I don't wanna be no lady,' the child murmured sleepily. 'I just wanna learn to be a good bow paddler.'

Rose had the luxury of coffee on the veranda when Josie finally dropped off. 'We can have coffee for maybe four, five weeks after the boat come,' Miri explained. 'Coffee and flour and green vegetables. Except he order something this time I don't know. Is called dehydrated potatoes. Nobody in kitchen knows what to do with potatoes.'

'I'll show you tomorrow,' Rose assured her. 'Leave the coffee pot, Miri. I feel like going on a binge.'

'*Aue,*' the other woman laughed. 'Better you drink *kaava.* Coffee drive you mad in moonlight. I hear somebody say that. I leave mug for Mister. He don't like cup.'

Live and learn, Rose sighed. Mister don't like cup! She stuck her tongue out at the open sky and poured herself a steaming black cupful—even spilling a little into the saucer as a sort of libation. She leaned back deep in the lounge chair and sipped and watched. The Southern Cross, deep in the sky. Venus, star of evening, sparkling bright—and far away. Sirius, the watch-star of the islands. All the panoply of heaven circled above her and intersticed her dream. Was it only a day ago that the world had been so shaken—her world? Was it only a night ago when she was forced over the border into womanhood? C'mon, her short-tempered conscience snapped at her, he didn't have to push very hard, did he? And then silently he was there.

'I smelled the brew,' he said. She leaned forward and filled the mug.

'Black? We have some powdered milk and lots of sugar, but I told Miri to leave it in the kitchen.'

'And a good thing,' he commented. 'We'd have all the insects within five miles charging up the stairs. Black is fine.' He settled into the other lounge chair. 'Lord, this is good. It's a pleasure to be able to relax again.' He stretched out, his long legs over-reaching the length of the lounger. They sat quietly.

'You've been working hard?' she asked. It was advanced casually, but she meant if for a flag of truce. There was no way her mind could sustain a steady hatred, with all burners going. And three months was a long time to get through.

'Yes,' he returned quietly. 'I've hit a snag.'

'Want to tell me about it?'

'Are you sure you want to hear?'

'Of course. I wouldn't ask if I didn't want to hear.'

He gulped down his coffee and refilled the mug, sitting up to face her as he did. In the darkness she could see only his outline, and the gleam of his teeth. So he's smiling, she thought—or getting ready to bite me?

'We have to make a killing with this book,' he began. 'I guess you realise that my former wife Helen just eats up our income with alimony payments. So I have to strike it big. Now usually I go for a straight adventure story. But to make this one movie-quality, I've got to add some sexy scenes. It's a must. Both my publisher and my agent say the same thing.'

'And?'

'And the *femme fatale* is just running away from me. I can't seem to meld her into the main theme.'

'Why don't you tell me about her?'

'All right. Why not.' He settled himself back in his chair again and began from the beginning, describing the plot, the main characters, and finally the woman. He talked for almost an hour, and very suddenly stopped in mid-sentence. She looked over at him. She had been half-listening, half-dreaming. He was running his hands through his hair. 'Damn! Of course!' he half shouted. 'That's why it won't come out even. I've got it now. Thanks, Rose! You certainly straightened me out in a hurry!' He jumped up and ran for his workroom.

'Yes, glad I could help,' she called after him. And then in a lower murmur, 'What the devil did I do to help? I never even said a word! Besides, it's a crazy plot. No self-respecting woman would act like that, ever. Well, hardly ever.'

But her coffee tasted sweeter, stronger, bolder when she went back to it, even though the entire cupful was cold. She looked around cautiously, and then laughed at herself. There was no need for caution. Josie was asleep. Giles was chained to his typewriter. Miri and the girls had all gone home. Giggling at herself, she leaned over the edge of the veranda and emptied her cup on to the ground. Then, hesitantly, she reached for his mug, filled it up, and leaned back to enjoy the flavour.

CHAPTER EIGHT

THE days that followed settled into a slow routine. An early morning swim, followed by breakfast. Lessons with Josie until the noonday heat brought everything to a halt. Naps for all. And then a time for exploring, usually spent with the child. Giles worked away, pounding the typewriter as if it were a mortal enemy. And then, a month after the freighter had sailed, Rose made a momentous discovery.

She had left Josie to struggle with a quiz on earth sciences, and walked down the hall to the bathroom. The door of his workroom was open. She stopped. The room was empty. Curiosity carried her across the threshold. Manuscript pages were piled helter-skelter. It was too much for her neat soul.

She leaned over and picked up a double handful of papers from the floor, shuffled them into some order, and searched the desk for someplace to put them. And immediately lost track of her original idea.

Squarely in the middle of the desk, in the only orderly area, was a small pile of envelopes, some unopened. Mail! For years she had sorted and classified her father's mail, and her fingers moved automatically to sort through this pile. Two letters from Papeete. Bills, apparently, with the little glassene slot to show an address. One letter from San Francisco in a bold heavy hand. One from New York, in a light feminine scribble. That last one was unopened. She checked the return address, just for curiosity's sake, she told herself. 'Helen Morley Gendron.' So his first wife still corresponded, and still used *his* name. She felt a little touch of

annoyance at that, and dropped the envelopes back
on the desk.

Something was nagging at her mind. She picked up
the envelopes again, and sorted out the two bills from
Tahiti. Something about them. What? She looked
them over carefully, tapping one of them against her
front teeth in an old familiar habit. Trying to start up
her thinking motor, her father always said. What was
it?

She scanned the top envelope again. Just a bill, from
Dupont y Freres, Victuallers. Nothing unusual, except—
the cancellation! Six days old! Six days ago the envelope
in her hand had been processed through the main Post
Office at Papeete. Six days ago! And what was it he had
said? 'There's no way off this island until the freighter
comes back, in three months?' Then how in God's green
world had this letter come all the way from Tahiti in six
days?

She could feel the wild surge of excitement run up her
spine. Information, wasn't that what she needed? And
here was her first clue. In some manner, mail had been
delivered to this island within the last six days. Oh, that
horribly monstrous man! There *was* a way! He had
trapped her into his blackmail arrangement because
she thought there was no way off the island. And he
had lied to her! Again! She slammed the letters back
down on the desk and then, for good measure, picked
up the neat pile of manuscript pages she had assembled.
It improved her feelings immeasurably to toss the pages
up in the air and let them find their own home.

'That's a big help, thank you!' He was leaning against
the doorjamb, watching her with those predatory eyes.

'It's no more than you deserve,' she snapped at him.
'It's——' She clapped her hand over her mouth. Don't
tell him about the mail, she screamed at herself. It can
only help *you* if he doesn't know that you know! Shut
up, little fool!

'I—I was walking by and thought I heard the wind blowing your papers around, so I came in to——'

'Yeah, wind,' he grunted. 'I saw you helping me out.' He stalked across the room and planted himself firmly in front of her. 'Why not try the truth for a change!'

'Why me,' she snarled. 'That's a commodity that doesn't get a great deal of use around here.'

'Why?'

'All right,' she shrilled at him. 'I'll tell you the truth! I was looking desperately for a way to get off this island. And I didn't find anything. And that made me mad. You deserved it!'

'You bet,' he sighed. 'Everything's my fault, right? I deserve every little torment your tiny mind can think up?'

'Right!' She tried to walk around him, indignation burning in her eyes. One of his arms stopped her.

'Whoa up,' he grunted. 'I wouldn't want you to think you can get away with everything in the world, Mrs Gendron. You deserve this.'

His hands swept into her armpits and hauled her up into the air until her nose was exactly at his level. 'Put me down you overgrown——' she roared.

'Run out of words?' He laughed. She kicked at him, remembering too late that she was barefoot. Her sensitive toes stung as they bounced off his hard kneecap.

'Put me down, you arrogant monster!'

'That's better,' he offered. And then the hands slowly levered her towards him until nose touched nose. She ducked her head, only to find his mouth had found its mark on hers. She squirmed against him, kicking, pummelling. But every move she made served only to exaggerate the pressure of his lips. Out of breath, she gave up, hanging in his arms like a big rag doll. And then a flash of fire, a spark of no mean dimension flashed between them. She found herself drowning,

drowning. Dissolving out of herself, invading the separate atoms of his being, being re-forged there as a part of him. The world rotated crazily. She closed her eyes to steady herself, only to find that the darkness accentuated the passions, the fears, the flaming pleasures that were running riot within her. Just when it seemed she could live no further, refuse him nothing, he set her aside and dropped her to the floor.

She leaned against him for support, struggling to regain control of her errant body. He kept a steadying hand at her back. She swallowed, gulped for fresh air, and peered up at him through her dishevelled hair He was guardedly watching. Attentive, she thought bleakly—perhaps even a little apprehensive? She forced herself away from him, even though her feet provided only feeble support. 'Damn you,' she muttered. He folded his arms across his chest and waited.

'Damn you,' she screamed, and ran for the door, tears streaming down her face. She stopped in the doorway and turned around. He held up both hands, palms facing her.

'I know,' he said wearily. 'Don't you ever touch me again!'

'Yes,' she sniffled. And then more determinedly, 'Yes, damn you!'

'And it seemed like such a good idea at the time!' She shook her hair back out of her eyes and searched his face for the sarcasm that wasn't there. Too overcome by emotions to make another response she whirled and ran for the bathroom. When she came back out ten minutes later and ghosted by the door of the workroom, he was sitting at the desk, his head down on his arms. Warily, she made for the veranda.

'You got something in your eye?' The little girl was sitting back in her chair, the completed test form in front of her.

'Yes,' Rose acknowledged glumly. 'Your father.' She

regretted the words immediately. There's no need to include the child in your feud with her father, she stormed at herself. Cut it out!

'You got Daddy in your eye?'

'No—well, yes. I had something in my eye, and your father tried to get it out for me. Have you finished the lesson?'

'Yes ma'am.' Two impudent little hands folded themselves angelically on the edge of the table. Suspicion reigned.

'No cheating?'

'Nope.'

'You didn't look at the back of my book for the answers?'

'Oh, is that where they are?'

'Don't be a smarty. Let me see the paper.'

Correction and discussions took them up to lunch time. They were alone at the table. Giles had disappeared somewhere, Miri told them.

After lunch she enticed the little girl to forego her nap. 'I've got a special class lined up for you,' she teased. Happy to be out in the air, Josie held her hand and skipped all the way down to the edge of the village. The *tahu'a* was waiting for them there, at the door of the largest hut in the area. He led them down to the shore. The tide was at its lowest ebb.

'Geography,' Rose announced, 'and History too.' The child laughed and looked around. The old man picked up a stick and began to draw. As he made his little symbols he sang them an explanation.

'Why it's the story of the Great Canoes,' Josie murmured as she watched him designate islands and currents and the history of the great Polynesian migration.

'Fom out of Havaki,' the old man chanted, and stopped. 'The old Havaki—the original land, no? From out of Havaki came the great canoes.' And the story

went on. How the first boats had followed the birds and
the wind and stars, found islands under their stationary
clouds, avoided the lands of the Melanesians, and
finally settled in Samoa and Tahiti. And then the
second wave, coming out of Samoa and Tahiti, stretching
east towards Easter Island, north towards Hawaii, south
to New Zealand, and back westward again, into the island
left behind them in the first migration. Bringing their
tapuus and their gods with them. Tangora, master of the
seas; Ora, the man-slayer; Tane the god of the land, and
the wild mad Pele, she of volcanoes.

The little girl watched, entranced, as the Pacific
islands were named and charted before her eyes. Rose
felt somewhat removed and watched casually at first,
but was soon drawn into the tale. Until it came to a
stop. Two other men of the village came up and said
something to the *tahu'a*. The old man reflected for a
moment before he answered. They did not like what
they heard, but they went away. The woman and child
stared at the diagram in the sand.

'What did they say?' Rose queried. She knew it was
something about the lesson, and she hated to think that
the old man might be in some trouble because of her.
He laughed at her discomfort.

'They say, *why teach the Great Path to a little girl*.'

'Is that bad? I suppose—it's something that only men
should know?'

The old man laughed again, and used his stick to
make a sign in the sand, almost a copy of the Egyptian
Tau cross. 'I tell them,' he continued in his dry voice, 'I
don't teach the child. I do what Pele tells me. I teach the
woman. You come again another day?'

'I—Josie?'

'You bet, Mommy. If that's what geography is, I like
it. How come my book only says what ar the fifty
states, and who was George Washington?'

'Well,' she stalled, 'there are different kinds of

history. And we have to bring you up as an American, you know.'

'Okay.' Rose was surprised again at the lack of argument. 'We can come soon?' the little girl queried. The *tahu'a* ruffled her hair with his big hand. '*Ea,*' he said. 'You and your mother. *Au revoir!*' He unfolded his frame gracefully and walked away.

'Shall we go home now?' the child asked. And tugged at her *pareau* when Rose didn't answer.

'What? I'm sorry, dear. I was looking for someone. What did you say?'

'I said why don't we go swimming,' the little girl laughed. 'There's Terri out there waving at me.'

Rose held up a hand over her eyes to shade them. The Polynesian boy looked just like all the village boys. Just the sort of person Giles would rather Josie not associate with regularly. Oh hell, she told herself, I'm the girl's mother. She gave the child a little shoulder-shove in the right direction. 'Go play with him,' she chuckled. 'I've got to see someone myself.'

She watched for a minute as Josie ran down the beach towards the other children. She felt no qualms at letting her go. There were ten to fifteen adults on various sections of the sand, and Rose had learned something early on. In Tahiti and the islands one never watched one's own child—one watched *everybody's* child. There were at least ten surrogate mothers out there now who were registering Josie in their care. And if nobody came back for her there would be a happy squabble among the ten as to which one would take her home for the night. And keep her for a week if need be.

Rose was smiling as she sauntered down the beach towards her quarry. Sam Apuka was working slowly but steadily on an overturned boat, pounding sennet into the seams. He looked up as she greeted him, and stopped to wipe his forehead.

'*Iorana,*' he offered, and waited for her to speak.

'I don't want to interrupt,' she said hesitantly. He shrugged, and waved a hand at the boat.

'No interruption,' he laughed. 'This canoe leaks when I go away, four—five years ago. Now I am back a month, it still leaks. I don't fix it today, maybe it leaks next week. Not important. Good you bring big hat. Sun is no good for *popa'a* heads.'

'I just wanted to take a minute,' she said, crossing her fingers behind her. 'Mr Gendron, he—he thinks we should have five letters, and we only have four.'

'*Aue*,' the big man said. 'I don't count. Maybe one is still in Maupiti, no? We go tomorrow. I will remember.'

'Oh, you're going tomorrow? I didn't realize it would be so soon.'

Apuka looked at her indulgently. The sort of look reserved for children, the mentally deficient, and curious young women. 'We go every week on Friday,' he said. 'The airplane brings from Tahiti in the morning. We pick up at noon, come back by nightfall. If it don't storm!'

And there, Mr Giles Gendron, she told herself. I've got you! There's a boat that goes out of here once a week, and makes an air connection! Well, Mr Gendron?

'You make funny faces,' Sam chuckled. 'Eh, we have big dance tonight. Dance *tamure*, no? You come?'

She smiled at him. 'No,' she returned. 'My husband says we cannot come when you dance the *tamure*. Tell me about your boat.'

'Better I tell you about *tamure*,' the Polynesian laughed. 'Miri and me, we dance. Big night. Maybe you don't have breakfast tomorrow. No cook.'

And how in the world do I get the conversation back where I want it? Ask? Come right out with it? 'That's a long trip to Maupiti,' she said. 'What boat do you use?'

'Long trip? You go top of mountains, you can see Maupiti. Nine kilometres, maybe ten. This village has one *pahi*, one ocean-going canoe.' He gestured down the beach to the old pier. 'Easy trip. Good wind, quarter of one day. Bad wind, we paddle. Half a day. No problems. One day we go, you come with us?'

And that does it, Rose told herself exultantly. All I have to do is come down some Friday morning, get aboard, and away we go. Yes, sure, her mind nagged at her. And right at lunch time Giles finds I'm gone, he gets on the radio, and the police know all about it. Damn! It's an answer, but not the *right* one. I don't have enough information. How do I get information? Newspapers!

'Sam,' she called, as if it were an afterthought. 'Can you bring me back some newspapers the next time you go?' Apuka looked at her strangely.

'Bring back newspapers every trip,' he said cautiously. 'He don't let you read? Bring back Tahiti newspaper, New York paper, Paris newspaper. Every trip.'

'*Aue*,' she sighed. It seemed to be the only word that fit the occasion. 'He doesn't tell me. That man!'

The Polynesian grinned at her, flashing his beautiful white teeth. 'Best way to treat *vahine*,' he laughed. He picked up his wooden hammer, his length of sennet cord, and went back to work.

She went back up the beach whistling. So! Somewhere in that house are stacks of newspapers. And if Inspector Tihoni is right, her father's case would certainly be in the headlines. 'I've got you, Giles Gendron,' she whispered melodramatically. And then, more honestly. 'Well, I might only have a hold on your little toe.' And then after a few more steps. 'They're all chauvinists—every darn man on this island!'

Josie came running up at her first call. The little girl seemed subdued. They walked around the bay, waded the sparkling little river, and then started for the stairs that led up to the big house. The girl took Rose's hand with both of her own and tugged them to a stop.

'Mama?'

'Yes dear?' She leaned against the rickety rail that lined the steps. The child was bothered by something, and *that* should be ironed out immediately.

'Terri broke his finger.'

'He did? How did he do that?'

'It was something he was doing in his boat. But his mother said . . .' A pause, while the child fumbled with her words.

'What did his mother say?'

'His mother said there are many accidents in the village this month, and it's all your fault. That's what she said.'

Rose stared down at the girl. Those huge eyes in that small face were immense, and worry-lines chased across her little forehead. 'My fault? I don't understand.'

'They said it was bad luck, because you brought Pele down out of her mountain, and nobody would have no good luck until somebody carried her back up to her— to her something. I missed the word.'

'To her *maere*. Her little temple. You don't believe all that, do you?'

'I don't know, Mama. But that's what they said. They wasn't angry or nothing, just sort of sad. You know?'

'It's all superstition, love. That's all. Just superstition. Do you think the *tahu'a* would talk to us the way he did today if he thought we had desecrated Pele's temple?'

'Desa who?'

'Desecrated. Did bad things to it.'

'Oh I don't know Mama. All I know is what they said. That nobody on the island could have good luck until Pele goes home.'

'You *must* see that it's all nonsense,' Rose insisted. 'Why, Pele's just a little *tiki*, a little statue. It isn't really worth anything, and there's no way it could bring luck, good or bad. I'll get Mr Apuka to talk to them. Come on now, we're going to be late for supper!'

She put one arm around the girl and started up the stairs. But as they climbed another thought started to whip around in her head. If Pele is all that unimportant, she asked herself, how come you hang on to it with might and main. How come you just don't pack her up her mountain and set her back up in her little temple? How come? But like all her other little troubles, she could find no answer for this one either.

Giles watched them as they climbed up the stairs. Standing at the front of the veranda he could see how close they were. How little giggles of laughter started up in one, and spread to the other. How they looked at each other. He nursed his drink angrily. What the hell is wrong with me! I had a lucky escape when she turned down my marriage proposal. Wasn't one mistake enough? All these years, and I've still got Helen hanging around my neck like an albatross. He tapped the envelope in his pocket, just to be sure it was still there.

'Daddy!' The girl hurled herself across the intervening space and was swept up in his arms.

'Hey,' he protested. 'Cut out the wiggling. We saw each other at breakfast, you know.'

'I know,' Josie teased. 'You didn't shave.'

'Did I forget again? Did I scratch you?'

'No, you didn't scratch me, but you gotta be careful with Mommy. Her skin is more tenderer than mine.'

'More tenderer? Where in the world did you learn that?'

'I dunno. I been studying hard. Mommy's got soft skin, but a hard heart. She stands over me with a stick and makes me study!'

'I do no such a thing, young lady,' Rose objected.

'Well no,' the girl confessed. 'It was the *tahu'a* that had the stick!'

'You mean to tell me the *tahu'a* has been teaching you?'

'I'll tell you, but first you gotta kiss Mommy.' The

girl wiggled out of his arms and took Rose's hand.
'Well?'

'Well indeed.' He looked over the little girl's head at
Rose's perfectly formed face. It was easy to read the
succession of expressions that flashed across it. First,
shock, then—fear? And then disdain, which gradually
changed as she looked down at the girl between them.
And then the look was—fatalistic?'

'Our daughter demands a free show,' he chuckled,
holding out both hands. Rose hesitated for a second,
pried her hand free from Josie's grip, and offered
both to him. He stood in place until Josie gave Rose
a push. She came into his arms reluctantly, but she
did come. 'Smile,' he whispered in her ear as he
pulled her close.

'I'd rather bite you,' she hissed back, baring her
teeth. Before she could recover her stance his lips came
down on hers, teasing, questing. He could see the
muscles in her shoulders stiffen as she prepared to
suffer but not give in.

'Remember the child,' he chortled softly as he came
back to the assault. She stood her ground until his hand
wandered down her back and gently caressed the soft
swelling of her hip. He could feel the jolt that struck
her. She actually jumped an inch, and then all her
resisting muscles collapsed. Instantly he pressed closer.
She sighed and gave herself up to the rising excitement.
He broke off the contact, upset at her reaction as well
as his own.

My God, he told himself, has it ever been like this
with any other woman? Look at her standing there,
trembling. She felt it, but she didn't want to. There's a
tear in her eye. What do I do now? Here's one of the
world's most desirable women, I can turn her on
whenever I want to, but she hates it!

He dropped his hands away from her shoulders.
'Sorry,' he mouthed. She blinked at the tears, and wiped

them away with a knuckle.

'What's the matter?' The girl tugged at Rose's skirt for attention. 'You got Daddy in your eye again?'

'I—I guess I have,' she murmured. And then in a stronger voice. 'Run along now, dear. Bathroom And scrub those hands. Hurry up.'

After his daughter disappeared down the hall he waited for her anger. It didn't come. She stood in front of him, back straight, heels together, head down, hands clasped behind her back. And said nothing. He fumbled for a conversational *entrée*.

'You're not wearing your new dresses?'

'No,' she sighed.

More silence. 'We have a surprise for you for supper, Rose. Tonight we eat beef, courtesy of Dupont y Freres.'

The name re-awakened her memories. Letters. She smiled down at Josie, who came up and presented her little hands for inspection before sitting down.

'Oooh. Steak.' Josie's eyes sparkled as she snatched up the seldom used knife and fork by her plate. 'We ain't had no steak for three months.'

'We haven't had any,' Rose automatically corrected.

'Yeah.' The child managed to squirt the words out of a stuffed mouth. Letters, Rose reminded herself. Newspapers.

'We have a small problem in the schoolroom,' she began. He put down his fork and looked at her.

'We are supposed to be conducting a class in current events,' she continued doggedly. 'We need some newspapers.'

'Ah!' He went back to masticating his steak. She waited. Miri appeared with the dessert, a fruit and cheese tray. Josie was keeping both ears perked to the conversation. Next time, she promised herself. You won't get away with this forever, Mr High and Mighty!

He went back to his workroom after supper. She

could hear him slaving away at his machine as she walked down the hall after sorting the laundry and folding it away. Josie had dropped off to sleep immediately, so she went back out on the porch.

Tired herself, she relaxed in the lounge, half asleep. A shadow darker than the night impinged on her consciousness. Giles was there, squeezing his bulk into the lounge beside her. 'Miri's watching from the corner,' he announced, and leaned over to kiss her gently. 'Hold my hand. Polynesians have a lot of faith in hand-holding, but not in kissing.'

Dazed, she put her tiny hand in his and they sat quietly side by side for about ten minutes. She stirred, tugging at her hand. 'I think we can stop now,' she announced. 'I'm sure Miri must have gone home by now.'

'What?' It seemed as if he were coming out of a daydream. 'Miri? She went home right after supper.'

She could feel the rage mounting. One fierce shake recovered her hand. 'Damn you,' she hissed. 'Damn you!'

'Don't sizzle,' he chuckled. 'What's one little kiss?'

'With you there's no such thing as little,' she snarled at him. She used one hand to scrub her lips clean. 'I've told you before—don't you ever touch me again!'

'Okay, okay,' he sighed. The silence hung about them for another five minutes. 'I've a letter from my wife— from my former wife,' he announced. She looked over at him. He was thumbing an envelope. In the early moonlight he had a silvery look about him. All the heavy lines in his face were disguised. Why, he looks almost handsome, she told herself.

'I guess you know that it's her alimony that keeps us broke,' he mused. 'The judge in New York figured she needed five thousand a month to live on, and another two thousand a month to keep Josie.'

She could feel a certain amount of sympathy for him,

but refused to make it public. He watched her hair blowing in the breeze, and then continued. 'That's the way the ball bounces.' It was meant to be lightly said, but she could hear the bitterness in his voice. 'The American court system has this thing about mothers and children. They don't seem to care how bad the home is, or how little attention the child gets. Custody goes almost automatically to the mother. And the father pays. No wonder there's such an epidemic of kidnapping—fathers looking for their right to be a parent, even though it breaks the law.'

'Is that what you did? Kidnapped Josie?'

'Yes. I had to do something. I picked her up at her school, went back and beat the hell out of that guy Helen was living with, and hopped a plane.'

'And that brought you to Te Tuahine?'

'Eventually. Three years ago. Helen's been looking for us ever since. Using my money, of course. This letter was quite a surprise.'

'How so?'

'She wants to marry the guy.'

'Nothing wrong in that, is there?'

'No, that's good fortune. If she marries him, the alimony stops. But she's too clever to cut off her income. She writes to tell me she's *thinking* of getting married, and if I were to offer her an appropriate wedding present, she just might do that.'

'Appropriate?'

'Money. She's looking for a lump-sum settlement and she'll let me off the hook. Only I don't have the money. If the Indians were selling Manhattan Island again, I couldn't afford to buy Battery Park.'

'Oh!' She could feel his discouragement. Silence again. 'But you expect to make a great deal of money from this book?'

'Hey, after all the help you gave me, it's a sure winner. But that's future income.'

'Is your—is Helen a gambler?'

'How in the world did you know that? That's where all the money goes. Into the Atlantic City casinos. If I could burn down the Boardwalk at Atlantic City I could save a bundle.'

'Then I think there's a possibilty, Giles.'

'There is? Did you know that's the first time you called my by my given name in some time?' The darkness hid her blushes. She huddled away from him, into the farthest corner of her lounge.

'I was only kidding,' he said. 'What's your big idea?'

'Why don't you offer her a gamble. Offer her a quarter or a half—or all of the rights from this book. Everything. Movies, royalties, spin-offs. All in exchange for your freedom now.'

'Good lord,' he said, surprised. 'That could run into a half a million dollars if handled right. Maybe she *would* go for that sort of a bet.' He thought for a moment, and then stirred. 'I think I'll write her immediately.'

He leaned over in her direction as if to kiss her again. She squeaked a denial and slid off the edge of her chair. She could see him shake his head as he held himself stiffly poised, and then relaxed into the chair again. They both stared out over the water towards the village, where the faint sound of music was swelling up. Figures could be seen moving in the shadows of a bonfire.

'From the sound of the beat they're dancing the *tamure* tonight,' he chuckled.

'Yes,' she agreed softly.

'There's going to be more than one baby made tonight.' She let the comment pass. The compelling beat of the drums, the sweet sound of the guitars, the sparkling heavens of night, all were conspiring to mesmerise her. If only it could be different, she told herself. If only we didn't have all this anger and deceit between us.

'Do you still hate me?' His words dropped through her jumbled thoughts and reverberated around inside her head. Do I still hate him? It was a strain now for her to recall that night. All the passions, all the pain. Do I hate him? Or do I hate myself?

'Yes,' she managed to squeeze out, knowing it was a lie. She could hear his hissing sigh. He shifted noisily and got up. For a moment she thought he was going to come over to her, but instead he moved towards the door of the house. '*Iorana oe*,' he said softly, and went inside.

'Live happily ever after?' She sighed softly as his back disappeared. And the tears came, like a gentle spring rain.

CHAPTER NINE

IT was pleasant sitting in the sand by the grove of Royal palms. The bay shimmered in front of her, caught at that moment of change when the incoming tide just equalled the outpourings of the little river. A couple of elders from the village waited at the end of the rickety old pier. Out beyond the reef she could see the *pahi*, the ocean-going catamaran. It was pointed up into the wind, its huge sail fluttering, as the helmsman waited for just the right moment to run the passage in the coral barrier. It would be a while, she knew from experience.

For almost ten weeks now she had made it a weekly practice to meet the boat, collect the mail, and look at the newspapers. Ever since the evening when they had argued, Josie had cried, and he had stomped off, to return moments later and fling a newspaper in her lap. She had struggled with her dictionary. Spoken French she could handle. The printed word was something else. But the search of the thin Papeete paper was fruitless. There was no mention of Jules Lambert, or his daughter Rose Harriet. No mention that is, except for the two big holes cut in the front page. Something had been taken out. Something almost two columns wide. When she threw the paper to the floor in disgust he had glared at her and given her that steely laugh that seemed to be his favourite these days. And so, to avoid more censorship, she had begun to meet the mail boat, scanning the papers before he got his hands on them. Sam Apuka had no objections. 'Big House is not my affair,' he offered. 'Make you feel good to help you man, okay by me.'

Out in the ocean, perhaps a quarter of a mile behind the canoe, she could see the rain squall. Totally defined in that vast ocean space, it raced towards the island, dropping its rain in a huge circle. The sun shone around and through it, creating myriad rainbows. The watchers aboard the *pahi* saw it too. The paddles came out on the starboard side, gently swinging the double bows around, holding everything steady. And then, just at the right moment, the helm came down, the two sixty foot hulls swung over, and the squall filled the sail. The *pahi* changed from a listless log lying quiescent on the surface, to a charging living thing, racing for the channel with a froth at its bows.

'They lose the wind inside the lagoon,' the voice said behind her. The *tahu'a* dropped to the sand beside her. 'Takes twenty, thirty minutes to paddle. I have something to tell.'

She gauged the distance and admitted he was right. The sail bellied and flapped, and six paddles bit the water, there on each side. 'Something to tell me?' I might as well humour the old man, she thought to herself. He really is a nice fellow, in spite of all this mumbo-jumbo with mad goddesses and looks into the future. She gave him her best smile.

'So,' he sighed, adjusting his position. 'Pretty soon is high summer. The longest day of the year, just before Christmas.'

Although she knew it was true, she just hadn't thought about it. Christmas in the middle of summer? Her Louisiana blood objected! 'Yes,' she said. 'I had forgotten. I don't know what we can do to celebrate Christmas here.'

'You should not worry,' the old man assured her. 'You be gone by then.'

'Gone?'

'Gone from the island, *tamahine*.'

'I don't understand.'

'No, of course you don't. There is much pain coming to you, but by Christmas you be gone from island, and rainbow will shine for you. Providing you do a favour—a little favour—for Pele.'

Oh no, not that again, she thought. He can't really believe in all this nonsense. She made a quick check on the canoe as it glided through the green water of the lagoon. Still fifteen minutes, no less. Oh well. 'What sort of favour does Pele want?'

As usual, he approached the subject circuitously. 'Pele, goddess of volcanoes,' he began, 'and Tangora, god of seas. Since creation they fight each other. Pele shakes the earth, Tangora waits. See over there, the black sand? From long ago, when Pele shakes the mountain and it erupts. Lava burns everything it touches, but in the end it runs into the sea, and Tangora puts out fires.'

'So Pele is the *bad guy* and Tangora is the *good guy*?'

'No,' he laughed. 'You get it wrong. There is no good, no bad. Pele is woman, Tangora is man. Woman rages and shakes world, but only to limit man sets.'

'Oh wow,' she giggled. 'What a blow that is for woman's liberation!'

He smiled at her. 'Not to laugh,' he chided, but there was a twinkle in his eye. 'Pele and Tangora, since world begins, no? But now look. Pele sees over all the islands. The ways of the *popa'e* rule. New strong God in heaven. So Pele sends message. Take me to the new land, she says. I will shake the mountains for a new young people. Take me!'

'Good Lord. You want me to—Pele wants me to take her to the States? I—wow. And then what?'

'And that is all,' the old man said. 'Pele will do the rest.'

'But I can't do that,' she stammered. 'She's a *tiki*, an artifact. There's a law about exporting artifacts.'

'Not to worry,' the old man sighed. 'There are friends

and helpers. A case will be provided. No questions will be asked. You will?'

'Why, I——' She stopped to consider. Why not? At the very least the *tiki* would remind her of her strange stay on the island. Why not? 'Yes,' she nodded. 'If I can get her through customs, I'll take her.'

'Good. *Iorana oe, Tamahine*. The canoe is landing.'

She passed him a smile again, got up and sauntered down to the pier. She was familiar with the crew, but there was still that little wall between herself and the villagers, that distance dictated by the stories circulating. About Pele and herself, of course. They waved, they spoke, but never came close. So when Sam Apuka vaulted ashore he was as welcome to her as anyone could be. He slung the mail sack down and emptied it. The crew was unloading stores.

'Here. Four letters for the Big House.' Sam was sifting through the little pile. 'One for the *tahu'a*. Hey! And one for me!' He handed over the envelopes to her, along with the three regular papers.

'One for you, Sam?' she teased. 'The girl you left behind?'

'*Aue*,' he laughed. 'It comes from the CEP. I bet they want I come back to work for them, hey?'

'Would you, Sam?'

He waved a hand around him. 'Go back when I have all this? And my *vahine* too? Hah!'

'Well thank God for that.' She thanked him and started back down the pier, scanning the letters as she went. All for Giles, of course. Two from New York. She recognised Helen Gendron's scribbles. The other from his publisher. One letter from Portland Oregon. I don't even know where that is, she mused. And one from San Francisco, from his agent. She tapped all four letters against her palm as she manoeuvered around a particularly decayed section of the pier.

Strange how much I know about him, and how little.

We hardly ever speak, and yet—the nightly ritual on the veranda goes on. For Josie's sake, of course. One kiss, and one bout of hand-holding where the little girl can see it. Nothing more. He talks more often about his book. Silly. He rambles on and on about a problem, solves it himself, and then gives me all the credit. I should have a hard job like that for the rest of my life! But the book is finished. Now maybe he can relax. He works too hard.

Back among the palm trees she looked up, and then made herself a little nest in the sand. You always look. Sitting under a Royal palm is reasonably safe; sitting under a coconut palm is suicide! She set the letters aside and unrolled the week's issues of the Papeete paper. Her French had improved considerably since she started her search. She thumbed her way through the first two days' issues and found nothing. In the third she had a nibble.

Banque Pacifique Tahiti Reopens in Temporary Quarters, the headline said. Laboriously scanning word for word she followed the one paragraph story. It only added to her puzzle. The original bank building had burned down, a case of arson. A new and temporary structure was opening next door. A picture showed the dedication. And then, the story recalled, 'Police believe they have the location of the embezzler, who made off with two million francs in cash and bearer bonds. The Banque is now operating under new management.'

And I should think so, Rose giggled to herself. Oh Papa, you told me it was only fifty thousand. How could there be two million francs in that little case? She shook her head, and went on. The rest of the papers told her nothing. She studied the advertisements on the last page. Four more days until December. The paper was dated November 26th. She shrugged her shoulders. The dresses were pretty, but beyond her ken. She struggled up, made a single bundle out of all the papers, and started up the beach.

When the shock hit her it was so great that she paused in mid-stride, frozen. The world was shut out. The children playing nearby were silent, even though their lips were moving. Oh God, she half-sobbed. It can't be! It was only once! She forced her mind to function. I came ashore on September tenth. It was September seventeenth when the Inspector left. Nothing happened in September. I was excited, disturbed. October? Nothing happened in October. Could I still have been disturbed? And now it's—now it's November. And nothing has happened in November! Oh God, no! Not this way! Almost automatically her hand went down to the slight mound of her stomach. It can't be, she assured herself. I won't let it be! But deep in her heart she knew it was.

He was waiting for her when she came up on to the veranda. 'Hi, mail-girl,' he offered. He had her drink in his hands, and almost dropped it when she pushed the little pile of mail at him.

'You look tired,' he said. 'Have a hard day?'

'I—yes,' she stammered, fighting back the tears.

'Come on over here and relax.' His firm hand on her elbow guided her to the shade and the lounge chairs. She collapsed into one, shuddering.

'Hey, are you coming down with something?' His solicitude was too much. She averted her head and let the tears come. He watched for a minute, then joined her on the lounger, pulling her up against his chest. As usual, he was dressed only in a pair of ragged shorts. She had not noticed it before, but the fuzz of soft curly hair that stretched across his chest at the nipples, ran down like the letter T to his navel. She rubbed against it for comfort. He cuddled her. Her mind ran like a caged animal. As if I didn't have enough troubles, she screamed at herself. There's no place you can run to escape pregnancy. You take it with you whereever you go. And *he* did it. What kind of a fool am I to nestle up to the man who did this to me? She sat up abruptly and pulled herself away from him. He opened his arms immediately and let her go.

'So,' he said, 'after all this time, you still hate me?'

'It's not something you would forget too soon,' she answered bitterly. 'Not if you were a woman.'

He sighed, picked himself up, and went back to the other chair. She could hear the rattle of paper as he attended to the mail. She sat quietly, still shivering, looking out over the harbour. Josie came running out of the house.

'Mommy!' She ran across the veranda and threw herself at Rose. They tangled in a happy pile, hugging each other desperately. 'You been cryin' again,' the girl accused. 'Did Daddy get something in your eye again?' Josie looked across at her father accusingly.

He held up both hands in denial. 'Not me! I didn't have a thing to do with it.'

'You better not,' the child threatened, and turned back to nuzzle Rose's cheek. He went back to his letters again. The little girl chattered merrily away. 'Miri showed me how to make *poi*,' she laughed. 'It ain't as hard as you said, Mom. I got it right for the first time, and we're going to have it for supper. Wonderful?'

'Wonderful.' It was impossible to sit next to this little bundle of dynamite and not join in. 'All wonderful,' she chortled. 'How did I ever get such a smart daughter?'

'The stork brung me,' the girl giggled. 'Did you know that Miri is making a baby? She just told me about it. Her and Mr Apuka.'

'Oh Lord,' Rose exclaimed. 'I can see we have to speed up your biology course, love.'

'Did I say something wrong? Couldn't Miri do it all by herself?'

'No, baby, it takes two.'

The girl collapsed in Rose's arms again. He lifted his

head from his reading to watch them. That's right, she told herself. It takes two. I can't blame him for everything. Well, I can but I shouldn't. Look at the furrows on his face. They're deeper than ever before. He works too hard—and worries too much.

'I have a letter from your—from Helen,' he announced. Josie clung more tightly to Rose. 'She agrees to the proposal I made her. Would you believe that, she agrees!'

'What proposal was that,' Rose asked, her curiosity unlimited. Why is it that every time he mentions his— Helen, I get angry, she asked herself.

'I told her about the new book,' he reported, 'and offered her fifty per cent of all the royalties and movie rights. She write that she has been to Simpson & Savage, and she likes what they already have. And she talked to Morrie Burnbaum, my agent. He told her about the two movie offers he already has. And she agrees.'

'She agrees? What do *you* get?'

He smiled for the first time. 'I get to read her wedding announcement in the papers,' he chuckled. 'And she agrees to drop all prosecution concerning the —er—kidnapping.'

'And the alimony?'

'It ends the minute she says *I do*. But——'

'Of course. There's a "but".'

'Well, Helen was always a cautious gambler. She says that *her* lawyer has drawn up a contract, and Morrie has okayed it. But she's coming here before she signs. She has no intention of casting herself adrift until she's seen that the last chapters are finished.'

'She's very trusting, too, I gather.'

'Very. I don't know when she's coming. I can hardly read her hen-tracks.'

'I hope she never gets here,' Josie said sullenly 'I hope her canoe leaks, and Pele gets her!'

'Josie!' Both adults spoke at the same time. The child sprang to her feet, staring at them with wide eyes.

'Well I do,' she shouted, and ran back into the house.

Supper that night was a silent affair. Josie refused to speak to either of them, even when Miri brought the *poi* to the table. Rose was quiet too, but for a different reason. Seeing Miri, so proud in her pregnancy, drove a sharp splinter into Rose's heart. All through the meal she sat on the edge of her chair, barely able to repress the shivering. He kept his eye on her, which only made things worse. It's not all his fault, her conscience yelled at her, but she refused to accept that judgment. It *had* to be his fault, she repeated. If I don't blame him, then I have to blame myself. And that would really crack me up. It's his fault!

And so to bed, where in the darkness, muffled by her own pillow, she could cry enough to ease the pain. The dreams came back. The taste of salt spray and death on her lips. The wild tossing of the little raft. The shivering cold of the tropical night. When sleep finally came it brought no rest with it.

Somewhere in the dark pre-dawn she felt a stirring at her bedside, and struggled to get one eye open. Josie was there, clutching her three-foot teddy-bear close against her chest.

Rose threw back to the corner of the sheet in invitation, and the child slid in beside her. 'What is it, love,' she asked softly pulling the small head into her bosom.

'When—when *she* comes, you won't let her take me. Please?'

'I—no, I won't let her take you.' I don't know how I'll keep that promise, but I won't let her take you, she promised again under her breath. I wish I knew an easy answer.

'And you'll be my Mama forever and ever?'

Rose hugged the little body tightly and sighed. 'Your Daddy has to decide that, baby. Now close your eyes and let's get some sleep. We have a great deal of studying to do tomorrow.'

'You mean *I* gotta,' the girl giggled, and promptly dozed off.

And now see what you've done, Rose lectured herself. It's not all that simple. Let him decide? Why did I say a stupid thing like that? I can't stay, not with——

Her hand slid down and rested on her stomach, and she dozed off herself.

It was a lethargic day that followed. Everyone in the house except Miri seemed to be infected with sleepy eyes. Rose struggled to keep Josie's nose in the books, but it was a losing battle. So when the flutter-sound came down the wind at eleven o'clock everyone on the island stopped to watch. As the noise grew louder even Giles broke away from his work and came out to watch.

'Helicopter,' he told them. 'That's an expensive way to travel around these parts. It must be flying in from Bora Bora.'

Very suddenly the Alhouette was upon them, coming in from the west over the twin peaks of the Sisters, hovering over the Big House, where there was hardly enough flat space to spin a top, and then coming to rest on the beach at the foot of the stairs. The motor noises dwindled, and only the whap-whap of the idle blades could be heard.

The overhang of the hill blocked off a good view of what was happening. The door of the helicopter opened and a woman climbed out, ducking her head under the threat of the big blades. A man in casual clothes—the pilot—climbed out of the other side of the machine and gestured towards the stairs. A second man, portly, white-haired, struggled out and looked around him. The pilot began to unload bags, stacking them in a pile on the sand. The other two started off towards the Big House.

'Ooh,' Josie said. She didn't sound happy at all.

'I can't believe it,' Giles muttered. 'It's Helen. A day after I got her letter, and here she is. Damn! Rose?'

He drew her aside, out of range of Josie's ears. 'I know it's an imposition,' he sighed, 'but I've got to ask. It will make things easier for Josie—and for me—if you would play my wife to the hilt while Helen is here. Please?'

She stared at him. The worry furrows were deeper than ever, but she was too sleepy to debate. 'All right,' she returned.

'Thanks,' he said laconically. 'It gives me another bargaining chip, if she thinks I've got a wife to take care of Josie.' His hand urged her back to the veranda, where the child was still waiting. Impatient, Rose rubbed her fingers along the plain gold ring she still wore on her right hand. Why am I concerned, she asked herself fiercely. It's only his former wife. Why should I care? There was no good answer, and the woman was coming up the steps.

'Giles!' The newcomer offered a cheek. He pecked at it. 'And Caroline!' She held out her arms to the girl, who promptly shrank away from her, dodging behind Rose's skirts.

'My name ain't Caroline,' the child muttered. 'Josie, that's my name. Josie.'

'No kiss for your mother?'

'You ain't my mother. Rose is my mother!' The two skinny arms came around Rose's waist, where she clung like a limpet. And then, to be sure her point was taken, 'Rose is my mother.'

'Well really, Giles. I would have thought you would bring her up better-mannered than this.'

'I did,' Giles said. His voice was like steel. 'We did. Helen, this is my wife Rose.'

'This *is* a surprise!' Rose took a deep breath and stepped forward, offering a hand. It was ignored. 'I had not heard you were married, Giles. What a—curvaceous creature she is. You should diet, my dear. Slim is the word in the world of society this year.'

'She's just the way we like her,' Giles snapped. 'And in our society, she's perfect.'

'Welcome to Te Tuahine,' Rose murmured. One eyeful of this tall thin creature was enough. One earful was one too many. The woman was dressed in pure silk, a flaming scarlet. It seemed out of place with her dark eyes, her jet-black hair, her aura of sophistication.

'You almost make me believe that you are Caroline's mother,' Helen commented wryly. 'Look at you both. Blonde hair, green eyes, wide smile. Where in the world did you find this pixie, Giles?'

'Come into the house,' Giles snapped. 'You *are* here for business, aren't you?'

'Oh yes,' Helen responded. 'Nothing but. The sooner I can get this over with the better off I'll feel. The pilot said he had to go over to Maupiti to refuel. He'll come back for us tomorrow morning. That ought to be enough time to settle things, won't it?'

'Come alone, did you? Where's your lapdog?'

'You mean Jim, don't you. You'll never learn to take him seriously, will you. He's a fine artist, a great talent, just waiting to be discovered. He stayed behind in Tahiti. He felt nervous about coming to this primitive little island. And besides, the bank man who offered us a helicopter lift, said that another passenger would overcrowd things.'

'I'm glad he stayed in Tahiti,' Giles snorted. 'Every time I think about what he did to Josie I get the mad urge to punch him out again. Come inside. Rose, could you have one of the girls bring us some refreshments? Rose?'

They all turned to stare at her. She was standing at the edge of the porch, her mouth half open, one hand holding gently to the roof pillar. Her entire world was concentrated in what she saw. Everything else was shut out. The rotund figure of the man was just now puffing his way up over the top stairs. The man arrived. There was no better description of it. He put both his feet together on the top stair, brushed off his white suit, took off his white Panama hat, and mopped his brow. A squeal of recognition vibrated in Rose's throat, and suddenly she was down the stairs and running full speed towards him. He turned around just in time to catch her in his arms.

'Papa,' she screamed. 'Papa! I *knew* you weren't dead. I *knew* it!'

'Rose. Darling Rose!' They hugged each other in a frenzy of happiness, swaying back and forth and ignoring the trio on the porch. When they stopped to catch a breath he beamed down at her. 'And I knew you weren't dead, Rose. But that idiot, Inspector Tihoni, didn't tell me about you until the night before last. Unbelievable! Here I am the hero of Papeete, and he waited for three months to tell me.'

'Oh Papa, I don't care how long he waited. I just— how did you get to come in—the police? They haven't arrested you?'

'Later, my dear,' he whispered in her ear. 'Later. You wouldn't believe! I am the best friend the police force ever had. Can you imagine that policeman? *Did you know*, he said, *that there's a Rose Harriet Gendron out on Te Tuahine? A beautiful young lady, with a beautiful daughter!* Pah! And what scheming have you been up to Rosalie?'

'Later, Papa, later,' she whispered, mimicking him. 'Oh my dear, I'm so glad to see you. So glad. Even if they arrest us both!'

'Hush,' he cautioned. 'There will be no arresting, *chérie*.' She took his immaculate soft hand and pressed it against her cheek, then drew him back up to the veranda.

'Don't tell me,' Giles chuckled as he came down a couple of steps to meet them. 'Mr Lambert?'

'Just so. And you are?'

'I'm your son-in-law,' Giles announced. 'What a pleasant surprise. Do come into the house.'

'Mommy,' Josie chimed in. 'This is *your* daddy?'

'Yes love, this is my daddy.'

'Then he's my grandfather, isn't he?'

Her father seemed to stagger, Rose thought. She helped him to a chair on the veranda. 'You're not well, Papa?'

'Oh I'm very well indeed,' he laughed, wiping his forehead again. 'But as you can see, for a man of my age to meet my daughter's husband and find that I am already a grandfather, *ma foi*. It takes some doing, that?'

'Oh you fraud,' she laughed. The clear unfettered notes flew up to the housetop. She had not laughed like this since—since long before they had come to Tahiti. And her father! He would never grow old gracefully, but would have to be dragged, kicking and screaming, into old age. Always a man for the ladies. Always forgetting—purposefully, on which side of sixty he stood! 'Take off your jacket, Papa. Josie, help your grandfather with his coat, please.'

She was all smiles as she turned back to Giles and Helen. 'You go ahead, darling,' she said. Put in all the charm, she commanded herself. Here's my ticket out of this place. Keep him sweet until take-off time! 'I'll get one of the girls to bring you both something. In your study?' There now. That sounded so much better than 'workroom'. A little class, that's what I need to add. Papa always brings out the best in me!

'Yes, in the study.' There was laughter behind the solemn words. He knows exactly what I'm doing, she told herself, as the pair of them walked off. A well-matched pair. Both tall and slim, walking like a panther and his mate. They look so well together. So why does that give me a pain?

Josie was chattering away with her new grandfather when Rose came back from the kitchen. And somehow *that* gave her a little twinge too. He's *my* father, she told herself angrily. I don't want to share him with anybody! What am I saying. I'm jealous of the little girl? She handed her father the tall vodka and juice that he preferred, and sat down across the table from him.

'Josie,' she commanded. 'I need to be alone with my Papa. Go help Miri in the kitchen.'

'I wanna stay, Mama.' The child's face screwed up almost into tears. But Rose was so excited that she failed to notice. The little girl's shoulders drooped as she walked away.

'Now,' she said softly. 'They can't hear in the study. Listen.' Briefly but completely, she sketched out her life for the past months, leaving out only that—terrible night—and her pregnancy. 'I didn't know where you were, Papa. I thought anything I said or did might compromise you.'

'So.' He slipped at his drink. 'Then you are not married. That is too bad, *chérie*. He is your type of man.'

'Nonsense.' She brushed aside any idea of painting Giles in better colours. 'I hate the man. Now, quick, tell me about you!'

Her father stretched. 'This is lovely,' he reported. 'It was a long trip, that. Now, where to begin.'

'With the storm,' she coaxed. She tucked her legs up underneath her and gave him a happy smile.

'So.' He reflected for a moment. 'Well, Rose, sending you off in the life raft was a foolish thing to do. No sooner were you gone than the yacht broke loose from the rocks and then winds pushed us up into Apiri Cove and smashed us up on the beach as pretty as can be. I managed to get off, and wandered inland until I came to a village. Two days later the police came, and took me back to Tahiti. I thought our goose was cooked. Mind you, there I am carrying the brief case with all the money in it, and they came and carried me off.' He stopped and took another pull at his drink.

'But this, Rose, you'll never believe. The night that you and I—er—left Tahiti, somebody set fire to the bank building. That Emile Lorange, you remember him? The bank president? He set fire to the building to cover some of his—er—financial transactions, and then he left on the Qantas flight to Sidney. It's—er—hard to believe, Rose darling, but he embezzled two million francs in cash and securities!'

'Papa? You mean that? The same weekend? Two millions?'

'All true, love. It made me feel—almost—in-adequate!'

'And then what happened?'

'Well, the chief bookkeeper had been out yachting with his daughter when that terrible typhoon came up, right? They welcome me with open arms. I reconstruct the books from what was left—and from memory, and presto—I am a local hero. And now that the bank is open again, me—I am appointed by the board of directors to be the new president. What do you have to say about that, Rose Harriet!'

'Oh Papa!' She was laughing so hard that her stomach hurt, and that brought her back down to earth. 'Oh Papa,' she giggled, 'Uncle François always said it, didn't he.'

'Said what, love. Your uncle was always talking.'

'He said that you dip your hand into a bucket of grease and come out with a pearl! You are the president? They've hired the wolf to guard the sheep!'

'Now, now,' he said, doing his best to appear dignified. 'It is not that at all, Rose.'

'Then tell me what it is. Quickly, Papa. It's almost time for them to come out.'

'Ah, Rose. This is, perhaps, the hardest part to believe.' He stopped to clear his throat. 'I am now a man of the world, you recognise, *ma petite*. I aid the police to track down that—that dirty swindler. I am an authority at the bank. And very suddenly it all feels very good. Your Papa has decided to settle down, Rose Harriet. To be a man of honour and distinction.'

Rose looked at him suspiciously. 'Another scam, or another woman?' she asked.

'Ah, how sharp the arrows,' he sighed. 'I am a changed man, my Rosalie. As it happens, also, there is a woman. The little widow Marceau—you remember her?'

'You mean the widow with all that money, Papa?'

'The very same, my dear. As soon as I get back to Tahiti with my lovely daughter, the widow and I will make the marriage, no?'

Rose shook with gales of laughter. My father is a changed man? Horsefeathers. But she remembered the widow Marceau very well indeed. There would be an iron hand under that velvet glove. Whips would be cracked. Paths would become extremely straight and narrow. And there would be no place for a twenty year old pregnant daughter! Rose winced as that idea drifted across her mind. But there could be a lot of loving, and Papa needs that! She laughed until tears came to her eyes. And then they talked, covering the details left out, the reminiscences recalled, until at last Miri rang the dinner gong, and they started for the dining room, arm in arm. In the hall they passed Josie, standing with her back against the wall, crying. But Rose was too far gone in her own needs and loves to notice.

The meal was later than usual. But when Giles and his former wife came out of the study Helen was smiling broadly and clutching a multi-page legal document to her very slender frame. There was chatter around the table, but most of it went over Rose's head. She was deep in her daydreams, sitting beside her father, and reliving all the joys they had shared. Why, I believe I worship my father, she told herself happily. Josie was very quiet too. She crowded her chair in beside her adopted mother, bent her golden head over her plate, and toyed with her meal.

'And so you see,' Mr Lambert said expansively, coming to the end of one of his interminable stories, 'We go back to Tahiti together, my lovely Rose and I, for the marriage. Such a lucky girl, the widow Marceau!'

'Papa, don't be such a complete egotist,' she teased him. 'You may be God's gift to the female sex—and then again—well, you are getting a little long in the tooth, remember!'

Her father answered something. She had no idea what it was. Her eye had been caught by Giles in that second before her father answered. There was a look of—loss—that was the word. Sadness. He held her gaze, almost as if he were trying to hypnotise her. She struggled to break free, and succeeded only when Helen caught at his arm and broke his concentration.

The little girl tugged at Rose's sleeve. She bent her head over to hear better amid all the noise. 'You're really going away, Mommy?'

She heard the words, but not the import. She was far too busy making up for the missed months, learning to love her father all over again. 'Yes,' she answered quickly. 'With my father for his wedding day. It's a very special day.' The child said not another word for the rest of the night.

An hour later, acting her hostess role to the full, she parcelled them all out. 'Papa, you'll take the —er- spare room. Helen, you'll sleep in Josie's room. Josie, you'll share my room with me. Now———'

'And how about me?' Giles asked, with a sound of mock grievance in his voice. She gave him her brightest smile.

'We're cramped for space, sweetheart,' she pouted. 'So I thought—just this once—on the veranda? Those lounge chairs fold all the way back, and perhaps you wouldn't be *too* uncomfortable?'

CHAPTER TEN

IT was an amalgam of many things that sent Rose into her first deep sleep in months. Meeting her father again, safe. The sleepless nights prior to this one. The excessive worry over her pregnancy. The wild wish that struck her at the dinner table, to know—to really know—what Giles thought and believed. Strange thought, that, considering how much she really hated him. But she fell asleep before Josie did, and awoke in the morning when the helicopter, coming back from its refuelling mission on Maupiti, buzzed the house and sent the teeming jungle birds into wild protests.

All the noise brought her up in her bed, startled. It took a moment for her to remember where and who she was. Amnesiac, she told herself, laughing. Josie was nowhere to be seen, and there was packing to do.

She jumped out of bed, wrapping herself carelessly in a pareau, and began to do just that. Someone had located an old battered suitcase for her. She stuffed it with her fanciest new underwear, added a few essential blouses and skirts, and snapped it shut.

I can get everything else—including a dress for the wedding—in Papeete, she told herself. And for travelling? Something cool but substantial. One of the sleeveless blouses she had made for herself, and a wrap-around skirt to go with it. And rubber sandals. Lord, won't it be nice to buy a pair of real shoes. And to have a steaming hot bath, with lots of bubbles! A day or two of relaxation, and then I'll go to Papa's wedding, and then—she stopped herself there, determined not to think a single moment beyond the wedding. There was something that her subconscious knew that her conscious mind didn't want to hear. Just as far as the wedding, that's the ticket. She slipped her feet into the thong of the rubber sandals and made for the door.

The others were already on the veranda. All except Giles.

'Ah, at last,' her father pontificated. 'I thought we would have to go without my Rose!' He offered her a big hug, and kissed the tip of her nose.

'Yes, do please hurry,' Helen said. 'I need to get out of this primitive backwater as soon as possible. Back to civilization and the bright lights, that's for me.' The woman's hand patted the briefcase under her arm as if it contained the crown jewels. And maybe it does, Rose thought. How in the world did Giles ever get caught up with her? Cold—even in the tropical heat of December. Every one of her words drips ice.

'The pilot is waving.' Her father interrupted her thoughts. 'We will go now, *chérie*.' He took her arm in a proprietorial way, and ushered her down off the veranda, just as Giles laboured up the steps in front of them, two at a time.

'Rose,' he called. 'Have you seen Josie? We can't find her.'

A chill struck at Rose's heart. Josie! In one overwhelming flash she recalled all the separate little scenes from the day before. All the times she had brushed the child aside. All the self-centred neglect. 'I—I haven't seen her,' she returned anxiously. 'She—I—I fell asleep very quickly last night. I thought she was— Miri?' The Polynesian girl had come up to them.

'No. Not in the village,' Miri reported. 'I don't see her at sunrise, when I come to make *le petit dejeuner*. Nobody sees her. Sam say he will send out searchers at once, no?'

'We can't wait for some silly child,' Helen snapped. 'Come on, Mr Lambert, let's go.'

Rose's hand itched, wanting badly to slap her face.

'Even if it's *your* silly child that's missing?' She made fists, tight tiny balls, looking for someone to pound.

'Ah, it is a small thing,' her father soothed. 'The island is small. There is no way to get off. Come on Rose, we go now.'

'Really,' Helen remarked in a slow drawl. 'I can hardly spare another minute in this—this island paradise.'

'No,' Rose said stubbornly. 'I can't go until I'm sure Josie is safe!' There was more than stubbornness there. All this time I've been blaming him for everything, she told herself grimly, and I didn't pay a bit of attention to my *own* responsibilities. The poor little kid! I knew she wanted me as a surrogate mother, and I just brushed her off. All because I was so wrapped up in my own concerns. Be honest with yourself at least, Rose. All because you wanted to retreat to your own childhood—to be safe and cosseted by your father—to go back to when life was simpler! Damn! The guilt feeling was too much for her to bear alone. She moved closer to Giles, pleading silently for his support. Without even looking, one of his hands dropped down on her shoulder and gently squeezed.

'I'm not going,' she confirmed. 'You go ahead, Papa. When I can, I'll come. After we find Josie.'

'You're sure, child?'

'It's something important, Papa. I *have* to do it. It's my fault. I'll come when I can.'

'Well——' Her father fussed with the idea, but a look at her determined chin convinced him. 'Of course, Roasalie. You'll come when you can.' He turned to Giles. 'And you, Mr Gendron. You will have good luck in finding your daughter, and you will take care—special care—of mine, no?'

'Yes.' Giles smiled for the first time that day. Her father cleared his throat, shrugged his shoulders, and started off. Why he's getting more Gallic every day,

Rose thought as she watched him disappear down the stairs to the beach.

Rose gave a weak half-wave, and wondered what was happening to her. At any other time, any other place, she would have followed her father off to whatever adventure awaited. But not now. Her feet seemed glued in place, and her conscience thumped on her with a myriad of guilty feelings. If only I had, she told herself, recounting the litany of things she *should* have done to reassure the child. But then, I never really thought it out. All the time I was accepting the child's love—yes, and giving in return—I never thought what would happen when it was time to go! 'There's another mess you've gotten us into,' she muttered in her favourite Laurel and Hardy imitation. It brought a weak smile to her face, but no more. Giles was coming back out of the house. She turned to him as naturally as if he were a friend, rather than the man she hated.

'What can I do?' she asked.

'Do? Why—it's no use your running up and down, Rose. We've got plenty of people for that. You can do the most good just by staying here and keeping track of where everyone else is. And, who knows, Josie might come wandering back at any minute. Why the devil are you crying now? You could have gone with your father. Maybe it's not too late?'

She put a hand on his arm. 'I'm crying about Josie,' she sniffed. 'I don't *want* to go with my father. If I had been a little wiser, Josie would still be here!' She was interrupted by a swell of sound from the beach. The helicopter pulled itself up, dipped a salute over the roof of the Big House, and headed westward for the gap between the Sisters.

'Here now,' he offered, wrapping her up in a comforting arm. 'It wasn't your responsibility. She's my daughter. I've been too damn distracted by all the fancy manoeuvring going on. I'm the one to blame. Now, I've got to get wheeling. You stay here, right?'

'Right.' Her answer was a soft murmur, but he caught it and returned a warm smile before he plunged down the path on the other side of the house. 'Where are you going now?' she called after him.

He stopped and shook his head. 'We have to cover all the bases,' he called back throatily. 'A couple of the men are dragging the pond behind the dam.'

'Oh God!' She stuffed her fist to her mouth. Dragging the pond! The girl wanted a mother. And what a terrible mother I've made for her! She found her way blindly back to the kitchen, where Moera was busy at the cooker.

'Men get hungry,' the young Polynesian girl offered.

'Yes,' Rose returned, and pitched in to help.

She worked hard until noon, and then went out on the porch as the workers came in to report, snatch at the lunch, and head back out again. Giles did not show up. After the clean-up in the kitchen, Rose stumbled back out on to the veranda and collapsed into a lounge chair. It was the first free minute since the helicopter had taken off. The first time to really think about her problem. And with nobody within a mile of the house, she brooded.

The child needs me. For some stupid reason she seems to think that I'm a nice person. Which I certainly am not. And that's not the whole of it. I need Josie as much as she needs me! And *there* was a revelation that startled her. I need Josie? Of course I do. I love that child as if she were my own. And how is that possible? She's the daughter of the man I hate. Well, perhaps hate is too strong a word. But at least I dislike him. And that's too weak a word. So I hate him. And why not, after all he's done to me!

Her hand wandered down unconsciously and stroked her stomach. God, what do I do now? I've got to leave this crazy place. I've got to get away from this man. But I can't really escape him, can I? I'll be carrying him with me, whereever I go. His son will look like him, and I'll be haunted for the rest—now why did I say his *son*? Maybe it will be his daughter! Another conversation flashed across her mind. She had been talking to Miri about the baby the Polynesian girl was expecting. 'And is not a boy,' Miri had laughed, 'I have to try again. no?'

Rose stifled the little sob that caught in her throat. In the end I have to leave. And that means Josie will have to stay behind. And there we'll be—me, his son, and Pele—wandering the earth like Judas? Condemned to haunt the world forever? She leaned back in her chair, and, unprepared for the attack, fell into the arms of sleep.

Giles came back to the house at five o'clock, worn to the bone. She was still asleep, sprawled over the lounger in wild sexy disarray. For a second he thought of waking her, of touching that soft creamy skin, of crushing her up against him—but he fought off the urge, the mad desire. He went into the house, showered, changed into a dry pair of shorts, and went out again. There were shouts, and a conch-shell sounded from the shoulder of Mona Aui. He shrugged his shoulders into a dry T-shirt and started off in that direction.

She woke up just as the sun tipped the top of the Sisters, spraying a rainbow of colour across the bottom side of the few fluff clouds which were hurrying southward. A pale pink glow illuminated the permanent cloud that stood over Pele's mountain. The cloud associated the name. Immediately she thought of the little *tiki* standing in her bedroom. Pele. And it awakened a suspicion.

She threw off the light cover that someone had draped over her legs and sprinted to the bedroom. In the half-light of dusk there were too many shadows. She pumped up the Coleman lantern and lit it. The white, almost fluorescent light, dispelled the gloom. A

quick look told her all she needed to know. The *tiki* was
gone. And what had Josie said? 'They all think you
brought bad luck when you brought Pele down the
mountain. You hafta take her back!' Yes of course,
Rose thought. 'You hafta take her back.' Josie has gone
up Pele's mountain to take the *tiki* back!

There was nobody else in the house. She snatched the
lantern, a packet of matches, and threw the remainder
of a cold supper into a pandanus-woven basket. Giving
no thought to notes for others, she grabbed up the
basket, raced out the door, and dived into the jungle
growth behind the house.

It was as much a struggle as it had been that first
time. The paths were still overgrown, and with the onset
of darkness the way became even more difficult. She
held the lantern up in front of her and struggled
upward, paying no attention to the barbs and briars
that tore at her clothes and scratched her legs and arms.
Occasionally there was a noise in the undergrowth that
startled her. Frightened her half out of her wits, if the
truth be told. But she kept going. It was fully dark
when she stumbled into the clearing half way to the top
of the mountain. Fully dark, and no moon. She made
her way cautiously over to the rock outcropping, and
crumpled up in a little heap, panting for breath. Her
shoulder was sore where she had carelessly bounced off
a breadfruit tree. Down below her she could see the
lights of the village and the Big House. There were no
lights on the other mountains. Evidently the search had
been called off. 'Oh Josie,' she moaned. 'You have to be
here. You have to!' And then swore aloud, in the heat
of her grief, 'I'll never leave you again, Josie. Never!'

It seemed right to say it, even though the saying
raised a host of spectres behind it. You can't have Josie
without Giles, she told herself, and laughed hysterically.
What in the world would I want Giles for! If there is
ever a man who—and suddenly even the artifice of her

fake marriage was too much for her. She struggled with the ring that he had placed on her left hand, tore it off, and threw the offending circlet over the edge of the cliff. And then it was time to go. She picked up the basket in one hand, the lantern in the other, and plunged back into the dense growth above her.

Giles came back to the house just after sunset. He could not disagree with the elders. There was nothing to be gained by further searching in the night. The house was dark as he stumbled up the stairs on to the veranda. 'Rose?' The house echoed silence. He went in, stomping down the hall to her room. His legs were tired, worn beyond belief. 'Rose?' He flexed his muscles, trying to readjust them. He muttered to himself as he wandered back to the dining room, and then out to the kitchen. The lamp smoked for a second, and then settled down. There was nothing to be seen. Nothing except the scattered remains of the supper. He snatched at a cold piece of rib, pulled a can of beer out of the cooler, and went back out on to the porch.

A cooling wind fanned his face as he leaned against the doorpost and scanned the world spread out in front of him. A few fires flickered in the village. Everything looked peaceful. What a deception, he told himself. Somewhere in all this blackness is my daughter! And if I had the sense God gives little children, I would have paid some attention to her instead of that stupid mother of hers. But I was too busy buying Helen off to notice. Where the hell is Rose?

He had nawed the bone clean. Disgusted with life, he hurled it out on to the hillside. It would be picked dry by morning. The tropical night was like that. Where the hell is Rose! The poor woman was—yes, almost as badly off as Josie must be—when I left her. Tired, dispirited, blaming herself for things that were not her fault! You're a fool, Gendron, to think you could blackmail her into being Josie's mother. An arrogant stupid fool. And if you hadn't seduced the poor kid—well, who knows what might have happened. Luckily she didn't get pregnant!

He shook himself, like a dog coming out of the water. Lucky? I've been nothing but bad luck to that poor kid—to that poor sexy woman! Nothing but bad luck! Somewhere in the back of his mind there was an itch he could not scratch. He finished off the beer, crushed the can, and set it down on the veranda table.

The bending over brought his eye level down far enough so he could see up the mountain. Up the mountain of Pele, where a single bright light glowered at him, blinked, and was gone.

'My God,' he shouted to the world. 'That crazy kid! Rose!' He roared it twice, and then twice again. The light was gone. He ran for the kitchen, for the spare Coleman lantern, the medical kit, and the emergency food kit. 'Think!' he yelled at himself. But the impatience—the driving mind-boggling impatience, was too much. Taking what he had already assembled, he ran for the mountain path.

It was almost midnight when Rose stumbled wearily to the lip of the crater. And still no moon. There was a dull outline of clouds in the distant east, and some of the familiar stars were blotted out. The sweet scents of jasmine, vanilla, gardenias, flooded her senses. She stood at the broken edge of the chasm and took deep breaths, pumping new life into her body. A slight breeze kissed her scratched and bleeding cheek. She pumped up the lantern again, and started down into the crater.

It was more difficult than the first time. Then she had both hands free, the moon was up, and she was not so driven by fear. Now all she could think of was the child. A mad litany repeated itself over and over again, so much so that she was not sure she was thinking or talking. 'Josie! Josie! Josie!' Just the name, nothing more. But if she were speaking, the name contained all the love, all the fears, that knit her to the little girl.

She was lucky, at that. The lantern both helped and blinded her, and she almost stepped into the lake before her tired senses told her she had reached her destination. She stopped and held the lantern high.

'Josie,' she yelled at the top of her voice. 'Josie!'

'Mama?' The voice was weak, filled with disbelief. 'You didn't go? Did you come for me?'

The sound came from her left, deep in the underhang of the cliff where Pele's *maere* stood. There was no more time for thought. She dropped the basket and ran. The darkness seemed to be filled with haunting dangers, but it parted in front of her, pushed aside by lantern light. And there, at the foot of the *maere*, was a crouching little body.

Don't get her excited, Rose told herself. Be calm. Don't let her know that you're frightened half to death! You're the adult. You're ten years older than she is. Get a grip on yourself. You're her mother!

The lecture helped. She set the lantern down on the smooth top of the *maere*, and dropped down beside the little girl. 'Josie love,' she coaxed softly, and opened her arms. A warm soft body crowded in on her, and a trembling voice wailed, 'Mommy, Mommy,' as the girl squirrelled against her, trying to bury herself in the softness. Rose squeezed hard. It comforted the child, and it helped *her* to control her shaking muscles.

'It's all right, baby,' she soothed. 'Mommy's here. Did you bring Pele back home?'

'Yes. She's up there.' The girl pointed. Rose stretched, just enough to bring her head to the level of the *maere*. Pele squatted there, teetering on the edge, shadowed by the bright light of the lantern. Oh brother, Rose sighed to herself. At this rate they'll have me believing in little volcano goddesses too! Keep your cool. Don't let the child know how frightened you are.

She dropped back to her knees beside Josie. Her searching hands found no broken bones, no cuts, no blood. 'You're not hurt, baby?'

'No, but it got dark, and I was scared to go back down. You didn't go in the helicopter?'

'Yes, I went,' she chuckled. That's it, her brain commented. Get a little humour in the situation, Rose. 'Yes, I went with my father,' she repeated. 'I'm not really here, you know!'

She felt a sharp pinch on her bottom. 'Hey, ouch,' she complained.

'You are too here,' the little girl laughed. 'You are too. I was cold, and you're so warm!' The child's head dived into Rose's breasts, seeking that warmth. Rose squeezed again. The tears stopped.

'I brought us some food,' Rose thought to say. 'Wait here a minute while I——'

'No, Mommy. If you're going someplace, so am I. I ain't gonna leave you go no more! Not ever!'

Without thinking, Rose helped the girl to her feet and drew her up close. 'No,' she assured. 'Not ever. Come on.'

They ate at Pele's feet. Cold barbecued ribs, little squares of Bonito, a papaya to be shared between them, and a drink of cold clear lake water, scooped up in their hands. And then they settled back, hugging each other.

'We'll wait until dawn,' Rose instructed. 'Cuddle up now and let's get some sleep.' The tiny blonde head nuzzled into her again, and the older woman did her best to recall some of the crazy little stories that her half-French mother had spun out for her in those long-ago days in Baton Rouge. Eventually Josie fell asleep.

It was too cold for Rose to do likewise, and she had too much on her mind. Besides, she had already slept the afternoon away. She sat up with her back against the *maere*, the child's head in her lap, and watched the stars over her head. Now then, she told herself. You've made the child a promise. Now what? She had no answer. No matter which way her thoughts ran, she always came up against the rock that was Giles Gendron. The man she hated. There was no answer to be had. Gradually she let her thoughts dissolve away into shreds, leaving her mind a complete blank.

That half-daze, half-sleep was suddenly disturbed. The Coleman lantern, faithful to the moment, rattled, hissed, blinked, and went out. Instantly Rose snapped to attention. The night noises seemed to be amplified. She could feel eyes watching from out of the darkness, feet rustling in the undergrowth. Be calm, she told herself. For the child's sake, be calm! 'Yeah, sure,' she muttered. 'Be calm. I'm scared half to death and you want me to be calm! If I want to scream I will. Just shut up!'

She lay Josie's head down carefully in the sand, stripping off her blouse to stuff it under the child as a pillow. The wind coursing over her bare breasts reminded her how cold a tropical night could be. She fumbled around in the dark, bumped into Pele's *tiki*, and found the lantern. A quick shake verified her fears. There was no fuel left in it.

Damn, she muttered under her breath. I've got to have—a fire! Of course, a fire. She scrabbled around on the ground. There were twigs, tiny pieces of long-dead bark, and a little farther away, a pile of sticks. It was the work of a moment to pile them all up against the foot of the *maere*. The matches eluded her tired fingers. It took a triple effort to steady her hands, scratch the match, and plunge the flame into the wood. Six matches later she was rewarded with a tiny blaze, a mere speck of flame. She settled back on her heels near it, trying to convince herself that she felt the heat. The flame grew a little larger. She turned to Josie, moving the tiny body closer to the fire.

Her fingers were shaking. Her whole body was

shaking, in the grip of a massive fear. I'm a city girl, she told herself. It will all turn out okay. It will! It has to! Now that I know, it has to. While she was rearranging Josie's sleeping form, her back to the fire, she heard the noise. Louder than the other night-noises. A thud, a sliding step on pebbly sand. She froze in position, too frightened to turn around, too petrified to make a sound. Frozen. She stuffed a hand into her mouth to stifle her screams. If it doesn't hear me, she told herself fiercely, it won't notice me. It must be a bear. There aren't any bears in the islands. They're——

'Rose!' The deep voice behind her was laden with relief, almost as if he had feared more than he saw. Her muscles relaxed, and the scream came out, welling deep into the crater, rebounding from the soft darkness of the lake, echoing from the sides of the old volcanic peak. And then she collapsed.

After that moment when he had seen the light on Pele's mountain, he had wasted not a moment. As a result, he broke into the clearing barely an hour behind her, and went directly to the rocky ledge. This *has* to be the place, he told himself. A shadow moved, off to his right. He swung around, both hands up. A face moved into the light of his lantern. The *tahu'a*!

'She has gone to Pele's temple,' the old man said. 'I came too late to stop her. And the little girl?'

'I don't know,' Giles sighed. 'We haven't found her. Rose knows something. I don't know what. She's— Josie *has* to be up here someplace. Where?'

The old man stepped forward fully into the light. He was wearing his formal cloak of bird feathers, and carried what looked to be a war club in his hand. He pointed up the mountain. They plunged into the darkness, toe to heel. The weight of the first aid kit swung heavily against his hip as he moved, trying to keep up to the old man. We've got to hurry, he kept telling himself as he drove his legs harder. We've got to find Rose! And Josie! Why in God's name did I put Rose first? That niggling worry in the back of his mind was still there. Why Rose? Why? She's only passing through. She's going to Tahiti as soon as we find the child. To go to her father's wedding. Hah! What a sharp old man that one is. And Rose? Like father, like daughter? Josie thinks the world revolves around her. That's why I've been so patient with the woman. For Josie's sake.

Like hell you have, his mind roared at him. Patient? If you had been patient, things might be a lot different right now. Remember what Rose called you? An arrogant man! And it's true. Don't kid yourself that you've chased all the way up this crazy mountain just for Josie!

The thought was like a slap in the face. He stopped in mid-stride, astonished. 'But she hates me,' he whispered. The solid darkness that was the *tahu'a*, ahead of him, disappeared around a corner. He hurried forward to catch up. The old man stopped suddenly, and Giles almost ran into him. Directly in front of them, under the lip of the cave roof, a tiny fire flickered, and behind it——

He ran the last few yards. Ran as if the devil were behind him. 'Rose!' he shouted. The tiny woman in front of him half-turned, screamed in wild fear, and started to collapse. He was at her side before she hit the ground, sweeping her up in his arms, treasuring her for what he knew was her full value—all his life and love and passion. 'Rose,' he whispered. 'I love you.'

One of her eyelids flickered. The eye slowly opened. And then the other. Eyes filled with astonishment and mad longing. 'What?' she croaked.

'Rose,' he repeated more loudly, 'I love you. I didn't know it until just this minute, but I love you. You have to marry me!'

She struggled up in his arms, sliding her hands around his neck, feeling the warmth of his broad chest flattening her breasts. Her shivering stopped. Of course, she told herself, what else could it be! She took a deep breath and kissed the tip of his chin. 'I'm glad, Giles,' she sighed. 'I don't hate you at all. I never did. I love you very much. And Josie too.'

An hour later her cuts and bruises had been seen to. The old man had brought the fire to a real blaze, and was now sitting with his back to them, cradling Josie's head on his lap. Rose curled herself up in Giles' lap and sighed a long thankful sigh. His arms were like a mighty bulwark, shutting out all the terrors of the night. And solving all my problems, she told herself fiercely. There was a warm glow permeating her being. Not fire-warmth, but rather man-warmth. Something she had heard about, but had never known before.

'You will marry?' the *tahu'a* asked.

'Yes,' Rose said dreamily.

'Wonderful,' Giles commented. His hand had been moving gently up and down her side, and now had come to rest just close enough to accept the weight of her generous breast. She could feel herself trembling again. Not shivering, trembling. He made concerned noises, not knowing the difference.

'Giles,' she offered hesitantly, 'I'm pregnant.'

'Wonderful,' he returned. His teeth nipped at her closest ear.

'It will be a wonderful little boy,' she dreamed out loud, 'and look like you.'

'Wonderful,' he repeated. He set her carefully aside, and began to struggle with the buttons on his shirt.

'Not possible,' the old *tahu'a* chuckled. 'Pele sends a girl.'

'Wonderful,' Giles contributed. He was trying vainly to stuff her into his shirt, but his wandering hands, reaching for buttons, sent explosions up and down her spine. Violent explosions!

'In that case,' she maintained primly, 'we'll just have to try again.'

A gust of wind swept across them. Inside his huge shirt she began to feel warm again. 'Don't forget,' the old man cautioned, 'when you leave the island you take Pele too.'

'Oh come on,' Giles snorted. 'That old superstition again?' The *tiki* swayed forward and backward, and then nosedived off its *maere*, straight at Giles' knee. He barely managed to get out of the way.

The old man chuckled. 'Pele say don't wait too long. I go down to the village. You come.'

'Yes, wonderful,' Giles said softly. His hand was still struggling with the shirt buttons.

'Maybe tomorrow,' Rose called after the old man. 'Maybe the day after tomorrow?'

The *tahu'a* waved to them in the semi-darkness. He had set Josie's head down gently on his feathered cape. They heard his laughter as he left. '*Iorana oe*,' he called.

Josie gave a little giggle, shifted on to her side, and began to snore. Giles' fingers were still at the buttons, undoing what he had worked so hard to do. Rose cupped his hands with hers, treasuring them for a moment, and then started to help him.

CHAPTER ELEVEN

THEY were married on the beach in Te Tuahine. The little chapel had been decorated. 'But it isn't big enough for the children to come,' Miri explained. And so the broad beach. The Anglican priest was a tall well-built Polynesian from Bora Bora, he wore a skirt of *pareau* cloth, and a frock coat. Sam Apuka stood behind the wedding pair, giving them a running translation as the ancient ritual, set in the Polynesian language, ran over their heads. She could feel Miri nudge her. 'I will,' she managed to squeak out. *'Ea.'*

There were blessings, and bowings and prayers. And then, in liquid English, the priest said, 'And I now pronounce you man and wife.' He beamed down at them, towering above their kneeling forms, and gently touched each of them on the top of their heads. He smiled out at the audience, and in melodic Polynesian, began a homily.

The audience shifted from foot to foot. A moment later, from the back of the crowd, a deep bass voice began to sing. Here and there, throughout the crowd, other voices joined in a haunting island melody. The priest continued for a moment, swimming against the tide, then gave up. He held up both hands and in a booming baritone, joined in.

'What's that all about,' Giles whispered to Sam.

'He about to make speech,' Giles laughed. 'Nobody wants speech, so we have *Himine*. Songfest. They sing something called "Now is the time for loving!"'

There was a small reception on the beach, and then Rose and Josie dashed up to the Big House, changing from the colourful *muumuus* they had worn for the ceremony, into more European clothes, for the trip.

The big *pahi*, decorated from stem to stern with streamers, signs, flowers, and love, awaited them at the dock. There were tearful farewells. Twenty-two paddlers—all the young men of the island, swept them out into the ocean for the trip to Maupiti, and the airport.

Giles stood beside her in the stern as they waved goodbye. 'Sam and Miri will stay at the Big House until we come back,' Giles explained to her.

'But I don't understand why we can't stay,' she protested. 'It's our home, isn't it?'

'I've told you why not more than a dozen times,' he teased. 'I want you where there are doctors and hospitals. And school for Josie. My daughter can hardly speak English. There's a house on the outskirts of Portland, Oregon, not half a mile away from an important person.'

'My grandma?' Josie prompted.

'Yes, love, your grandmother. My mother.' He tapped Rose on the tip of her nose. 'Any argument, lady?'

'Would it do any good if I argued?' she asked primly. She knew the answer already. If she did object, he would change his plans. But she had no intention of objecting. Life was perfectly wonderful, just being Mrs Giles Gendron. Perfectly wonderful! Just to complete the circle, she pulled Josie into the embrace they were sharing. The crowd cheered, and their long voyage had begun.

They found seats in the old airplane at Maupiti, and collectively held their breath as it wobbled bravely into the air.

'I'm worried about the *tiki*,' she told him. She patted the little case at her feet. It was an old leather container—a case for a cornet or trumpet, long disused. The *tahu'a* had produced it on their final day on the island. The little *tiki* fitted into it exactly, as if it had been carved in anticipation of this particular case. When he snapped the lid shut the old man pulled out an ancient Japanese writing brush and inscribed a complicated figure on its lid.

'Don't worry,' Giles chuckled. 'Forget everything except the trip.'

'Don't do that,' she snapped at him, brushing his hand aside. 'I didn't realise you were some sort of satyr. It can lead only to—to frustration, darn you. Josie's watching! Besides, if the customs people see the *tiki* we're in a lot of trouble!'

'Forget it,' he repeated. 'It's only a superstition.' But by that time their wheels had touched down at Papeete, and the little aircraft wandered up to the passenger terminal just as if it had a right to be there.

Her father was waiting inside the terminal. Her father, his new wife, and an official from the Mairie, complete with sash of office. The older man was looking a trifle subdued, but he hugged and kissed with French enthusiasm. Rose and her new stepmother took each other's measure at a glance, and liked what they saw.

'He is a good bank president,' the former widow Marceau confided. 'Who knows better how to guard the money than a reformed thief, no?'

'We've only got forty minutes,' Giles prodded. Qantas was the only airline with three seats open, and that only as far as Hawaii.

They needed hardly half that time. The official, in machine-gun French, raced through the civil marriage ceremony that made the religious service legal, and they caught up to their luggage just as the little trumpet case came sliding down the table. The inspector, a combination of Polynesian, Chinese, and French scattered through his genes, went through Rose's suitcase with meticulous care before making his chalk mark. His compatriot nudged him and said something about the time of flight. He laughed back as his hand was extended towards the little case—and stopped in midair. He stepped back from the line, bumping into the adjacent inspector, his big forefinger pointed at the little box and the symbol on top of it. If it were possible, Rose giggled to herself, he would actually have turned white. He held up both hands, and refused to touch another thing. From behind him a pure Polynesian looked over his shoulder and said, '*Sacré bleu!* Please! Take your luggage and go quickly!' Giles obliged, whistling as he went.

'Smart Aleck,' she told him fiercely as he stuffed Pele's box in the overhead rack.

They stopped over in Hawaii for two slow lovely days, before a flight offered to Seattle. It was a bumpy ride, but they hardly noticed.

'Don't you two gonna do nothin' but look at each other and sigh?' Josie complained.

'That's all,' her father admitted. 'You have to get used to it, baby!'

'Well, that's silly,' his daughter complained. 'If I didn't like you both so much I'd be mad. Even when we get to Grandma's house?'

'Even when,' Rose chided her. 'You don't mind staying at Grandma's for a few days while Daddy and I—er—get the house ready?'

'Nope, I don't mind. Grandma's got dogs and horses and pigs. You two will need glasses if you keep that up. It must be some eyestrain.'

'Read your book,' her father glared at her.

'Don't do that,' Rose told him, pushing his hand away. 'What do you think can be accomplished in a public airplane?'

'Ah, but we'll be home soon enough,' he leered. 'I want to keep you tuned up.'

'Well cut it out,' she chuckled. 'You know you can turn me on in a minute. Behave yourself!'

There was a two-hour stopover at Seattle. As in Hawaii, not a word was said about Pele, hiding in her little case. When they transferred to the local feeder line, Rose put the case at her feet. They flew south at five thousand feet, low enough to feel the air pockets as they skirted the fringe of the mountains. Josie fell asleep, and Giles was deep in a sports magazine he had picked up at the Seattle terminal.

Rose wiggled her hand free from his absent-minded clutch, and pulled the little case up into her lap. One of the snaps was bent. It took her a few minutes to open it, and lift the cover. The little faceless statue stared out at her, and seemed to be feeling its new environment, the new world all around it. It quivered slightly in its box, and the airplane took a wild diving swing away from its smooth flight path and readjusted to a new course. The air seemed bumpier than before. Rose stared out the window. The loudspeaker activated with a metallic click.

'This is your captain speaking,' the voice said. 'We have just made a course correction, at the direction of the Portland airways control, and will approach to the city from the far south. If you look out your windows to the north, you will see the reason for the change.'

Rose leaned over Josie's sleeping form and peered out the window. There, in the middle distance, surrounded by snow covered hills, a massive mountain top was stirring. Puffs of steam burst high in the air, and then suddenly there was a massive roar, the airplane was buffeted, and a great hole appeared in the side of the mountain. Giles put down his magazine and leaned over her to look.

'My God,' he said. 'Mount St Helens. The darn volcano is erupting! There hasn't been anything like that around here since—since God knows when!'

Rose squeezed back in her chair to give him room, and then glanced down into her lap. Inside her little travelling case Pele, the goddess of volcanoes, the *tiki* with no face, was laughing. Shaking the Earth!

Her husband pulled back and followed her glance. There was a peculiar—an unbelieving look on his face. As fast as her muscles could be made to move, Rose slammed the cover shut, snapped the locks in place, and let the whole thing slide off her lap on to the floor.

'Oh Lord,' she muttered under her breath. Her husband's face was inches from hers. 'It's only a superstition,' he chuckled. 'You're not responsible for all that!'

She sighed and took a deep breath, wishing she could believe him, but knowing that he was very wrong! '*Iorana oe*,' he told her.

'For ever after?' she queried.

'For ever after,' he repeated, and his lips sealed out all the sights, all the sounds, all the people, and locked them together in their own private world.

SHANNON OCORK

SECRETS OF THE
TITANIC

**The voyage of the century
—where secrets, love and destiny collide.**

They were the richest of the rich, Rhode Island's
elite, their glittering jewels and polished manners
hiding tarnished secrets on a voyage that would
change their lives forever.

They had it all and everything to lose.

"Miss OCork is a natural writer and storyteller."
—New York Times Book Review

1-55166-401-1
MIRA® **Available from October 1998 in paperback**

MARGOT DALTON

second thoughts

To Detective Jackie Kaminsky it seemed like a routine
burglary, until she took a second look at the
evidence... The intruder knew his way around
Maribel Lewis's home—yet took nothing.
He *seems* to know Maribel's deepest secret—
and wants payment in blood.

A spellbinding new Kaminsky mystery.

1-55166-421-6
**AVAILABLE IN PAPERBACK
FROM OCTOBER, 1998**

Jennifer
BLAKE

KANE

Down in Louisiana, family comes first.
That's the rule the Benedicts live by.
So when a beautiful redhead starts paying a little
too much attention to Kane Benedict's grandfather,
Kane decides to find out what her *real* motives are.

*"Blake's style is as steamy as a still July night...as overwhelming
hot as Cajun spice."*

—Chicago Times

1-55166-429-1
**AVAILABLE IN PAPERBACK
FROM OCTOBER, 1998**

EMILIE RICHARDS

THE WAY BACK HOME

As a teenager, Anna Fitzgerald fled an impossible
situation, only to discover that life on the streets was
worse. But she had survived. Now, as a woman,
she lived with the constant threat that the secrets of
her past would eventually destroy her new life.

1-55166-399-6
**AVAILABLE IN PAPERBACK
FROM SEPTEMBER, 1998**

JASMINE CRESSWELL

THE DAUGHTER

Maggie Slade's been on the run for seven years now.
Seven years of living without a life or a future because
she's a woman with a past. And then she meets Sean
McLeod. Maggie has two choices. She can either run,
or learn to trust again and prove her innocence.

"Romantic suspense at its finest."

—Affaire de Coeur

MIRA

1-55166-425-9
**AVAILABLE IN PAPERBACK
FROM SEPTEMBER, 1998**